She'd thought she could trust him, but it seemed that he was the same kind of cheating scum as her late husband...

Amanda saw him standing there—home safe. The sight of his tall, spare form, made her draw in a sharp breath to quell the rapid beating of her heart. "You're here," was all she said.

He stepped toward her but stopped himself before he reached her. "Yes, sorry to be so late but the sheriff and I were working on something."

He'd moved near enough that she caught the scent of perfume left on his person from an encounter with Mercedes Saldana. She remembered it from her husband's clothes. Recognizing the same odor she'd caught on Harvey after his visit to Artesia, her suspicions and temper went through the roof.

"Oh, believe me, I already know what business you and that sheriff had cooked up between you. And I know where you had it, too. I can smell it on you."

She stamped her foot. Her body shook and trembled all over until he worried she'd drop the burning lamp she held.

"It's not what you're thinking, Amanda—not at all." He stepped toward her. "I'll tell you about it, if you'll listen."

He wasn't sure she would by the wild fury he saw in her eyes. They might have been blue in the daylight, but they looked black as the ace of spades at the moment.

"A likely bunch of lies. You're carrying the stench of that woman all over you," she sniffed. "A woman can't trust any one of you men as far as she can throw you."

She stood firm but, in her trembling hands, the lamp shook and wobbled.

Reed took it from her. "Here, let me have that lamp before you set the place on fire."

"Well, I guess it'd keep that Saldana woman from moving in then, wouldn't it?"

She believes she's made a good marriage—but she never experiences the happiness or joy she expected...

Her harsh, forbidding husband makes Amanda Bradshaw feel more like a brood mare than a wife, and she never experiences the happiness or joy she expected. Though she's nine-months pregnant with her second child, he orders her to have a boy this time and leaves to go on a cattle-buying trip. Her labor begins, her small daughter is in danger, and Amanda prays desperately for help. When a dusty, trail-worn stranger rides up, she sees the kindness in his eyes and faces the fact that he's all she has. But will he stay to help?

He's an escaped convict—and her only hope...

Reed Twining spent several years playing cowboy until wrongly convicted of murder and sent to Yuma Prison. In 1893, he escapes and heads north to safety, until he finds a dying man who begs him to tell his wife he was robbed and murdered. A man who is honor bound to do the right thing, Reed rides in to find Amanda in trouble. Many men would turn and run—but not Reed. Still, when Amanda finds out who and what he is, will she order him to go?

KUDOS for *Ranch Wife*

In *Ranch Wife* by Ramona Forrest, Amanda Bradshaw is pregnant with her second child. Her creep of an abusive, cheating husband orders her to have a boy this time and then leaves on a buying trip, even though his wife is nine months pregnant and due to deliver any day. Not only does the jerk also order her to continue watering the garden—by hand carried bucket, no less—but he goes off and leaves her to fend for herself. Of course, he also gets murdered and robbed, so I guess he paid for his sins. Needless to say, Amanda goes into labor, unable to take care of her small daughter or herself. When a travel-weary stranger rides up to the ranch, Amanda know that he is her only hope of survival. *Ranch Wife* is a fine addition to this talented author's many published books so far. The story gives you a very realistic glimpse into just how hard life could be for women in the 1890s. I can't even imagine how difficult it must have been to be a pregnant woman in that time. The plot is well conceived and the story well written. – *Taylor Jones, reviewer*

Ranch Wife by Ramona Forrest is a realistic, if harsh, account of a married woman's life in 1890s New Mexico. Our heroine, Amanda, is married to Harvey, who appears to be a prosperous ranch owner. She moves from her beloved Colorado to New Mexico where her husband's ranch is located. Far away from her friends and family, Amanda is faced with the fact that her husband is cruel and forbidding, both toward her and their young daughter. Not only does he criticize everything she does, but he is unfaithful, and plunges his ranch into so much debt that, when he dies, the value of the ranch is barely enough to pay off the debt. The most appalling of her husband's actions is when he orders her to give him a son, then rides of to Albuquerque, hundreds of mile away just days before Amanda is due to deliver, leaving her all alone to fend for herself. While *Ranch Wife* is a historical romance, it is also an authentic look into the world of our pioneer ancestors and the brutal realities of life as woman in a time with females were little more than chattel, and every husband demanded that his wife bear him a son. How hard life must have been for these poor women, with so little control over their own lives. It's a wonder any of them survived. Forrest's characters, as well as her world building, have a definite ring of truth. One might even think she is a time traveler from the 19th century, she seems to understand these women's lives so well. – *Regan Murphy, Reviewer*

RANCH WIFE

Ramona Forrest

A Black Opal Books Publication

GENRE: HISTORICAL ROMANCE/ROMANTIC SUSPENSE

This is a work of fiction. Names, places, characters and incidents are either the product of the author's imagination or are used fictitiously, and any resemblance to any actual persons, living or dead, businesses, organizations, events or locales is entirely coincidental. All trademarks, service marks, registered trademarks, and registered service marks are the property of their respective owners and are used herein for identification purposes only. The publisher does not have any control over or assume any responsibility for author or third-party websites or their contents.

DEDICATION

I dedicate this book to a very fine woman named Vicki—a lady who generously displayed an act of selfless kindness and consideration to a total stranger, for no other reason other than to provide relief and comfort in a time of need. We are fortunate indeed for such as these in our society, and may she know many blessings in her life.

RANCH
WIFE

CHAPTER 1

Amanda Bradshaw walked out into the early morning sunshine, her small daughter's hand held snugly in her own. At times, she stopped and put a hand over her eyes to sweep a lingering glance past her immediate surroundings, out over the far-reaching landscape. The soft purples of the gentler mountains of southeastern New Mexico lay outlined in the distance but, as always, she searched fruitlessly for the sight of the ruggedly outlined mountains of the high Rockies.

Thinking of the immense, sharp, snow-covered peaks of those mountains reminded her of her childhood home. She sighed, squeezing her daughter's hand. "This isn't Colorado, is it honey?"

The child, Marianna, looked up, her expression puzzled.

Amanda tried to explain. "I know you can't understand how much I miss some things." The pain that lodged in her throat, as she remembered the place where she grew to womanhood, reinforced a deep longing in her aching heart. "Yes, my darling, you have no idea how terribly I miss the sight of those majestic peaks and deep green valleys." She smiled down at her child. "I can speak openly to you about it, but no one else." She sighed and murmured, "This is nice country, I suppose, but it'll never seem like home to me."

They opened the garden gate and entered. The small

family dog followed closely, eager to accompany them, but Amanda closed the slatted gate, locking him out. "We don't need Piddely digging in here, now do we?" she gently reminded Marianna, to ameliorate the child begging to have the dog with her.

As they walked between the carefully tended rows of beginning vegetables, she frequently bent down to draw her child's reaching fingers away from the feathery growth of new carrots.

Grasping at them with her chubby hands, the little girl grabbed at a feathery little carrot. "See mommy, I pick it!"

"No, Marianna, they're not big enough. We must wait."

The little girl looked up at her, her mouth firm. "Daddy wan' it."

"He'll have to wait, just like we will," Amanda reminded her. "Daddy expects this garden to provide most of what we need for the summer as well as the winter months." She snorted then frowned. "I certainly work hard enough to make that happen."

They walked on a few more steps. "We might get a good crop this summer, if it would rain more." She said it more to herself than her child, realizing they'd have enough for winter, but only if she carried water every day from the well that lay uphill from the garden.

That arduous task had become increasingly difficult with her burgeoning belly. Her next child would be a strong one, kicking so hard some days she ached with soreness from it. She placed her hand on the high mound, feeling the activity.

Stooping to pull an errant weed, she told the child, "Leave it to molder and rot away in the rows, that small bit of nourishment will help things grow."

"Rot, Mommy?" Marianna's face frowned with the question.

"Yes, it goes back into the soil and makes it stronger." She walked on farther. "As a little girl at home, my mother and I did the gardening. I know how it's done, but this soil is...different."

She moved along with the child, seeing small cracks starting again in the clay-filled soil, and groused, "I must haul water again today." Thinking how her arms would ache and her belly draw up into painful knots from the heavy buckets of water by the time she finished, tears filled her eyes.

The spring lay above the ranch house and the walk uphill, even with empty buckets, had become increasingly difficult for her. "Thank God, it's downhill when they're full."

Standing straight to ease her aching back, she looked about. They only employed two cow hands and she watched them ride to the southwest. Following their diminishing movements with her gaze, she saw the dim outlines of those far away mountains and was haunted again with intense longings.

Often, feelings of homesickness overwhelmed her. She nearly regretted her marriage, though she believed herself more fortunate than most women of her acquaintance.

Times were advancing near the turn of the century, it was 1893 and her husband owned a good sized ranch. A well-managed one, she believed, in this remote valley of southeastern New Mexico. That alone marked him a successful man. Wishing she could rejoice over the matter, she carried a load of guilt because she couldn't. Her marriage to Harvey had not brought the joy she'd expected and, in her deep disappointment, she realized she'd never felt that way about him, or her marriage.

A shadow loomed across the fence. Her heart leaped nervously in her chest as she drew herself up to face her husband. "You startled me, Harvey."

She hated that his presence made her feel inadequate, but it always did. Unfamiliar chills passed over her. *Was something wrong?* "Everything all right? You looked so grim at breakfast this morning."

"Of course it is, Amanda." He frowned. "I've business

to attend to in town this morning and wondered if you'll be all right here alone." His dark blue eyes wore those familiar shades of cold steel this morning as he stood before her, lips firm, hands on his hips, with his large form shading a part of the garden.

"Of course. We both will, won't we, Marianna?" She bent her fond gaze on her golden-haired daughter and stroked the child's head.

"I pick 'em, Mommy?"

The girl's voice faltered now in her father's presence. Her mind, bent on harvesting vegetables, she had a stubborn set to mouth, but she'd stopped asking and had gone silent. Clinging to her mother's skirts, looking up at her father, she said nothing as she faced him.

Amanda crooned softly to her, "No darlin', not yet. They're much too young, just like you." She swept down, picked up the child in her arms, and kissed her pink cheeks soundly.

"You're a spoilin' that child, Amanda. We don't want that, now do we?"

His jaw set firm in his square face, his eyes gone black with coldness, Harvey scowled. He was a strict disciplinarian, allowing no softness in rearing his children. He'd made that clear to Amanda more than once.

"I guess not, Harvey." She put her daughter down. "Will you be gone most of the day?" Roswell was over ten miles, and Artesia was about five. Either way, he'd be gone for most of the day and she felt a spurt of guilty joy about it. "I'll be just fine. Might need to carry water again, but I'll rest often."

"See that you do. The boys'll be out pretty far on the southern ranges today and won't be any help if you get into trouble." He'd often said he planned to take on another hand or two but hadn't, because hiring more men would lower his profits. His two men, down on their luck when he'd hired them, needed their jobs. When they groused about the extra work, he ignored their complaints. They stayed, and she often wondered why.

Amanda saw a softened look in his eye as he appraised her. When he took her in his arms at night and wanted her body, it'd never been the excitement she'd heard whispered about when women got together.

She was considered a very pretty woman, blonde, with a nice trim figure, but he never remarked on that or complemented her. His only comments were about how spoiled she'd been as a child. His constant criticism took any possible joy out of the relationship between them. If she'd been the apple of her daddy's eye and been mollycoddled growing up, Harvey only remarked how her folks had been way too soft in her upbringing.

She was his wife now and learning his ways. He'd seen to that. Slothfulness was not something he'd tolerate in anyone, including women and children. She stifled a frown as she waited for his next words.

"Well, Amanda, I'll be off, might be late afore I get back. I'll check over the garden next morning and see how you've done." Without another word, he turned away and headed toward the corral.

She watched his broad back grow smaller as he walked away and felt near tears. Did the man not see how difficult it was, keeping so many things done to his satisfaction? She bent down, tore another weed out of the ground, and ground it under her heel. "There, you nasty thing, you don't belong here, get out of my garden!"

She kept on in the garden until she saw him ride away on Spotty, his big strawberry roan. His solid form swung easily as he rode. A graceful rider, she supposed, and a handsome man, so people said. It didn't matter anymore. She no longer took pride in how fine her man looked in the saddle.

Unconsciously heaving a sigh of relief, she called her child. "Come on, little sweetie, let's go see what we can find for breakfast." She took her daughter's soiled hand and, along with the wiggling dog, they sauntered slowly to the house. A spacious home, it sprawled across a long, low rise. The high location afforded a nice view of the surrounding areas. But to her, nice though it might be, it was one more thing she couldn't appreciate, or even care about.

In the kitchen, she took out a loaf of freshly baked bread, sliced off two soft, thick slices, one for herself and another for her child. Opening a jar of dark of rich apple butter she'd made last year, she slathered it generously over the slices.

After cutting a slice into small, easy to handle chunks, she sat her daughter on a seat made higher by folding several thin blankets on a chair. "Here you go, honey, eat something. Then play with your toys for a while." She poured a small glass of milk for the girl and one for herself while wondering which hand had done the milking. She smiled, happy that it wasn't another chore left to her.

Marianna took up the bread her mother had cut for her and began eating while Amanda wandered aimlessly about the house, looking at things, her bread forgotten.

Their home—comfortable with enough furniture, pictures, rugs, lamps, and those small touches that made a house a welcoming haven—only made her realize she'd never felt they were hers. *Could that be the reason I feel the way I do when other women seemed content in their lives?*

Amanda tried to understand. Somehow, things on this ranch had no part with her, like they were not hers at all. Even the pictures on the walls had not been chosen by her. Everything had been in place when he'd brought her as a bride to this house, three years ago.

She heard scuffling and giggling at the table and smiled at the messy face of her child, as she slipped bits of bread to the dog. There was no one to see or make disparaging comments on her daughter's poor manners. "I'll clean her up after she's done, might wash up her clothes, too, if I have any strength left."

Delaying the wearisome task of carrying water for the

garden, she dawdled, hating the way carrying the heavy buckets of water made her swollen belly crawl into a tight, hard knot. That happened all too often these days, and when it happened, it worried her about possible harm to the unborn child. Harvey expected her to deliver a fine, healthy boy this time.

Hoping she'd be able to do that for her husband, Amanda shivered at the thoughts of seeing his face if she failed. He'd never raised a hand to her, but the man had other ways of expressing disapproval. How very well she knew that.

Amanda had inner convictions, too. Deep down inside rested a firm resolve that no man would ever lay a hand on her in anger. She'd never allow it and wondered why it ever crossed her mind.

After finishing her own slice of bread and cleaning her child's face with what warm water was left in the teakettle, she hugged her daughter and, settling in the wooden rocker, took her on her lap. "You're all nice and clean, love."

As Amanda softly crooned a few songs in Marianna's delicately molded ear, the soft body grew limp as the child slipped into a deep slumber. Piddely crept close and reached his damp little nose up to sniff the child's hand. Having the dog in the house was forbidden, too, but he lay beside the chair, staying close to the girl.

After laying Marianna in her small bed, Amanda returned to the garden. Disheartened at the sight of deepening cracks in the earth that seemed to grow wider as she stood watching, she shrugged and decided to get the job done. She believed the soil mocked her as it became harder with each passing day, forcing her to carry the water even more frequently.

She headed to the buckets, hung on wooden pegs. Even empty, walking up to the spring had become more difficult, but Amanda continually reminded herself she was a strong woman. She carried the heavy oaken buckets for nearly two hours. Each bucket carried less water these days because of the weight, but finally, the garden was moistened, if not flooded with the life giving water.

Her pregnant abdomen had tightened into a hard knot several times, making Amanda sit down to wait for the frightening, tensing sensations to pass before continuing on. Worn and sweating, she sat down on a nearby rock to let the soft breezes cool her heated neck and face. Her child might be awake by now and she needed to check on her, too.

The sound of hoof beats alerted her, quickening her pulse. *Had Harvey come home so soon?* Looking up, she saw the older ranch hand, Jud Turlock, riding up. A twinge of alarm flashed through her mind.

The man never missed a chance to get next to her if Harvey wasn't looking. It made her feel hunted and uncomfortable. She rose from her seat on the rock. "Why, Jud, I thought you boys were riding out south today."

"Well, I forgot somethin' and had to ride back fer it." His roving eyes held her in a heated gaze—one she unconsciously understood and found disgusting—then swept over her swollen belly. "See you've been a carryin' water again, too. Ain't that a bit much fer a woman in the family way?"

"What I do is no concern of yours, Jud."

Him mentioning her condition was unseemly, but she'd never relate this to Harvey, and the man knew it.

"Well, that husband of your needs to be doin' the carryin', instead of runnin' off to town ever chance he gets. I might just spend a little time helping you out. I'd carry plenty of water for you, spellin' you for a while, if you'd like the help."

He offered an ingratiating smile with his comment and edged his horse bit closer to where she stood by the large rock. She said nothing.

Receiving no answer, he turned away and rode his sweating sorrel gelding to the watering trough. He dismounted and tied the horse near where it could drink and, holding his eyes on her, came sauntering back. A man of medium height, solid build, sandy hair, and pale blue eyes, he wore a bushy handle bar mustache. She'd seen him preening that facial foliage many times and knew it was a thing of manly pride to him.

Jud came close to where she stood, too close for comfort. She caught the odor of male sweat and horseflesh. He'd tried to attract her interest many times. What his reason might be, she couldn't imagine. She'd never have to do with the likes of him. She'd never told her husband about the man's advances, believing Harvey would blame her.

What has this man in mind, standing close that way? Her heart rate increased along with her temper. She felt her skin grow cold with apprehension. He had no business being here and his behavior was insolent. "Just what do you want, Jud?" she asked, her face screwed tight and her teeth clenched.

"Well, right now, I'm aimin' to help you out some, ma'am." His thin smile was reminiscent of a coyote on the hunt. Though reasonably clean, the smell of the man made her feel ill. His coming upon her this way disgusted and insulted her. She clenched her fists as her anger increased.

"You can just get yourself back on that horse and ride on out of here. If I needed help, I'd ask for it." She growled the words as she smoothed her dress with nervous hands, wishing she had the ability to run. Either that or had packed a handy six-gun. "I've done enough watering for today." She turned toward the ranch house. "I must attend my daughter, if you please." She headed in that direction until she felt his strong hand clutching her arm.

"No you don't, ma'am. I know things ain't nice like they oughta be around here. I'm aimin' to help you out." Jud kept his grip on her arm. "You jest might be needin' my help one of these days."

His tone held the dark hint of secrets only he knew and she flushed hot. His implications angered her, though she had no idea to what he referred.

"You'd best release me, mister—right now." Keeping her tone low and as deadly as she could manage, she added,

"If I need any help, it won't be from the likes of you. My husband wouldn't approve of your laying a hand on me, either." She flushed, her face felt hot, and tears stung in the back of her eyes. "You'll be lucky to have a job, or even stay alive when he hears of this." She jerked hard against his tightly held grip on her arm.

Marianna toddled out the door, along with her dog, and ran unevenly toward her mother. "Mommy, we do garden 'gin?"

The hopeful sound of her voice told Amanda the girl saw no danger in her mother's present situation. Her only interest lay in pulling up immature carrots.

With the interruption, Jud released her arm. Perhaps the low growl from Piddely's furry throat had something to do with it.

Marianna looked at him. "Hewo, Mr. Jud."

"Hells bells, ma'am, no harm intended—just wantin' to help is all."

A sulky look crossed his face as he walked back to his horse and jerked on the reins. Climbing into the saddle, he rode out of the yard uttering muffled curses.

Amanda, unable to care about the expletives voiced before her, felt relief seeing him leave the ranch yard. Dared she tell this to her husband? She shrugged, frustrated, and muttered, "Never sure what might upset him, but this incident would for certain."

"Mommy, man go way."

"Yes, honey, he has to work."

She looked at her arm. The deepening bluish bruises had assumed the pattern of a man's fingers and the sight of it chilled her, and alarmed her. Could she explain something like that, if Harvey happened to see it? She knew she couldn't.

She took the girl's hand and walked unsteadily back to the house. In the coolness of the home, she sought one of the big leather chairs in the large main room used for resting and entertaining friends and neighbors. They seldom had visitors but she often sat there, reading with Harvey in the evenings.

She fanned her brow and closed her eyes. Carrying water was exhausting, and more so each time she did it. Worrying it might be damaging to her unborn child, she closed her eyes and dozed off to the soft, pattering sounds of her daughter playing with her old, worn, cornhusk doll. Her friend, Helen, had made it for Marianna more than a year ago and she preferred it to the finer one her father had bought at the general store in Artesia.

CHAPTER 2

Amanda's rest was interrupted by a low growl from the dog. She aroused further, hearing the sound of carriage wheels and the nickering of horses from the corral. Marianna lay asleep on the floor surrounded by the many objects of interest to her, a wooden spoon, old empty spools, and several items of doll clothes lying about in disarray. Her chubby hand rested beneath her cheek, and her rosebud mouth was slightly open.

Piddely, with hackles raised, stood growling at the door. Amanda walked to the door and opened it to see her friend and neighbor, Helen, in the act of climbing down from her conveyance. She stepped out on the wide veranda, or porch as her husband called it, to greet the woman. Helen's horse stood quietly at the rail out front, tail switching at the occasional blowfly. Piddely quickly changed his guarded stance and wiggled in welcome as he preceded her across the porch.

"Helen, it's so good to see you." She met her friend at the door, took her hand, and led her into the house. "I'm needing a bit of company right now."

"Thought to see how you're a doin', young lady."

Amanda noticed the sturdy woman taking in her heavy abdomen with the critical eye of a woman well trained in midwifery.

"Won't be long until you'll be a callin' on me, by the

way that baby's droppin'." Helen took a seat in the big sitting room. "Been a wonderin' so thought I'd best be payin' you a visit." She settled her good sized body into a large chair, wiped a touch of sweat from her brow, and patted her windblown, gray-tinged hair back into shape. "Whew, it's a far piece, drivin' over."

"Everything's all right, Helen, I keep busy most times. I'm a bit tired just now—finished carrying water for that darned garden again." Amanda heaved a sigh. "Sure wish this country had a bit more rain."

"You hadn't ought to be carryin' water at all, my dear, if you want to deliver a healthy child," Helen admonished. "You'd best have one of the hands take care of that, or that Harvey. It's not good for you to be doin' such heavy work, far along as you are." She frowned. "Want me to speak to him for you?"

"Please, if you think I shouldn't carry the water anymore, I'll do the telling. He always says I was spoiled and coddled at home, and he hopes to toughen me up some. But the baby does tend to tie up in a hard, tight bundle anymore, and I've worried about that myself. I thank you for the warning." Amanda wanted to get Helen's mind off her condition and changed the subject. "What have you heard about the dry spell we're having?"

Amanda had no trouble reading Helen's thoughts. Her warning about carrying the water came as no surprise. Straining her pregnant body lay heavily on the midwife's mind. By now everyone considered Harvey a real hard man and everybody around had hinted at it.

Helen smiled to cover her real thoughts. "Now, Amanda, land sakes, you know I'd never mix in anybody's personal business, but I do most of the deliverin' around here and thought to give you some good advice." She heaved a sigh and wiped her brow. "I'll leave it to you on the water-in."

Amanda laboriously got to her feet. "I've made some sweet cakes and if you'd have a bite with me, I'll make us some tea." She headed into the kitchen to put on a kettle just as Marianna sat up, looking about for her mother.

Helen took the child in her arms. "Momma's busy making us some tea, honey." She cuddled the little girl against her generous bosom.

Amanda, peeking in, heard her friend murmur aloud, "Wonder what that man'll do if he gets himself another girl?"

ℰℐℰℐ

It was nearly dark when Harvey rode in. Helen had left and Amanda had a roast in the oven for his dinner. She'd never felt any concerns over satisfying him at the table with her cooking.

He'd never complained once about the quality of his meals. *At least I've got that right.*

He entered the house, his tread slow and heavy on the wooden floor, and something in his demeanor caused her to raise her head.

At the sight of him, she knew something had gone awry. "How was town, dear?" she asked carefully.

"Nothing to get all excited about." He stood for a moment. "God, I'm hungry—supper about ready?" He looked her in the eye. "How'd the watering go?"

"It went all right—slower. I had to rest a lot more today. It hurt me and I had to stop." She disliked sounding defensive, but fear for her unborn child caused her to hope he'd glean from her words that she could no longer carry the water. If so, maybe he'd let up about it or lend a hand.

"Helen Ordway was here to see me," she continued. "And she told me to stop doing anything that heavy. Said I had no business doing anything strenuous, when I'm this far along."

She awaited his words on the subject. His long silence told her he'd never agree, but carrying the water made her strain inside and she was worried. Finally, he sighed and shot her a stern look. "You're right enough for now, though?"

"Yes, so far, I am." Hoping her expressed doubt might get through to him she decided to say no more about it. She also made very sure her arm stayed covered so the bruises from Jud didn't show.

"Well, you'll have to keep on with it for a few more days. I'm leavin' out on a cattle buying trip in the mornin' and I'd best get on with it so I can make it back before the child comes."

"Where will you go—how far away?"

"There's a good sized lot of Angus cattle for sale up north, near to Albuquerque. It's a far piece to go but they're of that mixed stock I've been wanting. Not many of them out this way yet, but they'd be real good on our kind of range." He washed up at the wash stand in the corner of the kitchen and, reaching for the towel, spotted the dog curled up beside his daughter. "What's this damned dog doin' in here?" His scowl set both mother and child on edge.

"He follows Marianna everywhere and she plays with him." Amanda's anger rose at his unfairness to his daughter, but she said nothing more.

Harvey shooed the dog out with his booted foot and Amanda heard the dog yelp after Harvey kicked the little creature outside and slammed the door shut

He softened his gaze as he turned to her. "Feels good to get home, wife." His warm words fell like stones upon her heart, knowing the unwelcome dog cowered outside in pain and rejection.

Harvey cast a hungry look at the table and headed for his usual chair. As he passed close to her, Amanda caught the clinging odor of a sweet, heavy scent, and recognized a strange perfume.

She shook her head in disbelief. Harvey would be the last man in the world she'd suspect of messing about with some woman in town, but still, she couldn't deny that she'd caught the odor of a very exotic perfume, thick and heavy, on his person.

That's no perfume of mine. I'd never wear anything like that. Frowning and puzzled, Amanda made haste to set the plates around while her mind raced with questions. Could he be involved with someone? From her own experience, she couldn't imagine Harvey interested in some other woman.

Turning her mind to getting supper on the table, she knew from her mother that the least hint of forthcoming food helped a hungry man wait for his supper. "It'll be a few more minutes, Harvey." She pulled down the flour tin and set to making biscuits, her best specialty learned from her granny up in Colorado. Her eyes filled with tears, remembering those gentle times at home.

Harvey moved into the sitting room to wait and slumped into a big leather chair, favoring the leather one with a reddish tinge to it. Marianna kept her distance, having felt rejection often enough to be hesitant in his presence.

The child went into the kitchen to stand next to her mother and hold onto her skirt while she strained upward to watch the making of the biscuits.

Amanda finished cutting them into rounds and shoved them in the oven. She took enough greens for small salad out of a box kept in the window. It hung to the outside for cooling. Her husband didn't much care for it, but salads were good for a body and she served them when she could.

She called supper. Sitting at the table, Harvey helped himself to plentiful amounts of succulent roast, and the potatoes, sliced and roasted in the oven. He completely ignored the greens. His expression worried her. He said nothing but something wore on his mind and, remembering the heavy perfume, Amanda began to worry. "Anything wrong, Harvey?"

"Nothing to worry your head about, my dear." He shoveled a huge forkful of meat into his mouth and sopped the juice with another biscuit. "Good fixin's, this is." He smiled up at her in appreciation and it made her remember the days when she'd thought how handsome he was when he'd smiled like that. He seldom did these days. Now he was plenty bothered about something. She sensed it.

Finally, Harvey pushed his chair back. "I'd best pack a few things. I'm in for a long ride and some it through some rough country. Might be, I'll hire a couple of wranglers to help me drive the stock back here while I'm at it, and if they turn out to be good riders, might keep one of 'em on."

He snorted. "What I've got here ain't worth a whole hell of a lot, might have to let one of 'em go. Best have a talk with them in the mornin' and line out the work before I leave."

If he did dismiss one of his hands, Amanda hoped it'd be Jud. The man was a constant worry if he saw a chance to bedevil her when Harvey's back was turned. He felt he could get away with it, knowing she'd never said a word to her husband. Harvey walked slowly to the bedroom and pulled down his leather pack. Amanda wondered how his big roan could carry all that and him, too. Spotty was a good horse, but Harvey was a big man.

℮ↄℯↄ

The next morning, as the beginnings of a soft pink-shaded daylight eased away the purple shadows across the eastern slopes, Amanda stood on the wide veranda with Marianna clutching at her skirts as she waved goodbye to her husband. Why the child had gotten up so early, she didn't know.

After he rode out of sight, the little girl tugged on her skirt. "We go pick, Mommy?"

"No, not today, lovey—looks like we might get some rain." Looking hopefully at the gathering clouds on the western horizon, she felt optimistic. The rain usually came from that direction. "Lord, I hope so. I can't keep hauling that water much longer." Her stomach crawled into a painful knot, just thinking about it.

Later, Amanda saw the two cowboys saddling up. "They should have been out hours before this. They take advantage of Harvey and that's something I certainly *will* let him know about." She smiled, hoping that information would get Jud fired.

"I'd be glad to see the last of that useless cowboy." A woman ought to be able to rely on her husband to handle things, yet she was reluctant to say one word about Jud's insulting actions to Harvey.

Another detail that seemed to miss Harvey's eye were the frequent disappearances of Jud when Harvey left the ranch. Buddy Long, the other hand, had proven more reliable, but he followed Jud at every turn.

"Where do you go when you disappear, Jud?" she wondered. "He's lucky the boss don't catch on. I mind my own business and he can mind his."

At the sound of horse's hooves she waddled to the door and opened it. Young Benny Ordway pulled up.

"Why, Bennie—hello." Surprised, Amanda waited to hear why he'd come. She'd be in need of his mother right soon, the way things were headed.

The boy, about age ten, dismounted, strode manfully to the porch, stopped, and stood at the bottom of the steps. "Howdy, ma'am," he said, his hat hastily doffed in respect. He couldn't keep his young eyes from her burgeoning belly no matter how hard he tried, and Amanda clamped her lips, struggling to hide her mirth at Bennie's youthful struggle with embarrassment and curiosity.

"Benny, nice to see you." Her voice filled with expectancy, as she waited for him to reveal the purpose of his visit.

Piddely let out a protective growl.

"Uhm—uh, ma'am, my mom sent me over to tell you she's taken real poorly just now an' hopes you won't be needin' her anytime soon." His freckled young face flushed

beet red up into his sandy-shaded hair. He scuffed his boots
in the dust, trying to keep his eyes off her condition.

"I'm doing real fine right now, Bennie. Tell your mom
not to worry her head over me when she's feeling so bad."
She didn't feel as sure as she sounded but she wasn't about
to lay guilt on a sick woman. "Won't you come in and set a
spell? I made some cookies yesterday."

As she spoke, Marianna toddled out to clutch onto her
skirt, alternately hiding and peeping out at Benny with her
big, blue eyes. The little dog moved close to her side and
took a protective stance.

"Uh, well, thanks, ma'am, for the offer, but I'd best be
getting' back. My mom might be a needin' me," he remarked over his shoulder as he headed for his sweating
horse. "I'll need to water old Jip, here."

"Help yourself," Amanda replied.

Remembering the cookies, she asked, "Will you take a
few of these cookies off my hands? You folks'll need something with your mother sick."

"She'll be real thankful for such, ma'am." He led the
animal out to the horse trough. "I'll just tend to my horse
right now."

Amanda put together a good sized pack of her latest
batch of sugar cookies, dusted with sugar granules. She
handed them to the boy as he sat his horse and figured part
of the sweets wouldn't make it home.

"Thanks, ma'am." He tipped his hat just like his father
always did and, nudging Jip in the sides, rode out of the
yard. His going left her feeling empty and terribly alone.

Amanda peered out at the rising storm, and hoped Bennie would make it home before it rained. Satisfied she'd
have a few days respite from her garden work, she turned
her attentions to the child. They sat together looking at an
old magazine. Remembering her life as a child in Colorado,
she remarked, "Be nice if we had a new one sometime." She
got a pair of scissors. "Let's cut some dolls out of this book,
sweetheart, shall we?"

Amanda used the time to think of her girlhood home. How she'd loved the soaring heights of those high Rockies. They'd lived right beside them and in the summer months their cattle grazed up in those high lost valleys.

In time, she saw that Marianna was asleep with the dog beside her, the torn old magazine at her feet. Amanda shrugged at the peaceful sight, curled up in a chair, and cuddled her huge abdomen. Would this child be the son her husband waited for?

CHAPTER 3

Reed Twining sat his horse, a nondescript black he'd found behind a shabby-looking general store on the outskirts of Yuma. It'd been tethered there with a rope and he'd helped himself.

"They'll have me for horse thievin' too," he uttered with a bitter laugh. "Things couldn't get much worse for me, anyway. I guess I'm just damned lucky this nag was wearin' a saddle." He rode over another long mesa, working his way north, carefully avoiding ranches, villages, and towns, as he rode.

He'd felt bad takin' the horse if it was some man's livelihood, even if it wasn't much of an animal. "I had to get away—or die in that filthy damned hellhole." He felt his desperation justified, in part, the things he'd been forced to do.

Enough things had gone against him this past year that he'd developed a deep mistrust of most people and, in particular, lawmen. Escaping that bastardly hot cell in Yuma made everything else pale in importance and he'd done it regardless of what he'd had to do. Stealing a horse hurt him way down deep. He felt he was as honest as the next man, but circumstances had dictated otherwise. His very survival had taken the upper hand.

After he felt he'd ridden far enough, he'd spent a few months at a ranch in the eastern part of Arizona. There, he'd earned enough to get newer clothes and outfit himself with a better saddle and a pair of pistols barely worthy of the name Colt, but they'd fired when he'd tried them. He'd liked the ranch well enough, but when they'd started wondering about him, he'd left in the night.

He'd been on the run for nearly a year, and had worked his way this far from Arizona and the hated Yuma Prison. His goal pushed him to make his way to one of the far northern states. It was late spring now, and if his luck held, he'd maybe get to Wyoming before it got too cold. "That ought to be far enough."

Reed didn't know the country hereabouts and, at another time, would have thought how good it looked for ranching. Those thoughts were forgotten now. He'd given up on his long held dream, since he'd run into that mess in Prescott.

The local sheriff in that town had taken the other side of things and he'd gotten a long prison sentence for trying to save a life. The injustice of it rankled deep and the bitterness in his heart had grown during his long months in a hole dug out of rock with evil, rusted iron bars placed squarely across the front. "Damned place wasn't been fit for hogs, let alone men."

His thoughts ran riotous and he paid little attention to where he might be as he entered a long narrow canyon. Enjoying the shaded coolness of the high walls, he decided to stop for a long cool drink from the stream running along beside the trail. "This is down low and nearly out of sight. Maybe I'll snare a rabbit for something to eat while I rest up, won't need to make a lot of smoke."

Hearing a shot ring out, Reed halted. "What the Hell?"

The icy feeling of recapture made him wary and careful in his movements. He pulled his horse into a copse of thick growth. Dismounting, he held his hand close over the horse's nose, lest he whinny and reveal their presence.

Hearing no further gunshots or noise, he tied his nag to a small tree and peered out enough to see the dust of two horses racing down the trail away from him. "What the hell was that all about?"

He stayed cautious. Not knowing the circumstances of what had just happened, he waited and watched.

After an hour, he led his horse out onto the trail and mounted. Riding a short distance, he suddenly felt tired, shaken, and off center. Hearing the gunshot had come too close for comfort. Upset, Reed decided to rest a bit, maybe snare that rabbit he'd been thinking of.

The canyon was cool and pleasant, aside from that gunshot, and he wanted to enjoy it. He'd seen the two men ride away. They seemed to be in a hurry and probably wouldn't be back. Reed's hands shook as he dismounted. Thirsty and dry-mouthed, he wanted a drink of something besides the fusty contents of his canteen. Hearing the gurgle of a nearby stream, he led his horse down to get a drink and fill his canteen with fresh, icy water.

When the horse snorted and shied back, nearly pulling the reins out of his hands, Reed looked to see what had spooked the poor nag. Stepping close to the water's edge, he saw a man lying in the shallows of the stream, face up, blue with cold, or dead. Reed looked closer. Dried blood had crusted on the man's chest and trails of red had seeped from his wounds into the water, coloring it for a ways until it became diluted and disappeared.

He left his horse upstream to drink and knelt down beside the wounded man. "Mister, you been shot. You alive?" He shook the man, trying to rouse him if he lived. His face was ashen in color, blood oozed from his lips, and he felt cold as ice.

Reed believed him dead until he heard a soft moan. Leaning closer, he saw the man's eyelids flutter and open, trying to see.

"I'm here to help you, mister." Reed comforted the man and helped him as he raised his head from freezing cold water in the snow-fed stream. Darkened, steel-blue eyes opened and fixed on Reed's face. The lips, blue with cold, seemed too frozen to move, yet the man attempted speech.

"Thank God, you've—can you get word—my wife—" He barely managed the faint words, but Reed heard him well enough. "—a ranch along the Pecos, a woman alone, little girl, a baby coming. Bradshaw place."

Reed tried to move the man, but he moaned in pain, indicating his refusal. "Please—let me lay—been here too long now. I'm near gone. They robbed me and killed me."

He lapsed into silence and, as Reed held the man's head out of the icy water, he saw the life force leave the body. A mysterious thing to see, he'd seen it before and it never failed to amaze him. He had no idea why, but it'd always struck him that way when he'd seen a man leave this life and go into the unknown.

"Poor cuss, what a hell of a way to go." Reed decided to haul the man out of the stream and, after a difficult struggle, dragged the body out onto a bit of soft sand. "Sand sure beats the hell out of all the rocks he was laying on. Poor soul near froze to death in that water."

Looking around, he spotted a big roan horse, grazing off down the canyon a ways, and guessed it belonged to the dead man. "Reckon I could try to haul the dead man back to his ranch. It'd put my travel plans off by several days. And then again, the local sheriff around this area ought to be notified of this killin'." *But it won't be by me.*

Reed faced a daunting dilemma. Though it was in his nature to do what was right, that very thing had already cost him dearly. Riding to tell a sheriff anywhere about a killing was just asking for trouble and a whole lot of problems he'd never asked for. A convicted and escaped murderer would be instantly guilty to any sheriff, and Reed knew it. "Would posters be up this far from Yuma?"

Shaking his head, he tried to decide what to do.

His imprisonment had been a terrible travesty, being innocent as he was. But in that small town of Prescott, Arizona, with everyone speaking against him, he'd had no chance. That farce of a trial was over so fast, he'd known right then, it had to be a cover-up for some crony of the sheriff.

Seeking the dead man's ranch and speaking to his wife would suffice. He no longer trusted doing what seemed right. He'd suffered enough trying to be a good man. Now, he'd look out for himself.

Seeing no one about, Reed dragged the dead man off into the bushes, sweating with the effort. Bradshaw was big, and moving his flaccid body took a lot of strength. After searching his pockets, he hauled over enough large rocks to cover and protect the man's remains. "Ought to be enough to keep the critters off until the wife decides what she wants to do about him," he muttered through clenched teeth.

He mounted his ragged horse and headed for the big roan. The animal still wore his saddle and bridle, along with a good sized pack. "Might use some of that chuck if he's got any packed in there. He won't be needin' it, and I damned well do."

Reed was a long and lean kind of man, and his travels had made him more so. He couldn't remember when he'd had a full belly.

It took him only a few moments to catch the horse and check over the pack. He shoved the few items from the man's pockets into the large leather pack and took some tough jerky from the grub bag. Looking the animal over, he decided to ride him and give his own miserable nag a well needed respite.

After searching the sky, taking his sights from the sun and the lay of the land, he re-filled the man's good sized canteen. Reed climbed out of the canyon and headed the horse southeast to find that ranch along the Pecos and deliver his sorrowful news.

He was sorry to interrupt his trail to the north, but he'd promised a dying man and wouldn't go back on what he'd been asked. He'd get back on the trail north as soon as he could. He picked his way and, according to the lay of the sun, decided he was headed the right way. "This ought to get me somewhere near the place he said his ranch was."

He didn't look forward to telling the wife about her husband's murder, but the man had asked this of him with his last few breaths and Reed was a man of his word.

He found the roan a decent ride and relaxed. By nature, the horse knew exactly where the ranch was, and Reed felt relief he wouldn't have to ask questions of anyone. If someone saw him riding a dead man's horse, it wouldn't look good and that worried him some, since he no longer believed any story he'd tell would be credible.

He'd already found enough trouble to last a lifetime. Maybe when he got near, he'd let the horse go and follow the animal to his barn, riding his own horse. "It won't look so bad that way."

With that decided, he let the horse have his head, settled into the nice rig the dead man had owned, and drowsed in the saddle. Relaxing to the sway of this horse's gait, he felt an unusual sense of comfort. He'd satisfied his hunger a few times from the jerky found in the saddle bags and took several deep pulls from the man's canteen as well.

What lay ahead, he had no idea, and the unknown aspects of the situation had him doing a lot of deep thinking, but he kept on riding.

❧❧

The big horse always headed to the southeast and Reed let him find his way. The roan usually chose a decent trail and, late one afternoon, they came over a rise, and Reed saw a group of ranch buildings spread out below. There were hay fields, corrals, and trees planted about the house. It looked to be a prosperous set-up. When the roan picked up his head, snorted, and quickened his pace, Reed knew he'd found the right place.

He changed horses and headed down.

CHAPTER 4

Amanda paced about the kitchen, frequently looking out the window. Harvey should have returned by now. He'd been gone nearly six days and she'd heard nothing from him. Fretting, she lumbered slowly about, running her hands through her hair. "If he's injured or dead somewhere, how would I know? Is he driving his new cattle back to the ranch? Is that why he's delayed?"

The last day or so, her swollen belly had made any sort of water hauling impossible, and she'd been unable to water the garden. If it didn't produce enough for the winter, she could no longer worried about that, or how Harvey's eyebrows would narrow with his cold, metallic-blue stare of disapproval.

Those oaken buckets were heavy. She was long past caring about his displeasure, any more than she gave a damn about that blasted garden.

Occasional bouts of passing labor pains spread over the past several days had given warning—her labor loomed close. She couldn't think anymore as she continued to pace about.

The midwife was ailing and Harvey hadn't come home. She hadn't seen either of the ranch hands all day, or was it more? She wasn't sure, but they were gone. The last she'd seen of them, they were headed into the nearest town wearing their best clothes.

On the positive side, the older hand, Jud, hadn't pestered her. She'd had enough of him, too. The man never missed a chance to make her feel hunted and uncomfortable.

Thinking of the two hired hands, a shiver passed through her. She spoke aloud to break the awful silence. "I'm alone, and with the midwife ailing, who'll go for the doctor in Artesia if I begin labor?"

Fear and a feeling of isolation struck a pang through her body. Her forehead felt like ice as she watched her two year old daughter, Marianna, playing with her few toys scattered about across the living room floor. Her small dog, Piddely, stayed close beside her.

Frowning, Amanda tightened her jaw, thinking she'd give Harvey a full accounting of those ranch hands. They'd certainly tended to nothing in his absence and it bothered her that the horses had looked her way for the past several hours, nickering and stamping about in the corral. Amanda knew they hadn't been fed since sometime yesterday, and ranch animals came first.

She shrugged and headed out to take care of that and the rest of the livestock, as well. There were chickens to tend, eggs to gather, and the cow to milk. She wiped away a weary tear as she waddled out to do the hired hands' work.

Her daughter followed her, and the fluffy little dog followed the child. Amanda shied away from the horses, they were big strong animals and their hooves were sharp. But stock horses were valuable to a rancher and must be cared for. Shrugging in futility, she went to work.

With gritted teeth and wrinkled brow, she saw no signs of fodder in the slatted feeders, and her anger exploded. The neglected animals rooted uselessly in the corners for something to eat. Her face burned with disgust at the extra work laid on her. *Everything is more difficult with me getting so heavy.*

She lumbered to the barn, grabbed up a huge armful of hay, and carried it laboriously to toss into their manger. The horses pushed up, nickering, nipping, and nosing each other out of the way, to start munching. She made several trips, with the prickly hay scratching her arms, to satisfy them. She stood for a while, leaning on the rail fence, breathing deeply, watching them take big mouthfuls, and dropping hay on the muddy ground in their eagerness. "Wasteful creatures," she said, panting for breath.

The horse trough sat half inside the corral and a wind-mill kept the water pumping all hours of the day or night, so that worry was taken care of. It overflowed constantly and kept the nearby area muddy. She'd often seen how some of the horses enjoyed standing in the soft mess, and Harvey had informed her mud was a comfort for trail worn hooves.

Marianna headed straight for the mucky mess. "Stay out of that mud, sweetie," Amanda warned. "I can't clean you up with all I've got to do."

She didn't bother with oats. She'd reached the point of gasping for breath, feeling worn to a frazzle, by the time she finished with the hay.

They kept about twenty hens in a snugly built chicken coop, ensuring an adequate number of eggs. Coyotes often lurked about, catching the odor of easy prey. She'd heard them out on the hillsides, yipping in their high staccato calls, but hadn't heard any unusual squawking or fluttering of wings from the poultry enclosure, and knew they were safe.

She found the chickens out of water, cracked grain, and mash. Sighing with fatigue, she found a bucket, toted water for them, and spread a generous amount of grain about on the ground. The chickens acted like the starving creatures they were, flocking close to her feet and her daughter's, as they scrambled frantically for the grain. Wings outspread, flapping and raising dust, they excited Marianna.

"Look, Momma, chickies pick in dirt!"

"Yes, little darling, that's the way chickens eat." Amanda patted her daughter's blonde head, taking a mo-ment's respite as she leaned against the gate, letting the cool breeze fan her forehead. She put a hand over her eyes to sweep an occasional searching glance past her immediate surroundings, out over the far-reaching landscape. The soft purples of the gentler mountains of southeastern New Mexico lay outlined in the distance, but they weren't the raggedly outlined mountains of the high Rockies.

She sighed and, squeezing her daughter's hand, she said it again, "This isn't Colorado, is it, honey?"

Most of the animals were fed now, but that all this work had been left for her when she was in this condition, made her stamp her foot. "Wait until I get my hands on those two! And this *is* something I can tell Harvey!"

After refilling the mash feeders, she gathered the eggs from the nests into her apron and headed for the house. For now, she felt satisfied the animals had been tended except for the cow. By the way she hung her head and lowed, she was hungry, too. If Amanda found the strength, she'd do the milking later. Marianna toddled along beside her, babbling, "We go pick, Mommy?"

"Not right now, dear. I know you love the garden, but we have these eggs to put away." She nodded to the clutch of eggs nestled in her apron.

In the house she laid them in a basket and after sitting at the kitchen table for a moment, left Marianna playing on the floor, and went back out with a shining pail to milk the cow. The cow's udder, swollen and tender with milk, made her grit her teeth at this additional cruelty. She fed the cow and watered her, another burden thoughtlessly placed on her.

After milking, she lugged the pail inside. Exhausted, she couldn't find the energy to heat the stew for herself and her daughter. Instead, she sank into the nearest chair and wiped her brow. "I'm completely tired out. My head is spinning. I've got to rest."

She closed her eyes, put her head back, and sighed. "God, help me."

Marianna played with her doll, while the dog lay faithfully beside her. Amanda dozed off, faintly hearing, but not comprehending, what the child uttered. *"Chickies?"* as she pattered toward the door.

ↄ⁄ↄↄ⁄ↄ

Wakening with a start, Amanda felt a stab of pain, beginning low in her back. Her eyes flew wide in alarm. "God, no, it's begun. I know it has, and there's no one here to send for the doctor!"

Amanda's heart raced. Childbirth, though not new to her, was a situation fraught with unknown dangers. She'd heard too many stories with bad endings and, being alone as she was, those images loomed terrifyingly close. With no one to help her along, and no hand to send for help, the terror of her situation dawned fully upon her and sent her heart tripping rapidly in her chest.

As another pain struck her, she cried aloud. "Oh God help me—what am I to do?"

Looking about for Marianna, she saw nothing of her. The doll she'd played with lay carelessly tossed on the floor, and the front door was ajar. Struggling to her feet, Amanda made her way slowly to the door as another sharp cramping pain began. She stopped, gripping tightly to the door frame, until it eased off. Reaching the porch, she called, "Marianna?" Her voice sounded thin and weak, even to her own ears.

She heard no answer, but looking toward the corrals, she spotted her child beside the water tank, sitting in and playing with the soft, dark mud. Mercifully, she was outside the corral fence, but those horse's hooves were just inside. The dog stayed just outside the mess, watching, listening, and wagging his tail to the babbling voice of the little girl. She happily played with handfuls of mud. Her face and clothing were already smeared with the filthy muck as she pasted it on the water tank.

"Oh no!" Amanda cried, but her voice closed off as another pain took her. Emitting a deep, heaving groan, she sank to the porch floor as her vision blurred. After it passed, she worried. *This is not the same as last time. It's coming on too fast. Everything's gone wrong. I'm alone, the midwife's not here, and I can't take another step to reach my child. I'm about to deliver this baby out here on this blasted porch!*

Her heart raced, and her breathing increased to sharp panting. This labor was different. All the horror stories Amanda had ever heard rose up to haunt and terrify her. She was in real trouble and there was no one about to turn to. Afraid and unable to reach her little child playing so near the sharp horse's hooves, Amanda searched frantically about until, in utter desperation, she squeezed her eyes shut and prayed aloud. "Oh God, please help me!"

Another cramp came—so hard, it left her gasping. Recovering from that, she heard the sound of slow hoof beats and looked up. Clearing the mist from her eyes, she saw a lanky, raggedly dressed rider enter the yard on a scrawny looking black horse. But he led another horse, so familiar it took her breath away. She gasped. "That looks like Harvey's horse." Panting the words as shivers of pain and alarm coursed through her body, she tried to get up but couldn't.

The rider drew up in front of the porch, and Amanda watched a tall man, dressed in trail-worn clothing, swing a long leg over to dismount. He removed his hat as he headed for the steps and greeted her in a soft, slow voice. "Howdy, ma'am, this the Bradshaw place?"

She watched his eyes narrow as he approached. Seeing her lying on the porch, like she was, and panting in pain he had a raft of questions, "You having some trouble here, ma'am?"

"Yes sir, I'm in a lot of trouble," she panted. "Who are you?" she asked, though at this moment, she really didn't care.

Whoever he was, even appearing down and out and raggedly dressed, his eyes conveyed an innate kindness she hadn't seen much of lately. He looked a decent sort and mighty darned good to her at the moment—she was no longer alone.

"I'm Reed Twining, ma'am, just traveling through the area. I came to bring you some news, but I reckon that can wait a bit." Coming closer, he squinted at her. "You in some kind of trouble—how can I help you?"

"I'm afraid my time has come. There's no one here to help me, and no one to send for the doc."

Fearful her condition might scare the man away, she knew that if this stranger rode away, she'd die out here, right on this porch. And her little girl—what would happen to her?

Cautiously, Amanda watched his eyes as he took in her advanced state of pregnancy and, when another pang seized her, it left no doubt as to her problem. Her face felt like ice, sweat broke out on her brow, and her heart tripped in fear that the man, seeing a woman in labor, would turn and run like hell, and she'd be alone again.

She readily welcomed the man's words as he said, "This porch is no place for a woman in your situation. All right if I help you get inside?"

She'd barely heard him say he had news. His being here meant she had help, and she was in no position to be fussy about it. But, worry over her child came first. "Yes, I thank you, but my little girl is sitting in the mud out by the horse trough and—I—I can't get to her. Could you see to her first?"

She saw him take in the child and her situation. Marianna sat busily squishing mud through her tiny fingers, squealing with joy.

"Ma'am, she looks to be fine for now. Let's get you inside." He stepped onto the porch and reached down with long, brown hands to lift her to her feet. "Just step along unless you're hurting again."

She allowed his touch and welcomed the strength of it, as he led her slowly inside and eased her carefully into Harvey's favorite chair.

"I'll see to the child, now, and the horses," he said and turned to leave.

She watched his lanky frame walk out the door. Heaving a sigh, she settled into the chair. *Who is he and why is he here?* Glad not to be alone, she didn't think on it any further or remember the prayer she'd uttered.

Another sharp pain tore at her, and the warm, wet flow of her water leaked out and down into the chair. "Oh no, my water's broken in Harvey's favorite chair. He'll be madder'n a hornet when he sees what I've done—hope it's not ruined."

Babbling her worries aloud, she tried to get up and fell back. *This baby's coming along too fast, way too fast—not like it was with Marianna.* Her heart rate increased with worrying about her unborn child. *Will he be all right or subject to some horrible condition?*

She felt utterly helpless with all the things she'd heard. Now, thanks to her errant husband and two useless cowhands, she was left to the mercies of a total stranger. *This trail-worn stranger is the only help I've got or likely to have.*

Amanda considered the challenges facing her, her frantic mind swirling with how to get a woman's help in bringing this child into the world. She couldn't imagine allowing any male other than a doctor that kind of personal contact. Not her husband either, for that matter. The very thought of it shocked and horrified her in the extreme.

She hadn't seen the ranch hands for a day or more, and this stranger off the trail wouldn't know where the midwife's ranch was located. Nor was there time for him to go searching. She pondered and fretted until another pang seized her. This one lasted so long she feared her child would arrive in the chair where she sat. More fluids seeped out. She feared it was blood. That would really damage the fine leather of Harvey's favorite chair.

He'll be very put out about it. She had that to face, along with being in active labor, a strange man in the house, and her child wallowing in the mud. Seeing the tall stranger come carrying her daughter upon to on the porch, Amanda burst into tears of relief.

Marianna's dress dripped with sticky mud. And her face and hands were smeared with the clinging mixture, as well. Her shoes were unrecognizable, with large chunks of the stuff plastered to them.

Reed stood her on the porch and said to her, his voice very gentle, "Little darling, stay right here until we see what your momma wants to do about you."

He brushed off some of the mud he'd gotten on his clothing from Marianna, before he entered the house and came to Amanda. "Your daughter's got herself into a mess, needs a bath and clean clothes."

"Thank you for bringing her up. I was worried about her being so close to the horses out there." She panted as another pain seized her. "If you can get some warm water from the stove well in the kitchen, I'll find clothes for her."

She forced herself out of the chair. The dripping fluids had wet her skirts, and the way they flapped and dripped across the solid wooden floor as she walked, embarrassed her, but there was no help for it.

She made it to the small chest where Marianna's clothes were kept as another sharp, tearing sensation took hold. Frozen in pain for several minutes until it let up, she pulled a drawer open and took out several items, hardly aware of what they were. She staggered into the kitchen and laid them on the table.

Her thinking had gotten completely muddled by pain and fear, and the sight of a strange man moving about on the porch with her child was unnerving, in spite of the fact that she was glad for his presence. With her oncoming travail of childbirth, she'd have welcomed anyone but Jud. At that thought, she shivered in disgust.

Hearing the man's soft voice, speaking gently to her child on the porch, Amanda turned in the chair she'd sunk into. He'd removed Marianna's shoes and outer clothing, and entered, carrying her in his arms. The little girl seemed completely content to be held by him.

Would a child know if someone is a decent sort? Amanda wondered. But some inner instinct told her the child knew better than she did about that. She couldn't re-call Marianna's own father carrying her about in that man-ner, not ever.

Amanda watched as Reed set Marianna in the center of the table. She'd have some cleaning to do when she was able but, at the moment, she felt only gratitude at having her child safely in the house.

The girl chattered gaily. "Mommy, I dig, and see hors-ies." She gazed lovingly at Reed while she rattled on about the mud. He set a pan of warm water on the table, found a cloth, and began the job of cleaning her. He took her little under shirt off and washed her face, then arms and stomach and on down to her dirt crusted legs. Her feet were clean, but the shoes lay on the porch in ruins.

Amanda appreciated that he never went close to the child's under drawers and they were none too clean. She'd attend to that. Unbelievably, had it not been for the intermit-tent, stabbing pains, Amanda would have enjoyed the last few moments. The man seemed at ease with the child and handled her gently.

He found a brush and untangled her long golden hair. "My, what a pretty little lass you are," he said softly to Ma-rianna as he put on the girl's nightgown. Without thinking what it was, Amanda had brought it to the kitchen.

"You're very gentle with children, aren't you?" she said.

She looked up into his eyes, deep-set, dark brown, nearly black, like his hair. His long jaw had a thick growth of stubble, but looked firm. There were indentations along both sides of his face, and his hair was sorely in need of a trim. It made her wonder if he had a family. She decided that if he did, he hadn't seen them for a while.

"Never had much to do with 'em, ma'am, but she's a tiny little thing an' a body has to be a tad careful."

"Could have fooled me—" she replied as another sharp pain shook her to the core. She tried her best to hide it from him and the child.

"You're coming right along, aren't you?" He nodded to the dampness on the floor. "Maybe closer than you think." He took the little girl in his arms again. "If that soup on the stove is for supper, maybe this little one'd eat a bite and take to her bed for the night. Might be a good idea with what's ahead."

The sun was nearly down, Marianna's bedtime was near. With the baby coming tonight, having her asleep would be best, but Amanda chilled at his words. He meant to help her deliver the baby, and she knew full well by now, she had no choice but to allow it.

Horrified, she struggled to keep her head on straight as she murmured, "Yes, it's ready. You're welcome to have some with her. I won't be eating. I couldn't, but I'll get the bowls and slice some bread."

She moved to the cupboard, took down what was needed, and made it to the table before she had another spasm. After it let up, she sliced the bread and got out the spoons. "I think that's it. Please eat as much as you like, there's plenty." She staggered off to her husband's ruined chair and eased her pain-wracked body into it.

Listening to the sounds of the man feeding her child and her babyish conversation with him during the meal, Amanda realized he had a way of charming her young daughter and she was glad of it. The man was a godsend to her right now and she appreciated that he'd come her way

CHAPTER 5

It was getting dark outside. Reed took the child in his arms and asked Amanda during a quiet moment, "Where does she sleep?"

Amanda pointed. "First small room down that hall on the right. She has a low bed in case she falls out at night."

He brought Marianna close and leaned down, holding her small body near enough to say goodnight to her mother.

Amanda kissed Marianna's pink cheeks. "Sleep tight, sweetheart." Murmuring thanks to Reed, she caught the male odor of him as she looked straight into his eyes. Fear lay there, and she understood it. He faced a situation no decent man ought to, and she was helpless to change what was happening.

He carried the girl to her bed and settled her down to sleep. She'd had plenty of outdoor activity this afternoon, and sleep would come easy. After a few crooning words from him, Marianna dropped off to sleep, a smile across her face.

He came back to the young woman. "She's a right nice child, your daughter." He added, chuckling, "Sleeps with an old corn husk doll. Is that the right one?"

She didn't seem to hear his question, and he voiced another concern. "Ma'am, where're your hands?" He'd already noticed how unusually vacant the ranch yard seemed, and wondered.

"My husband left to buy some cattle up near Albuquerque, and they rode off somewhere yesterday. I'll have plenty to tell my husband when he gets back!"

Her anger had flared to the point she'd forgotten she was in labor. Reed held back a smile. The little woman had spirit, and plenty of it.

He studied her. She needed him right now, more than she knew. Though he was a stranger, she faced trusting him with her life. Was she frightened by his appearance? Did she see him as some wild, strange male off the ranges, darkly weathered, and trail roughened? He didn't know, but he was someone who planned to do what he could. And he was scared to death himself with what he faced.

She settled a bit and took a closer look at him. "Reed is your name? I think that's what you said."

"Yes, ma'am."

Maybe he should have told her about himself, but the way things were progressing, his life story didn't make a lot of difference. She faced a tough night and that *was* what mattered. She wouldn't want to know the truth about him in any case, and he figured to be on his way in the morning, after he told her his news. She'd never have the embarrassment of facing him later on with memories of a night such as this one would be. He nodded his head, having decided that was the best for them both.

"Did you find enough for supper?" she asked then remembered about Marianna's doll. "Yes, she prefers that corn husk doll to the nicer one."

Reed hid a smile. Food, and perhaps a doll, were safer subjects for her than discussing what he'd need to do for her right soon. Maybe she couldn't bring herself to mention what lay ahead, but the way she trembled and suffered in her labor, he believed she'd be rapidly coming face to face with reality.

He wasn't too sure how he felt about this business, but he was here and planned to do his best for her. He answered her query about the supper. "Yes, ma'am, and it was right fine eating. It's been a while since I've had any home cooking. Mostly ranch chow, these past few months, or whatever I could scare up out in the brush. Traveling as I am, you don't hit towns much." He rolled his hat around his hands. This situation had him in as a big a twist as it did her.

As Amanda's labor intensified, the fear of having a strange man attend her birth became less important. She twisted in pain and tried to hide it from him. As the intensity increased and the labor prolonged, he waited for her go-ahead. She'd had a child and must know what to do. He didn't know much about it, but she'd need what help he could give.

He reached to take hold of her when she was about to stumble to the floor during an especially severe contraction, but she shooed him away. Having a strange man as a midwife probably remained completely unbelievable for her. He'd seen the look of a trapped wild animal cross her face more than once as she looked frantically about, searching for help. Seeing no one else, her eyes sought him. He hadn't run off like the hands, or her husband, for that matter.

Another pang tore through her with an intensity that left her panting for breath. She looked at him, a question on her lips. "If she's asleep, will you help me get the bed ready? I've things washed up and ready." Nervous, she babbled on. "My neighbor was going to help me with the birth, but she took sick and hasn't gotten better that I know of. Said she'd send word if she was feeling better."

As her misery mounted, it turned into anger toward her husband. "Those cows could have waited, but instead, Harvey's gone off for some fancy breed of cattle, right in my time of need. He's left me in a situation no decent woman should have to face." She gasped and nearly doubled over as another pain tore through her, reinforcing her desperate plight. "Oh, God help me!"

She reached the bedroom and Reed followed, hesitant to enter a room so personal to a married woman.

"I'll just wait out here, ma'am."

"I'll need your help getting this bed ready, if you will," she said, finally accepting her need of him. The birth drew closer, timidity and shyness no longer had a place here. He saw she'd finally faced it with that last tearing pain. Now she was a woman in the agonizing throes of labor, brought down to the unforgiving bed of childbirth. Anything could happen, and she had no way to stop it.

He came into the bedroom, looked around at the bed, pictures, rugs and heavy, solid furniture. "Nice room, ma'am." He looked at her in the gathering darkness. Her pale face and blonde hair, dampened by the sweat of her labor, couldn't hide the lovely contours of her face. *She's a fine-looking woman, even now while she's going through a particular kind of hell on earth, with this child she's having.* "I'd best get a lamp lit. We'll be needing some light, I reckon," was all he said.

"There's enough light to make up this bed before it's too late." Her voice sounded firm enough as she indicated the old, faded sheets she'd prepared. She handed them to him and told him every move to make until it was ready.

He'd never had a hand in preparing a birthing bed and he caught her sly smile about it. She might be relieved to find comfort in the fact that he was far more nervous than she. Most men would have tried to run for help.

"Ma'am, you must know, I've never had anything to do with what's going on here, calves, a colt or two, even sheep, but a human baby, oh my God, never!" His sweating face and trembling hands bore out the truth of his words. "You need help, and I'll do what I can for you, but I'm no doctor."

Amanda answered in between her panting breaths. "Maybe—it's not so—different—I don't know—but there's no one else. I'd be obliged—if you'll do what you can."

Looking into her eyes, acceptance, along with her fear of the events ahead, were there for him to see.

"I don't have too bad a time of it, so they tell me," she offered from panting lips.

He appreciated her kindness in that she sought to comfort him, seeing his shaking hands. She'd never seen him before this day, but he'd come, and they were in this together.

He left the room to find the lamp. Before long he found one on a shelf in the kitchen and struck a match. He returned carrying it high, letting it shed light across the bedroom. "I put some water on to heat out there. I hear it might be needed."

"That's good," Amanda replied. "The midwife boils the scissors in it, says it needs that kind of cleaning before you cut the cord."

"The cord?" He felt his panic rise. *What the hell is she talking about?* The room spun around a bit and he feared he'd pass out realizing he'd have to cut something.

"Yes. It connects the baby to the mother and has to be cut." His face had gone icy at those words, but she went on to explain. "There's a part that comes after the child is born. Cutting it won't hurt me or the baby. It needs tying off. One close to the baby, and one in another place, and cut in between."

She must have learned these things from that ailing midwife. He needed to know what to expect, but her instructions weren't making him feel any better.

"I might be able to do it myself, but I don't know how I'll be when it's over," she whispered as another spasm shook her.

"No matter, ma'am, if that's what needs doing, we'll get it done then." He'd recovered his nerve enough to prepare himself for what lay ahead and do what he could to help the woman. He straightened his shoulders and seeing the clothes she wore, suggested, "You might want to find something better to wear, ma'am, I reckon that dress'll be in the way, won't it?"

"Thanks, I'll just change right here if you'll give me some privacy."

He quickly left the room and shut the door. He wanted to light a cigarette in the worst way, but worried the way things were going, there wasn't time for a smoke.

She stepped to the door wrapped in a loose cotton nightgown, and called him just as another pain of devilish intensity struck her. She cried out with the depth and sharpness of it and nearly fell to the floor.

He rushed in and caught her. "Best get yourself on the bed now, before you have this baby on the floor." He helped her crawl onto the sheets they'd readied only moments ago.

"I needed to push that time. I think this child is coming."

She wanted to scream. He could see it building in her, but probably didn't want to awaken Marianna with too much noise, so she softened her cries to deep, animalistic sounds as she thrashed her head about and moaned.

"Not that time?" He looked into her stricken eyes. It was near time for him to get very personal, and he was in no hurry. "You tell me when, so I can catch the little tyke when he or she makes their way into this world." He knew pretty well what he had to do. "I'll go right quick now and get the scissors ma'am. Might be using them real soon by the way things are shaping up."

"Yes, it won't be long no—o—o—o—w."

Seized with a massive wave of pressure and pain, she panted for breath, sweat dripped from her face and hair as she thrashed about, flipping her head from side to side, unable to stop.

Reed stepped close, and placing a solid, strong hand on her forehead, he crooned softly. "It's going along nice, I think, ma'am. No need to worry now, just keep on working just like you've been doing." He smoothed her forehead with gentle hands, stroked her damp, silky hair, settling her a bit before he ran to the kitchen for the scissors and rushed back to the bedside.

"It's coming!" She moaned and grunted with another contraction until she gave a huge push with her tensely bunched abdominal muscles. He laid the scissors down, and whipped her gown out of the way to see a crown of dark hair come into view.

She stopped for a moment, eyes closed and panting, until she gave the final tremendous push. Reed reached out to catch the slick little body in his hands.

He gazed in awe at this new human being until the huge, snakelike, bluish cord came out attached to the child. It lay there, pulsating like a live thing. He stared at it for a moment. *Oh God! I've got to cut that!* He turned his attention back to the baby wriggling and squirming in his hands.

The newborn let out a loud angry, gurgling cry and Reed, seeing fluid in the tiny mouth, instinctively turned the baby face downward on the palm of his hand. Fluid slipped out and drained away. The slightly oversized genitalia proclaimed his sex. The child squirmed and snuffled for a bit, yet seemed to breathe well enough to pink up in color.

After several of his angry cries, Reed wasn't worried about the baby's state of health. "Ma'am, you have a son," he told her and laid him on her abdomen as it was the best place he found to attend to the cord.

He took the two thin bits of string she'd gotten ready and tied the now quiet umbilicus in two places, one very close to the child as she had ordered. Taking the scissors, Reed severed the child from his mother.

He wrapped a strip of clean cloth around the child's cord site, and wiped the small body gently with a soft rag dipped in warm water. After he wrapped the tiny boy in a softly worn blanket she'd prepared, he laid him in his mother's arms. "Here you are, ma'am, meet your new son."

She took the child and nuzzled her nose against his soft cheek. Looking up at him, she said, "Thank you."

Unshed tears lay in her eyes and tired and worn from her travail as she had to be, he saw a glow of happiness spreading across her face as she murmured to her child.

Reed turned his attention to the mother. Uncomfortable at the extra amount of tissue and drainage, he didn't know if it was too much or about right. He guessed that was the same as he'd seen with cattle, and it was natural, or he sure as hell hoped so.

He took the liberty of washing her down and, as she lifted herself, he removed the soiled linens from beneath her body and laid clean linens under and against her swollen and torn flesh. After padding and covering her private area, he pulled her gown down and covered her with a blanket. He took the baby from her, jostling him gently in his arms. "You'd best rest awhile, ma'am. You did a fine job bringing this little feller into this world."

She looked at him with tears in her eyes, but said nothing.

"You take your rest now, ma'am," he whispered and left her to sleep.

Reed gently cleaned the baby as much as he felt comfortable doing and wrapped him in clean, warm clothing. His gentle jostling had put the babe to sleep. He laid him in the cradle she had close by and drew another blanket over him. "You'd best rest a bit, too, young man."

Reed looked down on the sleeping woman. The dark circles beneath her eyes spoke of the difficult work required to bring a baby into this world. He wanted to reach out and smooth her hair, but thought better of it and left her to rest. Looking again at the sleeping baby, he murmured softly, "Poor little man, your daddy's gone and your momma's left alone with the care of you."

There was no hurry to tell her she the news he'd brought. Seeing things were quiet for the moment, he walked out on the porch and sat down to think. "Time enough in the morning for something like that."

For a ranch, the place seemed nearly abandoned. *Too damned quiet around here for a working cow outfit,* Reed mused, watching the quiet of the nighttime ranch yard. *No sign of hands about or neighbors coming around. Who takes care of things in the boss's absence, if anyone?* He had a lot of questions, but no ready answers. He pulled out his tobacco, rolled a nicely rounded smoke, sat back in one of the handy chairs, and lit up.

As the smoke curled upward, he continued his thoughts. *This is a right nice place from the looks of it, but something's sure as hell not right around here.*

His deeper instincts were usually right about a lot of things. But why bother worrying about this place? It wasn't any business of his, and he'd be hitting the trail again as soon as he'd told the missus his news.

CHAPTER 6

Reed relaxed, sitting on the porch in the glow of a softly star-lit night. A slip of moon appeared to be rising and after a bit, he drowsed off to the soft sounds of a hoot owl proclaiming his territory. The clopping of hooves moving slowly into the ranch yard awakened him. Ever aware of his own personal situation, he sat up straight, hidden in the shadows and on the alert.

Watching and waiting, he saw the beginning light of the coming dawn in the eastern sky and wondered, *Who'd come riding in late in the night like this or so early in the morning?*

Reed sat quietly in the darkness of the porch watching the two riders move slowly to the corral, unsaddle their horses, turn them into the corral, and slip quietly to the bunk house. He decided they must be some of the cowhands that rode for this outfit. It wasn't his business where they'd been, but men coming in this late didn't strike him as right.

Morning was soon enough to get into these things. He'd see what happened then. He drowsed off again until the thin wailing of the newborn child awakened him.

Reed knocked at the bedroom door. Amanda answered immediately and said to enter. Like any new mother, she'd awakened instantly to the tiniest sound from her newborn's cradle.

"He needs his momma," Reed said as he came closer.

She flushed at the smile he gave her in the dimness of early morning. He decided she might be uneasy at his presence after last night. She'd rested some, and being a young, healthy woman, he noticed her color and strength had improved.

The baby fretted and waved his tiny fists in the air. Reed picked him up and, holding him carefully, brought him to his mother. Amanda looked at him, her eyes softer this time.

"Thanks, mister—I owe you a world of gratitude."

He believed she meant for everything he'd done, caring for her daughter as well as attending her.

"Think nothing of it." He flushed and went on. "Please, ma'am, don't take on about what happened here last night. It was human thing, and natural, that's all. Think nothing more about it. If I was a help to you, so be it. I'd be mighty obliged if you'd see it that way." He nodded and bent his dark eyes on her to emphasize his meaning.

"What is your name again, sir? I think you may have told me but I don't remember."

"Name's Reed, ma'am. Reed Twining."

"Would you have any objection if I call this boy after you? I'd see it as an honor, and I'd like to do that." She frowned, "Harvey might have a name he wanted, I don't know, but not for this child. I'm determined to have my say about the naming of him."

"Why, ma'am, I think that'd be just fine, but if you knew everything about me, you might think to change your mind on that."

His face flushed but he was pleased all the way through by her thoughtfulness.

Amanda straightened herself in the bed. Her chin went up. Her voice deepened and took on strength. "I don't think so, Mr. Twining. I know people, too, and no matter what lies in your past, you *are* a good man and I know it. My son will honorably bear your name and be proud of it." Then the fussing of the baby took precedent and she indicated she wanted to feed him.

Reed hastily withdrew. "I'll be sitting on the porch, then," he said as he left the room.

Amanda wanted to try getting up when Reed had gone but, unsure of the state of her clothes from the aftermath of giving birth, stayed put. She didn't want him to attend her any more than he already had. But in any case, she had to care for this new child as well as the other one, fast asleep. Thinking of the birth, she flushed hot, remembering his attentions to her during that time.

Responding to the snuffling, frantic cries of her newborn, Amanda guided the wriggling infant to a swollen breast and felt his seeking lips catch hold. "Hello, little Reed, what a fine big boy you are. Your daddy'll be mighty proud of you."

But thoughts of presenting this boy child to her husband brought her no joy. It was expected and she'd done his bidding.

Reed sat in one of the rustic chairs on the porch, taking in the cool morning air. It'd been a long night for him, and he enjoyed the good, solid feel of accomplishment. It was over now, so he relaxed and smiled, pleased with himself. "Who'd ever think I could do something like that," he uttered as he fell into a soft sleep in the quiet of the very early morning. A rooster began his early morning crowing but he barely heard it.

෨෨෨

Dozing on the porch, Reed never felt the first rays of sun on his face, or the soft breeze that wafted across the ranch yard, but he did awaken to the sound of carriage wheels coming into the yard. Alarmed, his pulses leaped up and he waited; his survival instincts on full alert, as the buggy came to a halt.

A slightly overweight, middle-aged woman alighted carefully and turned to the young boy who did the driving. "Bennie, you go tend that horse now, while I check on the missus."

Spotting Reed, she stopped. Her eyebrows raised, she faced him, her work-roughened hands on her hips. "Now, who might you be, young man?"

He recognized authority in her voice. "Just passing through, ma'am—name's Reed Twining."

"Missus, inside?"

"You'll find her resting in her room."

The woman's face blanched white at his words and Reed understood her alarm. A ragged stranger on the porch shouldn't know where the missus rested. It was more information than she'd expected to hear.

Reed smiled inwardly. *Yes, ma'am, I know where she's at. A whole lot happened around here last night.*

Her eyebrows shot higher and her jaw clamped shut. The lady barely nodded to him as she hurried into the house, almost slammed the door, and, no doubt, headed straight into the bedroom.

Amanda awakened in the dimness of the morning light to see her midwife, Helen Ordway, staring down at her. Then she watched the woman's eyes widen as she focused on the tiny newborn snuggly tucked in beside her.

She touched Amanda on her shoulder, as if to reassure herself that her friend had survived. "Merciful God, you've had this child all alone!"

Amanda sat up in bed, fully awake now, and cried out, "Helen, oh God, I'm glad to see you!" She flushed a dark rose shade of embarrassment, "I know how things look, Helen." She looked her in the eye. "I needed you desperately last evening." Tears filled Amanda's eyes as she straightened herself in the bed. "There was no one to send for you and no one here to help me when things got started."

The tears fell, though she tried hard to hold them back.

Helen gulped before she began her questioning in an almost whispering tone. *"Who* is that strange man sitting on the porch out there?"

Amanda hadn't felt any alarm at all and, seeing Helen's curiosity rising to monumental heights, sought to settle the woman's worries. "You want to know what went on around here last night, and something definitely did." She pulled her gown close around her neck and indicated the sleeping infant, tucked in beside her. "Meet Mr. Reed T. Bradshaw."

Helen gently scooped the babe up in her arms and began her inspection, as much in her capacity of a midwife as of a friend. "Why, Amanda, he's absolutely beautiful, looks right fine." She opened his soft, worn blanket and inspected the tiny body beneath the binding to check the severed umbilicus. "I see he's got the thread tied on his cord right enough. Who did this, Amanda?"

"That stranger out there came along right when things got real bad. I couldn't get Marianna out of the mud or get myself into the house. It may not seem right to anyone else, but last night, that man out there on the porch saved my life and my daughter's life, too." She shrugged, but her chin was firm. "I had no choice in the matter and I thank God he came when he did."

"Who is he?" Helen's face had gone ashen. "And what went on around here last night?"

"I have no idea who he is, but I know what kind he is— that's enough for me. Marianna took to him right away." Adamant, she looked into Helen's eyes. "I believe a child knows if a man is good, maybe better than us."

Helen only nodded, but Amanda knew she had more questions.

"That man out there came along just in time for me and to rescue Marianna from that mud out by the horse tank. He gave her a bath, fed her supper, and put her to bed, too," Amanda went on. "I had no other choice, right then, Helen, I was so far gone in labor, I couldn't even walk!" She stiffened her spine as she remembered and considered how it might look. "I had no one to call or send for help! And now that it's over, having time to think, I can't imagine how I could tell any of this to Harvey!"

Her anger grew, knowing he'd take things wrong. He'd gone off and left her alone at a critical time—her back had been squarely against the wall and she'd defend her actions to him or anyone else. She'd done what she had to for her own survival, for that of her daughter, as well as her newborn.

Helen shrugged. "Well, what's done is done. Let's get you cleaned up then. Childbirth is a messy business, at best." She pulled back the heavy curtains, letting in some badly needed light, and dug out some fresh clothing from the large wooden chest

"I don't want to think about what happened last night," Amanda said. "I can't right now, but I'm going to be fine, Helen." Remembering the gentle care she'd received from the stranger, she went on, knowing she was repeating herself, "I was afraid when my labor started, so hard and fast, nothing at all like Marianna's birth. There was no one here. I don't know what would have happened yesterday, if that man hadn't come riding in when he did."

The conversation halted as Marianna came into the room dragging her tattered blanket. "Mama, where man go?" She saw Helen, and stopped. Then she spotted the sleeping baby wrapped in his blanket held in her mother's arms. "Ooh—dollie?"

Her blue eyes grew large and she approached the small bundle slowly, questioning, her small hand outstretched.

Amanda patted her on the head. "Good morning, dear, look what came in the night. You have a baby brother. Want to see?" She looked to Helen before letting the little girl get close enough to touch her brother.

At her nod, Helen took up the infant and held him close enough for Marianna to put one tentative finger on his cheek.

"Baby?" She giggled, and questioned what lay uppermost in her child's mind. "Man go 'way?"

Helen's eyebrows raised in surprise. "Seems that feller out there has made a friend for himself with this one."

She nearly giggled at the way the child had taken to him.

"He's sitting right out on the porch, Marianna." Amanda gave her daughter a quick kiss before she turned and ran out of the room and out onto the porch, her newborn brother immediately forgotten.

Soon the two women heard sounds of her childish chatter and Reed's deep answering voice. Bennie had come on the porch to sit with Reed and Marianna spoke to him, too. Amanda held back her smile.

They heard her say, "Hi, Bennie."

Her voice held a newly found shyness, and Amanda smiled at Helen. "She took to that man right away and it sounds like she likes that Bennie of yours, too. I'm afraid my girl's got an eye for the boys."

"Never mind about that child," Helen replied. "Now you tell me everything, that went on here last night, and don't be shy about it. And I'll need to check you over to see how you are."

Amanda told her the best she could how things had gone and her helpless embarrassment at the man's intimate attentions. "He was gentle and very kind. He never made me feel wrong about his helping me. I'll thank him until my dying day. If you can't understand that—"

Ready tears filled her eyes.

Helen ignored the tears, said no more about Reed, and became all business. "This birth will need to be registered in Artesia. I'll attend to that for you—that's about all I'll have to do with this case."

The examination and cleaning done, Amanda straightened her gown and lay relaxed on the bed, her infant in her arms while Helen busied herself collecting soiled linens. He'd stacked them in the corner after he'd cleansed her and

changed her linens. She flushed hot at memories still fresh
in her mind.

They heard a knock outside the bedroom door. Helen
opened it to see Reed with Marianna in his arms. His face
wore an embarrassed flush. "Come to see how the missus
might be doing."

Though uneasy about how she'd feel about him this
morning, Amanda smiled to see that he stood his ground.

"Sir, she seems to be just fine, and that baby is too,"
Helen answered.

Amanda smiled at Reed. "How is it you came to be
here at this ranch, like you were?"

"I've my reasons." He faced Helen, though his eyes
tended to stray toward Amanda with the infant bundled in
her arms. "If you'd come outside with me for a minute,
ma'am, I've something to say."

Amanda had no idea what he had to say, but his quiet
manner to Helen told Amanda it was best be said out of her
hearing.

Helen complied. "Hold on while I put this child in his
cradle so his mama can rest."

She took the baby and laid him in his cradle then followed Reed out to the porch, leaving a puzzled Amanda
resting in bed.

It was coming up a glorious morning, with the sun well
up by now. Bennie sat petting the fluffy Piddely, who
stayed close against Marianna's side. Reed smiled at the
sight of them then opened the conversation.

"Ma'am, I came here with some mighty bad news for
the lady, but after seeing the fix she was in—well, as you
can imagine, it had to wait. Now that things are settled with
the child and all, she'll need to hear what I have to say."

Helen's face grew pale and her body stiffened. "My
God, man, what is it?" Even young Bennie sat at attention
in his chair, all ears. Seeing that, Helen held up her hand.
"Hold on a moment. Bennie, why don't you take Marianna

off to play, and you'd best keep her out of that mud by that watering trough."

The boy scrambled off to comply, though Reed saw by his disappointed expression that he was every bit as curious as Helen, to hear what Reed had to say.

With the children out of earshot, he went on with his story. "A few days ago, I came across a man shot and dying. He'd been robbed, he said, and with his last words asked if I would please tell his wife what happened." He looked at her with regret on his face. "I didn't know what to do, so I covered him with enough rocks to keep the critters off and came to tell his wife what'd happened and see what she'd want to do about him."

"And you walked in on a woman about to give birth. Lordy man, that'd make most men turn and run,"

Helen had a friendly shine in her eyes as she faced him. With those words of quiet praise, Reed hoped he'd made a friend.

If she knew he was an escaped convict, what would she have to say about that? He had no plans to enlighten either woman and would soon be back on the trail north, so it didn't matter in the least.

Marianna came running up to the porch. "Weed, I wan' eat." Helen looked surprised at the child calling him by name, but said nothing as the little girl ran into the man's long arms.

He picked her up and said to Helen, "If you're hungry, maybe we all could use a bite. I'll see if I can scare up a few vittles for the lot of us." With Marianna in his arms, he headed into the house and into the kitchen.

Helen followed him in and sat down. He set the child in a chair while he dug around for something to fix. Helen sat at the table watching his every move. It didn't bother Reed at all as he took out flour, bacon, eggs, and a pot of lard. He rolled up his sleeves, cut thick strips of bacon, and after getting the huge iron stove roaring, set the skillet on and filled it.

He found the coffee pot and filled it from the water pail, now nearly empty, and set it to boil. Then he measured out enough flour for a huge mess of biscuits.

Marianna, mesmerized by his deft actions, had never seen a man working in a kitchen before. That was obvious to Reed. Bennie stood in the doorway, his eyes also wide. When Reed asked him to fetch a new bucket of water, he raced to comply.

Reed turned to Helen as he set about mixing the biscuits. "There's time enough to tell her what I came for. It'd be best if you were here for that. She'll be needing a friend about then, I reckon."

After kneading the dough, he rolled it out and used a water glass to cut it into thick rounds. The bacon was sizzling and snapping and he deftly turned the strips before shoving the biscuits into the oven. He peeled and sliced several potatoes and after removing the bacon, poured the slices into the pan of grease. With them frying, and the biscuits baking, the smell in the kitchen was mouth-watering.

Amanda eased quietly into the kitchen and stood in amazement, watching the stranger work in her kitchen as if he belonged in it. Taking in the odor of the forthcoming breakfast, she had to swallow a few times to handle the saliva from her hunger. After the trials of labor, she was ravenous.

She stood there in silence, watching this raggedly dressed man move about with practiced ease in a woman's domain. He took another frying pan and poured beaten eggs into it and, with the biscuits ready, he said to Helen, "If you'd know where the plates and things are, the food is pretty near ready."

"You bet I do, mister." She jumped to the task and set the table in short order.

Bennie and Marianna helped her with it and the boy whispered to his mother, "Ma, I ain't never seen a man cooking before."

"Son, there's aplenty you haven't seen before. Set and eat now, and didn't I tell you never to say ain't."

Her admonishment, softened by an indulgent smile and soft caress across his sandy-shaded hair, brought a flush to his cheeks. Reed smiled to see it and at her reply to the boy. He took a plate, filled it with a bit of everything and, taking some utensils in hand, said, "I'll see if the missus might want to eat something." He headed toward the bedroom, but Amanda stepped out.

She smiled at the amazed look on Reed's face. "I'll sit at the table."

A shade of embarrassment flashed across his face, "Sorry, ma'am, didn't see you were out here."

Amanda looked at him. "Good morning, Mr. Twining, did you get any sleep at all?"

"Not a lot. But I'm fine. How are you now?" He looked from her to Helen.

"She'll do fine...Mr. Twining, is it?"

He reaffirmed his name as he took in the refreshed appearance of Amanda. *How could you possibly be all right after what you suffered in having that baby?* She'd slept enough to ease the dark circles from beneath her eyes, and Helen had brushed her shinning golden locks. He found himself amazed that a woman could go through what she had in bringing forth a child and look that good the next day. Shaking his head in amazement, he decided women were amazing creatures. They had to be.

CHAPTER 7

Y ou look right fine this morning, ma'am," was all he
could think to say as he handed her the filled plate
and pulled out a chair.

She somehow understood the look of wonder across his
face. "Thank you," she replied, her voice wavering as she
looked him in the eye, expressing far more feeling than required for a casual complement, and slipped into the chair.

"How's the little one this morning?" Reed asked her.

"He's just fine—hungry. Did I tell you his name?"

"I believe so." He flushed, feeling the heat rise up into
his shaggy hairline. The older children sat quiet, listening to
their exchange. "I'm real honored by that, ma'am."

Amanda sipped her coffee, feeling herself and her life
returning to normal, though with a new child to care for, it
would be harder.

"You've done so much for me, I couldn't think how
else to thank you." Taking a bite of her food, she looked at
him, her eyebrows raised. "I must say you're a handy one in
the kitchen. This is mighty good."

Reed saw to it she had plenty before her and turned his
attention to Marianna. He handed her a filled plate. "Here
you go, sweetie."

Bennie helped himself and loaded his until it nearly
spilled over.

Marianna looked up at Reed. "Where baby?

"He's resting right now." He patted her shining hair. "You're momma will bring him out after a while. Remember, she's got that new baby to tend to now, and she'll be needing you to help her with him."

She fastened her big blue eyes on him. "I hep Mommy?"

Looking at the little girl, a feeling of child hunger rose within him. He envisioned Marianna grown into a lovely young girl, and himself with a shotgun, running off her many amorous young suitors.

Amanda got busy with her breakfast and took several bites. "You are one good cook, mister. This is better than I make, or could it be because I'm so blessed hungry?" She smiled at him. "I'd like more coffee."

Reed grabbed the pot and poured another brimming cup for her.

Amanda, remembering Bennie's hurried visit to say his mother was ailing, stopped eating. "Helen, how are *you,* then?" she asked. "After Bennie's visit, I was worried."

"I had some kind of pain in the belly. Hit me bad for a while, but it's gone now and I came quick as I could, being as your time was so close." She sighed and smiled. "I arrived a mite late."

Amanda finished her breakfast and went into the bedroom. Baby Reed had awakened and begun snuffling and rooting about for his own nourishment. She took him up and settled back to feed him.

Helen had completed a very thorough exam, but hadn't said a word as to her condition and Amanda began to worry. When her friend came into the bedroom, she asked, "Was everything all right, then?"

"Right as rain, lady." Helen smiled. "Looks like you've begun your healing real fine." She cast her eyes on the feeding infant. "How's that boy this morning?"

"Hungry," she giggled in her relief and joy. "Harvey wanted a son real bad. He'll be happy to see this little fel-

low. Hope he'll like the name. I called him after that man
out there. It was the only way I could repay him."

Amanda saw a shadow pass over Helen's face at the
mention of her husband. Something about it made her wonder. When she finished feeding the baby, Helen reached
down and said, "I'll take him."

She took the boy, laid him across a generous shoulder,
and patted long enough to hear an explosive burp, then laid
him back in his cradle. He slept soundly again with a thin
trace of bluish milk draining from his tiny pink mouth.

Saying nothing more, Helen helped Amanda get into a
clean gown then told her, "Reed has something to say to
you."

Puzzled, Amanda frowned. "Yes, he said that. What
could he have to tell me?"

Helen hadn't said anything, but Amanda felt a chill,
remembering that strange look on her friend's face.

She took Helen's arm. "Let's get out of this room. I've
always hated this dark bedroom. Harvey always keeps it
closed up tight. I'm glad you've opened things wide so a
body can breathe."

With her arm in Helen's, she returned to the kitchen.
Marianna and Bennie sat side by side, eating their breakfast
and talking to each other. Reed sat at the end of the table,
his hand on a cup of coffee. His plate was empty.

The children got up from the table together and when
Marianna asked to go outside and play with Bennie, she
asked Reed instead of her mother.

Amanda wondered at the strong attachment the child
had formed to this total stranger. He'd be leaving shortly
and she realized she'd feel a good-sized loss herself, when
he was gone—maybe every bit as much as Marianna.

Reed looked at her. "Ma'am, why don't you sit down?
I came here yesterday to give you a message, but things
happened." He flushed. "My news had to wait a bit, but
with the little ones outside, it's time to have my say."

Amanda felt her blood grow cold at the tone of his voice and the sober look on his face. She took Helen's hand, waiting for what he'd come to say.

Looking Amanda in the eye, his voice low, he began. "Several days ago, I was coming through this high walled canyon heading generally north, when I heard a shot. I hung back, being I didn't know what was going on." He hesitated a moment. "I waited for a while until I heard horses riding away. Seeing nobody around, I went on down the trail a bit." Reed cleared his throat and grimaced. "I heard a creek running just below the trail and went down to water my horse and have a drink. When my horse shied back, I saw a man layin' there in the creek, half froze or dead.

"That water was running real cold the way it does in those canyons," he continued in his soft, deep voice, laying out the grim scenario as he told the young mother of her husband's death.

He regretted the look of shock that came over her face, and the way she turned ashen. Tears flooded her eyes as she dropped her head onto the table and sobbed. Helen, white-faced herself, moved close, and put an arm around Amanda's shoulders.

Reed wasn't sure how to proceed now that his story was told, and a sobbing woman made him uneasy in the bargain. This sort of news had to be devastating to a young wife and new mother. With this loss, the young woman was left alone in the world, as far as he knew, with two babies to bring up.

He went on to finish his story. "Ma'am, I went through his pockets and brought what was there. I never looked at it, being private and all, but his things are in those saddle bags that were on that big roan horse out there." He rose up, eager to get the story finished. "I'll go fetch it in for you, ma'am."

Amanda raised her head to look at him. In her chalk-white face and stricken eyes, he saw a look that befitted the size of her loss. Her eyes, filled with tears, brimmed with more to fall. Unable to find words of comfort, Reed shrugged and headed out the door.

He left the house and almost as a unit, both women rose from the table and moved to the kitchen window to watch the man walk out across the wide ranch yard. His stride, long and purposeful, took him to the barn where he entered and disappeared.

Helen broke the silence between them. "You all right, Amanda?" Trying to find words of comfort, she offered, "I'm real sorry, dear. This is mighty hard news for any woman. You know me and Herb'll do what we can to help out." She indicated the two children playing in the yard. "Seems like it'll be mighty hard for you now, raisin' the two younguns on your own."

"I don't know what I'll do, Helen." Amanda turned to her friend, her tear-drenched eyes beseeching answers. Wondering how to proceed, she said, "Harvey made all the decisions around the ranch, and now suddenly, everything is up to me." The tears came again.

"Something has to be done about this, if Harvey was robbed and murdered, the law must be notified," Helen avowed, as if to make things right.

Amanda couldn't think of anything to say in reply. Nothing made sense right now. She needed time to think, and time to heal from her labors of last night. Thinking about her situation was more than she could do at the moment.

"The law needs to know what happened to Harvey," Helen went on, verbalizing her thoughts. "Laws a mercy, a man's been robbed and murdered. They'll need to arrest and hang the man who did this. Can't have that sort running loose about the country."

But to Amanda, her words meant more responsibility thrust on already overburdened shoulders. "Would you know—who to tell?" Her words were halting as she dried her eyes. Helen would think her tears were of sorrow, but deep down, she knew they were of fear. How could she get along without Harvey managing things? She'd never handled anything in her life outside of taking care of a garden, a house, and her babies.

She tried to be ashamed of her real feelings, but hard as she tried to deny it, a great sense of relief had rapidly come flooding through her at the news she no longer faced Harvey's harsh, forbidding control. Feelings of elation weren't far behind. *Nothing can stop me from returning to my beloved Colorado.*

"I wonder if Reed would stay on here until I decide what to do?" Amanda queried, half to herself, half to Helen.

She'd grown to rely on a total stranger in a very short time, though she knew almost nothing at all about him.

"He seems a good sort." Helen, always willing to help, sounded positive. "He's a right nice gent, quiet manner and ways. You've a handful to deal with after hearing this kind of news. That man out there just might be an answer for a while, dear. He certainly was last night."

"He does seem to be a good sort. Marianna took to him right away," Amanda agreed. "I couldn't believe the way she let him carry her around. I've always thought a child had a sense about a person, no matter what is said." She kept seeing her daughter nestled in the man's arms. She'd rarely gone near, or been held, by her own father—but then, Harvey had always been cool and distant toward his female child. The poor little thing had learned to keep her distance.

"Wonder who had it in for Harvey or who'd know if he had money on him?" Helen's brow furrowed with the question. "Could be a lot of people, if they knew he was set on buying cattle and carrying a wad of money." She looked at Amanda. "Never found any money on him?"

"Didn't he say he never looked?" Amanda's head came up reluctantly. A sick feeling ran through her. She looked at Helen. "You don't think it's possible—

"Would he show up here like he did, bold as brass?" Helen stared at Amanda, a question in her eyes.

e/ɔe/ɔ

Reed walked out of the ranch house, intent on fetching the saddle bags for Amanda. He looked about the place as he walked to the barn where he'd tossed them yesterday. Smoke poured from the bunkhouse this late in the morning. The hands hadn't stirred themselves yet, and it was long after they should have gone about their business.

The worthless bums didn't know their boss was dead. Things had been left undone in the short time Bradshaw had been gone, and any stranger off the trail could see the state of things on this ranch. It angered the hell out of him.

He told himself it was none of his business, but Amanda, being a widow now, faced the job of running this ranch alone. She'd never get anywhere with hands this irresponsible. It was more than his sense of right could handle.

He found the saddle bags. She could look in it on her own and dig through the contents he'd found on Bradshaw along with the rest of it. *She'll need to decide what she wants to do about his body. I've done what I came for.*

Reed thought of getting on his miserable nag and riding away, but found it hard to consider. For some reason, he felt tied to the place after all that had happened in the night. Everything depended on what that little woman had in mind. "She's had a hell of a shock for a woman in her situation. I'd best hang around awhile and see how things go for her."

Thoughts of leaving any woman alone in such great need hurt his sense of what a man ought to do. Amanda needed help. He'd easily seen that last night, and this morning, he felt reluctant to leave her in such a sorry situation.

As a new mother, she was extra vulnerable, and now a widow to boot. He saw the little girl growing up without a father, and his newborn namesake as well. *Am I crazy in my thinking?*

"I could offer to stay on here a while 'til she gets a handle on things," he muttered aloud.

Already, he'd warmed to the place. It felt like home, a place where he could settle down, earn some wages, and maybe stay on a while.

He stepped up onto the porch and re-entered the house carrying the saddle bags that had been Harvey Bradshaw's.

"Here're his possibles, ma'am." He laid the heavy, leather-pocketed bags on the table. "If he carried money for a cattle buy, it might be inside there, but he did say he was robbed. I didn't think it right to dig into it," he explained further. "Well, except for the jerky. I helped myself to what was in the grub sack."

He laid the linen bag, containing what was left of the dried, hard jerky, on the table and stood back.

Amanda had never looked into any of Harvey's personal things during their life together. In his cold way, he'd let her know it was none of her business and she'd never have dared intrude. Even now, slowly opening the straps, and remembering his hard, taciturn nature, she felt uncomfortable invading the man's privacy.

"It seems strange to look through his things," she said, hesitant as she reached into the leather bag.

First, she pulled out a box nearly full of shells for his six-gun. Then, there were papers, folded and in a large envelope. She laid them aside without looking at them. Clean handkerchiefs, socks folded and rolled neatly, and matches were removed next. Near the bottom, she felt a bit of metal and withdrew a small bit of jewelry. Holding it up for inspection, she frowned. "Looks like an earring, but is there another one?" She dug about in the leather bag, came up with nothing more, and wondered, *Was he planning to surprise me because of the baby?* Puzzled by the strange earring, thoughts of searching for the money had escaped her completely.

"I wonder what this is about. This earring was never one of mine."

She held it high to the light. It was made of finely drawn gold filigree, formed in a lacy rounded pattern with a tiny bell in the center. She shook it gently and heard a softened metallic ring, merely a tinkle, yet musical to the ears.

Amanda frowned in her confusion and felt her scalp prickle. Finding an intimate thing like that among her husband's things didn't set right. Aside from sobering thoughts of how it got there and what should be done about it, she realized she actually knew very little about her husband's intimate feelings. He'd never confided any deeply personal things to her, not even about his parents or upbringing.

Helen sat at the table with her and Amanda easily read her facial expressions and thoughts. She had them, herself. Too painful to mention, she still wondered, *Did that tight-fisted cuss have another woman somewhere?* The night he'd returned from town, and before he'd left on his cattle buying trip, she'd caught the heavy scent of an exotic perfume. It was nothing she would have worn. Harvey had been living in this area for many years. Did he have someone hidden away somewhere? Amanda shook her head in disbelief. Harvey was such a hard man, certainly not one to run after a woman.

Many times, she'd wondered how he'd managed to charm her into marriage. He'd been a graceful rider and a handsome man. Everyone had said the same. But none of that mattered anymore, because many long months ago she'd stopped caring or taking pride in how fine her man looked, in the saddle or out of it.

She'd managed to cope with his demanding ways and quite well, she'd always thought. In her girlish thinking, she'd always believed that marriage brought a woman a kind of fulfillment, or happiness. With Harvey, it hadn't been that way, and deep within herself, she'd come to believe she hadn't been woman enough. *Did my marital short-comings make him look elsewhere?*

CHAPTER 8

Amanda forced her thoughts away from the earring. She had more important worries. What to do about bringing Harvey's body home for burial and, as it was murder, someone must notify the law. Her shoulders sagged, contemplating all that lay before her.

Alone, two children to care for, and a ranch to run, she had an idea close to her heart—escaping to Colorado. She couldn't make good on her deepest desire at present. It was too soon. She needed time to think, and to regain her strength.

Amanda turned her attentions back to Harvey's belongings. "There is certainly no money in here. If it was bandits who robbed and killed him, they must have known he'd planned to buy cattle—how else would they know to target Harvey?"

Tears of anger and frustration filled her eyes when a loud, solid knock on the door, interrupted their discussion. Reed opened the door. Jud and Buddy stood on the porch, and the sight of the two errant cowhands made Amanda's temper rise.

Seeing Reed, both men stopped. Staring for a moment, Jud looked past Reed to Amanda. "Is the boss back?" he demanded, his tone forceful. "I see his horse out here in the corral. What's going on around here and who's this here dude?"

Ignoring the poorly dressed stranger who faced him, Jud stood wide-legged, his chest puffed out, directing his query to Amanda.

She rose slowly from the table to come and stand next to Reed, and faced Jud. "My husband's been murdered out in some canyon to the north of here, and this man has come to tell me about it."

Amanda saw Jud's face go white. "My God! Aw—ma'am, now you don't say." He stood there, struggling for words, twiddling with the battered, wide-brimmed hat he'd quickly doffed. "What happened?"

"Harvey was shot and robbed on his way to buy that herd of Angus-mix he wanted. It was way north of here in a canyon toward where the cattle were, up near Albuquerque. Reed here, Mr. Twinning, came across him just before he died."

Her tears were held, she wasn't about to cry in front of this disgusting cowboy. Knowing Jud, he'd likely see this death as an opportunity for his own designs. After the many times he'd deviled her in Harvey's absence, she knew he'd see this event as an advantage for himself. The thought of it made her feel ill, deep down in the pit of her stomach.

Reed faced the two. "Fellas, it looks to me like things have been let go around here. The missus right here had to tend the stock on her own yesterday while she was feeling poorly." He bent a dark look on Jud. The accusation hung in the air between them. "Where were you two?"

"Can't see as how it's anything to do with the likes of you, mister."

Reed turned to Amanda. Seeing her distraught look, he offered, his voice steady and low. "I'll stick around awhile if you'd like."

Without giving it a moment's thought, she answered him. "Yes, please, if you'd consider it. There is so much to tend to, and I hardly know where to begin."

A look of defeat cross Jud's face and Amanda could almost read his thoughts. This new man, Reed, stood in his way of getting next to her now that he had the chance. Instead of a sober, hard-driving boss like Harvey, he faced a shaggy-looking stranger off the trail, standing in the doorway like he already had the run of the place. She could barely hide her spreading grin.

Jud got off his high horse in a hurry, shuffling his feet, and his hands trembled. "Aw, say now, ma'am, now, no need to go taking on another hand, Buddy and me can handle everything, just like we been a doing."

At his words, fire flashed from Amanda's eyes. "Like the way you've been doing for the past week?" she demanded. "I nearly killed myself doing your work out there." She moved closer to Reed. "As far as I'm concerned, neither one of you is worth your hire and right here and now, I'm asking this man, Reed, to be my foreman as long as he'll stay around. If you two can't handle that, you're free to leave."

The cry of her newborn son broke into the thin, tight air of tension. Amanda turned to Reed. "Will you handle this? I must see to my child." And without waiting for his answer, she walked slowly away to disappear into the dark corners of her bedroom.

"Aw, she's gone and had that baby, now ain't she?" Jud exclaimed.

"Looks like she has," Reed replied. "I guess doing your work for you yahoos, plumb wore her out and brought her to her bed. Nice going, you two." His disdain for the two men, echoed in the words he flung at them. "Men, I've never cared one way or the other about being a ranch foreman, but I've been asked." He pointed his outstretched arm across the broad valleys to the south and west. "If this place is as big as it looks, we'll need another hand or two. I've no call to argue the point, but going off leaving the place in the hellish mess I found it yesterday—what the hell were you two thinking?"

"W—we were on the south ranges the past two d—days," Jud stammered. "Being that was where Harvey sent us." He pawed the porch with his booted foot. "Boss never said to stick around the ranch house whilst he was gone."

Jud evaded Reed's eyes. His face had gone a deathly pale. The man was lying in his teeth. Reed also figured Jud needed this job and was afraid he'd lose it.

"You were gone off more than two days according to the missus. I found her laying out on the porch, here, dying of pain and tuckered out from tending to the stock you left to starve." He drew in his breath and tightened his face. "If the rest of the place is as this bad off, we'll be making some changes around here right soon, unless I miss my guess."

Amanda's light step sounded on the porch, and she came out carrying her new child.

"Might get some rest, ma'am," Reed said to her. "You look some pale."

"I'm fine—better every hour." She looked at Jud and Buddy, her head up and her chin firm. "You boys all right with Reed, here?"

"I guess we'll do what has to be done, ma'am." Jud replied, his face tight with anger.

He wasn't about to let on how he felt but, by his look of disdain at his new boss, Amanda knew he'd do what he could to get shut of the man. Reed looked like some no account saddle tramp, and it made Amanda smile that Jud now had to answer to a rag-tag stranger off the trail. And she wouldn't hesitate to tell Reed if Jud deviled her whenever he got the chance. She nodded her satisfaction and went back inside, leaving them to sort things out.

Reed stood, his feet apart. "I'd like to ride out with you and get a feel of the place. Let me know which area you're heading to, and I'll ride along unless I'm needed around here today," he said, then went on, "Right after you do the chores around here."

He nodded to the livestock, eagerly awaiting attention.

Jud answered for the two, his chin out, "Sure, mister, we'll take care of everything. Looks like your outfit don't amount to much. Maybe we can fix you up a mite before we start."

He indicated the scrawny black nag that was new in the corral. Reed smiled, knowing Jud hadn't yet seen the pathetic saddle and tack that went along with the horse.

Helen approached. "Reed, that murder has got to be reported and I can't do that alone, been feelin' real poorly myself."

He turned to the men and shrugged. "For today, you fellas had best get along with what you're doing. I'll ride out with you as soon as I can. Hold off on anything else until we decide what's to be done about the lady's husband. It's got to be reported."

"Sure enough, it does," Jud replied. "There's a sheriff in Roswell or maybe it'd be better seein' the sheriff in Artesia. He's a good man and it lays closer. He'll know what's to be done." He shook his head. "Sure too damned bad. Harvey was a hard man for sure, but square all the way around."

"Thanks, man," Reed said. "Good advice, I'll speak to the lady. For now, just go on and tend to things, if you will."

Jud and Buddy headed back to the bunk house, with Jud mumbling loud enough for Reed to catch a few words. He smiled, hearing Jud's complaint, as the man scuffed up dust and kicked at any wayward rock in his path. "Now ain't this a fine little bucket of cow shit! She's gone and put this God-forsaken saddle tramp over us and dammit all the way to hell, it ain't right, not a'tall!" He kicked an additional clump of sod as he walked. Anger had turned his face a fiery red as he repeated his angry words to his saddle mate. "Bud, it just ain't right, no how!"

If Jud burned with rage and disappointment, Reed felt no pity for the man. He had it coming for the way the place lay neglected. Buddy, appeared to be a meek tag-a-long sort. One who easily accepted orders from anyone, and that included the reluctant Jud, his co-worker.

Reed felt ill at ease as he deliberated his fading options. If he was to help Amanda as her foreman, he couldn't keep heading north like he'd planned. The lady was in a rough spot right now, being a new mother and all, and he disliked leaving her alone with the two useless hands. Yet, going to see a sheriff about a murder was asking for trouble. He'd have to chance it, or cut and run. Sweating a little, he poured a cup of coffee and sat in the kitchen, his mind lost in thought.

Helen came out with an armload of soiled linens, and by the look on her face, had forgotten he was here. "Oh, Reed, did you get things squared with those boys out there?"

"Best I could, until we decide what to do about the la-dy's husband." He fingered his ragged hat, wanting to get things out on the table. "Jud suggested the sheriff in a place called Artesia. If he's the one to see, I wonder if you'd drive in with me. I don't know where it is, for one thing."

"Guess I could, if Amanda's right enough on her own here. Might be she could use some goods as well—won't be traveling for a while yet." She took a cup of coffee for her-self and sat down. "Been feeling poorly myself lately, but whatever's bothering me is gone for now." She wiped a bit of sweat from her brow and Reed noted it wasn't all that warm, inside or out.

Amanda was in the bedroom, tending her baby, and he spoke more freely to Helen because of it. "I was working my way north, figured to get there before the cold comes again." He paused. "It wouldn't be right to leave this wom-an alone since she asked me to help out. I'd appreciate any advice or help you can offer." Reed wondered what she'd say if she knew what he was running from. It wasn't the way of folks to ask, and she wouldn't. "This place needs a firm hand, by what I've seen," he added.

"That Harvey wasn't one to spend money on good help." Helen tried to avoid sounding overly disparaging about Amanda's dead husband, but she couldn't completely conceal her feelings about him. Reed had already gotten the idea that Amanda's husband had been a cold, demanding sort. He'd also noticed the newly made widow didn't seem especially overcome with sorrow for her loss.

Helen lowered her voice. "Harvey was a severe cuss, and I often wondered how she managed, being married to him." She grinned at Reed. "It feels pretty good to get in a lick or two about the man while Amanda's still in the bedroom." She sipped her coffee, set her cup down, and headed to the bedroom. "I'll see what she wants to do."

After several moments, Helen emerged carrying the baby, and Amanda accompanied her, fully dressed, with her hair combed and brushed into shimmering gold. The dark circles had faded some from her eyes.

After nodding to Reed, Amanda looked across the ranch yard to see her daughter and Bennie playing with a few old horseshoes. "They seem to get along well enough and having another youngster to play with is very nice for Marianna—doesn't come about all that often for her." He noticed the dreamy smile on her face watching the two children at play.

Amanda directed the next comment to him. "Reed, I know the authorities must be told and Helen says she'll go in town with you to see Sheriff Toliver. I only met him once, but he seems a good sort and he'll know what to do."

She sensed a deep reluctance in him. It was nothing he'd said, but rather a feeling she got. "Is that a problem for you? I see how your clothes look. Would it help if I found something more presentable for you to wear?" She had in mind some things her husband hadn't worn in years. She guessed he'd worn them when he was a younger man, and certainly a slimmer one, and that too, was something he'd never discussed with her.

"Well, that would help." In fact, different clothing might be a lot of help, almost a disguise. Encouraged by the thought, he squared his shoulders, firmed his jaw. "There's more about me I haven't told you and I'd feel like a liar if I

didn't come clean with you since you've asked me to stay
on a while. I like your place here and I'll do what I can for
you. But when you know all about me, you'll agree it could
be a problem for me, going in town dressed as I am."

He had a hesitant look on his face, but Amanda saw
him as a good man—after he'd helped her the way he had,
she knew it down deep. "Can you tell us what's bothering
you? I want to know. I've already trusted you with my life.
No matter what you have to tell us, in my eyes you'll never
be anything but a decent sort—never."

Helen sat listening. Reed saw, by her narrowed eyes,
she'd had some worries that something wasn't right about
him. The women quietly waited to hear what he had to reveal.

"It isn't easy to say, and you likely won't be wanting
me around after I tell you about myself," Reed said, twisting
his worn, sweat-stained hat about.

"Why not let us do the judging of that?" Amanda felt
her heart pulse rapidly as her alarm rose. Could his telling
about himself mean her only source of comfort and help
could be slipping away? Near panic took hold of her at the
thought of it.

Reed looked at the two women with much the same
feeling. They held his future in their hands and seemed like
family, especially after last night. He swallowed and began.

"I'd been traveling about for a couple of years, just seeing the country so to speak, when I took a job near Prescott,
Arizona, about three or more years ago, working a ranch
there." He cleared his throat. "I had a friend. We'd only
known each other for a few months, but worked together
and got along. On days off, we used to spend time in a place
called Whiskey Row." Grimacing, he took a deep breath
and continued. "That's a street full of saloons they have in
that town. Famous, so they say."

He paused and flushed. "Jim took up with one of the
bar girls they kept around. He'd even been thinking he'd
marry her and get her out of the place." He shook his head.

"Seemed like the owner had his eye on her, too." Reed stopped and sighed. "You ladies sure you want to hear all of this? It won't be the best story you've ever heard." He paused and waited for their answer.

Helen spoke up. "Get on with it, Reed. We know how you men-folks are about things like that."

The accepting look on her face kept Reed going. "One night, my friend was taking up her time, well, I mean not going upstairs or anything, just sitting there and talking. The bar owner, seeing she wasn't taking care of business, if you get my meaning, got right in his face and told him to get the hell out." He flushed, looking at Amanda. "Pardon, ma'am, for the cussin'."

Reed actually blushed with that part of his story and Amanda appreciated the fact he was sensitive to her feelings on such a subject.

He went on. "Well, Jim shoved the bar owner out of the way, and the man pulled a gun on him. My friend wasn't armed right then, so I stood up for him. There was a scuffle. Not much of a fight at all, but I heard a gun go off in the middle of it. When the smoke cleared, my friend lay dead on the floor and my gun was missing from my holster.

"When it showed up, laying on the table next to me, it'd been fired and the bar owner swore to the sheriff I was the one that did the shooting." Reed felt good telling it like it'd really happened. He held his breath, waiting for their reaction.

"Well, what happened then?" Amanda wanted to know.

"Wasn't anything good for me," He snorted. "They held a trial right quick, and with all the testimony said against me, I got sent to Yuma Prison for a long stretch." He shook his head. "No man should ever be shoved into a dug-out cave with iron bars across the front, just like a dog. That hellhole wasn't fit for man or beast, and being alongside of a river, Yuma has got to be the hottest, muggiest, place this side of hell."

"How'd you get out?" Helen asked.

"I watched and waited until I found a way. They trusted me for some outside work, and during a scuffle between two other poor souls, I took my chance." He shrugged. "That was over nine or ten months ago, and I've been running like a coyote ever since. Worked on a ranch in the eastern side of Arizona for enough to buy a few things I needed, but as you can see, it didn't come to much."

He waited for their response. If it went against him, he'd just leave out and go north. What else was there?

Amanda broke the heavy silence. "I don't care what you've done in the past. I only know what you've done for me." She smiled at Reed. "After the way my child took to you, you can't be an evil soul. It's not in you to be a killer and I'll never believe it."

She looked at Helen, waiting for the woman's verdict.

"I'll have to agree with Amanda, Reed, but I do see how it might create a problem going to the sheriff, wouldn't it?" Helen uttered a small laugh. "We need to decide on some way to let that sheriff know about Harvey's murder." She frowned. "And those two cowboys out there know too much about you already." Her brow furrowed in thought as she said, "You'll need some fixing up and a different name before we go see the sheriff."

CHAPTER 9

If Jud thought it'd get you shot or arrested, he'd ride right to town right now and blather everything he thinks he knows to that sheriff," Amanda said with a wry smile.

"He's a hateful man. I never told Harvey about it, but he's been bothering me for months. My expecting a child never stopped him from trying to get close, or putting his hands on me, either."

She pulled up her sleeve and the sight of healing bruises on her arm set Reed on fire.

Seeing that, he felt the heat rising inside himself. "Holy hell—"

Amanda put her hand up. "Never mind about that." She was adamant, not wanting to waste time talking about Jud. "I just wanted to explain these bruises. He came across me while I was watering that blasted garden several days ago. Grabbed me by the arms and wouldn't let me go, until he saw Marianna come out. I'd never told Harvey about it. He'd have said I asked for it. Jud makes me feel uncomfortable, but I'm not afraid of him."

His face turned white with anger at her words. "Uncomfortable! Hells Bells! Why that dirty low-down, sneaking—"

"Reed, I've got bigger problems than Jud," Amanda said. "He's really nothing to worry over. Harvey got upset over everything, and it never took much to get him that way." She couldn't hide the bitterness in her voice. "He'd have blamed me anyway."

Reed knew by her tone that Jud had made no impression on her, other than disgust. "He won't be bothering you again, ma'am." He cast a glance at her, his chin and wide mouth set firm. "Long as I'm around, I'll see to it, and you won't need to worry about telling *me* if it happens again."

"Thank you for that." After several moments of thought, Amanda brightened. "Let's see what we can do about fixing you up a bit." She smiled. "You can be my brother. His name is Leroy Hardesty. You can use that name while you're around here, if you like." She couldn't help uttering a small laugh. "Wouldn't Leroy get a kick out of this? He was always one for pulling tricks on us. He's some kind of lawyer now. Read the law with a man in Durango for a couple of years, left the ranching to Dad and Harry, my other brother." She frowned in fond remembrance. "I always called Harry, old sober-sides. He was so bossy, especially to me."

Reed frowned and shook his head in wonder. He faced being a damnable liar, on top of an escaped convict, and hated it—all the while realizing it would be a great disguise. "You ladies amaze me. I thank both of you for believing in me. It's been mighty hard trusting anyone after the deal I got in Prescott." He smiled back at them. "What kind of duds are you dragging out for me?"

"They were Harvey's but he'd put on some extra pounds in the past few years and couldn't wear them anymore. They're yours if you won't mind wearing them." She got up slowly from her chair and headed into the dark bedroom.

Helen rose, holding the sleeping infant, and followed. "I'll tuck this little mite in his cradle."

Reed watched them go.

Amanda came out with an armload of things and laid them out on the newly cleaned table for his inspection. He saw several shirts, woven, patterned, white, and big enough to fit his tall, angular frame. He'd always been slender and strong as cured hickory, though he appeared especially gaunt these days. Time in prison and being on the run hadn't allowed regular meals.

The pants looked long enough at first glance. He shrugged and picked them up. "I'd like to give them a try, especially these." He indicated the black trousers with a tiny gray stripe woven in them. He felt a flush of excitement, looking at the finery. They had a dressy look about them, and he was eager to wear something without ragged edges for once.

Amanda went back and brought out a pair of shiny black boots. "Harvey had several good pairs of boots, but one's enough to try, I imagine."

He rose from the chair. "Got a place I can try these duds on?"

She pointed to the kitchen stove with the reservoir of heated water. "If you'd like to wash up a bit, the horse trough might not be good enough." When he held a bucket of steaming water, she pointed down the hall. "Go all the way down the hall there and take the last room on the left. I've put the clothes in there for you. You should find everything you need. We used it if we had overnight guests and that's only been once since I've been here."

Reed headed down the hall and Helen asked, "Are you thinking of letting him stay inside this house at night, down there in that room?"

"Hadn't thought about that, but I just might. Jud will likely try to kill him if he stays in the bunkhouse," Amanda replied, a look of worry on her face. "You don't think Reed's dangerous, do you?"

"No, not in the sense that he was sent up for murder, but think of it—he *is* a man, isn't he?"

"I hadn't really thought about it in that way, Helen. And besides, after the way he took care of me last night, it's a complete wonder I can look him in the face at all." She flushed. "But I believe he meant it when he told me it's a natural thing and not to worry over it. The way he was about everything he did for me, has helped me handle the situation, Helen." Amanda shrugged, her hands splayed outward. "I don't know how to think about it now. But at the time, he seemed like the finest doctor in the land and I'm very grateful to him."

Helen made a face of regret. "Sorry I couldn't have been here for you, but it's past now. No need to be dwelling on it, is there?"

Amanda kept looking down the long hall, waiting for Reed to make an appearance in Harvey's clothes. "Wonder what's keeping the man." She went on in her worry over the clothes. "Maybe he isn't happy about wearing a dead man's things. You suppose that's it?"

Then she went on, deep in thought. "In all the time I've known Harvey, he never seemed the sort to wear fancy duds like those. I wonder what he was like in his younger years." She sniffed and raised her head. "I wonder what made him so cold, like he was."

"Honey, that's something neither of us will ever know, isn't it?"

Their conversation went unfinished as they heard the sound of boots coming down the hall. When Reed appeared, he hardly seemed the same man.

"Not a bad fit, a bit loose, but if you're of a mind to let me have the use of them, I sure do thank you, ma'am." He stood before them, awaiting their comments and inspection.

Amanda couldn't believe the difference clothes could make in a man's appearance. A tall, slender, broad-shouldered man, he wore the finely striped trousers quite well and, with the crisp white shirt and narrow string tie, he looked like a different person. She felt a smile of wonder cross her face, "You look like a banker, a business man, and maybe even one of those fancy-dude gamblers."

He held the nicely cut black jacket by the collar, casually flung over the shoulder. "The coat fits right fine, too, ma'am." He'd shaved, left a small mustache, and wore the fine leather boots.

"How about the boots? Harvey had very narrow feet."

"As it happens, so do I," he commented. "No wonder they fit like they do." He held out a shining boot and hiked up the trouser leg to gaze at it.

The door opened and Marianna entered with Bennie right behind. Her dress was soiled with dust and bits of hay, but no mud. The dog clung close to her and, seeing Reed, let out a low growl.

The little girl gazed at Reed in amazement. "Weed, you look all pitty!"

He reached down and swept her up in his arms. "I do, do I?" He grinned, white teeth flashing against his deeply tanned face. "Only girls can look pretty, Marianna." He laughed, his head thrown back, his voice full and deep-throated as he expressed his joy in the child. He held her out from him and looked into her eyes. Amanda couldn't take her eyes off the two of them.

"That man certainly seems taken with your daughter," Helen whispered to Amanda. "I wonder if he's ever had children."

Amanda flushed as she turned to Helen. "She's taken with him, too. Was right off and, at the time, I was mighty glad to see it. Reed washed a good peck of sticky mud off her before he fed her and put her to bed; and that naughty rascal loved every minute of it."

She smiled. "It's too late to start for town before to-morrow. Will your family worry if you don't show up at your ranch tonight?" She'd formed an idea. "Stay the night. I've plenty of room here. We've never had all the rooms full, not since I've been here." She didn't try to hide that small note of sadness in her voice.

"I'll stay. Bennie might like more playing time with Marianna." Helen smiled an indulgent smile. "I'd say they both could use more of that."

"I'll shuck off these fancy duds and see to things outside, since the boys have gone out to the south today," Reed said.

He went back down the hall and Amanda, gazing after him, heard Helen say, "Looks to me like this stranger from nowhere has already taken over a lot of things around here." She grinned. "My dear, you're recovering nicely from the childbirth and all, but you've got your husband's murder to think about and this ranch to run." She patted Amanda on the shoulder. "I know it's a heavy load you've got right now, but aren't you putting a lot of your needs on a man you don't even know?"

Amanda made no reply as Reed returned, wearing his usual trail-worn rags and said to Marianna and Bennie, "Why don't you younguns come on with me and we'll go see if the stock's been tended."

Marianna jumped to grab his hand, and Bennie followed close behind.

Amanda and Helen watched from the kitchen window as the trio went together across the yard. Marianna's mouth was moving constantly and Piddely kept close to her with a wary eye on Reed.

"What do you think of that?" Amanda commented. "Maybe I'm crazy to hire a man from out of nowhere, but I feel right about it, Helen. I do."

"I can't tell you either way about that, whether it's right or wrong but I respect your feelings about it. He did come right out with his story, didn't he?" Helen replied. "I'd best fix a few vittles now to bide us over 'til supper." She glanced at the papers lying on the table and then at Amanda. "Have you looked at those things, yet?"

"No, I haven't, but guess I'd better. I'm not sure about looking at business things. Harvey never involved me in any of his affairs and, at home, my father never said a word in front of us about his running the ranch, either. I guess he felt those things were for the man to attend to as well." Amanda sighed. "My mother never had to face being a widow, either."

She slowly, almost fearfully, opened the large envelope with bank markings on the outside and withdrew the papers. Carefully, she spread them out on the table. After scanning the contents, she looked at Helen, puzzled. "Looks like Harvey borrowed a good deal of money to buy the stock he was after. Come look at this, Helen." She indicated a legal-looking document. "What does this mean?"

Helen took her time looking at the papers and finally raised her head, a frown across her face. "Looks like your Harvey got himself deeper in debt than anyone knew, Amanda." She scanned the sheets intently. "In fact—my stars, it looks like he's gone and borrowed this place right into a hole in the ground, if this amount is what he owes." She wiped the sweat from her brow again. "I think you'd best get into Artesia to see the banker that wrote out this paper."

"Oh, now what?" Tears filled Amanda's eyes. "I wouldn't know where to begin with something like that." She shook her head in futility. "I imagine the men will have to have wages one day soon, won't they?" She felt tired. Facing the loss of her husband, his running of the ranch, and now more problems, she felt completely overwhelmed. "I don't know how Harvey paid the men, how much, or even where he kept money for that."

Feeling completely lost, Amanda put her head on the table as her shoulders shuddered with deep, tearing sobs. But in doing so, deeply held feelings, long suppressed, slowly emerged and were washed away. Her outpouring of tears were those of a frightened woman's sorrow and fear, certainly, but within herself, they brought release from months and years of pent up frustration, homesickness, and disappointment. She felt lighter because of it, but knew she could never reveal those feelings to her friend.

Helen tried to lead her toward the bedroom where a nice clean bed awaited. "Honey, don't take on so. We'll get it sorted out. You'd best go rest a while before that baby needs you again."

But Amanda held back. "I can't sleep now with all I have on my mind, Helen."

She straightened her shoulders, ready to face her newer misfortune and the inner, scalding knowledge, that her husband had not told her the truth about much of anything.

She turned from Helen and looked out the kitchen window. A warm glow suffused softly through her body at the sight of Reed carrying a huge armful of hay, heading for the horse corral. Bennie hauled a partial bag of grain along beside him. Marianna followed them both, her little mouth going a mile a minute.

Helen joined her at the window and they stood watching.

The scene before her looked clean and right to Amanda's anguished mind. With no thought that the cowhands should be doing those things, she only felt the rightness of it in this moment. Enthralled at the sight of that tall, raggedly dressed man doing things on her ranch took her thoughts away from the newer crisis of the towering debt against it.

It made her forget everything, but not for long. Her mind returned to dwell on that mysterious earring. It clung in the back of her mind and never left her thoughts for long. Something definitely wasn't right about it. *Had her husband found another woman?* Those thoughts ran against everything she'd thought sacred in her marriage, and made her sick inside.

Amanda sighed and turned to watching Helen make something to fill those empty stomachs. It was coming on noon. The trip to Artesia tomorrow ought to be very interesting, and hopefully informative. She hoped it would be.

Helen got out enough for a meal and stopped. When Amanda saw her sit down and put her head in her hands, she asked, "Are you having that trouble again, Helen?"

"It's that same faint twinge of pain that I been getting across here, lately." She indicated her lower abdomen. "If we have the time, I hope to see the doctor. Maybe he can tell me what this is. It's got me some worried."

Amanda sat Helen in a chair. "You poor soul, you've got a tough fight on your *own* hands, if it's anything serious." She turned to finish what Helen had started. In short order, she finished heating the gravy and meat, ready to pour over biscuits left from the morning meal.

When Reed entered with the children, he saw her busy at the stove and questioned her. "What on earth are you doing? Should you be up and busy so soon, that way?"

Amanda ignored his query. She had more important things on her mind. "Reed, we finally went through those letters. Seems Harvey went heavily into debt for those cattle, but it's much more than that. He borrowed way more than enough to buy cattle. He's left this ranch deeply in debt."

Reed shook his head. "That can't be good news when you're left with the two children to bring up," he said. "Any way I can help with this?"

"Might help more if you were a real good lawyer."

Amanda shrugged as she said it, and Reed laughed. "My daddy was a banker back in Kansas. He'd know how to deal with this. He's gone now, most all are, so I've heard."

"How come you're out here, running around playing cowboy, then?" Already a man of mystery to Amanda, she hoped to learn more.

Reed grinned at her. "I was just a dumb kid back then and wanted to see the West after seeing shows about it in our town. Ever hear of that Wild West show put on by Buffalo Bill Cody? Showed how he took on Yellow Hand, roped wild buffalos, rode broncos—even had a real Indian chief in the show. For a young boy, it was a great adventure, and seeing that show put a lot of wild ideas in my head." He sighed. "It was never as exciting as the shows made it sound but, in my travels, I've found these western states are truly wonderful." He paused for a breath. "It's a great country we live in," he said then grimaced. "Excepting Yuma, and thereabouts, hanging's better than that hell hole."

Amanda set the food on the table. "Did you learn enough from your daddy to help with this bank business?"

"Likely not enough to suit my father. He wanted me to go off to Boston for better schooling, but I was too smart for that. He had to make do with what was there in Wichita." Reed laughed again, feeling happy and comfortable. It'd been a long time since he'd had that feeling and he reveled in it. "I've sure learned a mighty lot of other things, though."

Bennie and Marianna came into the kitchen. "Weed, we eat?" She turned her blue eyes up at him with her question. Amanda watched him warm to the child as he listened to her. "I hungy. Bennie, too."

Helen raised her head, "It's ready, just sit at the table." To Amanda, "You sit for a while, my dear. You'll be overdoing."

Reed took Marianna up and sat her in the chair with folded blankets. Her piping young voice said, "Fanks, Weed."

They heard the baby cry and Amanda went in to him.

Reed dished up the food and put it on the table for the children. Helen sat down again, fanning herself, and carefully wiping perspiration from her brow. Reed frowned as he observed her. Her meager efforts at the moment had quickly become too much for her. He had a bad feeling about it, but made no comment.

Later, with Reed and the young ones outside, Amanda came out. She felt rested and carried her son in her arms. He squirmed and made the soft, puling sounds of the newly born. She carefully took a seat at the table. Her eyes were red from crying and she didn't try to hide it. Helen fixed her a plate and set if before her.

Amanda looked up at her. "Thanks, Helen. You feeling a little better?"

"Some. If we have time, I want to see the doctor about this."

Amanda nodded, ate a few bites, then went on about the papers. "Reed says his father was a banker. Maybe he understands these things. Anything he knows will be more than I do."

Reed entered the kitchen, and she asked him about it.

"I've had some training in the law, maybe enough to help some, but I was too smart to learn much back then." He scoffed at himself as he looked at Amanda. "If there *is* anything to be done, I'll try to help."

"Well if you're to be my brother in this, you'd best have a letter giving you the power to act for me or to take information. I don't know what's going on or how bad my situation might be."

She handed her son to Helen, went to a desk, took out writing materials and got busy.

Would they believe he was her brother? With rising alarm, she remembered that Jud and Buddy knew he wasn't. She couldn't think further on it, but the lies would rise up to haunt her later. Reed too, she was sure.

She finished a letter of introduction for him to show the banker if identification should be required. Feeling very tired, Amanda rose from her chair and handed it to Reed. "I am going to bed now. It's been quite a day." She nodded to Helen and smiled at Reed. "I think we'd both feel safer if you were in the house. Please take that room down the hall, where you changed clothes. It may not seem right to some, but it seems right to me, and who's to say different?"

CHAPTER 10

The next morning, with the sun peeping over the faraway eastern mountains, Helen and Reed climbed onto the padded seat of her rig. Helen's mare, rested and pawing at the earth, was eager to be off. By instinct, the horse wrongly believed she headed for home, and Reed could hardly hold her back.

Before they drove away, Helen issued stern orders to Bennie. "Now son, you're the man around the place until we get back, and it's likely to be late, being it's a far piece into Artesia. You watch out for Marianna, keep her out of the mud and such, and do what the missus tells you. She needs her rest and for you to help out and see to the chores." Her voice was firm. She meant business and Reed held back a grin, seeing the boy's young chest swell with importance at her words.

"Yes, ma'am, I'll mind what you say." He scuffed his boots in the dirt. "We'll be fine here, Mama, just you be careful out there."

After they drove away, Bennie stood watching them and Amanda's heart went out to him. With a catch in her throat, she noted how the boy worried about his mother. He was coming along in growth and would be a fine, strapping young man one day. She sat on the porch holding her baby, with Marianna pressing close against her. The little girl wiped tears away at Reed's leaving and reached her small hand to touch the newborn's soft pink cheeks.

Amanda shook her head in mild shock. The change in Reed this morning, as he stood before her in Harvey's clothes, affected her in some way she didn't understand. She knew for certain, no man could have looked better wearing the fine clothes he'd put on last evening and again this morning.

She'd also noticed he'd trimmed his shaggy dark hair, shaved, and kept that fine moustache across his wide mouth. Just that much change gave him a totally different look— definitely that of a man of substance, and she easily believed his father had been a banker. The son looked like one, too.

The look of confidence in those deep, dark eyes left her puzzling at the mystery of him. And, unwillingly, she noticed how deeply she'd been affected. The sight of him had sent heated thrills zinging through her body once again this morning. It upset her. A newly made widow with a host of problems shouldn't have such feelings.

Frowning, she wondered why this man affected her that way. It wasn't right, certainly not now. She was a widow with a small child, recovering from childbirth. She'd never had such feelings before or even knew they existed. It puzzled her, embarrassed her, and made her wonder what it meant.

eɔeɔ

As they moved along the rustic track that passed for a road, Reed remembered the boy's concern over his mother and realized he worried a great deal about his mother's health, maybe more than she did herself.

"Is your boy aware of your illness?" he asked her.

"I reckon he is," Helen replied. "I sent him over here the other day to tell Amanda I was ailing."

Reed flapped the reins over the mare's rump, to pick up their pace. She had slowed when they turned toward the opposite direction from her home ranch. "I believe your Bennie is a mite worried about you."

"I guess his fool head isn't as far in the clouds as I thought. My baby's growing into a man—makes me feel proud and grateful having a boy like that." She smiled up at Reed, her satisfaction as a mother written on her face.

They drove along a dusty trail with two worn ruts from wagon use. Reed handled the reins and, wearing the borrowed fine clothing of yesterday, he smiled to himself, pleased, feeling like a banker's son again.

He glanced at Helen. "May I see those letters or notes? Might be I could make some sense of what's going on, if I have a look."

She dug them out of her reticule and handed them over.

After handing her the reins, he read them carefully. "My God Helen! That damned fool took out enough money to buy that stock several times over!"

What Harvey's reasons might have been, he couldn't figure. He hadn't seen any recent improvements around the place, and he'd only kept the two hands. He shook his head. Maybe the banker would be of some help.

As they drove on, the sun gave off enough heat to make the day pleasant. Birds sang in the trees and flitted in fright from the scrub bushes along the sandy trail as they passed. Now and then, a wild creature crossed in front of them, riling the old mare a bit. Once a coyote, several rabbits, even a lone pronghorn leaped across ahead of the rig. It made for a pleasant ride. Reed felt so relaxed, he nearly fell asleep.

"Don't forget the name you're using—Leroy," Helen reminded him. She grinned as she said it. "Seems unreal, doesn't it?"

"Right now, everything does." He chuckled. "One day I'm running from the law, and the next I'm someone's long lost brother. I want to help the little lady, I do, but I hate more than anything, being a damned liar. It galls me all to hell." Reed had retrieved the reins and held them in one hand as he gazed about the landscape, seeing brush, scrub, few trees, and very little water. "This range here abouts doesn't look all that promising to me. How many cows was Harvey was running?"

"Never heard anything about that one way or the other. He only kept the two hands, though." She squinted against the sun as she answered. "The Pecos River runs through the ranch in places—makes for good grazing in spots."

Reed acknowledged her reply with a nod. "Need to get a good look around, right soon." He frowned. "I get the feeling things are not what they seem in the light of her husband borrowing so much against the place." Hearing no answer, he flicked the reins over the mare's back. "How far is this berg we're heading to, did you say?"

"About 5 miles or so." She said nothing more for about an hour until she remarked, "We're nearly there now, just over that small rise ahead." She looked him in the eye. "I'm trying to figure you, mister. You've changed your way of talking along with the fancy duds. You're different in more ways than one." She chuckled, "You sound as fancy as you look—makes a body wonder."

He smiled, knowing he did look like a different man with the changes in his appearance. He felt different and the change of clothing *had* wrought a change in his manner of speech, if not everything else about him. Reed shrugged, but made no reply to her comment as he drove.

"I'll introduce you to the banker," Helen continued. "We've known him quite well over the years. A person they're familiar with might be some help in figuring out what Harvey was up to. It's a good place to start." She handed him the documents with a smile. "You'll need to carry these, being the widow's brother."

He took the papers and laughed. "You're a cagy one, ma'am."

When they topped the rise, he saw the small town of Artesia laid out below. A small stream shimmered in the distance, meandering along the side of the street. The place boasted many trees, some lining the streets, with more out among the stockyards and barns. "Looks rather prosperous," he commented. He flapped the reins over the mare's rump again and went on down.

They drove past several saloons with nothing much going on inside. A horse or two was tied out front, but no music or loud talk poured out of the doors. Too early in the day, he decided.

Artesia boasted two general stores that appeared to be stocked with all manner of goods required by folks in the immediate area. Large metal stock tanks sat gleaming in the sun. A plowshare sat in the weeds alongside the first store. The second store had a pair of ladies dresses in a fly spotted window and hats made to go with them, or so he surmised. Seeing it gave him a warm feeling. Being on the run so long, he'd missed seeing the small ordinary things of life. It felt good, entering a town this way, in spite of the worry he was about to put himself in jeopardy of arrest

Helen pointed. "See that stonework building up ahead on the right? That'll be the bank."

"Where's the sheriff's office? I believe we'd best let them know about Amanda's husband, first off."

Reed worked to quell the cold feeling of edginess that had settled in his bones. Lying to a sheriff and a banker sent his nerves zinging. After keeping a tight lid on his worries, long subdued and hidden, he'd allowed himself to fall into a trap. He now imitated the prosperous-looking brother of a rancher's wife, if only for this trip. It worried him more than plenty.

"It's just across from the bank there."

Helen roused him from his unsettled thoughts, pointing out a rough-cut building, stout and solid with a row of narrow windows. The solid steel bars firmly placed in them gleamed in the sun as they passed. The bars plainly faced the trail as they entered the small town and the sight of them hit him with freezing memories he'd rather forget. He shook off an involuntary chill.

People bustled about on the streets doing their business. Only a few bothered to take a look at the new rig pulling in. "I'll pull up to the sheriff's office first. We'd best go in and make a report." Terse and direct in his speech, it was a way he hid his internal stress. With his sorry history, he had plenty to hide.

He tied the horse and helped Helen down. A wince of pain crossed through her, and her hand crept to mid abdomen.

She passed it off, saying nothing of it, but only, "If we have time, I'd like to visit Doc Cutler about these pains I been a having lately."

Reed nodded. He planned to see that she did.

"I've known the doc from attending a birth or two. I've only seen him once for myself. But being pain free at the time, the doc had no symptoms to work with."

Her words told Reed the woman was very worried. He believed it was more for her family than herself, if trouble lay ahead.

They entered the sheriff's office. A young man at the desk looked up. Seeing Helen, he rose politely from his chair and greeted them. "Howdy, folks, how can I help you?"

Reed spoke up. "I'm Leroy Hardesty, late of Colorado. We've come in town to report the finding of a dying man, actually, my sister's husband, Harvey Bradshaw. A stranger riding through brought us this news along with Harvey's horse and pack. Said he'd covered the man with enough stones to keep the animals off and was kind enough to bring his belongings to the ranch."

He went on to describe the location of the canyon as best he remembered. "It's someplace northwest of here. Not sure how far, but we were told it was a two day ride. The man said Bradshaw lived long enough to ask him to inform his wife, and he's done that," Reed said and went on to explain his presence. "Amanda Bradshaw is my sister, but she wasn't able to come in town."

"I'm a deputy here, Bart Day. Sheriff Toliver is out on a case just now, but he'll likely be back soon. Tell me every detail you can remember, if you will. It'll need investigating, of course, so we can take care of the matter."

Reed thought the man was being a bit full of himself, maybe to impress the lady, but nevertheless, he proceeded to lay out the location and any other particulars he remembered. Reed went into detail about where the drifter had said the remains would be found. "I'm not at all familiar with your state, and this location would be impossible for me to find." He used the finely drawn words that made him sound like an eastern dude.

The look that flashed across Helen's face at his talk told him she'd have more questions, but she'd have to get used to the changes in his looks, speech, and his mannerisms if he was to portray the educated brother of Amanda.

During the interview, Reed surreptitiously kept an eye on Bart Day, searching for signs the deputy recognized his face from a wanted poster. He scanned the walls for any sign of one if they'd gotten this far. With a sigh of relief, he saw nothing on the walls about an escaped murderer from Yuma Prison.

"Stay around a while, if you will. Sheriff's due in anytime now." The deputy rose to shake Reed's hand. "Nice to meet you, Mr. Hardesty. I met your sister once, real pretty woman."

Leaving the sheriff's office, they moved the small rig across the street nearer the bank. He carefully helped Helen down. "I'd like to water this horse before we go in." He unhitched and led the sweating mare down toward the left side of the street where a long watering trough sat. Mud had collected around it and the windmill that fed it pumped steadily away in the slight breeze that kept the blades slowly spinning. "Need to tie that thing off once in a while," he muttered as the mare plunged her nose deeply into the water then raised it before she began drinking.

Helen waited on the steps of the bank, chatting with a couple of ladies. He saw her nod in his direction and knew she included him in her talk. Maybe it'd help if folks believed he was Amanda's brother. He hoped so. The mare finished her drink and, with water dripping from her muzzle, he led her back toward the bank and tied her to the hitching rail.

He stepped up onto the dusty boardwalk to enter the banking establishment with Helen. That his heart raced did not surprise him. He wasn't given to lies and his pretending to be Amanda's brother was a big one, one he couldn't get his conscience around.

They entered and Helen asked a young man behind a window if they could meet with the banker. He left, went into an office, and returned with a middle-aged, portly gentleman, balding on top and sporting a small, neat mustache. His clothes were neatly pressed and his hands were pink and clean. The fancy gold-lettered name on his door said: Harry Blankenship, Manager.

Helen held out her hand to the man. "I'm Helen Ordway from the K Bar O, and this is Leroy Hardesty, the brother of one of my neighbors." After he took her hand and nodded in greeting, he ushered them into his office, closed the door, and bade them to take seats. Reed held his counsel while Helen went on to tell him of the situation at the ranch and of Harvey's death. "We've seen the sheriff's deputy about this, since a crime has been committed."

They sat in comfortable padded chairs for this meeting and Reed found it a pleasant relief after the long buggy ride over rutted roads. "The man who found his body brought his belongings to the ranch house a few days ago and informed us of the death." He reached into the reticule. "I have some questions about these papers Harvey carried and believe you might help us understand their meaning." He handed the sheaf of papers to the banker.

Blankenship opened the papers, scanned them, and nodded. "I remember these, of course. Mr. Bradshaw came in to take out this loan about two weeks ago, I believe." He coughed and held a handkerchief to his slightly puffy lips. "Excuse me," he murmured and continued. "Harvey seemed somewhat upset and under some sort of pressure, but I granted the loan. As you can see, it was in addition to two other loans he'd made previously." He shook his head at the news of Harvey's demise. "Really sorry to hear of his death—murder, you say?"

Reed nodded. "He was carrying a good sum of cash for a cattle buy, Mr. Blankenship. It must have been a case of robbery, as there was no money found on him, according to the man who found him."

"Are you sure the man is telling the truth?"

Reed snorted in disdain. "Most robbers wouldn't ride for two days to tell the man's wife of his death, now would they?"

"Not likely, but the sheriff will want to speak with the man." His chin was firm and protruded a bit as he looked Reed in the eye. "If a local rancher's been murdered as you say, we can't let a thing like that go unpunished," he added, picking up the sheaf of documents. "As far as these papers go, I'm sorry to say, this ranch is in deep financial trouble. I never understood why the man needed so much cash. And now, with his death, it leaves his widow in a rather poor financial situation. Is there some reason she hasn't come in to see me?"

"Yes sir, she has just given birth to a son, and traveling is out of the question for a while." Helen provided those details. "Harvey wanted a son, and now, he'll never see his boy grow up—too bad."

The banker rose from his chair. "Sorry, folks, this appears to be a rather devastating situation for the widow since, of course, these loans must be repaid."

He shrugged and splayed out his hands, indicating there was no other choice in the matter. "I wish we could be more help in this." He reached out to shake Reed's hand and, nodding to Helen, indicated the end to this particular conversation.

They left the bank and stood for a moment on the wooden sidewalk. Helen repeated her previous words, reflecting her wonder. "You not only changed your clothes, mister, you've change your way of talking and everything else about you." She waited for his explanation.

"My daddy was mighty big on learning, ma'am," he drawled and grinned at her, knowing she had good reason to know more about him. "Actually, he sent every one of us away to school in Wichita. I trained as a lawyer, maybe enough to set up a practice, but foolish me, I wanted to see some of this country before setting up anything permanent." He uttered a futile laugh. "After what happened to me in Prescott, I most certainly see the need for a good lawyer in some parts of this country."

He heard his stomach growling, "We ought to get a bite to eat, maybe before that sheriff gets back." He dug in his pockets, and pulled out a few coins. "Not much to work with, I'm afraid."

"I'll take care of it. You're getting in so deep with all the fabricatin' you've had to do lately, you deserve a good feed." She looked at him and laughed then indicated a small place down the street a ways. "My old Bessie'll be all right here for that long."

Her mare stood there, switching flies and trying for a few blades of grass growing along the sides of the boardwalk.

They crossed the dusty street and entered an eatery called La Cantina. It looked mostly empty being early afternoon. A few scattered diners sat at small tables. And along the rustic bar, a couple of men sat in conversation, half empty glasses in front of them. For some unknown reason, Reed felt a chill cross through his body as they entered the place.

CHAPTER 11

They took a seat at a table covered with red-flowered oilcloth and Reed took up the tattered menu a small boy laid before him. As he worked to decipher the offerings, Helen said. "Just ask for *La Especial.* That's what you'll get anyway. They only make one or two things a day, but it's usually good eats." She grinned. "I always enjoy something I don't have to make myself."

"I help you?"

A soft voice caught Reed's attention. He looked up at the young Mexican woman standing beside them, waiting expectantly for their order. Reed took in a pair of decidedly beautiful wide-set eyes of shimmering, smoldering ebony and caught the exotic scent of freshly used Mexican hand soap on her person. She emitted a heavy, musky kind of perfume, as well as the scent of clean clothing as yet untouched by the odors of the busy kitchen. A shiver passed through him when he heard her soft breath while she waited.

Helen ordered for them both. *"Dos especiales, por favor."*

The girl gave Reed a long slow look before she nodded and turned away to the kitchen. Unable to look away, his masculine eyes followed every step. Her swaying gait, undulating bottom, and tiny waist did not go unnoticed.

"That is Mercedes Saldana. She's something, isn't

she?" Helen said. "I hear every man around this area has tried to court her, but she never takes up with any of them," she murmured low. "I've heard certain other things too, but then, it may just be gossip." With a sly smile, she added, "I don't get into Artesia too often."

Reed nearly snorted his reply, "Any man with blood in his veins would be chasing after that one. She's a real beauty—no doubt about that."

Yet she emitted an air of mystery about her and he'd also noticed her long, intricate earrings. An unwilling thought crossed his mind, remembering the one found in Harvey's saddlebags. He shook his head in disbelief. *Would a lovely young girl like that waste her time on an older married man?*

He said nothing of his thoughts, but his interest had been aroused. His mind encompassed the vision of this lovely female creating a stir among lonely males. He imagined wild music playing at night, and this lovely *señorita* moving slowly about the cantina, bending over tables to take an order and displaying enough of her feminine charms to drive any man crazy for her. *God, she'd entice the devil himself.*

Reed watched the girl at every opportunity as she moved about the room, tending other patrons. His interest, however, was not that of a man seeking comfort in the soft arms of a beautiful female. Before long, he realized his interest was not one-sided. She'd taken notice of him, also seeking to catch his glance at every opportunity.

Her figure was full and he decided that, especially for his benefit, her swelling hips undulated in an exaggerated way as she walked past him. He believed it to be practiced and deliberate. Her shimmering hair swept across her shoulders in a dark, glossy, cloud. *My God! Looking at her, a man could fall in love so damned easy.* He couldn't stop his thoughts and remembering the intricate gold earring, he wondered, *Could Harvey have fallen into an illicit relation-*

ship with this woman when he had such a fine little woman at home?

Reed knew men and how easily a man could become entangled if the temptation was enough. Mercedes brought their food to the table, but before setting Helen's plate down she placed his plate before him very slowly and shot him a sultry glance that sent heated flames racing wildly through his entire body. *This woman can curl a man's toes forward and backward.* The fire burning in those black, sloe-eyes gave off an exciting message that could light a burning torch inside a man.

She left their table and walked away with a sinuous, suggestive gait that had him longing for the wild, passionate promises he imagined beneath that wildly patterned skirt. He wiped his brow and noticed every other male in the cafe watched her as well.

Helen noticed and patted his hand. "Cool down, son." Seeing the interplay between Reed and the lovely *señorita*, she'd also noted the heated effect it'd had on him. "She's surely a beauty, isn't she?"

"Phew, I'll say she is. A damned little pepper pot, that one!" He flushed a deep red as he dug into his platter of tacos, rolled tamales, and crispy tortillas. He covered it all lavishly with a spicy sauce that burned all the way down. He hadn't tried the scalding chicory-type coffee yet.

"Watch out for that one, Reed," Helen cautioned. "She's broken more than a few hearts around Artesia." She took a healthy bite of tamale. "Miss Saldana's a mighty hard case. Her father beat the daylights out of her a year or so back, but he learned his lesson, too. That woman does exactly what she pleases and cares for no one—might take up with a man, but never for long.

"How do you know that about her?"

"Everyone knows about it. Of course, it's mostly gossip when you live out so far, but cowhands talk a lot. Mercedes Saldana is one of a kind. Seems to believe she's above the law and takes orders from no man." Helen kept her voice low, "Won't do to make an enemy of her either. People have been found dead, and that includes her father."

She didn't say anymore but Reed's imagination, fully aroused, gave him the idea he'd found a path for further investigation. Harvey Bradshaw's murder wasn't far from his thoughts.

"What's on your mind, young man?" Helen must have read his face and seen the change on it. "Don't you go tangling with that one. She'll tear you up and spit you out like so much half-rotted meat when she's done with you."

"You think so?" He smiled at her, but his face had set with a coldness and resolve he didn't try to hide from Helen.

His look made her curious. "What've you got in mind?" She flushed. "I know I shouldn't ask. It's not my business, but I think you're a mighty fine young man in spite of your past," she went on. "If you got any ideas of tangling with that woman, you'd best know, you'd be tangling with a wildcat."

Reed made no answer. Helen shrugged and changed to a subject closer to her own needs. "If we got enough time, I'd like to pay the doc a visit."

"We got enough time and more if you need to see him."

They finished the meal and Reed rose from his seat. Helen followed his lead and laid enough money on the table to take care of the meal and enough extra for the *señorita*.

They walked out the door, but not before Reed caught a glimpse of black eyes gleaming in his direction, and a good shot of naked shoulder from a blouse pulled low. As they left the Cantina, he fought the arousal the sight had wrought.

He'd formed uneasy feelings about Amanda's husband. The man had borrowed far more money than what he needed for his prospective cattle buy. Someone knew about it, and murdered him for it, but why? Considering the intricate golden earring and the possibilities associated with that bauble, could that lovely female have had a hand in Harvey Bradshaw's murder?

With a fine wife like Amanda at home it didn't seem reasonable to him, yet under certain circumstances, few men were impervious to the wiles of a beautiful woman. Knowing that Bradshaw was a rigid and severe sort, it seemed even less likely. But an idea had formed in his brain and he was of a mind to follow through on it.

Deep in thought, he walked with Helen along the boardwalk until she stopped and indicated a sign. The faded lettering said: Henry Cutler M.D. They climbed up worn and sun-bleached steps to reach a weathered door and entered. An older woman met them inside, a questioning look on her face.

"I'd like to see the doc, if he's in," Helen said.

"Why yes, he just got in from tending a patient all night, but he's still awake." She turned away and entered a door across the room.

In moments the doctor came out, his face drawn and gray with fatigue. He shook Helen's hand. "You need to see me?"

Helen stated she had recurring abdominal pain and the doctor indicated the inner office. "Come in, we'll have a look." They left the area and Reed took a seat to wait.

After about a half hour, Helen returned, her face more than pale. She merely said, "Let's get the visit to the sheriff over with. It's getting late."

Helen fought tears and staggered in her walk down the steps. Reed reached a hand to steady as well as to comfort her. She wasn't ready to tell him what the doctor said, if she ever would. "We'd best head for the ranch after seein' that sheriff," was all she said.

Entering his office, they found the man sitting in his chair. Reed stepped up and shook his hand. "Sheriff Toliver?"

"You're Bradshaw's brother-in-law. Humm—didn't know he had one. Deputy told me of your visit, damned shame about old Harvey. If there isn't any more you can add to what you've told my deputy, I'll contact the sheriff in Albuquerque about it. That canyon has to be up near there somewhere, but you can't say exactly where it is, that right?"

Reed shook his head.

Then sheriff asked a few more questions then sighed. "I'll do what I can to get his remains home to the ranch." He paused in thought. "Don't know where that drifter got to, you say?"

"Didn't stay long enough for more, in a big hurry to get up north, as he said—must be half way there, by now." Reed, rather terse, spoke no more than he had to. Lying this way hurt and he wished to hell he'd never started.

The interview was rather short to his way of thinking, especially for a murder. He collected the mare, hitched her onto the small carriage and they drove away toward the ranch. Reed handled the reins and they left at a good pace, the mare being well rested and heading home.

They drove in silence, but Reed's mind hung on Helen's ailment. He needed to know what was wrong. "All right Helen, what's going on?"

"I am a mite worried, Reed. Been having a pain right here." She indicated the lower right abdomen. "Not all the time, but I've had it three or four times so far and it's worrying me. Can't stand up straight when I get it."

He'd held off asking about her visit to the doctor but when he heard her utter a deep groan, he needed to know more. "News not so good, then. What did the doc tell you?"

"Well, after he poked and prodded around like they do, he said he thinks it is my app...something, but wasn't completely sure."

Tears filled her eyes. "He said it's something that gets infected and, in larger towns, doctors have begun doing an operation to remove it when that happens." She shook her head and shrugged. "Of course, he's never done such an operation, only heard of it."

Helen's worried expression tugged at Reed's heart-strings. "What if you get the pain again?"

A dark foreboding crept over him and settled deep in his bones. He'd had the feeling the diagnosis wouldn't be good and her dismal words confirmed it.

Her lower lip trembled. "He said to send for him right fast and don't try to come in to him because travel in that condition would be more dangerous for me. He's contacting a doctor he knows in Albuquerque. Said the man might know what to do about it." She paused, drawing in a deep breath.

Reed whistled low. "Sounds pretty bad. Sure sorry to hear about it."

"He also said this app—y or whatever it is, usually causes death when it ruptures," she went on as they rode over the bumpy, wagon-rutted trail. "If he *could* operate, I can die from that too, but might have a fair chance. He also said, if nothing is done, I'll die or be very sick for months on end. He's heard of it going both ways."

She drew herself up, and stiffened her spine. "I told him, if you can get out there in time, come prepared to do what you must. I have a son to bring up and my husband needs me." She shrugged at the futility of her situation and lapsed back into a stony silence.

Reed easily sensed her deep fear and made a remark he hoped would help. "I happen to know a bit about this condition because it happened to my sister a few years back. There was a small hospital in our town and I went with her." Hoping to give her some encouragement, he added, "They did that operation and she lived through it."

"Our doc's never done it, or ever seen it done. He said time was even more important since I've had the pains several times already."

She fought to keep the worry from her voice, but he heard it, and had seen her wipe sweat off her brow too many times already. "I know you worry over your family and not for yourself, being the good woman you are, but if it happens again, will you send Bennie for me and someone else for the doc?" He didn't give her a reason for his request, but he'd seen a few things in his years of travel, and believed he could lend a hand.

She turned to him. "Why send for you?"

"I've been around a lot of things and might be some help to the doctor." He smiled at her. "I'd like to help out if it comes to that."

Helen smiled at him. "Mister, you're a darned site bigger mystery than you let on and you know it."

Reed said nothing, just kept on driving.

CHAPTER 12

Sometime after dark, they pulled into the Bradshaw place. Reed helped Helen down, steadied her on her feet after the long ride, and sent her into the house. "I'll see to the mare and how things are out here." He watched her walking slowly to the house and wondered, *Is she stiff and slow from the long ride or is it something else?*

He unhitched the horse and led her to water. In the fading light, he noticed hay in the slatted manger for the horses and that the chickens had been watered and fed. "Good boy, that Bennie." He didn't consider the two cowboys.

Looking at the bunkhouse with the faint spiral of smoke curing upward, he guessed the two men were having their supper. He muttered, "We'll ride out tomorrow, make no mistake about that, you two."

***

Helen entered the house and, seeing the warm light coming off the lamps and catching the tantalizing odor of a cooked meal wafting in the air, she cried out, her voice dragging with fatigue. "It smells good enough in here to tempt the devil himself, Amanda. It plumb makes my worn and worried soul faint with hunger"

She looked overly tired and grabbed on to nearest chair. Amanda watched her collapse into it.

"Lord a mercy this was a terrible long day for me."

Seeing her friend's white, worn face, Amanda stopped rolling out the biscuits and went to her. "Helen, what is it?" She sat in the next chair. "You're white as a ghost."

"Just very tired, I've been poorly, you know about that, and I haven't got all the way over it, not yet." She directed a tired smile at Amanda. "Any coffee on that stove?"

Amanda had made a fresh pot. She got a cup, poured it full of deep rich liquid, and set it in front of her friend. Full of worry and curiosity about the onerous debt against the ranch left by her husband, Amanda left off her questions. Helen looked on the verge of collapse. Was it fatigue or something else? She put a hand on her shoulder. "Maybe a bite of supper will help you feel better."

Helen looked around. "I'll bide until Reed comes in and we eat. Where are the children? And I mean all of them—don't see a one."

"Marianna has Bennie in one of the bedrooms we use for storage. They are playing, and baby Reed's asleep," Amanda informed her with a smile.

Feeling stronger and better, Amanda felt she could stand up to anything Reed might have to tell her. With her head held high, she'd already decided if she lost the ranch, she'd head for Colorado with her children. It might seem like giving up to some, but her years in New Mexico had never been happy and returning to her beloved Colorado would be no hardship to her.

How often had she searched the long low mountains of New Mexico, wishing to see once again the height and grandeur of the Rocky Mountains of Colorado? She'd never feel at home until she could see them every day.

Helen sipped her coffee. As the rich dark liquid filled her with strength and comfort, she sat straighter, seeming to regain some of her former vigor. Amanda watched her with anxious eyes, yet kept glancing toward the door.

Helen smiled. "You're keeping watch for that man to come walking through the door, I see." She looked at

Amanda and nodded. "Looks to me like that Reed feller has become pretty darned important around here."

"I'd have to say, he has." Amanda blushed but stiffened her stance. "He showed up when I was at death's door, and my child, too. Of course, he's important, at least for right now. He'll be leaving soon enough." She frowned. "I wonder how I'll get along, then"

Her face felt like ice if she gave thought to not seeing that lanky figure about the place ever again.

The thumping of boots sounded on the porch and Amanda's head snapped up. She felt her chest expand as she drew in her breath and waited for Reed's appearance. Was it to learn what the banker had said of those loan papers, or what?

She smiled, forgetting her own fatigue from caring for her children and worrying over the ranch.

Reed came in, his long body filling the doorway. Smelling the food already prepared, he looked at Amanda, a glow in his dark eyes. "Something smells mighty fine in here, ma'am." He smiled at her, white teeth flashing from a broad smile.

Then with a quick look at Helen, he directed his attention to her. "Feeling poorly after the long drive, ma'am?"

"A bit, but this coffee sets me to rights quick enough. I'm better by the minute." She nodded at a chair. "Set to the table, son, chuck'll be on right soon at the rate the missus is going."

He looked around for the children. "Kids okay—help you, did they?" He saw a healthy rush of color in Amanda's cheeks and wondered if the heat of the stove made her flush rosy that way.

"How was the visit in town?" She looked him in the eye, needing to know what lay ahead for her ranch.

"No better than we figured." He frowned. "Something's not right about all this borrowing. Your husband has taken out large amounts over several months, far more than needed for any cattle buy, no matter how big that herd might have been."

He felt bad saying these things, but they had to be said. "Sorry for no better word than that. Helen was with me and heard the same."

"Reed had no problem convincing the banker or the deputy either that he was your brother." Helen chuckled. "Never heard such fancy polished up words out of a man's mouth, either."

Amanda let that comment pass. Bewildered by her many losses, she couldn't take it all in. "What about Sheriff Toliver? Did you see him?" Her blue eyes darkened with that query and a tight lipped expression came over her face. Her hands gripped the back of a chair.

"Yes, for all the good it did. He'll contact the sheriff in Albuquerque about finding your husband's body, and about hunting down the party that robbed and killed him."

"Suppose these cowboys here let on in town you're not my brother?" Amanda envisioned trouble ahead for her new ranch foreman if that happened.

Reed shrugged, but he had no answer to her query. "I'd better go shuck these fancy duds before we eat. I'll be seeing the boys in the morning and get them sorted out. They're in from the southern ranges. I believe that's where they've been today." He rose and walked down the long hallway.

"You know, it near drove that man crazy, having to lie that way," Helen said. She grinned at Amanda. "At the bank, Reed sounded like a banker himself and at the sheriff's office, too. He's not telling everything about himself, but after the way he's helped out around here, I'll never see the man in a bad light."

Amanda nodded. "I'll never see him that way, ever. I just hope he'll stay long enough to help me get back to Colorado. If this ranch is lost to the bank, I'll have no choice but to go. Truthfully, I've never been happy living on this Ranch."

Helen nodded. "Likely it was your husband made you feel that way. Everybody knew him for a hard sort. I imagine you found that, yourself."

Amanda merely shrugged, not knowing how to speak of her dead husband. She certainly knew how she felt, but voicing it was a different matter.

The both heard Reed come down the hall. He'd opened the door to where the children played and they heard Marianna's happy chattering. Soon Reed came back in, wearing his worn outfit with the little girl in his arms, clinging to his neck. He sat at the table after placing the child in her padded seat. Bennie quietly found a place at the table, but said nothing as he bent a worried look on his mother.

Shortly, Amanda noticed Reed's speech had slipped back into the role of drifter, only needing to change his borrowed finery for his own ragged things to complete the transformation. A shame, she thought, remembering the fine picture he made in the slim stripped pants and shining boots.

Amanda dished out the food. "Time everyone ate. It's been ready for a while." She started to pick up the platter of meat and Reed jumped up.

"Here now, that's way too heavy for you to be lifting." He took every dish she'd readied and put them on the table. Then he reached for the big enameled coffee pot and set it on the table far out of Marianna's reach.

"Weed, I have coppee?" her plaintive voice queried.

"No, you may not," her mother replied. "It's not good for little girls."

With that, they enjoyed a good meal of roast beef, hot biscuits, and thickened gravy over potatoes. They had no greens, but Reed's mouth watered as he noticed a crusty pie sitting on the side board, just waiting.

As good as the food tasted, it was basking in the fine, glowing warmth of family that made this meal enjoyable and satisfying. It'd been a long time since Reed had been close to anyone. He'd nearly forgotten the way being part of a family made a man feel. Once again he felt himself rising to the challenge of helping this woman sort out her troubles and face the future on her own. Going north to escape the possibility of capture and arrest had left his thoughts completely.

Surrounded by people so newly met, he felt a strong desire to protect and take care of this young woman, her trusting little daughter, and now a newborn boy that bore his name as an honor to himself. His chest swelled with resolve and pride, two deeply intense feelings he'd not known for many years. He had no money to offer, but he did have plenty of strength and knowledge.

Ideas had already formed in his mind. He wanted to solve the questions surrounding the murder of her husband and, after the enlightening trip into Artesia, had a very good idea where to begin.

CHAPTER 13

In the early morning, Reed roused out and breakfasted. Dressed in his worn clothes, he headed to the bunkhouse. He didn't see Amanda but he'd heard her infant cry in the night a time or two and surmised her rest had been broken in the care of him. He felt his chest swell a bit. *She named him after me, now that's mighty fine.*

He knocked on the door of the bunkhouse and walked in. Jud raised his head off his pillow and snuffled. "Who'n hell is it?"

Reed faced the men as they lay snuggled in their bedding. His face felt tight as a drum and, with lips tightly drawn across his gritted teeth, he snarled, "You boys'd better haul-ass if you want to stay on here." Venom dripped from his tongue. In utter disgust at the caliber of these two hands, he added, "I'm riding out with you fellers today to get an idea what's going on with this ranch. The boss put me in charge so let's get at it. If you're hungry, grab some jerky, because you lazy bastards should've been up long afore this."

He turned and went out, heading for the corral. Seeing Spotty, Reed figured he'd use Harvey's horse since he was the foreman and had the right. His own sad nag wasn't worth a hill of beans on his best day.

Minutes later, the two cowboys shuffled out, hair awry and shirttails hanging out. Jud came up to Reed. "Sorry boss, we didn't get in till late yestidy, and there wasn't no food fit to cook when we did. We got us a few complaints ourselves." He wheezed and coughed. "That Harvey was a slave driver figuring us two being enough to handle a place this size." Grumbling, he headed for his tack. It hung in the barn on wooden pegs. Buddy, never one to raise a fuss, went along saying nothing.

Jud made no comment about Reed saddling Spotty and Reed didn't especially care what he thought. "Just how big is this place, if you know for sure? Reed had long wondered, and now as foreman, had the right to ask as many questions as he chose without sounding too nosey.

"It runs about four sections, pretty much square the way it's laid out." Jud told him. "Ain't none of it government lease neither. Old Harvey had a right good sized outfit for this area, so I hear. Pretty dry for decent grazing, but he'd put in several good sized water tanks, an idee he got from Arizona folks. And then there's the Pecos River running through in places."

Reed decided the man knew a lot more than a regular hand ought to know, but let it pass. That bit of knowledge only added to his decision to help Amanda get things put to rights. "Let's get out there, then—long day ahead."

The three of them rode to the south for a few hours before they saw any cattle at all and spotting a small bunch in a grassy box canyon, Reed commented, "How many head did you say Harvey was running?"

"Never said," Jud returned. "Seems he was losing some right along, but it never seemed to bother him the way it ought."

Reed took another tack. "Ever know what Harvey was running off to town for?" He laughed a bit. "Like something personal, maybe?"

A peculiar look crossed Jud's face. "How'd you get an idea like that?"

"Something I ran up against in Artesia is all." He looked Jud in the face as they crossed a dry stream bed.

"You ever think he might be seeing some woman, there? One he'd have to spend a lot of money on maybe, trying to hold her interest?"

Jud flushed under the scrutiny, looked away, but said nothing to enlighten Reed.

തൽൽ

Amanda stood at the kitchen window with her baby in her arms. She'd watched as the men rode away. Seeing Reed on her husband's horse didn't bother her at all. But the easy swing of his broad shoulders, even dressed in his faded rags, bothered her plenty. She realized that just looking at him did strange things to her insides and, though she fought the strange sensations that lanky man caused to rise inside her, she continued to watch until he passed from view.

Both older children were asleep, and so was Helen. Amanda turned away from the window murmuring, "Wonder what this day will bring?"

With the men gone, she relaxed. After all the worries of yesterday, she'd wearied thinking of it and took an immediate sort of comfort holding and caring for her infant. Maybe she shouldn't have placed a total stranger in charge of things, but who else could she have asked? Jud? Never!

That single earring hadn't left her mind for long. She'd considered it endlessly, even imagining her husband in another woman's arms. But finding it so unlike that cold, harsh man she'd come to know, she refused the image.

The baby asleep, Amanda laid him in one of the big chairs and paced about the kitchen, her mind in a constant whirl. She'd always hated the way Harvey's presence had made her feel inadequate. Somehow, it always had. Feeling relief that she no longer had to worry about Harvey's opinions of her shortcomings, she shivered, remembering the softened look in his eye at those times he took the notion for intimate relations.

He'd never been one to kiss or offer compliments to her, or try to arouse a sense of need in her. She'd never felt a hint of passion to make their time together a good experience. With Harvey, she'd been a failure as a wife. Intimacies with him had been embarrassing and uncomfortable. Never the excitement she'd heard women whisper about when they got together.

She'd always been considered a very pretty woman when growing up, honey blonde hair with a nice trim figure. But he never remarked on that or seemed to care. His only comments were about how spoiled she'd been as a child.

Harvey's coldness of nature, and constant criticism had killed any possible joy in any relations between them. Remembering the day he'd come riding into their ranch to buy livestock and stayed around to pay court to her, she couldn't imagine how she'd ever thought him handsome and a fine prospect for marriage.

Amanda sniffed, her head held high. If she'd been the apple of her daddy's eye, and he'd mollycoddled her growing up, it had seemed normal and proper to her at the time.

But once married, she'd learned that Harvey was not the same sort of man as her father. She'd learned his ways soon enough, he'd seen to that. Slothfulness was not something he'd tolerate in anyone, including women and children. She stifled a frown, remembering how he'd boldly declared she'd better throw a son this time. Girls were nothing but trouble, he'd said. He needed sons, and a lot of them to work the ranch and cut down on the hiring.

But now, as a widow, she no longer had to please the man who'd become a stranger in every way. Amanda felt a smile stealing over her face. Harvey was gone, and deep down, she found it difficult to mourn his passing.

She puzzled again over the earring. Harvey had never been much for physical intimacy aside from satisfying his own needs, and nothing more. She found it nearly impossible to believe he sought his comforts elsewhere. Yet what *did* that intricate and finely wrought bauble mean? It had some sort of significance and meaning, but what? And for whom?

Helen appeared, rubbing the sleep from her eyes, looking for coffee and catching the odors of recently cooked food. Seeing the young woman sitting in the kitchen, she remarked, "Up early, aren't you? What's going on in that head of yours, Amanda?"

"Just thinking, sorting things out. It's hard right now, with all I've got ahead of me." She sighed and looked at her friend. "I'll be strong again, and ready to handle things, but I have so many questions—things to find out. I need time to get everything straight in my head, and I mean aside from the workings of this ranch." She rose to fill her cup. "Maybe I can get things figured out with Reed's help, if he stays long enough." She sat down with her coffee. "He's just ridden out with the boys."

Amanda felt she needed to explain. "I grew up on a ranch, but my father never allowed or encouraged me to get involved with what he referred to as 'man's work.' Females took care of the house and belonged there. He'd said that more than once." She shrugged, her hands splayed out. "I learned to ride a horse, but that was about it as far as running a ranch went." Her head held high, she admitted, "You know, Helen, I really have no longing to live this life, not really, never have." Her friend made no comment as Amanda went on, musing aloud, "Maybe I could make a living here for my children."

Without realizing it, she'd included Reed in those thoughts. Could she do it *without* a man? She shook her head, knowing she couldn't.

Helen sat in a big chair nursing a cup of coffee, still half asleep. Amanda hadn't heard her say what the doctor had said about her spells and, curious to know, she gently nudged her shoulder. "Helen, you see the doctor yesterday?"

"Well—yes, I did."

"Would you mind telling me, if it's not too personal?"

"He told me it's appen-d-something. He said I might have to have an operation if it happens again, but he's never done one like that. Not good news for me, is it?" Helen looked her in the eye. "I'm not so afraid of dying, people do it every day, but I worry about my husband and Bennie— he's so young."

"That's worrisome, for sure." Amanda, at a loss for words, wanted to help. "Did he say what to do, if the pain comes again?"

Helen repeated the doctor's warnings, then she told Amanda, "Reed said to call him, as well as the doctor. That man seems to know a lot about quite a few things. You suppose he knows something about this, too?"

"Too? Why do you think he knows so much about everything?" Already confused about the man, Amanda was eager for further clarification. "He asked you to call *him*?" she asked, puzzled. "I find that hard to understand, but everything I've learned about Reed has been to the good so far." She frowned. "I wonder why he'd know about something that serious."

"Who knows, but I took it as a good sign, for whatever it means. Now let me rest for a moment, dear." She moved to one of the big chairs in the larger room, lay back, and closed her eyes.

Amanda left her to rest and decided to check out the garden. She took up her baby and, holding him close tiptoed outside. It was quiet out there too, with the other children asleep and she wanted to see if any plants remained alive. She hadn't watered them for a very long time. Unable to carry that heavy oaken bucket anymore, she felt no guilt about it.

No more would her husband give her his dark, steely-eyed look of censure. Watering the garden had been much too difficult for her so late in her pregnancy, but he'd never let her off that job. She recalled his last words to her. "See that you do."

For that reason if no other, she felt a burden lifted off

her shoulders. "I'm free of that look." She smiled to herself. "If that makes me an unfeeling wretch, I really don't care."

No one could hear her words. She spoke them freely and almost laughed into the silent air around her as the delicious elixir of freedom took possession of her mind. The very thought of it lent her the strength she required for what lay ahead. She hugged the joy of those feelings close to her heart.

Remembering how Reed had looked in those fancy duds, a wild stir of excitement crept through her. "He looked so fine, like a banker or a lawyer wearing them." She laughed and the sound of it filled the air with music. She hadn't laughed like that in a long, long time.

Approaching the garden gate, she saw things growing very well. The soil was more than damp around the tender shoots. "Someone has watered these plants, but who? Reed? No, couldn't be, he was gone all day yesterday."

She didn't enter the garden, but turned away and hurried back to the house, her brow furrowed with the new question. "I've got some help I don't know about. I can't for the life of me figure out—who?" Her question remained unanswered as she returned to the house.

In mid-morning, as she stood alone in the ranch yard with Piddely, Amanda said her goodbyes to Helen and Bennie. Marianna had cried herself to sleep at the loss of Bennie as a playmate and Reed was out with the boys. Walking back to the house, Amanda felt terribly alone, and a sense of desolation washed over her.

Within the hour, she had fed her baby and changed him, as well as the linens on her bed. Hearing the sound of horse's hooves clopping into the yard, her head came up and her heart raced in anticipation, thinking it would be the lanky Reed.

She chided herself, knowing she ought to be ashamed of thinking such a thing, being a new widow and all, but she couldn't help the excitement that being near him gave her.

He'd been her hero, appearing when she'd needed someone desperately. She honored him for that and felt close to him.

A shock passed through her at seeing who'd come to her ranch. It wasn't Reed, with his long legs and wide smile. Disappointed, suddenly fearful, and with a tightened face, she watched Sheriff Toliver ride in. *Has he come to arrest Reed? If so, then where will I be? What will I do then?*

Feeling selfish in her worry about the loss of Reed, her heart raced as she waited. She hadn't realized until now how quickly she'd become dependent on a man she barely knew, in spite of how greatly he'd helped her.

Toliver pulled up, dismounted, and tossed the reins over the hitching rail in front of the house. Hat in hand, he faced Amanda on her porch. "Howdy, ma'am, I've come to speak with you about the loss of your husband."

Waiting for her reply, with one spurred boot on the first step, he doffed his hat and rolled it, his fingers edging along the rim. Amanda, seeing that, wondered if he was nervous. He looked it.

"Won't you come in sheriff...Toliver, isn't it?" Her tone was cool as she led the way inside,

"Yes, ma'am, that's my handle, Jonas Toliver."

As he entered the home, he appeared to take in the comforts, decor, and furnishings. She hoped he thought it suitable as he followed her to the large sitting room that sported several chairs. She took a seat in the soiled chair, carefully covered with a folded blanket, and bade him take another.

"How is your investigation coming, then?"

Amanda tried to keep from clenching her hands on arms of the chair in her worry about Reed riding in dressed in those ragged clothes. The lie about him being her brother had her plenty worried. If discovered, it could send Reed straight back to that dreadful prison after all he'd done to help her. She hoped the sheriff wouldn't stay long.

"Ma'am, I know about the heavy debt your husband has piled up against this ranch and how it leaves you and your children in a bad spot." He flushed at revealing private information, but Amanda supposed he had a purpose in his line of conversation.

"My deputy contacted the people in Albuquerque and they have wired to say they found his remains. My man's bringing him home for burial. He's on the way now."

"Thanks for telling me." She was quiet for a time then said, "I guess he ought to be laid away in the Artesia cemetery." She paused, trying to keep her thoughts on the real purpose of his visit, knowing he looked for information.

She decided to inform him of her surprise at the situation. "I should say, sir, it came as a great surprise to me and my brother about those loans." She flushed and flung out her hands. "We aren't decided yet how to proceed with something like that, and we're not sure if I can hold on to this ranch, because of them." She faced him, her instinct for survival rising to the fore. "I don't understand why he needed so much money. He never spent much for things around here that I could see."

"I have a good idea about that, too, and find it a painful subject to bring up, you being a new mother and all." He paused then went on. "You ever suspect him of seeing another woman anytime during your marriage?"

"No, I never did, but—" She flushed again and admitted, "When we went through his saddlebags, there was something—" She rose to get the errant earring. It lay inside a box on her chest in the darkened bedroom. She left the sheriff, but returned quickly. "I found this with his things, sir." She held it out to him.

Toliver took it and held it out. Looking at it carefully, nodding his head as though he knew something about it. "I've never seen this particular item before, but have seen similar items on a certain suspect I have in mind. She always wears fancy earbobs. I've seen them often enough. I have an idea about this and if I may, I'd like to tell you what I suspect." He cleared his throat. "Your husband may have gotten involved with a woman I have under suspicion. I won't go farther into it right now, but would you consider letting me have this?" He held out the fancy bit of jewelry. "If what I believe is true, this bit of jewelry may be the small piece of the puzzle that helps clear up this situation and likely several others as well. It might help me make a connection if I could have the use of it."

"Certainly, you may."

Amanda said it automatically. In shock at learning the sheriff also considered the possibility of her husband's infidelities, her mind went reeling. That he could have been unfaithful came as a complete shock since Harvey had never been much for the physical side of marriage. She'd been glad of it. All the hoopla about intimate relations between a man and woman never made any sense to her after her own experience with marital intimacy.

Supposedly Harvey had gone to the bank for a cattle loan. Amanda remembered the lingering odor of that heavy, musky, perfume on him after that last visit to Artesia, and finding that beautiful earring tucked into his saddle bags made her wonder over and over if Harvey could have bought a delicate, feminine creation like that for another woman. It amazed and angered her to think of it, but she hid her feelings from Toliver as best she could.

This sheriff seemed a decent sort to Amanda. He might be tough in his way, but she felt certain he wasn't the kind to say anything like that about her husband if he wasn't sure of his words. Hearing these suspicions from him added up to one more shock. Upset at the information Tolliver had brought, and along with everything else that'd happened in the past several days, she sat staring into space until she heard his voice again.

"Mrs. Bradshaw, I'd like to speak to your brother if he's here."

At those words, an alarm went raging within her that nearly took her breath away. The unwilling lies they'd both told closed in, choking her. They'd come too close for comfort.

"H—he rode out to the south ranges with the cowboys t—today," she stammered, barely keeping a straight face. She felt a great sense of relief that Reed was absent. "Did you want him to come in to see you when he can?"

"Why yes, if you'll ask him." As he turned to leave, Marianna came toddling out on the porch, dragging her blanket and rubbing her eyes. He stopped and said, "I've never seen Harvey's little girl, in fact, I know almost nothing about the man. He sure enough left a pretty widow, ma'am, if you don't mind my saying so." He flushed. "Like any man, I appreciate the sight of a fine-looking woman."

Amanda shrugged in reply to his complement, yet felt a glow of warmth in hearing it. She'd not felt beautiful for a very long time.

"Mommy, where Weed?" Marianna looked expectantly about, dragging her blanket, her finger in her mouth.

Amanda laughed, trying to hide her nervousness about the identity of Weed. "Honey, he rode out with the cowboys today." She hoped to turn her daughter's thoughts in another direction. "Are you hungry, Marianna?"

"Who's this Weed, person?" Toliver asked. "I hadn't heard of any riders around this neck of the woods by that name." He cast a warm smile on the little girl. "And who's this pretty little lady?"

"She calls one of the hands that. His name is Reed, but she has trouble saying it." She patted the child's shining halo of golden hair. "This is my daughter, Marianna. Sweetheart, say hello to the sheriff."

"Hewo," she murmured, barely seeing the sheriff as she looked about and asked again. "Where Weed? I wan' see Weed."

"She's sure taken a liking to the man, whoever he is." Toliver chuckled as he turned to mount his horse. "I'll just water my horse and be off. Nice to see you, ma'am, an' sorry for what happened to your husband. We're working on that, never fear."

She stood on the porch and, with a sense of relief, watched him ride away. She waited until the dust from his horse's hooves had settled before entering her house again. It bothered her to have lied to a good man. She knew Toliver to be a very fine officer of the law and had an awful fear it'd come back to haunt her. It'd certainly mean trouble for Reed.

CHAPTER 14

The sound of her fretful newborn took possession of her thoughts and, putting aside her fears of the future, she hurried inside to tend him, leaving her daughter playing in the yard with Piddely.

Amanda wished for the sight of Reed more than she ever imagined she'd look for any man, especially now that she was a free woman. "Everything is closing in on me and now the sheriff is out here with his questions." She sighed. "Reed, where are you?" Her thoughts raced as she fed her new son. "I did smell perfume on Harvey the last time he went to town. It must have been the day he borrowed that last money for those Black Angus cattle he wanted." She sat up straight, her jaw tight. "It burns me clear through that that cheating bastard treated me like a hired hand and a danged brood mare, and all the while I never suspected a thing. It never entered my mind he'd be one for chasing women."

The more she thought about it, the angrier she became until all those pent up emotions held in reserve came flooding through. She doubled over in tears of frustration and anger. Marianna came running into the house and seeing her mother in tears, began crying in sympathy.

"Mommy, hurt?" A child's security is their parent and seeing her mother sob helplessly and looking distraught, brought fear to the girl. She found a cloth and handed to her mother. "Here, Mommy." Her childish voice came through the tears until Amanda just had to smile. She caught her daughter in her arms and hugged her close.

"I'm just fine, little one. Don't you worry about me, my little darling."

The closeness of her daughter pressing against the infant angered him until he squirmed and let out an angry squall of indignation.

Marianna wriggled off Amanda's crowded lap and turned her attention to her tiny brother. "Ooh, baby cry, Mommy."

"Yes, honey, he's a man too, and that's what they do best."

She knew her words were an unfair judgment of the entire male species, but at the moment she felt incredibly angry toward the entire lot of them. She'd been ill-used by one of them—her own dead husband.

He'd never made her happy in their marriage, not once that she could remember. And this sleeping boy in her arms belonged to that mysterious male gender she knew so little about.

She shook her head in bewilderment. Her own father had been a distant sort, too. He may have spoiled her, but she'd never had the fatherly warmth from him that Marianna had received from Reed. Considering those things, she wondered about her mother's happiness as a wife.

She laughed at herself and felt better all the way around. She guessed crying had a healing element in it. Frequently during the sultry afternoon, she went about her work keeping her eye on the southern horizon, looking and waiting for the moment when that tall, wiry man called Reed would ride in.

Remembering the way he'd taken care of her in her hour of need, she murmured, "Maybe they're not all so bad." She took her now sleeping newborn into her dark bedroom and tucked him in his cradle.

cↄↄↄↄ

Reed rode into the ranch yard about dusk. Amanda stood in the kitchen window, the light of a lamp glowing behind her.

At the sight of his tall form, a feeling of warmth swept over her. An innate sense of completeness filled her at the sight of him. Watching him at every opportunity had become a conscious habit, one she reveled in.

As he unsaddled the sweating roan, she felt thrills sweeping through her, watching the way his long hands smoothed and caressed across the horse's back and his sweating flanks. He wiped the horse clean of dust and sweat from the day's ride, while those wild thoughts she couldn't stop raced through her mind. *How would it feel if his big hands did that to me?*

Going into the barn, he hauled out large armfuls of hay and threw enough into the manger for all the horses. They crowded around munching on the sweet-smelling, mountain-grass hay. Harvey usually bought it when he didn't get enough from his hay fields. Smiling, she stood there, wondering about Reed, but came to no conclusions.

Jud had gone on to the bunkhouse to make their supper and left the care of the remaining tack to Buddy. Continuing to watch, she saw Reed wash his face and arms in the horse trough. *He's so terribly thin,* she mused. He slicked back his hair before heading for the house, hat in hand. His sun-darkened face had an honest, solid look to it. Watching him, she realized with a start, *He's a very handsome man. I never saw him that way before.*

With a rising excitement she didn't understand, she met him at the door, anxious to see that long, lean face again and look into those dark eyes. He looked tired and worn from all day in the saddle. A few errant droplets of water lay among the fine hairs of his arms and dripped off the ends onto the floor. Without a word, she led him to the table and the place she'd set for him.

Marianna spotted him. Squealing in delight, she squirmed out of her chair to run and grab his hand. "Weed, where you go?"

"Things need attending to, little darling."

His voice was deep and soft. No wonder he was able to attend her during childbirth and manage to make her feel comfortable in spite of how personal he'd had to be. Amanda flushed, remembering how those long warm hands had taken care of her personal needs. How he'd cleansed her and placed the clean linens beneath her.

He gave Amanda a broad smile as he played with the girl. "Everything all right with you, ma'am?"

"I'm fine, Reed, better all along." His dark smile had her heart beating near out of her chest as she dished up a plateful of beans, stew, and fluffy biscuits. "You'd best eat a bite, you look a mite hungry." She poured him a brimming cup of coffee and set it before him.

"I reckon a man could get used to this, ma'am." He gave her a wide grin and dug in. Marianna pouted, went back to her seat, but spent most of her time looking at him and watching him eat, hardly taking a bite of her own meal.

"Honey, you'd best finish your supper," Amanda reminded her, but she hadn't finished her own meal either. She sat at the table, in a dreamlike state herself, comforted by the presence of this kindly man who'd come from nowhere to become the most important person in her life.

The swiftness of the changes in her life hadn't completely sunk in. Recovering from the birth of her new son and the loss of a husband were more than Amanda could take in right now. And for one magical moment, she forgot it all. She sat in a dreamy trance of unreality, enjoying the peace and comfort of sitting at this table, in this situation, at this time. She felt overwhelmed by the rightness of it.

Remembering the sheriff's visit, reality came crushing back. She hated what she had to say. "Reed, the sheriff was here. He'd like to talk to you a bit more. He has some ideas, mostly about what my husband was up to before he was killed. Seems to think he knows who's behind it."

"What does he want with me?"

She noticed his face had gone a few shades lighter, and his hand clenched tightly about the fork he held.

"He didn't really say in detail, but he has an idea about that earring. He wants you to come in town again. You ready for that?" She paused and frowned. "I'm really sorry we've gotten you into this mess. It's not right for you to have to pretend you're my brother. It's going to come out, something like that always does, and it'll hurt all of us. I know it will."

"I'm sorry we started that, too." Reed said as he took a few bites of a biscuit smothered with marmalade. "This is mighty good chuck, ma'am. It sort of makes up for all the lying I've had to do." He grinned at her. "If things seem right, I just may come clean with the sheriff. He's got a lot on his plate right now in solving this murder, but I believe he's a square shooter." He loaded another biscuit with butter and went on eating.

"You're very brave to even consider that, yet it might be for the best. I never was one for lies, myself, and it's bothering me, same as you." She took a biscuit herself, broke it open, and buttered it as the steam rose into the air. "I'll stand behind you all the way. If that man knew how you'd helped me, he'd know you were no killer." Remembering words like that might be alarming to a young child, she shot a quick look at Marianna. The girl quietly slipped bits of food to Piddely, totally unaware of their conversation.

"Ma'am, even a killer might have been moved to help. You were in a bad way that night."

He flushed with the memories of those hours. He'd never forget it himself. At times, he wondered: If he had a wife of his own, would she have a child for him and suffer that way in the doing? Would he have the courage to put a woman through that? He smiled and shook his head, knowing full well, that at certain times a man couldn't stop to consider things like that, not when a woman took his eye and wanted him.

Amanda had turned rosy, too, but she looked him in the eye. "Most men would have turned and run, and maybe robbed the house before they left." She laughed. "You can't make light of the kind of man you are, mister, but I'll swear to your innocence before any judge in the land."

"Those are mighty kind words, ma'am." He looked at her with the kind of warmth she'd never caught from any man, certainly not Harvey Bradshaw.

The light in his eyes sent thrills coursing all through her body again, and a wave of heat shot through her until she had to muffle a gasp. This man made her feel things she'd never known. She felt especially shy as she murmured, "You could call me Amanda. I think we know each other that well."

She felt embarrassed saying that and turned to her daughter. "Marianna, why not finish your plate? We can't be wasting food on that dog." Most of her daughter's food sat on the plate, untouched.

"Mommy, I tired." She got up from the table and moved against Reed's leg. Gazing up at him, she wheedled, "Weed, would you tell me a story from my book?" Her big blue eyes entreated and begged. Amanda watched him melt at the child's request.

"Honey, Reed is very tired from riding all day." Amanda hoped to spare him extra effort after a taxing day.

"Not so tired I can't read to this little charmer." He took her on his lap. "Now where is this book you're talking about?"

As she jumped down and raced to get it from her room, Amanda scolded, "You are spoiling that child."

With that, she realized she'd parroted her dead husband's very words, spoken only a couple of short weeks ago. She left Reed alone and went about cleaning the kitchen. The baby had proved to be a peaceful infant unless he was hungry, and she was grateful for the few extra moments it allowed her.

Marianna returned with her tattered book and Amanda watched this kindly man take her on his lap and read to her as if she were his very own. Her heart swelled at the sight of it, and her daughter indulged herself in his father-like attentions. She'd had little enough of that from her own.

In surprise, Amanda saw Reed take the little girl to her bed and tuck her in, just as he had on the night of his arrival. *What sort of man is this?* she mused as she gave her kitchen the finishing touches and set out sourdough to work for the morning batch of biscuits. The baby awakened with cries of hunger and, unable to imagine nursing her child in front of the stranger, she took him into the dark bedroom to change and feed him. She finished, lay him back to sleep, and went out.

With the house quiet, and Reed sitting at the kitchen table, she indicated a chair in the sitting room. "Why not sit a while and rest yourself?"

Where he'd sleep tonight hadn't been mentioned and remembering Helen's admonishment about having a strange man sleeping in her house, she was undecided about it.

She began with a query. "How did you find things out there? I've never ridden out with my husband and have no idea about anything as far as livestock or even the problems with raising them. I feel lost and unsettled about this place, Reed."

Her situation was dire in many ways. She had no real means to provide for her children on her own and he was well aware of it. His protective instincts rose as he gazed into her trusting eyes. "It's a mighty fine ranch, ma'am, as far as I can tell. I didn't see a whole lot of cattle the way we rode, but the boys say the rest are to the west of what we saw today."

Returning to what lay uppermost on her mind, she asked, "Will I lose this place?"

"It's too early to tell about that." He paused to ask, "You say the sheriff has an idea about what's going on with the loans and all?" He sat across from her, looking into her eyes, and lost his train of thought.

Amanda was young and fine-looking, for all she'd had to bear. She'd been strong in the face of everything, and Reed remained amazed at how well she'd recovered from her night of travail in bringing forth her son.

He decided women, with their limited strength and their softness, were actually tough as shoe leather in quite a few other ways. Helen, too, in the face of an impending death sentence, had thoughts only for that of her husband and son.

Amanda's voice broke into his thoughts, returning him to the question at hand. "Yes, the sheriff wants to speak to you about his ideas," she said. "Do you think you could be my brother again and go see him?" She frowned. "I know you hate the idea of it, but we've done it once and maybe seeing him could help us."

With her words, she'd included him in her future. He wondered if she realized what she'd said

"I'd have to wear those fancy duds again." He smiled at the thought and Amanda felt her heart leap at the way his white teeth shone against his sun-darkened skin. "I'll do it tomorrow then," he said. "Best get things moving if there's a chance to save this place."

She found she was more than eager to see him wearing those fine clothes again. His dark hair and eyes looked especially good against the black serge jacket, the charcoal striped trousers, and that neat string tie against the whiteness of the shirt. He did look like a banker, or lawyer, or maybe some fancy gambler as Helen had said. And to Amanda, he looked like a man who belonged in clothes like that.

She decided on another matter, too. Her head went up, and her chin firmed. "Reed, if you'd like, you may sleep in that back bedroom. I know it's probably not right, me being a lone woman and all, but I'd be pleased to know someone is in the house at night. I'd feel better knowing you're close by."

She flushed and felt the heat of it rise up her neck, but she didn't care. She had no one, really. This stranger had become the only friend she had outside of Helen. Her real brothers were far away and she hadn't seen them in years.

"I'd be mighty pleased, ma'am. And don't worry about having me under the same roof." Reed put his hand to his mouth and yawned. "It's been a while since I had a decent shelter over my head, and that bed's a nice one."

CHAPTER 15

Morning saw Reed dressed and ready to head into Artesia. He wore the fine looking outfit as before and, feeling like the fraud he was in them, stood before Amanda. "As much as I appreciate the use of these clothes, I'm a damned liar when I put them on and use your brother's name."

She nodded in understanding. It had to be that way for now so she made no comment as she busied herself at the stove. Amanda sympathized with him about the lies and fraud of the impersonation, but it'd been started and she didn't know how to stop it. Was it also a fraud that it seemed right having this man sit at her table and her cooking his meals?

Watching her make his breakfast filled him with contentment. After a decent plate of bacon, eggs, potatoes, biscuits, and coffee, he was ready to head into town. With all the unreality he faced in town, sitting here with this woman seemed very real. But it had him worried. *Where's this going? If I stay around here this way, I'll end up in Yuma Prison again, sure as hell.*

Amanda heard the baby cry and went to him. Marianna came out, rubbing the sleep from her eyes, and dragging a tattered blanket along the floor. Spotting Reed dressed so finely, she ran to him. "Weed, you all pitty again!"

She clung to his hand and he saw in her eyes, she wanted to be held on his lap.

He took her up to sit on his knee and told her, "I'm going into town today, little darling, a man's got to look his best." He gave her a hug, rose from the table, and set her in her own chair. "Here you go." He set a plate of breakfast in front of her and buttered a biscuit. "Your momma's in the back with the baby."

He put Harvey's fine beaver hat on his head and made ready to hit the trail to Artesia as Amanda came out, carrying her son.

She handed him a few bills. "Can't have my brother hit town without something in his pocket."

"I do need it, but taking money this way makes me feel lower than a damned snake."

"You'll never be that to me, Reed. You've already earned more than I could ever pay to my way of thinking, and I'm not speaking of your job as foreman." She looked away in embarrassment. "Now get going, and let's hope that Sheriff Toliver has figured out who did this to my husband. He seemed to know something. Maybe you can find out what's going on. I mean the borrowing as well as the killing."

"I'll do what I can and, if it feels right to me, I'm likely to come clean with that sheriff. It'll come out about who I am in time, anyway, and I'd like to be on the right side of that man when it does." With that, he shoved the hat on a bit tighter, glad of the decent fit, and went toward the corral.

Amanda stood at the kitchen window watching his every move as he rode away. Her infant son lay snuggled in her arms fast asleep, his little belly filled with mother's milk. Marianna tugged at her skirts. "Momma, we go garden?"

"Yes, honey, in a minute." She barely paid her daughter any heed while she watched that finely dressed gentleman ride out of the ranch yard sitting on the big roan. *He sure cleans up nice,* she mused, unable to take her eyes off

Reed as he rode away. *I'll never stop believing he was sent to me.*

"Garden, Mommy?" Marianna was restless, she'd tired of her toys and that green and growing place had always drawn her attention.

"In a minute, dear." She absently patted Marianna's head until Reed was out of sight then turned her attentions to the little girl.

They walked out to see the garden. Again, she saw it damp and the planted vegetables bursting with new growth. "Who waters this garden?" she wondered, but with baby Reed awake, squirming, and struggling, it was soon forgotten. "Marianna, we need to tend this baby right now. We'll come back later.

ℰↄℰↄ

As Reed rode away on the big roan, he saw Amanda standing in the kitchen window and it gave his lonely heart a twist. That fine-looking woman had watched him ride away. In his lonely travels, nothing like that had ever happened. Moved deeply, he felt his heart swell and vowed to be worthy of her trust. He'd help her if he could find a way. *That woman's placed a lot of trust in a total stranger.*

Going back to Yuma Prison would be a hellish price to pay for it, yet the way he felt right now, even the threat of that wouldn't prevent him staying around. "You must be all kinds of a fool for what you're doing, Reed, you dumb son-of-a-bitch."

He rode at a good pace. Harvey's roan had a fine, soft gait, and Reed enjoyed the feel of the wind in his face. The glory of the rising sun covered the early morning with shimmering gold. Right now, the way things were, everything was right with the world, and his heart was full to overflowing.

Artesia was a good five miles or so, and he hoped to

get back tonight. He enjoyed sleeping under the same roof with Amanda. It wasn't in the same bed, though he'd given some thought to that, too. Seeing the daily improvements from her recent childbirth, what man wouldn't? Amanda was a fine, beautiful woman. Staying around, and working for her gave him the feeling of being a family man. The child, Marianna, was drawn to him and looked to him for the things a father could give a child. That small thing made him feel like a father, if not a husband. *Amanda Bradshaw trusts me in spite of knowing all about me, well, almost all.* He smiled and nudged the roan onward.

He reached Artesia, rode over the ridge and down into the town with troubled feelings. He risked too much riding into this town, dressed in another man's clothes and pretending to be someone he wasn't. His thoughts were disturbing. *Lying was never my style. But I guess a few months in a hellhole of a prison might warp any man's sense of right and wrong.*

Reed rode on until he spied the barred windows of the jail. With his heart thrumming heavily, he pulled the roan to a stop in front of the sheriff's office, dismounted, and tossed the reins over the hitching rail. After several attempts to slap the dust off his clothes, he went in.

Sheriff Toliver sat behind the desk, his sleeves rolled up as he bent over some paperwork. His sweat-stained hat hung precariously behind him on a rack of deer antlers mounted on the poster-cluttered wall.

Looking up, the sheriff grinned. "Howdy there—Hardesty, is it?" He rose up and reached a hand to Reed for a friendly shake. He turned to introduce him to a young, lanky, blond-haired man sitting at another desk. "Meet Alonzo Allen, my other deputy."

Reed acknowledged the deputy with a handshake. "Howdy," he said, watching the man's eyes for signs he'd seen the wanted poster on him. Then he turned to address the sheriff. "Amanda said you wanted to see me."

He hoped his inner turmoil was hidden well enough. An experienced sheriff usually had an eye for things like that and Reed disliked his feelings of uncertainty. As he stood there, he couldn't prevent his eyes from scanning the numerous, tattered wanted posters tacked to the walls

"Sure do," Toliver replied, drawing Reed's attention away from the posters, "I'd like a confab with you about several things if you've got the time." A tall, spare man, he moved from behind his desk, closer to Reed. Motioning to a couple of nicked and hard-seated chairs, he offered, "Have a seat." He settled in one of the chairs and Reed took the other. "Have a good ride in?"

"Yes, of course." Reed wasn't one to spend time on useless talk and got right down to business. "You've got something on your mind. Amanda had the idea you were onto something in this case or have some idea what's going on. Is that right?" While he wanted to get to the heart of the matter, he continually searched Toliver's face for signs. For what exactly, he didn't know, but he hated the lying situation he'd gotten into and wanted to come clean with this man. *Dare I tell him the truth about myself and trust my fate to his discretion without ending up back in Yuma Prison?*

"Now that you're here," Toliver replied. "I'd like to go see that banker again. He knows a plenty—hell of a lot more than he's telling. Might learn something there. I've heard a few things about him, too, and I'm pretty sure the damned fool's got himself mixed up with the Saldana woman, to boot."

Reed found that amazing. "The banker? He doesn't look the type?"

"Any man can be the type if he's got an itch that ain't being scratched."

Reed shook his head as they walked out into the dusty street, heading for the small financial institution. Entering the dimness of the bank, they asked the same nicely dressed young man—at a desk now, sporting thick sideburns and an air of importance—if they might see Harry Blankenship.

The fellow knocked on the banker's imposing door and entered. Moments later, he ushered them in to see the banker.

They found him leaning back in his office chair, feet up on the desk, with a sly smile across his lips. Seeing his visitors included the sheriff, he sat up straight, put his feet on the floor, and rose to greet them.

"You needed to see me?" he harrumphed in his most imposing tone. "What can I do for you?" He sat down and swiveled his body around a bit in his padded office chair and indicated two lesser chairs for their convenience. Reed wondered at the sudden pallor of his face: *What do we know, or need to know, and why in the devil does this man look so pale?*

"Got a few minutes?" the sheriff asked. "I've a question or two, and I'd like some answers."

Reed noticed how quickly his slanted, blue-eyed look and forceful tone had pushed the banker off center.

The man gripped the edge of his desk with whitened fingers. "Always got time for the law."

"Well, Blankenship, we're after more information to begin with. As you're well aware, Harvey Bradshaw's been shot and killed out in some canyon north of here." He stopped. "You do know that, don't you?"

Blankenship seemed to believe the sheriff meant more than he said with that statement and grew red in the face. He continued to hold his anger inside as he replied, "Of course, I know it! Everybody in town knows it. Just what are you implying with talk like that?" Reed heard the small tremors of fear creeping into the man's voice as he continued. "Toliver, what are you getting at?" The banker's face was screwed up tight and his voice had grown tinny.

"Maybe quite a few things, but so far, I'm just looking for facts, not gossip. But I have to say, I've heard a plenty of that, too," the sheriff asserted, his voice in a lowered, confidential tone, as he pushed his advantage.

Reed noted Blankenship's features becoming ever paler. His sweating face required a discreet mopping of his brow. "I'm not sure what you're referring to with a remark like that." The banker seemed desperate to know what the sheriff had on his mind.

From what the sheriff had imparted to Reed, Toliver intended to prod the reluctant banker for several reasons, gossip being only one of them.

"Were you aware that Harvey had something going on—with a certain young woman?" Reed asked, stepping into the conversation. "You loaned him a lot of money. Didn't it occur to you that it might be used for something other than improving his property or buying cattle?"

"It's hardly my business to control a man's life or his social activities. I'm a banker, not a minister!"

"You surely must have known all those loans were more than that ranch was worth and could never be repaid," Reed countered.

Blankenship reared to his feet in anger. "You two can leave my office! I am an honorable man and a competent banker. I won't sit here and listen to these unfounded accusations."

"A man usually tells his banker why he wants a loan," Reed kept on in a quiet, even tone. "He's gone now as you know, and you're free to speak about the details with me, his brother-in-law and, under the circumstances, to an officer of the law." His voice, credible and insistent, sounded very much like a well-educated brother, acting on behalf of his widowed sister.

"Well Harry, tell us. Did Harvey take out a loan for the cattle he was fixin' to buy, or not?" The sheriff jumped back into the confab and pressed Blankenship for an answer

"That's private business, and none of yours—either of you." Blankenship slumped back into his chair. "I'll not discuss a man's private or business affairs, dead or alive." He stood his ground on that, looking from Toliver to Reed. "And I won't tolerate this kind of talk from you or anyone else digging into how I conduct my banking affairs." His flabby chin quivered, and his hands clenched the arms of his chair, as he went on. "I've got a position to uphold in this town and, small though it may be, I'm a respected man around here." His indignation rose higher as he worked to throw off the heavy cast of suspicion emanating from the steely-eyed sheriff.

"Lately, when there's money involved, things have been happening around here, people have been getting themselves killed." He straightened in his chair. "And I happen to know you've been seen visiting that black haired devil-witch, Saldana. Every time a man gets himself tangled up with that woman, somebody gets killed, and you damned well know it."

"What I do in my private life is no one's affair." Blankenship blustered. "You got no call to make a statement like that to me."

"I wonder what your wife might have to say about that."

Blankenship clutched the arms of his big chair, his knuckles white. "You bastard—you'd better leave my wife out of talk like that!"

Reed noticed he dabbed again at the sweat breaking out again across his soft, pale forehead.

"I'm trying to run this town, keep the killing down," Toliver affirmed. "And now I've had to send a man damn near to Albuquerque to bring back Bradshaw's body and find the sons-a-bitches that killed him. Man's been robbed and who'd know better than you if he'd borrowed a bundle of money to buy cattle. How's that set with you, Blankenship?"

"The family knew full well what he borrowed on his ranch, Toliver."

"His family had no idea about any of those loans, but they know it now the man's dead, don't they? Murdered for his money, for God's sake!"

"How is it my business to know what happens, once they leave this office?" Sweating profusely, the banker rose again from his chair, softened his speech, and in his best conciliatory tone, added, "Hell, man, we can get to that later, can't we?" His whining tone echoed that of a beggar.

Toliver shot a look of disgust at Blankenship, and, as a parting shot, he tossed out his final words. "You bet we'll get into this—later."

Blankenship stepped toward the door, as a silent suggestion that the men should leave his office, and held out his hand to offer a parting shake.

Reed ignored it but Toliver shook the man's hand as he said, "I been a hearin' some on Bradshaw's nightly activities." He looked at Blankenship. "And he isn't the only one. The man borrowed so much, and so often, the ranch will likely go under, and somebody in this town knows all about it." He put his hat on, sauntered out of the office, shoving it firmly onto his unkempt hair.

Out on the boardwalk, they headed across the street. "Blankenship's been sipping drinks and who knows what else with that overheated Mexican hussy," Toliver told Reed. "Now I'm hoping maybe you can shed some light on things. That is, if you get the chance with her." He sniggered, "And I think you will."

"You don't plan on going easy on me, do you? You tell me she's stuck that little knife of hers into a few other gents around here, and now you're telling me it's my turn?"

Laughing, the men continued down the boardwalk.

"My wife is a goldmine of news around this town," Toliver said. "There's plenty more from what I hear."

If Toliver knew my history, an escaped convict and possibly a killer, meddling in his efforts to solve a man's murder, how would he be then?

CHAPTER 16

W e need a better place to talk. Let's head down for a bite at the La Cantina." The sheriff laughed. "I've more than one reason for patronizing that joint."

He adjusted his battered, sweat-stained hat on his head and motioned Reed to accompany him. They continued along the street.

"What I'm thinking is this. That fool, Bradshaw, went and got himself tangled up with this woman at the Cantina." He pulled out the lone earring they'd gotten from Amanda. "If this fancy little doo-dad does what I think it will, we'll know for sure. Of course, being able to prove she was in on the killin' is another matter." He gave a disdainful laugh. "Oh, she's a real looker, that's for sure, but for a long time I've suspected that Mexican she-devil of having a hand in several dirty dealings around Artesia."

Reed chuckled. "I've already met that lovely creature and if I can help in any way, you know I will."

Toliver nodded. "She'll be looking for a man with money, always does, and more folks than me will say the same. Too often, they end up dead and she manages to profit from it in some way." As they neared the Cantina, Toliver grinned. "She'll take to *you* right enough. Wearing them fancy duds will lead her right to your door unless I miss my guess." He glanced at Reed, his eyes narrowed. "You game?"

"Hell, yes. She already put the shine to me when I was in here with Helen the other day." Reed chuckled. "I didn't pay her any mind right then, and had the idea she'd have happily slit my throat for it by the frosty look in her eye."

"You'll have some fence mending to do, then." Toliver nudged his shoulder. "But if she thinks you're good for a few pesos, she'll keep at you." He paused before they entered the place. Soft strains of Mexican music echoed from within as Toliver hesitated. "Let's walk on a ways. We might want to discuss this a bit farther." They walked past the Cantina and found a quiet bench. "Let's set awhile."

Reed waited to hear his thoughts, all the while thinking he just might take the chance that he'd be safe in telling his story to this man. Nearly desperate to reveal his true identity and get shut of the lying, he'd strengthened his feelings that Toliver might believe in his innocence. After having the chance to know the sheriff better, Reed believed the sheriff was a man he could talk to.

Toliver interrupted Reed's thoughts when he pulled the earring from his vest pocket. "I'm going to drop this fancy doo-dad where she'll find it. If it goes the way I figure, we'll see a tie to Bradshaw. You'll be my witness on it."

They turned back and entered the Cantina. Near the noon hour, hungry patrons slowly filed in, taking a table, laughing, talking, and fingering the tattered menus. At their table, Toliver tucked the earring behind the sugar bowl and winked at Reed before looking at the menu a young boy had set before him.

Reed chuckled. "Helen says just order *la especial*. It's what they serve anyway." He never bothered to look at his own menu.

A soft shuffling sound and the essence of a heavy, exotic perfume indicated the approach of the Saldana woman. "I take you order, s*eñores*?"

She spoke in a soft, slightly accented voice that dripped

with seduction. Everything about this woman implied beguiling suggestions of unimaginably wild sexual delights. Her every move, gesture, intonation, and sexually explicit glances promised it.

Reed raised his dark eyes to hers, lowered his eyelids, and nodded only slightly, sending the lovely *señorita* a heated, smoky message no woman could miss. "Yes, ma'am, I'd sure like your *especial.*"

By the rapid intake of her breath, he knew she'd caught his meaning.

"*Si,* it shall be as you weesh, *señor,*" she whispered, lowering her long silky lashes very slowly, and thrusting out her finely shaped breasts. The soft, fullness peeked over her low cut blouse. Turning to the sheriff, her tone became infinitely cooler. "And you, sir?"

Toliver ignored her rebuff. "I reckon I'll have the same, miss."

Still miffed after her last efforts to entice the sheriff had failed, she regarded him with icy disdain. Toliver merely smiled.

The men understood each other. Reed saw that the lovely Mercedes Saldana reeked of savage revenge for the sheriff's refusal of what she'd freely offered. Toliver's thoughts of bringing her down made Reed smile openly. Hatred and cunning emanated from her as she sauntered away from their table, her hips swaying, rolling, and undulating enough to temp the devil himself.

"Whew! That's some package you're dealing with, Toliver. I believe I'll just reach for the sugar when she brings my coffee." Reed smiled, completely at ease with this man of the law. He shrugged and decided. "When we have a chance, I've a few things to say to you on my own."

Toliver nodded but said nothing in reply.

The plates came, heavily laden with a very fine selection of tacos and enchiladas, heavily laced with fragrant, green chili sauce. A pile of thick, warm tortillas on the side added to the meal. Reed waved his hand. *"Señorita, cafe, por favor."*

She came with the coffee. After a sizzling glance in his direction, she sidled close and, leaning slightly against him, poured a brimming cup of the dark, chicory-flavored liquid. Reed reached for the sugar bowl, and the earring slid into view. He made no notice of it, but Mercedes gasped at the sight of it and quickly reached out to grasp the intricate bauble.

"Oh, *señores*, I look long time for thees. I think it lost."

She put the lovely earring it in her pocket and walked away, her steps a little faster with a good deal less of the enticing sway.

Toliver looked at Reed, a satisfied smile across his face. "Let's eat and get to hell out of here." He dug in, smiling, "I don't give a hoot in hell who owns this place. This is damned good chuck—best in town."

"Coffee sure as hell isn't."

Reed drank it anyway and ate his meal in silence. His thoughts swirled madly about while he considered the sheriff's reaction to his story. His feeling that he'd found a friend in Toliver and, being sick of his deception, made him decide to tell the truth about his past. He'd lay it out on the table regardless of the consequences.

Toliver paid the bill, and Reed enjoyed several more enticements from the exotic *señorita* before they walked out onto the boardwalk. The sheriff said, "You had something to say?"

"Yes, I have, and I gave it a lot of thought before I made up my mind," Reed began as they walked slowly toward the sheriff's office. "I'm not Mrs. Bradshaw's brother, for one thing, but I *am* the drifter that found her husband lying in that creek, dying."

He felt his nerves tighten and his tension soar, waiting for Toliver's reaction.

The man remained silent except to say, "Go on, there's more, of course."

"A lot more—ever hear of a sheriff called Emmet Miller, of Prescott, Arizona?"

"Well, yes, I have, but only a few words of gossip."

Toliver waited, his brow furrowed with a look that told Reed he understood he faced a man who carried a heavy burden. They reached a handy bench and sat down. No one was near and, while Reed told his story, he curtailed his talk if someone walked past. "Well, that crooked bastard railroaded me into Yuma Prison well over a year ago—more now, since I'd been on the run for over ten months when I found Bradshaw in that creek."

He gritted his teeth and hardened his resolve. "I'm Reed Twining, an escaped convict, sent up for murder." He went on to explain the details of his conviction and the circumstances of the incident that led to it. "They sent me up so fast I had no time for a defense. I've studied the law myself. The whole thing was illegal as hell and I knew it, but with everyone in town in the sheriff's pocket, I had no chance."

"How much law have you studied?"

Reed was amazed at his question. "I could have opened a practice most anyplace back then, but being young, I wanted to play cowboy for a while." He flung out his hands, laughing at his boyish ideas.

"Damned if I don't believe you, Reed. I know a decent man when I meet him. If anything comes up about your convict status, I'll do all I can for you. Hell man, I need your help in this Saldana case." Toliver shook his head and placed a friendly hand on Reed's shoulder as he voiced his own pressing concerns.

"That evil bitch is guilty as sin, and now we know for sure, she played Bradshaw for a fool." He rose from the bench. "Let's get back."

And together they walked on down the boardwalk to enter the sheriff's office.

Reed settled in a chair. "What's next in this case?"

He'd relaxed considerably at the sheriff's acceptance of

his history. The feelings of closeness and comradeship nearly overwhelmed him.

"I've checked as far into Saldana's background as far
back as possible," Toliver said. "I'm of the belief she's trying to retrieve an old Spanish land grant that once belonged
to her family. She believes her father's land was taken away
by the *gringos*. A good part of this entire area at one time
belonged to the Saldana family, I know that much. How
they lost it is another matter. I've consulted several men
who've studied the history of these land grants and received
their replies."

"You believe she's trying to regain those acres by any
method she can devise, including murder?" Reed asked.

"It's crossed my mind all too often. Why else would
she be involved in the things I believe she's guilty of? Her
father gave her a severe beating for sleeping with a man
about two years ago. I have to say, he didn't live very long
after that. Fell off his horse, the cinches had been cut—who
cut them, we never found out."

"How would that get her land back?"

"Well, that wouldn't, but it shows us what a loving little sweetheart Miss Saldana is, now doesn't it?" Toliver
laughed. "We're dealing with a woman who'll stop at nothing. Like a rattlesnake, she'll strike at anyone who steps in
her path. Her father believed he had control of her and, to
his sorrow, found out he didn't. She uses men and no doubt
hates their guts, and all the while she's giving them the time
of their life."

He chuckled. "She's dynamite in the bedroom, I've
heard from several men." Growing serious, he added, "She
takes up with a man if he can further her ambitions, and I'd
swear on a stack of bibles, she's never given a damn for any
of them."

"And you want me to do what—"

Toliver burst into a hearty laugh. "Sharp as hell, aren't
you, Reed? But, who else? She's taken a fancy to you—
thinks you're Amanda's brother and by the looks of you, a

man with some money. But if she believes you can pay off
the debt to the ranch, she'll never get her hands on it and, if
so, that makes you an adversary." He grinned at Reed. "But
be warned. Before she kills you, she'll shine up to you to
get what she can from you. She'll use all she's got on you,
and son, that's a plenty!"

Toliver grew sober. "So you see, Reed, if you aren't
careful, you'll be a laying out on the range somewhere with
a damned bullet in your brain." He narrowed his eyes as he
glanced at Reed. "Or she may use that sharp little knife she
carries hidden on her body somewhere. But first she'll get
what money you have if she can. You might be safe enough
till then."

"Ha!" Reed threw up his hands. "With what money I
have, I'll be safe for the next decade or two—if she only
knew." He laughed, but he could feel the icy shivers of his
impending death filtering slowly through his body. "There's
no way in hell I'd want a damned thing to do with that
woman. Yet you're asking me to take a chance like that?"

"She'll be looking for another victim, and she's already
set her sights on you. I've seen her shine up to men before.
It's how she operates."

"I've seen an example of her work myself on Harvey
Bradshaw. I'm not interested."

"Don't forget, you're trying to help that nice widow
woman out at Harvey's ranch, Reed. What about her and
her children?"

"How will my getting killed help her?"

The bitter taste of disaster rose in his mouth. Rather
than embark on this deadly mission, he longed to ride back
to that ranch and relax under Amanda's care, hold that little
girl in his arms, talk to her, and pet that silly little dog.

The ranch hands needed lining out, and he hadn't seen
the whole of the ranch, to know what work was needed. *I've
got a lot of work ahead of me, if I'm to try and save that
placed.* He grimaced. "Getting next to that overheated little
Mex is not in my plans, no way in hell."

Toliver's next words brought him back to the present. "Reed, she'll likely kill that Bradshaw woman out there, if she thinks that'll get her hands on that land. That ranch out there was, at one time, a part of that Spanish land grant she's trying to regain."

Reed sat in shock as Toliver changed the subject. "Blankenship is mixed up with that conniving bitch, too."

"So you said. What gives you that idea?"

"I hear things, people gossip, and Blankenship's wife, snooty as hell to my wife, has no idea what her man is up to." The sheriff sighed. "What that really means in hen talk, I don't know, but from what I hear the chickens are coming home to roost on that banker, pretty damn soon. Every time I see Blankenship's wife, she's a wearing that damned hat, a sitting on her head of tight curls with a peacock feather sticking out like a damned rooster tail. She tries to be so damned toney, sticking it to my wife, letting her know she ain't good enough to belong to her snooty clutch of damned old settin' hens."

Reed heard the pain in Toliver's voice at the treatment of his wife. He patted his shoulder hoping to ease the man's discomfort. "Don't tell me she pays heed to that kind of talk."

"Well, you figure something's afoot when those gossiping fools at the aid society are spreading rumors. And if they're affecting my wife, they're affecting me."

He hurt for her. Reed saw it plain as day on the man's face.

"Blankenship's wife thinks it has to do with a wayward sister of hers," Toliver went on. "Says her sister's been taken into the world of sin, that they're keeping it from her, and whispering it behind her back." He grunted and pushed his hair back. "She said it was Nellie Hamblin that told her."

Though it seemed trivial to Reed, this tough sheriff loved his wife and her pain was his. He decided that with the right woman, any man might feel that way and he gave a quick thought to Amanda. A woman like her made it easy to understand how a man might care that much about a woman.

"How does this affect the case with the Saldana woman?" Reed asked.

"Not much, except the town gossips seem to know the banker's been consorting with the Saldana hussy," Toliver replied. "What my wife's been hearing has nothing to do with her sister. Those gossiping biddies are talking about Blankenship's carousing with that Mexican she-devil. When she finds out, it'll ruin her, not to mention him." He frowned. "I almost feel sorry for the snooty baggage, and him, too."

Deep in thought, Toliver tilted his chair perilously back and slung one lanky leg over the edge of his desk. "Blankenship's got himself into a bushel basket of hell with that black-eyed bitch. If Bradshaw was murdered, it sure as hell is her that's behind it."

Toliver straightened in his chair and checked that the deputy was in the back and out of earshot. "Proving it's the problem. She gets a lot of help from someone in this berg. Probably it's that big Mex, Ramon, that's always at her beck and call. If she's after Harvey's ranch, she's more'n likely to get a hold of it if those loans put it on the block."

He shook his head at the deviltry of the black-haired wench. Reed nodded, but said nothing. He wanted to get back to the ranch, but Toliver impatiently paced about his office, obviously waiting for something, and Reed felt reluctant to ride away just yet.

"I'm waiting for another report from Albuquerque on the finding of Bradshaw's body," Toliver explained. "I sent a man there with orders to bring him back if at all possible for burial, but haven't had any further word by wire as yet. I have the feeling the Saldana woman is at the bottom of several unsolved murders here-abouts, including the death of her father."

Reed nodded, understanding that the real cause of that

death lay buried in murky details from the many relatives and their conflicting stories. It was impossible to get to the bottom of that morass. He nodded. "It appears the man used corporeal punishment on his wayward daughter and paid for it with his life. From what I've already seen, I'm certain that she-devil would be up for it."

Toliver agreed. "I know damned well Mercedes Saldana is behind Harvey's borrowing all that money at the bank. That black-eyed female is after his ranch—sees herself as the owner of the vast estancia of her forbearers." He went on, talking out his suspicions. "As a law man, I've seen motivation at the crux of many a crime and looks like hers is a deep, long standing one that drives her to murder and theft to get what she's after."

The office door opened. A boy entered, doffed his hat, and handed a slightly crinkled message to the sheriff. "This came a bit ago."

"Thanks son." Handing the boy a small coin, he sat back in his chair to open the envelope. He pulled out the telegraphed message and, after scanning it, handed it to Reed. *Body recovered stop slug that of Springfield rifle stop returning with remains stop.*

"Nothing new there. Hells bells, must be dozens of those rifles around." Toliver frowned as he pored over the telegraphed message, trying to remember who owned one of those guns, or more importantly, who didn't.

Reed shook his head. "Might be another piece to the puzzle, but near everybody I know has a rifle like that." He rose, shoved his hat on. "Thanks for the chuck at the Cantina. I thank you for your understanding about my past and taking me into your confidence on things. I'd best be getting back ho—to the ranch." He'd almost said home before he caught himself.

Toliver held out his hand. "Hold on, son. Not before you have another *especial* at the Cantina."

Reed blew out his breath and sat back down. "She's got to be stopped then, hasn't she?" He wiped his brow and leaned forward, elbows on his knees. "So tell me, how in the hell do I proceed?"

"She'll let you know what she wants right enough. All you need to do is go set in that Cantina alone. No need to do a damned thing. She'll do it all, if she thinks you've got a few dollars. Or who knows? This time, it just might be your good looks that's got her all hot and bothered."

"I'm not sleeping with that snake for you or anyone else. I don't care what the hell she wants." Reed felt a pain go deep in his gut and rip through him at the turn things had taken. He changed the subject. "So enlighten me on this land grant business. What gives her the idea she's entitled to any of it?"

"I've checked with the Solicitor General of the Territory of New Mexico about that grant. In his letters, he explains that her grandfather had full claim to the land, but in the years that came after, that grand old man, Pablo Morales Saldana by name, got a bit confused in his later years and let family members take his land from him, bit by bit. Her father, Anton Mora Saldana, lost what was left in a card game to a *gringo*, a sad story, but not unusual by any means."

Toliver sighed. "What's really sad is that she is in no way entitled to any land in this area. The woman has delusions of regaining ownership of the original acreage that made up her grandfather's Spanish land grant. She can't face the reality of her situation. In no way does she see herself as a lowly peon."

"It is sad. But that sort of determination, or delusion, makes her dangerous as hell, and you want me to get involved with that murderous bitch?" Reed smiled at Toliver and shook his head. "I see my life coming to an end, but I'll gladly do what I can for Amanda Bradshaw, and more than that." He drew a deep breath and made his decision. "Sheriff, I certainly appreciate your feelings regarding my personal situation."

He reached out and firmly shook the sheriff's hand.

"I'll do whatever the hell I can. Just might need to go have some supper a bit later on."

He rose along with Toliver. They walked out to the street and Reed took his leave. He knew what he had to do and it made him damned uncomfortable. His insides felt like ice thinking of the deadly female he'd soon face. Only remembering the plight of the young woman he'd ridden away from in the early morning, kept him on track.

Reed headed to the Cantina for a bite of supper though his deepest desire was to be in the saddle and heading "home." Amanda's ranch had already become that and more to him. His thoughts were of a soft, feminine woman with shimmering golden hair, her little girl, and an infant that bore his name.

CHAPTER 17

With reluctant steps, he approached the Cantina and the intense ordeal he faced. Entering, he took a small table with seating for two. It was covered with woven material, reflecting the wild color of Mexican décor. He removed the Silver Beaver he wore and set it on the side. It'd been Harvey's and he worried only slightly that the Saldana woman might recognize it. The air felt cool as it dried his temples and the slick, dampened black hair where the hat had rested. Tensed, he waited for the seductive attentions headed his way.

"Ah, señor, what is your pleasure?" Heavy, sensual perfume preceded the soft, ingratiating voice at his elbow. He looked up into two dark pools of heated seduction and felt an icy shock slither through his gut. He also recognized the lone erring Harvey had left in his saddle bag. The lovely Mercedes wore both of those damning earrings and moved her head a little extra so the tiny bells tinkled softly. She stood before him wearing the evidence that proved she'd had a hand in Harvey Bradshaw's murder.

"La especial, por favor, mi señorita," Reed answered and, acting on his purpose, he looked deeply into her eyes.

The unwelcome surge of his pulses sang through his body as he surveyed the voluptuous beauty, her bosom heaving. *My God, what a lovely devil, she is!*

She bent low over his table to retrieve the menu and

gave him a full and lingering look at the rounded mounds of her lovely breasts. He took in the scent of the deep, musky perfume emanating from her clothes and soft, warm, inviting body, some that came from her flesh, and some from a bottle.

She was unbelievably exciting, downright intoxicating to a man long denied the comfort of a woman's body. His pulses raced and he felt it in his throat, his belly, his groin, and his increasingly shortened breath.

She sauntered away, her swaying hips promising everything within a man's imagination and beyond. Reed shook his head, remembering his purpose. *This woman could tempt that goddamned snake out of the Garden of Eden.*

He wanted to laugh at his foolish male self as he remembered the bleeding and dying body of Harvey Bradshaw. Those memories dashed ice water on his heated response to Mercedes and helped him get a grip on his wayward thoughts. He steeled himself inwardly to do battle with a cold and deadly reptile, wonderfully disguised as a warm and desirable female.

In time, she brought his heavily laden plate and set it before him. "Here is for you, *señor*." Her voice went singing into him and set his male heart racing. She flashed her full bosom before him once again when she poured him a cup of the thick, dark, Mexican-style coffee. "You like dance, *señor?*" she cooed softly.

He shot her an intense look of appreciation. "Might be persuaded."

With a sex-laden smile from his lips that he hoped might curl her oversexed toes, he turned to his plate. Ignored, for the moment, she sniffed and undulated away to attend another table.

Reed finished his meal, eager to leave the cloying air of the cantina. Heading for the ranch was on his mind, but that wouldn't get him the vital information the sheriff wanted. *He believes in me enough to use me in helping him solve this murder. I'll need to play along and help the man.*

He shoved his fancy hat on and, laying a few dollars on the table, slowly sauntered toward the door. Amazed, he spotted Jud and Buddy out of the corner of his eye. His temper rose like a blowing dust storm at the sight of those two going off again, leaving Amanda alone to fend for herself with her little ones. He ambled over to them and, in a low, hissing voice, snarled, "I'll deal with you miserable sons-of-bitches later."

Jud, obviously under the influence of a few belts of whisky, snorted back at him. "Just what the hell game you a playing there, mister foreman, all duded up like that?"

"What I do is none of you're damned business, you lazy no-account bastards. See you back at the ranch."

He sneered at them, all the while knowing they would happily expose him if they knew what he was about. He left them speechless and open-mouthed, exited the Cantina, and turned his thoughts to the job at hand.

How would she contact him? He'd have to wait and see but figured it wouldn't take long. He looked like a man of means in the clothes he wore, or she wouldn't have bothered with him. Not flattering but, in her case, he didn't mind. Since any dealings he had with her could very easily spell his end.

He walked slowly away and, within minutes, heard the whisper of skirts behind him and felt a soft hand tuck into the crook of his arm. "Ah, *señor*, why you not wait for me?" She pulled him to a stop and faced him.

Reed removed his hat. "Howdy, ma'am. Wondered if you'd show up. I like to keep my business private, out of places, and off the streets, if you get my meaning." He took her arm and they kept walking. Though he appeared outwardly calm, he felt those insidious touches of ice curling inside his gut. With a friendly smile, he looked down at her. "Now, where's all this dancing, you mentioned?"

"Ah, *senior*, my place is good for you?" She hooded her eyes and heaved her lovely bosom in a way no man could miss. He caught himself before he gulped at the sight.

It had been a long time since he'd seen anything so soft, female, and inflaming—too damned long for his own good. He fought his wayward thoughts and rising response to this alluring woman.

"For dancing?" He uttered a slight laugh of disdain and removed her arm. "I'm not much for small talk, Miss Saldana. It's not dancing I'm after." He gave her a smoldering gaze. *Two can play the seduction game, missy.*

"You come with me. We speak of—business perhaps, before maybe, *señor*—other pleasures." She tugged at his arm and he allowed it. Glancing furtively about, he caught the shadow of a man following along behind and felt no surprise. It'd be her style.

She led him along the boardwalk. Unsure of what to expect, he patted the slight bulge beneath his fancy coat, thankful for the small derringer the sheriff had made him carry. He might have need of it. But one murder charge against him was more than enough in his life and he'd be loath to use it.

They walked slowly, with Mercedes clinging to his arm and pressing herself against him. In time, they turned down a darkened side street and, as they moved, she pressed her body even closer until they came to a good sized, low-slung house.

It wasn't too dark to see a finely built Mexican casa, constructed of thick adobe with a rusty, red-shaded, tiled roof. The wide eaves kept the rain from washing the adobe. He wondered if perhaps it had been treated in the traditional way with milk splashed over it many times until it dried to form that softly shimmering patina. In the rising moonglow, the expansive home stood proudly, graced with big, smoky-shaded cedar trees and splashes of vibrant Bougainvillea shrubs scattered about.

She drew him to the thickly carved door, opened it, and ushered him inside. The gleaming floors were of polished adobe-like squares called Saltillo tiles. Thick, carved Mexican furniture sat placed according to need. Numerous and colorful woven rugs lay scattered about on the floors. Rich wall hangings, lamps, and gleaming brass objects proclaimed it the home of a wealthy woman rather than that of a poor waitress from a cantina. Reed realized she must be the owner of that establishment to afford a home like this and worked there for her own purposes, one he'd now become entangled in.

He saw no other person about as Mercedes led him to a large leather sofa where she indicated he take a seat. As he slid into the butter-soft leather, he felt her warm body slink down close beside him. He sat back, his legs crossed at the feet and his arms spread wide, awaiting her next move.

"*Señor*, I bring you drink."

She slipped away to a table filled with finely decorated bottles and poured him a good-sized glass of tequila. Handing it to him with a thick slice of lime, she sat beside him again, aligning her body close and touching him in as many places as possible. He kept his hands to himself except for taking the tequila.

"Is good, no?" she inquired as he sipped the heady and fiery liquid.

Her voice, soft as feathers, sent added shivers spiraling up his spine. He felt considerable more than that as the heat of flaming desire rose within his body. He nearly cried out, *Oh Lord, what man wouldn't want some of this?*

Reed fought to keep his head on his shoulders in spite of Mercedes looking deeply into his eyes and murmuring things in his ear, offering everything his mind could envision. The memory of Harvey Bradshaw's wounded body lying flat out in that icy creek was all that kept him from falling into that lovely pit of destruction. He shivered with the pain of his burning desire and fought to keep his head.

"*Mucho frio, señor?*" she asked, uttering her musical, tinkling laughter, knowing and loving her effect on this man, or any man.

She enjoyed it, exulting in the power it gave her. Reed heard it in her soft, purring tones.

He ignored the question, set the glass down on the table, and turned to face her., trying to cool the situation. "What did you wish to discuss with me, my dear?"

She brushed her breasts across his chest and moved her eyebrows in a most suggestive manner. "You like to help me with my *rancho, señor?*"

"You have a *rancho*? How might I be of help to you?"

Of course, he knew it would be money, and a lot of it. He'd become the smitten lover, and she had to believe it. He cooled rapidly at the mention of money, as he looked deeply into her eyes.

"If you help me, I will have the place of my forefathers. It was for me, but is gone now. *Gringos*, they take it."

She fought the anger in her voice, but in her soft tones, now gone sulky, deep and cold, he heard the nearly rabid seething of an intense anger. She tried to hide it, but her need to reclaim what she believed belonged to her was written on her soul.

"Tell me who took it from you—someone who lives here?" He knew that to be impossible as it had happened many years ago, but was curious to hear her beliefs on the matter. He wanted to know what made her think she was entitled to any of it.

"All dead now, but is mine! I must have it return for my people."

Her voice raised a notch higher, and though she kept her control, Reed easily saw she was rife with fanaticism about the reclamation of the land grants she believed had been stolen by the hated *gringos*.

"What does the law say about it?" A dangerous topic to bring up to a woman possessed, but he wanted her reaction on that, too.

"*Gringo* law is no fair for our people. They take it from us! We have nothing, now senior. Nothing, *nada!*"

Inflamed by her unreasoning fury, her eyes flashing with it, she turned to him, and he saw the glitter of hate mixed with intense greed glowing on her face.

She lowered her voice, returning to her silken tones, as she wheedled softly. "You like help me? I make you very happy, *señor*, like no other man. *Si*, like no other man ever." She moved, allowing her blouse to gape wide open with her breasts fully displayed for his gaze. And they were indeed lovely. Creamy and firm, the rose-tipped nipples were surrounded by deep brown areolas with tiny pale islands floating there. She breathed her next words. "For you, *señor*, it will be my great desire, my deepest pleasure." She groaned softly with her promise.

The sight of those lovely breasts would make any man cry out and he nearly did. But Reed got hold of himself. He wasn't having any of it, knowing he'd end up lying in a ditch somewhere with a fatal bullet wound.

"If you need money, I'll see what I can do for you. I will, but now my dear, at this moment, I must see a man. He's waited all day to see me and, unfortunately, I must leave you now, my lovely *señorita*."

He let his voice take on the solemn tones of deep regret as he gazed into her dark eyes like a lovesick calf. He kissed the silken back of her hand.

How Reed extricated himself from the lovely clutches of Mercedes Saldana and managed to get to the door to take his leave, he wasn't exactly sure. But when he found himself out on the street in front of her home, gulping in the cool, fresh night air, he felt like he'd escaped prison all over again. He'd made the lovely Mercedes several promises he wouldn't keep. But she'd never know about that until it was too late for her.

"I'm becoming a damned good liar." He grimaced at the thought and headed toward the main street of the small town, wanting to find the sheriff, yet knowing they dared not be seen together after where he'd been.

Looking discreetly behind him, he felt sure the man who'd followed him and Mercedes earlier, followed him still. Being seen in the sheriff's office or anywhere near, could get him shot clear through, same as all the others she'd done away with. He knew enough about her now to believe it.

"Whew! That devil-woman offers a man everything she's got on a golden platter! But thank God, I kept seeing Bradshaw all shot up and that's enough to keep any man on the straight and narrow," he muttered, careful not to be overheard if anyone was near. "Wouldn't want to give people ideas unbecoming."

Laughing with relief that he was safely out of the devil woman's clutches, he decided to find his horse and ride out to the ranch. It'd be very late when he got there, but he needed the clear, clean air of the ranch after his encounter with the Saldana woman. Her sultry presence had left him feeling unclean. Whether the feeling was physical or mental, he couldn't be sure, but he felt dirty as hell, all the same.

Thinking of the gentle softness of Amanda Bradshaw, he smiled into the darkness. *He'd never once seen anything unclean or devious in that lovely woman's open and honest face.*

Wondering where Jud and Buddy were spending the night, he knew it wouldn't be on the trail to the ranch and it got him fired up all over again. "Damned sons-of-bitches!" he muttered, thinking of that soft, gentle, and blue-eyed blonde woman left alone with a newborn to attend the many chores.

He reached the stable where he'd left his horse earlier, long before going to the Cantina for dinner. Walking into the soft warmth of stabled animals munching hay and making their usual sounds was, as always, a comforting place. He heaved a sigh and reached for his saddle. As he grasped the saddle, he heard a sound and froze. "Who's there?" he asked. His heart pounding, his hand left the saddle to clutch the little revolver.

"It's Toliver and I'm curious as hell about how things went this evening." He chuckled. "Meet up with the woman in question?"

"Hell, yes, I did. And, as expected, she got right to the

point in asking for money, gave me a whole lot of come-on along with it. My God, man!" He blew out his breath. "That's a hell of a lot of woman, and I was getting damned ready. If I hadn't seen Bradshaw like he was, she might have sunk those long claws of hers into my hide, along with how many others?"

"Too damned many. See anything that might help us in getting to the bottom of things?"

Toliver stood shadowed in the straw littered barn, his eyes glittering in the shards of moonlight that filtered through a slot in the barn roof. Reed, mighty glad to see him, felt his tension drain away. The sheriff had become a friend. "She was wearing both those fancy gold earrings, if that's any help." He snorted in derision as he said, "Looked like they belonged on her, even tinkled a bit."

"It sure as hell ties her to Bradshaw as far as I'm concerned, but not enough to convict her of anything." Toliver moved a bit closer and lowered his voice. "Anything else?"

"How about everything she's got to offer if I help her get the family *estancia* back for her." Reed laughed softly. "The woman's got no idea she was talking to the poorest of saddle bums in addition to the rest of it."

"Best keep an eye peeled then. She's sharp as hell and that fancy set of duds will only take you so far."

It warmed Reed all the way through that Toliver liked him, believed his story, and planned to do some investigating to overturn an unjust murder conviction against a man he considered a friend.

"I've been followed so she might know we've been talking. I need to head out to the ranch and see to the place. My hands are in town here so the little lady is left alone out there with her babies and that don't set well with me."

"*Your* hands?"

"Yes," he said then went on to explain. "When I came to tell her about her husband, I found her alone and about to have that baby. I helped her out that night, and right now she's relying on me to set things right around the place."

Reed flushed red enough that the dusky interior of the barn couldn't hide it. "She's asked me to help out as her foreman until she decides what to do with all the debt and shady business about her husband. She's placed a lot of trust in a complete stranger and I don't aim to let her down."

He reached for his tack again, but Toliver placed a hand on his shoulder, halting him. "You helped her having that baby?" He went pale. "I'm not sure I could have done that. What a man!" He shook Reed's hand. "Thanks son, for helping me in this and don't worry about that Prescott business. I'll make some inquiries about the man there. His work'll catch up to him—you can't be the only one he's railroaded."

He slapped Reed on the shoulder and with his departing grin a mile wide, he left him to finish saddling his horse. Leaving town, Reed rode through the darkness, worry nagging his gut. He was getting in deep with the sheriff's scheme, and that black-haired she-devil, when all he wanted was to be on his way back to the woman with golden hair, her small girl, and newborn baby boy.

CHAPTER 18

Amanda felt very alone. Earlier, she'd seen the cowboys heading away and, seeing they wore their best clothes, surmised they were headed for Artesia. They hadn't said a word to her either way, and Reed had gone to see the sheriff.

That had her feeling uneasy. She understood that the boys needed some time away as much as anyone and hadn't had much time off under Harvey, but it angered her to be left to do all the chores again.

"Things need taking care of around here, and with Reed gone, those boys need to be here," she groused as she fed the baby and tucked him in his crib. "My, oh my, you certainly are growing, just like those weeds in the garden." That was another chore she faced. Though some kind soul seemed to be doing the watering, and the blasted weeds grew right along with the vegetables.

Marianna busily tore the clothes off her doll, and Piddely stood wagging his tail, ready to help her. She smiled at the sight of the two playing together. "At least the dog can be in the house without anyone being upset."

How well she remembered hearing him yowl in pain when Harvey had kicked the little creature out the door. Thoughts of release from Harvey's frequent and severe glances of censure frequently brought a smile to her lips. His tightly enforced regiment had kept her in a state of constant tension. But now her hidden feelings of resentment were gone. "I don't care if I lose this place," she huffed. "I wasn't happy here and won't mind leaving if it comes to that."

It felt good to voice her feelings aloud since there was no one to hear. "I was a poor specimen of a wife, always was. Well, so be it. I know one thing! It'll be a cold day in hell before I get myself tied up in a spot like that again. I wonder what it was that made me think being married was right for me in the first place."

She remembered back when she'd thought Harvey was handsome and a man of substance as a ranch owner. Moving to far away to New Mexico had seemed exciting and grown-up. How eagerly she'd looked forward to being a successful rancher's wife and having a home of her own to manage.

She laughed aloud at her foolishness then grew sober. *That's one thing I've learned. There's no man who'd be right for me. I don't have what it takes to be a wife and never did. I've learned that much about being married, and I must say, it's more than I ever wanted to know.*

She shuddered, remembering moments in Harvey's infrequent, passionate embraces. "Never again," she muttered with her chin in the air. "If he was seeing some other woman, I'd be very surprised." She frowned as she talked it out with herself. "But he was a man, so who knows? I've never had to consider such a thing before and don't know how to feel about it." She chuckled, exalting in her new-found freedom. "Whoever the woman was, she's lucky she didn't marry him." She chuckled again as she twirled about the kitchen, enjoying the feeling of near weightlessness.

When she felt this way, the impending loss of her ranch easily stayed in the back of her mind. Doing the chores was no real hardship for her these days, though it wasn't right, and she wouldn't hesitate to let Reed know about it.

Later that day, hearing the sound of wheels, she looked out to see Bennie driving Helen into the yard and stepped out to greet them. Marianna, seeing the carriage, ran out, excited to see Bennie again.

The boy handled the reins, proud as a peacock with his grown-up responsibility. He pulled the old mare to a halt, and Helen carefully climbed down. Amanda thought her movements were slower than usual.

Helen turned to admonish her son, "Now, Bennie, you see to the horse while I have a chat with the missus."

Amanda stood on the porch. "Come in and sit a while, Helen. It's so good to see you." She raised anxious eyes to her friend, wondering how she was doing with her frequently occurring belly pain. But courtesy dictated that she wait for the subject to come up.

Helen came up the steps to take Amanda's hand. "How are you doing then, my dear?" She wiped beads of sweat from her brow.

"Good, about as expected I'd say," Amanda replied. "Come in and take a seat, I made some cookies."

She headed inside and Helen followed. Marianna ran out to climb into the buggy with Bennie, crying, "Make horsey go, Bennie, make her go!"

Amanda smiled, watching the children with an approving nod.

"Land sakes, those two get along real nice now, don't they?"

Amanda heard the note of hope in Helen's voice and figured Helen thought of Marianna as a wife for her Bennie one day. She decided mothers were like that the world over. Her visitor took one of the big chairs in the sitting room, but not the one covered with a folded blanket. Amanda took that one. She'd been unable to figure a way to get rid of the darkened stain put there the night her son was born.

Outside, Bennie drove around in circles to please her daughter and they heard her delighted squeals.

"He's a nice boy to put himself out that way, Helen." Amanda turned her attention to her guest, unable to wait any longer to ask, "How are you making out with those pains, any more lately?"

"Just a few twinges off and on." Helen waved away the worry of it and changed the subject. "How's that new son of yours? I'd like to see how he's doing." She looked at Amanda. "And how is it with you? Enough milk?"

"I'd say so. He's filling out real nice. His eyes are still blue, and they're taking on the dark-steely look of his father. I can't help hoping that's all he takes from him." Amanda laughed away her concern. "The color of his eyes reminds me of my own father's a bit, too. Funny how that works out."

"Where's that Reed feller?" Helen was point blank with her questions and curiosity creased her brow.

"He's in town helping the sheriff with some wild idea the man has. It's got me some worried because Reed's planning to tell Toliver all about himself." Amanda paused, frowning. "He said he might if he thinks the sheriff will believe his side of things."

"You could lose the only help you've got if it goes against him," Helen countered. "I looked about as I drove in. Place looks empty, no cowhands around, nothing going on and you sitting here with two younguns all alone. Don't hardly seen right, somehow."

"I saw the cowhands heading to town this morning, after the early chores. I can't remember when they've ever had a day off. I can handle things now if I have to, but if Reed gets himself tossed in jail, I'll be alone for certain." She frowned and looked out the window. "I wish my real brother *would* show up. Not likely, since he has a busy law practice in Fort Collins and, of course, he's got no idea what's happened here or even that I need him."

Helen changed the subject. "Well, let's have a look at this baby and I'd like to be sure you are healing well enough yourself." She rose from her chair and headed for the bedroom.

Amanda followed her, went to the window, and drew back the heavy drapery, allowing in a bit more light. "It's brighter with these back," she said, trembling inside as she looked at the big bed, remembering more than she wanted to.

Helen looked down at the sleeping babe. "My, he's filling out just fine." She smoothed the fine dark hair on the infant's head. "Nice, healthy baby."

"I don't need an examination," Amanda told her. "I know how I'm supposed to be after a child comes." She stood firm. "Everything is right on track. I'll be back to normal right soon, I'm sure of it."

Helen shrugged and they left the bedroom. "I guess you'd know if things were a kilter. You can always send for me if I'm needed." She changed to a quieter tone and asked, "What about this drifter, this Reed feller?" She flushed in asking, but it was on her mind. "He did say he was wanted for murder and I can't help wondering about that. Are you all right with him staying here, and under the same roof, if I don't miss my guess?"

"He's been nothing but a gentleman to me and certainly to Marianna. I worry that Jud might try to do away with him if he stayed out in the bunkhouse." Amanda smiled and heaved a sigh. "After all he's done for me, I can't believe he'd be the sort to kill anyone, certainly not me. I have to trust him, Helen. I have no one else."

"I'm glad to hear your feelings on it. I feel that way, myself. He's a gentleman in more ways than we know by the way he was at the banker's office. You should have seen him right then, Amanda. Sounded like a fancy, highfalutin' lawyer himself.

They moved to the kitchen and looked out the window to see Marianna and Bennie playing in the yard with Piddely yipping excitedly at their heels. "The children do get along nice, don't they?" Helen said, wiping a bit of sweat from her brow again.

"Helen, you're not feeling well, are you?" Amanda had a terrible feeling about her friend. She faced a dreadful ordeal and Reed was gone to town.

"I get this pain across the belly now and then, but it's not like it has been, so maybe it's nothing."

Amanda made no reply to that as she set out a plate of freshly baked cookies and poured Helen a cup of coffee. She went out on the porch and called the children. Heart in her mouth, she wondered what she'd need to do if Helen took worse. *She's trying to make light of it, but Reed told me what she faced.*

The youngsters piled into the house. Bennie flushed red as he looked at the plate of sweets. "Thanks, ma'am. These look mighty good." He filled his hands with the sugar-coated rounds. Marianna copied his every move, filling her smaller hands before running back outside. Piddely sniffed the floor, licked the crumbs, and followed.

"Well, I'd best be getting' on back," Helen said. "Had to see how things were for you."

Amanda saw a wince of pain cross her face as she straightened up but didn't know what to say about it. The way Helen acted, with so much pain, real trouble was coming for her, and soon. She looked to the horizon, hoping for signs of Reed, but it was too early. He'd be gone all day and likely more than that.

"You'll send Bennie for Reed if you have another attack, won't you?"

"Yes, he seemed to know more about this stomach pain business than he was telling, and to tell you the truth, I trust that man as much as you do." Helen's lips made a firm line across her face. "But, my dear, Reed's taking an awful chance telling about himself to that sheriff. I sure hope he makes out all right."

"It's got me worried sick, Helen. I can't imagine trying to get along here without him." Amanda flushed at the admission, but in her heart she'd already faced that truth. He'd come to her rescue, and in her present situation she needed someone she trusted—she needed him.

She'd also faced the fact that a woman had little chance to survive in this world without a man to help her, in spite of her fanciful ideas about owning a dress shop in a town somewhere. She hid it from Helen, but it hurt to know a woman's life is always held in some man's hands. She hated the thought of it.

After another friendly hour, Marianna stood beside her in tears as they waved goodbye to Helen and Bennie. Amanda squared her shoulders. She not only faced all of the chores this evening, but for certain, she faced a future alone with two children to bring up. "I've got to pull myself together. There has to be some way out of this dreadful mess Harvey has gotten us into. Feelings of exhaustion and hopelessness crept over her as she fed her child and nursed her baby. All the while she waited to hear the sounds of Reed returning from Artesia.

❧❧❧

Reed urged his horse along, eager to reach the ranch and see to things, but more, to feel the welcoming warmth he'd found inside that home. The moon cast enough light that he easily kept to the trail and Spotty knew the way in any case. Relaxing in the saddle, he lapsed into a half-sleep until the sharp crack of a shot rang out and he felt the sharp tug as a bullet ripped through the fabric of the nicely cut coat he wore. Instantly alert, he realized he was the target. "Hell's bells, she's after me already!"

Bending low over the pommel, he urged the horse into a good, ground-eating lope. Riding the saddle low, leaning to the side, he looked back in the darkness. Seeing anything was futile. Reed saw no flash of metal, spark of gunfire, or anything to answer the question that rose in his mind. *Who in hell's after me?*

It could be anyone, from the resentful Jud down to the man who'd followed him about Artesia. It was certain that someone had him in their sights. He believed it had to be the man who'd kept watch as he walked with the Saldana woman. Maybe he was her man, if she had one.

Reed rode hard until he'd gained enough distance to pull off the trail into a small copse of trees. Dismounting, he stood in the shaded area and looked back along the moonlit trail. He finally saw a faint, shadowy figure on horseback pull to a halt. The shooter stayed nearly a quarter mile back. Reed didn't recognize the shape of the person and had no clear idea who it might be. But he had a new enemy. Someone was out to kill him or drive him out of the country.

When the dark figure turned back toward Artesia and rode away, Reed waited a bit longer. Sure his nemeses had gone, he continued on his way. He never came close to sleep after that but frequently looked back along the trail behind him. He didn't know the hour he made it into the ranch yard but it was very late and rather noisy. Quelling the welcoming whinnies between the horses was impossible.

He put things away and tended to the horses. Finding the entire lot nearly out of everything, he loaded their manger with hay. Subduing his anger at the missing hands, he headed for the house. A welcome feeling of homecoming enveloped him. A lamp burning in the window shed a light that warmed him all the way through. He'd been gone from his own home for several years and it'd been a long time since anyone had cared enough to place something so welcoming in a window just for him.

He entered quietly and stood for a few moments taking in the softly lit kitchen and the lingering odors of the last meal. Everything in this house seemed to welcome him. The little girl's toys lay scattered about and Piddely rose from his pallet to come wiggling with his low growl of greeting.

Amanda came out of her bedroom, carrying her own small lamp. She wore a robe snugly belted about her shrinking waistline. Her pale, honey-shaded hair cascaded down her back and, looking at her, dressed that way and so soft and sleepy-eyed, Reed felt his heart beat like a trip hammer. He surmised she usually let her hair loose for the night that way. The difference between this woman and Mercedes Saldana was striking, and the comparison shocked him.

The sight of her, so sweet and clean, gave him a sudden, strong urge to reach out and take her in his arms. Was it just the warmth and welcoming of his coming home, or the look of her all soft like she was that made him feel the way he did just now? He wanted to hold her tight against his body to feel the softness of her. He wanted to bury his nose in that glorious head of hair and breathe in the scent of it. He swallowed the lump in his throat and managed a soft, "Hello," before laying Bradshaw's fancy hat on the table.

Amanda saw him standing there—home safe. The sight of his tall, spare form, made her draw in a sharp breath to quell the rapid beating of her heart. "You're here," was all she said.

He stepped toward her but stopped himself before he reached her. "Yes, sorry to be so late but the sheriff and I were working on something."

He'd moved near enough that she caught the scent of perfume left on his person from an encounter with Mercedes Saldana. She remembered it from her husband's clothes. Recognizing the same odor she'd caught on Harvey after his visit to Artesia, her suspicions and temper went through the roof.

"Oh, believe me, I already know what business you and that sheriff had cooked up between you. And I know where you had it, too. I can smell it on you."

She stamped her foot. Her body shook and trembled all over until he worried she'd drop the burning lamp she held.

"It's not what you're thinking, Amanda—not at all." He stepped toward her. "I'll tell you about it, if you'll listen."

He wasn't sure she would by the wild fury he saw in

her eyes. They might have been blue in the daylight, but they looked black as the ace of spades at the moment.

"A likely bunch of lies. You're carrying the stench of that woman all over you," she sniffed. "A woman can't trust any one of you men as far as she can throw you."

She stood firm but, in her trembling hands, the lamp shook and wobbled.

Reed took it from her. "Here, let me have that lamp before you set the place on fire."

"Well, I guess it'd keep that Saldana woman from moving in then, wouldn't it?"

Her words, sharp and painful, as she bit them off, spoke of her hurt and bitter disappointment in his betrayal.

Reed realized she had no claim on his attentions or personal life, but it hadn't entered her mind in her fury. "I see you've an idea what's been going on, then. Got that from the sheriff, I guess."

He thought she might be cooling off a bit, or hoped she was.

"Some of it, yes." She sniffed again and turned her eyes away from him. "Why are you riding in now, in the middle of the night? Why not spend the night with her if that's what you're looking for?"

"I'm not after her or anyone else, my dear. I hurried back soon as I could, seeing as how the boys were in town kickin' up their heels."

He let the cowboy vernacular creep into his speech. It seemed to help his case, though he couldn't imagine why.

Amanda slumped into a chair. "Did you find out anything to help with all those loans?"

Defeated, she sat there looking up at him. A small amount of hope lay in her eyes along with a great amount of mistrust.

"We know for certain the Saldana woman wore those earrings. The sheriff and I went to have a meal at her place. When she spotted the missing one we'd placed behind a sugar bowl, she grabbed it right off the table and claimed it.

That gave us a bit of solid evidence." He went on to tell her about his own encounter with Mercedes. "I got away safely tonight, but someone took a shot at me as I rode back to the ranch."

She leaped up and moved to his side, her face pale and tightened with worry. "Are you hurt?"

He pointed out the burnt slash through the arm of the jacket. "No, but this jacket might need a bit of mending."

She turned a ghastly white at the sight of the bullet hole and nearly fainted. Reed leaped to steady her, but instead, gathered her into his arms and spoke softly to gentle her. "Here now, I wasn't hit. You'd best sit back down. You're not altogether back to normal yet, are you now?" he whispered in soft comforting tones as he edged her toward a chair.

She felt so soft and good in his arms, he held her against his own solid frame a whole lot longer than needed. And with a giant leap to his racing heart, he noticed she wasn't trying to move away. Clinging to this moment of delight, he held her closer, patted her hair, and smoothed the soft fabric of her robe down her back, hoping to settle some of her anger and suspicion.

"It's all right Amanda," he crooned softly in her ear. "Whoever it was never got close enough for a good shot, and I'm not hurt." He continued to hold her since she hadn't resisted. "Might have a little mendin' job for you, though." Against his better judgment, he pulled her ever closer. She felt so good pressed against his body that he kept her there, struggling with himself to keep from going for more.

"So you say. You men take so many chances, and we women get to sit home and worry about it. Not fair, is it?" Stiffening within the circle of his arms, she pulled back enough to look up at him. In the soft lamp light, she smiled at him.

"You feel so good to me right now, I hate to move away, but I must. This isn't right, it can't possibly be right."

"Why do you say it's not right for me to hold you in

my arms?" He looked down into her eyes. "You're a mighty special kind of woman, Amanda."

"I've never felt I was special, Reed, not even as a girl at home, in spite of Harvey always saying my folks spoiled me." She looked directly up into his dark eyes. "But when you hold me like this, I confess I feel that way. Could it be it's you who makes me feel warm and safe, and special?"

She made no move to leave his embrace and he smiled to himself, realizing he comforted her with the same patience he'd used a few times on a wild young colt. He could scarcely believe she'd allow his touch and stay within his arms like she was. It filled his heart with certain tender feelings he'd never known before. He had no idea what was happening to him, but something sure as hell was.

As she murmured her confusion against his chest, she nestled her cheek even closer. *Oh God, he smells so good.* This man had some mysterious essence that held her transfixed and, in spite of the errant perfume, she couldn't tear herself away. She found a kind of comfort and safety in Reed's arms she'd never expected or imagined possible. Feeling it now, she knew it was something that had been missing in her marriage.

Her smile had set his lonely heart on fire and it wasn't lust or sex that took him by surprise, but the sweetness, the femininity of her and the companionship she freely offered that filled his heart. She cared enough to get angry about the perfume left on his clothes by the Saldana woman, and she worried about the shot that tore a hole in his jacket. He saw that as a sign she cared about him and drew her ever closer for a moment. After a while, he released her and eased her into a nearby chair.

"If being held by me makes you feel special, it's my pleasure. I'd have to say, holding you in my arms that way gave me a mighty good feeling, too." He threw his head back and gave a small chuckle of joy.

Amanda watched his throat move, saw the outline of the solid muscles of his shoulder and arms. Oh, how good she'd felt against his body, and the way it thrilled and burned her way down deep inside. When he'd held her against him, she knew it wasn't just the way he looked in those fancy dude clothes. It was much more than that. It was him, the feel of him, the smell of him, the solid way he took care of things. Reed was a man you could trust. It was that and everything else about him.

CHAPTER 19

They were alone in the quiet and dark house. Unable to stop herself, she rose from her chair, went to him and, without thought, pressed her face against his chest, and nestled into his arms. Settling a bit deeper, the feel of him caused that strange turn in her belly again and the heat of it flashed through her. Something about him seemed to set her on fire, way deep inside.

Shocked by how she felt, she gasped, "I must get some rest." Flustered and embarrassed by her outburst of emotion, she sought to draw away from him.

Seeing her face burn with a rosy shade that even the dim light in the room could not hide, he held her tight. "Please, Amanda, not yet. Don't be afraid of me. I care about you and want to help you. We have many things to work out."

He released her and his tone became serious. "I need to know your plans if you lose this place. And before you answer, remember the sheriff and I are working to prevent that."

Flushing, she moved away and sat back in the chair. "In truth, I've never liked it here, and if I lose this ranch, I'll gladly return to Colorado." She held her head high with her admission. "This ranch is not a happy place for me. Never has been."

"Sorry to hear that," Reed replied. "But at the moment,

we ought to try and recover the value of this land and the stock. You'll need all of that to raise these children. If, as we suspect, the Saldana woman has succeeded in drawing your husband into a relationship and into such enormous debt he'll lose this place, it's my guess he'd be losing it to her."

He cleared his throat. "Toliver believes she is under the mistaken idea that her father held all this land under a Spanish land grant and lost it to *los gringos*. She believes it was cheated away from him and it's her goal to regain it—she as much as admitted it to me."

Amanda heard the changes in Reed's tone and diction. He sounded like a lawyer or banker, and it left her so puzzled she barely heard the words he spoke.

Finally, lowering her voice to a whisper, she asked, "Who *are* you, Mr. Reed Twining?"

"What do you mean?"

"You may be a drifter and escaped convict right now, but you haven't always been, have you?" She sat across from him with that stern look he'd come to know, settling firmly across her face.

"As I have said before my father owned a bank in Kansas and that life is not unfamiliar to me, I confess. But after school, I wanted to see the West, play cowboy, and live the life. A boy's fanciful dream maybe, but that's what I did for several years." He shrugged and gave her a rueful grin. "Until I run into a wayward sheriff in Arizona, that is."

"I can tell that much by your speech." She flushed and added with a smile, "Dressed the way you are and talking the way you just did tells me you're not the same man who rode in here a few days ago." She felt the heat rising up her neck. "And you got here just in time, Reed."

By the snuffling, angry sounds from her bedroom, a few immediate things needed attending. "I'd best see to my son, but I'm glad you made it back safely." Still heated from their encounter, she told him goodnight and walked into the darkness of her room.

She reached for her child, put him to her breast, and let her body cool, her mind settling with the nurturing and care of him. Yet all the while, her thoughts remained on that strange man living in her home just down the hall. He excited her and intrigued her to the exclusion of all other thought.

Reed sought his lonely bed and lay in the darkness, pondering what had just taken place. There was something new and wonderful in his life. The memory of Amanda close in his arms, and wanting to be there, had taken him by storm. So female, so soft, and in pain for so many reasons, she looked to him for protection and his heart swelled with the kind of feelings he'd never known before. *What the hell have I gotten myself into?* He lay awake far too long and worked to sort out his twisted life.

ℰꙮℰꙮ

Reed stepped out on the porch in the gray of early dawn. He hadn't slept much, but felt rested enough. No smoke poured from the bunkhouse and he surmised the cowboys were still away. His dander up, he groused, "This whole set-up is intolerable, but those men are all we've got for the moment."

Piddely sat near his leg licking his paws. Reed reached down to ruffle his neck fur. The scene around him looked so peaceful, he felt like sitting in one of the chairs and dozing off instead of getting things done. But heaving a sigh of contentment, he stepped off the porch and went to the corrals. He tossed hay for the livestock, flung a few handfuls of corn to the chickens, and grabbed a bucket to milk the cow.

After he took the milk and eggs to the kitchen, he walked over to check the garden. It looked mighty dry as it hadn't rained for a week. Wondering how the plants were able to attain such growth, puzzled him since Amanda hadn't been in any shape to carry water. While wondering about that, he heard the pounding of hooves in the distance. Hurrying back to the ranch house, he saw Bennie come flying into the yard. Seeing Reed, he pulled his lathered horse up as near as he could get.

Reed faced the boy. "Son, what's got your tail in such a curl?"

"My mom's been taken real bad, Reed, an' she said I was to fetch you. One of the other fellas rode for the doc." Breathing hard, his face tight with worry, he dropped to the ground on trembling legs, fighting tears, his face drawn and pale. "She said you wanted to be told if she took bad again." He raised his face to Reed, a look of hope on his boyish features.

His desperate face and hurried words touched Reed. He reached down to pat the boy's shoulder. "Yes, I told her that, so let's get busy." He hurried to enter the house.

Bennie followed him, after tossing the reins of his heaving, blowing horse over the hitching rail in front of the porch.

Amanda came from her room, carrying the baby in her arms. Spotting Bennie, her face felt like ice. With her heart thrumming madly in her chest, she asked, "What's happened?" But she knew why he'd come.

"It's Helen," Reed said. "She's taken bad this time and I asked her to call me if it came around again."

"We'll all go. I'm not staying behind! Will you hitch up the buggy? I'll get us ready in here."

By the set of her jaw and the look on her face, he knew not to utter a word of protest. She'd regained most of her strength by now and her determination to go to her friend would not be denied.

"I'll get right on it, Amanda."

He went out with Bennie, told the boy to water the sweating horse he rode in on, and caught up a horse to hitch up to the buggy. Between the two of them, they got things ready.

Amanda raced through the house to prepare for the

journey, fighting back tears. No time for crying now. It was close to five miles over rough roads, and they'd need things. She ignored the crying of baby Reed. He'd have to bide until she got her daughter moving and fed. She went to awaken Marianna.

Within a short half hour, they'd piled into the small buggy and began the journey. Amanda, tense with worry over Helen, sat beside Reed, her hands clasped tight around the baby's wrapped form as she fed him. He'd had to cry until they were started off and he wasn't too happy about the wait. Having no other options, she kept herself covered as best she could while he nursed.

Marianna, delighted to see Bennie again, pouted because she couldn't ride with him, but Amanda was firm. "You just sit on the other side of Reed and help him with the driving this morning."

The little girl smiled happily and soon Amanda heard them chatting together while she tended her baby.

The buggy wheels ran smooth until they hit a rock or deeply worn rut. She felt the jolts, but her healing had progressed to the point she could shrug off the roughness of the trail. "As good as it feels good to be out of that house, I'm sorry it has to be on an occasion like this."

When baby Reed's stomach was filled, they pulled off the rough trail until she tucked him into a padded box behind the seat. The jostling of the uneven trail didn't seem to upset him and he quickly dropped off to sleep.

Worried, she knew full well with this last onset of pain that things could go badly for her friend. Helen had repeated the doctor's words as she'd remembered them and Amanda knew what to expect, little of it hopeful and all of it frightening. Bennie rode beside them, his face a tight mask of fear.

Reed drove with quiet expertise, urging the horse along, avoiding the worst of the trail when he could, yet he drove in haste. She sat close beside him and their shoulders touched continually. That closeness sent the warmth and strength of him into her and it felt good. The touch of him allowed some recapture of the magic of last evening when he'd held her in his arms.

His masculine scent soothed her in subtle ways never imagined or expected. His very nearness was reassuring, like his being beside her was saying everything would be all right.

Marianna sat on his other side and the little girl's pattering voice created a quiet distraction for her worries. Baby Reed lay quiet in his box behind the seat. The jostling of the buggy made for a quiet, pleasant trip, except for her concerns over Helen.

It was mid-morning when they arrived at the K Bar O Ranch, Helen's home. Her husband, Herbert, rushed across their wide-slung porch in greeting, glad for their comforting presence. His anxious face confirmed the seriousness of Helen's situation. Reed stepped down with Marianna and, as he lifted Amanda down, she asked, "Will you carry the baby in for me, please?"

At his nod, she rushed to her friend's bedroom to find her covered with a thin sheet, pale and sweating. "How is it, Helen?" she asked, kneeling beside the bed, unable to conceal the worry she felt. Being close friends, she didn't need to.

"I'm so glad to see you, dear. Is Reed with you?" She doubled up for a few moments and then relaxed again.

Amanda wiped her dripping brow. "Yes, we're all here, baby too. He's bringing them in."

"He's a dear man, that way." Helene grimaced a moment. "I'd like to see that baby."

She smiled in spite of everything she faced. Amanda, so awfully frightened for her, wanted to cry. But she firmed her chin and maintained a brisk and efficient manner. "Has someone gone for Doc Cutler?"

"Yes. Herb sent for him right away, but it's a long way to Artesia, and a long way back. He'll be lucky to get here by nightfall." The doubt on her face spoke volumes about her feelings of hopelessness.

"We're here and we'll do what we can." Amanda did her best to sound hopeful. "When did this begin?"

"Just this morning before sun-up, we sent Bennie for you and one of our riders for the doc, right away."

Amanda smiled down at Helen. "Let's see what Reed has to say. That man is a constant surprise to me. One day he's a destitute drifter and the next he's a banker's son, or looks like one."

"He's certainly a man of many talents, as I said before," Helen replied. "I saw that when we were in town— any idea about your husband's killer?"

Amanda believed she sought to take the attention away from her own perilous situation. "Yes, Reed's told the sheriff everything about his own problems and they're actually working together on some plan they have."

She frowned. "Remember the earring? They put it behind a sugar bowl at the Cantina and that floozy, Mercedes Saldana, was overjoyed to find her lost little bobble."

She couldn't keep the anger and disgust from her voice. "They believe she took money from Harvey and any other man fool enough to mess with her. She's got some crazy idea of restoring a Spanish land grant her family lost. In truth, it was never stolen from them, but lost in a card game, or the last of what they hadn't already sold away."

"I'd heard of her reputation with the men folks, Amanda," Helen agreed. "I reckon everybody has, but I'd never heard of her doing anything like killing to get what she wants. Must be she didn't think my man had enough money to draw her attention." She chuckled until another deep twinge took her.

Amanda wiped the sweat from Helen's brow with a handy bit of cloth dipped in cool water.

"I don't know how this whole business will end, but it seems every man she has to do with, ends up dead."

The thought of Reed lying dead out on some lonesome trail made her blood feel ice cold.

Helen reached out a hand. "What's wrong? You've gone so white."

"Nothing for now, but I worry about Reed. She thinks he's a prosperous banker or rancher. He told me she's already asked him for money and he made her some kind of promise." Her eyes narrowed and she whispered, "She left a heavy dose of perfume on him. He got close enough to her for that."

"And you got close enough to him to notice it, didn't you, my dear." Helen smiled, but went on, "Mercy, she's after Reed, then?" Helen said then hushed as Reed entered with the baby in his arms.

Looking at the fat little face, she cried, "Oh, my stars, he's fillin' out real nice." She tried to get up, but Amanda touched her shoulder to stop her.

"Just rest yourself. I'll fetch him." She rose to take the boy and hold him closer for Helen's inspection. "Where is Marianna?"

"That little charmer is busy with Bennie," he replied with a grin. "No worries there."

Helen smiled. "Those younguns sure do get along nice."

Again Amanda heard that hopeful declaration about their children getting together some day. Her own babies weren't big enough for thoughts like that.

The baby squirmed, arched his tiny back, and let out a yowl of impatience. "He's hungry again," Amanda said. "I'll go tend him."

Reed took the chair at Helen's bedside and leaned toward her, his brow furrowing. "How long has this been going on?" After she told him, he said, "I understand you can have these episodes several times until that last one. Never know for certain, but I'd say you are most likely, very close." He didn't try to hide his look of worry from her. "We'll have to wait for the doc, but soon as he gets here, I may be of some help to him. I've seen this before—in my sister."

"And how did that turn out?" Helen's voice held a deep tremor of fear.

"She was a very sick girl for a time. We were almost too late."

He patted Helen's shoulder, pulled the shades close, placing the room in semi- darkness, and left her to rest. He took a seat at the kitchen table with Herb. They chatted about ranch details, avoiding discussion of their deeper fears.

Amanda sat in the front room, holding and rocking her infant. The children ran in and out according to which game they played. "You kids had best keep the noise down and let Helen rest while we wait for the doctor," she admonished.

Helen slept for an hour or two, and lay awake a few more, until finally, the welcome clop of horse's hooves entered their yard. Reed and Herb met the doctor as he alighted from a small, solidly built carriage.

"How is our patient?" Dr. Cutler asked, as he hauled his bag out from behind the seat and headed with them to door.

His coat and hat were layered with dust. He stopped to remove the coat and shake it outside. The hat, he slapped smartly across his thighs, to remove some of the dust, and tossed it onto a chair as he entered the sitting room.

Herb led the way into the darkened bedroom. "She's right in here, doc."

Reed nodded for Bennie to take the doctor's horse, unhitch him, and lead him to water. The boy hurried to comply and left the sweating animal standing in the shade with an armful of hay to eat.

Reed's heart went out to the frightened boy who hurried to finish with the horse and hang close enough to hear what the doc might have to say, hoping the man could help his mother.

The doctor shooed the husband out, but not Reed. Bennie stayed close outside the door. Cutler knelt at the bedside to examine his patient. "Same as before, is it?"

"Yes, but it's a bit worse this time. I can't stand up straight at all, do my chores, or anything else, Doc." Her white, fear-filled face turned to him with hope in her eyes. "Can you do anything for me?"

"I've received letters and very detailed instructions from a doctor in Albuquerque. He sent me everything he had." He looked into her eyes. "We'll have to remove your appendix, Helen."

Reed listened as he explained the prognosis, with and without the surgery, gave her the choice, and warned her, his voice soft and low, "Tell me your wishes and I'll abide by them, but only with surgery, will you have a decent chance."

"I've already done my thinking on it, Doctor, most of it after what you said the other day in town. If you believe it's my only chance, then will you please go ahead? I've got my family to think of." Helen set her jaw. Her eyes looked about and, seeing Reed, she asked, "Will you send Herb in here, please?"

He called her husband in, left them alone, and faced the doctor.

"You asked me to call on you if this happened again. I'm calling," Cutler said, his voice steady. "If you know anything about this, I'd appreciate your help."

"I know a bit. My friend at school studied to be a surgeon. I helped him a time or two. My sister had this very thing, and I helped with her surgery the one time. I won't hold any instruments unless I have to, but I'll help out."

"You're ahead of me then. All I have is what Dr. Evans in Albuquerque has told me by letter, but he gave good, detailed instructions. We've got to go ahead. As I see this situation, it's the only chance she's got."

Reed stood ready to help. "Lead the way. I'll do all I can."

They went together into the bedroom and laid it out for

the husband and wife. "It's her best chance," Doctor Cutler said. "We'll do our best for you," he said, including Reed in his statement.

Helen looked up at Reed. "You?"

"I know a little about this. I've seen it done before."

"And the patient made it, you said."

He nodded and smiled down at Helen, hoping to give her courage in the face of difficult odds. "Yes, she did."

"We'd best get at it," Cutler said. They left the room and went into the kitchen. Pointing to a narrow table sitting beneath a window, he said, "That's the closest we'll have for a suitable table to operate on."

They placed the table in the center of the kitchen and cleaned it with lye soap. He directed the husband to get what linens they had on hand, then opened his medical bag, and took out a separate bag of instruments. "Set these things to boiling," he told Reed.

Reed got the fire stirred up until it roared, filled a large pot, and set it to heat. The doc laid out what he wanted him to boil and pulled out dressing materials that appeared to be strips of torn sheeting. "Get a flat iron and heat it on the stove. We'll need to iron these dressings."

"Iron them, why is that?" Reed asked.

"Kills the little critters we can't see, the ones that cause sepsis, meaning infection," he said then added, "Sounds strange, but it works rather well and that's what's important. It's a new tool for us in the rustic medicine we practice so far out from the bigger cities."

Bennie stood against the wall, and Marianna shrank against his side. She sensed the seriousness of the situation and her eyes were huge. "Bennie, what doin?"

"Aw, nuthin', no need for you to be worrying. The doc's gonna fix my mom, is all." Reed nodded for him to take her outside. Bennie complied, taking her hand he led her outside, escaping the flurry of activities. "We'd best stay out here unless they call us."

Reed and Cutler prepared to do an operation they both

feared could fail, yet feared more, not to try. Soon, with the instruments boiling, the table padded, and a pile of ironed strips of sheeting ready, they helped Helen to the kitchen.

She walked slowly, bent over from the tenderness of her affected abdomen. Her eyes were filled with determination. "I must see Bennie before we do this," she said, having already spoken with her husband.

Reed called to Bennie. "Your mother would like to see you, son."

He went to her, with Marianna clinging to his side, seeing his mother standing in the kitchen, pale and sweating in pain, and their kitchen side table readied for the surgery. His eyes grew large. He'd seen the table filed with jars and what-not but he'd never seen it looking like that. He was tight as a bow string and fighting back tears. "Mom?"

"Son, they're going to take this thing out of me that's been making me hurt so bad and I won't be sick any more. You be a good boy now, and watch out for that little girl, won't you?" She patted his head and smoothed his hair as she always did and smiled at Marianna, hanging on Bennie's arm.

Bennie bit his lip and tightened his jaw. His young boy's face had gone white. "Yes, Momma, I will."

"Now you two go out on the porch and wait until they're done." With Bennie gone, she indicated for the men to help her onto the table.

The Doctor nodded to Amanda. "We'll need to get some of these things off her, if you'll help." The men left the room while Amanda and Dr. Cutler cut away part of her gown and covered her with a sheet. Then he called them back.

Her husband stood by her head and touched her cheek. "You'll be fine, dear, I know you will." His own face looked as white as Bennie's while his lips whispered a prayer he'd be proven right. "I don't think I can get along without you, Helen."

Reed understood his thinking. Life without his stalwart

woman would be unthinkable for Herb. Surprised, Reed realized he felt that same way about Amanda.

Amanda stood away from the bustle, watching the quiet efficiency of that mysterious man who knew so many things. Reed had nothing to his name, yet he'd become so important to her sense of well-being, she never wanted him out of her sight. She didn't know near enough about him and was curious to learn every imaginable detail. She'd never felt this sort of pride or amazement in a man before. But she did now. It swelled and grew within her heart as she watched Reed work with the doctor to save a friend's life.

CHAPTER 20

Doc Cutler approached this unfamiliar work with calm confidence. He spoke quietly, smiling down at Helen, giving her what hope and confidence he had to offer. "We'll do our best for you."

She nodded her acceptance. Her face was pale, yet firm with determination. Reed saw a tear escape, run down the side of her face and into her hair. Cutler handed a small bottle of ether and a medicine dropper to Reed and gave detailed instructions as to the approximate number of drops needed.

Then he addressed Helen. "We're ready, my dear. Just breathe this medicine in real deep until you fall asleep."

Cutler placed a thinly folded cloth over her nose and nodded to Reed. Reed slowly dropped the strange-smelling liquid over the cloth and, at length, Helen's eyes closed. They saw her body go lax and Cutler signaled him to halt the drops. Reed felt the mounting tension.

What they were attempting was more than he'd anticipated, yet it was what he knew they had to do. His jaw tightened as they watched a deepening unconsciousness take hold of Helen.

In addition, Reed felt a bit of dizziness come over him after catching more than one whiff of the ether. A few more and he'd be on the floor, himself. He stepped away from the table.

The doctor went to the sink. He washed with the strong lye soap, he'd found and carried along on every call, and signaled Reed to do the same.

Cutler pulled the sheet away from Helen's abdomen to just above the pubic area, and pushed what remained of her nightgown to a high chest area with the breasts covered. Conscious of a woman's modesty, he tried to comply with the standards of decency. He pointed to the lower right portion of the abdomen and said, "That's the area. The appendix lies beneath here." He turned to the sink and washed his hands once again. "Sorry for the interruption, but this sort of washing has proven to be very effective in preventing sepsis in the incision."

He uncovered the instruments laid out on ironed sheets and placed on a small table he'd set close. Selecting a razor sharp scalpel, he said in a low voice, "Wash again Reed, and then sponge the blood. There will be quite a bit."

When Reed was ready, Cutler began a diagonal cut across the soft, female flesh of Helen's lower right abdomen.

Amanda sat quietly in the kitchen, as far back as possible. She didn't want to miss seeing Reed work with the doctor. Though a thing like this was completely new and strange to her, she believed the men were sure and competent in their movements. As they worked over her friend, amazement and pride in that lanky man standing at the doctor's side filled her all over again. She heard their murmured commentary, as they went about the business of saving a life. Without conscious thought, she considered Reed her man. Who he was and whatever he'd done before he'd come to her had never mattered. He'd ridden into her life when she'd had no one, and if he left her now, after all that had happened, to ride north as he'd planned, she would be lost.

It was no longer because of the ranch. The thought of losing him struck a chill so deep inside, she shuddered and was glad there was no one to notice.

Reed sopped the blood as Cutler went deep enough to slice a small opening of the abdominal covering. "The doc in Albuquerque said there will be several other tissues here but if we are lucky, the appendix should pop up with a bit of pressure on either side of the incision." He cut a bit more, lifting out several strings of fat-laced tissue until he was ready. "I'm into the abdominal cavity now," he calmly informed Reed. Gently pressing on either side of the incision, they were rewarded as a red, swollen, and puss-laden member—looking much like a very infected, swollen finger—slid into view. "Good God, it's huge!" Cutler exclaimed. "I'd say that explains her pain level," Cutler told Reed. "I've never seen anything like this, not in all my years of training. Now it must be tied off and removed." He carefully reached under the inflamed, swollen finger of infected tissue and brought it farther into view. Taking a ligature of catgut he'd boiled and threaded on a needle, he ran it beneath and at the base of the appendix and with a few quick turns, neatly tied it off.

"Get a cloth beneath it, Reed. When I sever it, we want to prevent that putrid matter from infecting her abdomen any more than it has already. She'll have trouble enough recovering from the infection this thing has carried, but I'd say she has a decent chance to do so."

Reed slipped a folded, ironed cloth beneath the swollen appendix and received the foul mess as Cutler severed it. He laid it in the sink and re-washed his hands as he watched the thing oozing enough death-dealing poison to kill more than one human. "I believe you got it just in time, doc."

With his comment, he heaved a sigh of relief, picked up a bit of cloth, and wiped the sweat from Cutler's brow and his own. It'd been way too close, he knew it—they both did. But now Reed felt the soaring elation of knowing that Helen had a chance at life.

"God willing, I hope we have," Cutler agreed. "She has a rather decent prognosis now."

He took some of the gut and sewed the inner tissues

closed. Then, with more of the dark thread he'd prepared, sewed the outer incision closed.

After washing again, Reed mopped any errant blood that escaped until Helen began moaning.

The doc nodded to him. "Two drops—no more."

Helen quieted enough with those few drops. Cutler finished his work, dressed the neatly sewed incision with the ironed sheeting strips, and covered her with a blanket.

Calling in Herb, the men lifted her and carried her to her bed. Amanda had stripped it and remade it with fresh bedding. As soon as Helen lay in the cool sheets of her own bed, she began to stir and moan.

Cutler took her husband aside. "She's got a good chance at recovery, Herb. We got it out in time—my God, we were *just* in time."

The man shook the doctor's hand with tears in his eyes and went out to call Bennie.

The doctor stood over Helen, watching her regain consciousness. Amanda sought Reed as he sat in the kitchen. "That was the most wonderful thing I've ever seen. You ought to be a doctor yourself. You were very good at helping Dr. Cutler."

"I'd seen this done once before and wanted to help the doc if I could, being it was his first time operating for something like this."

He tried to play his efforts down, but Amanda wasn't having it. "I know what I saw, and again, you came to the rescue. He needed you with him, he needed you very much." He didn't miss the approving shine in her eyes, or the hush of respect in her voice as she came close and took his hand. "You never fail to amaze me, Reed," she went on. "I don't know you well enough, but you're no saddle bum and no killer either. I know that much."

"You know plenty about me, I've told you just about everything."

"Just about?" Amanda asked, smiling, but their conversation was halted as Doctor Cutler addressed her.

"Sorry to interrupt—you're Harvey Bradshaw's widow, aren't you?"

"Why yes. Why do you ask?"

A pang of worry struck her, along with a bit of shame that she'd forgotten her life with Harvey in the past few days. The doctor's serious look made her shake inside and her hands, hidden in her skirts, clenched tight, awaiting what he had to say.

"I need to inform you that a deputy from up north came along with the sheriff's man, returning your husband's body to Artesia." He paused, looking at her. "They asked me to make a positive identification, which I did."

This sudden bit of information struck Amanda like an avalanche. Except for the onerous burden of debt he'd left her, she'd nearly forgotten she'd had a husband in the events of the past three-four weeks. Ashamed that she'd forgotten Harvey that fast, her face flamed with guilt, yet she held her head high. Her feelings had altered considerably, knowing he'd been seeing another woman and had borrowed away any security for his family in the bargain. Beneath the surface, she'd been reveling in her new found freedom and, for that and that alone, she tried to rake up the proper amount of guilt as she responded to the doctor's information.

"Did the man from up that way have any idea what happened or who killed him?"

"That wasn't discussed before me," he replied.

She became thoughtful. "He'll need to be laid to rest, of course." She looked to Reed without a second thought. "What'll I need to do? I suppose he'll have to be buried in the town cemetery. We haven't a place at the ranch."

Amanda returned her gaze to Dr. Cutler. "Thank you for telling me." She immediately wished she could discuss this with Helen, but that was out of the question.

"Could you stand a drive into town tomorrow?" Reed asked. "It'd be almost twice as far as the drive here."

Dr. Cutler intervened. "She shouldn't subject herself to that. It's too far for a new mother. How old is that child?"

"Nearly one month now, and I'm recovering very well."

"I forbid it and Helen would, too, if she had a say." Cutler smiled at her. "Child, I don't need another patient and there's no way you can help your husband now, is there?" He turned to Reed. "You're her brother. Why not handle this for her? She can go in later on and visit the grave." He turned back to Amanda. "I did hear they had no information, so far, as to who killed your husband. But of course, they didn't discuss that with me as that was not my purpose for being there. The sheriff would be the one to ask."

Amanda realized that the lie about Reed being her brother was still alive. She didn't want to deal with it now and merely replied, "Thank you, Doctor Cutler. I'll abide by what you say." She smiled at him and hearing the snuffling and fussy cries of her baby, left them to care for him.

"I'll go in as soon as I can," Reed said. "But let's see this business through right now."

Hating the tangle of lies he'd willingly created, Reed felt the encroaching tentacles of it reaching out to entrap him even now after he'd told the sheriff his story. He heaved a sigh. He'd get his identity straightened out as soon as he could.

At the sound of Helen's moaning they turned their attention to her. Reed saw her eyes open and heard her mumble, "Is it over?"

She saw her husband standing at the foot of the bed and smiled up at him. "I'm awful thirsty, Herb, got any water on you?" She closed her eyes and rested for a few moments before speaking again. Rousing, she saw Reed and Dr. Cutler. "Well?" she asked.

"We got it in time, Helen," Cutler answered. "You might be pretty sick for a while, since it was mighty close. But I'm happy to say, you've got a real fighting chance."

Reed stood back, watching doctor and patient. Cutler pulled the blanket and sheet down and pushed her partial gown up just enough to reveal the mound of ironed sheeting he'd used to bind her abdomen. "Might bleed through a bit, dear, but we got her sewed up tight," Cutler said.

Reed thought he saw a tear escape from Cutler's eye.

"Thanks, Doc. And you too, Reed," Helen murmured. She groaned as she moved. "Hurts a mite, Doc."

"You need to move about some," Doctor Cutler told her. "Helps the circulation and breathing. We'll help you with that."

He had her hold a pillow over her incision and, with that held snugly in place, he and Reed reached beneath her hips and shoulders to help her slide onto her left side. He then placed a pillow between her knees.

"Thanks, Doc, oh my, that feels so much better." And she promptly drifted off, still somewhat under the spell of the ether.

A bit later, Amanda came in and knelt at the bedside. "Helen, you're going to be just fine, I know it, and so does Bennie."

She pulled him forth, and he reached out a hand to his mother.

"Are you going to get well, Mom?" Bennie's voice, tight with the anxiety he manfully tried to hide, was a bit high.

"Yes I am, son. The big worry's over now and the doc said I can't ever get this again."

Bennie fought a tear and reached out to pat his mother. Marianna stood back, quiet, her big eyes staring at all the excitement. Amanda's eyes were wet, too.

She turned her attentions to fixing something to eat. "I'll make us a bite. We haven't had anything for too long."

Now that the big worry had been taken care of, nourishment came next. Amanda found a loaf of bread and a roasted haunch of meat and got busy.

Reed sat on the porch with Herb. "Tell me, any cowhands around to hire? I've got a couple of men I may have to replace."

Herb looked him in the eye. "Amanda hired you, Helen tells me, right off the trail. She told me everything else too, so no need for you to lay back on anything you want to say. She sets a lot of store by you, son," he went on. "After your work in there with the doc, I'd stand behind you against a whole damned pack of sheriffs and all their deputies. You can count on me if you ever have the need."

"Thanks, Herb. I'm damned sick of lying about being her brother and wish to hell we'd never started it." Reed paused and looked the man in the eye. "The sheriff knows all about my running from the law. I took a liking to him and trusted him enough to level with him. We're working on bringing the killer of Bradshaw to justice, but we've got a ways to go on that."

"Anybody in mind, he's looking at?" Relaxed now the operation was over and things looked pretty good, Herb leaned back in his chair, crossed his legs, pulled out the makings, and rolled himself a smoke.

"Ever hear of that Saldana woman?" Reed leaned forward. He rested easy himself, now the operation was over. His other secrets were out, too, and it felt damned good. He took a big breath and let it out slowly.

"Who hasn't? How's she mixed up in Harvey's killing?" Herb bent close, not wanting Bennie or Marianna to hear their talk. The children had left the house and were running about in the yard with a lantern. "I've heard a plenty on that one. Just about any man around here can tell you an earful."

Reed saw a twinkle in the man's eye as he admitted, "I've met up with her myself," he said. "She's a handful." He laughed. The woman wasn't done with him yet, and he knew it. "We've an idea we're working on."

But he knew better than to blather about on about it. Gossip spread faster than a prairie fire on these lonely ranges. He didn't know Herb well enough, and his own situation was edgy at best.

"Helen told me you're not Amanda's brother, but hasn't said a lot more."

Reed saw the unanswered questions in his eyes. "No, I'm not, just happened along at a critical time for the lady."

"She told me about you bringing in that baby, too. Man, you've got more guts than most to handle a thing like that. Don't know if I could."

"You'll never know unless it happens to you, and if you're lucky as hell, it won't." Reed grinned. "Named that boy after me, and didn't know she was a widow at the time." Proud of the fact, he felt his chest expand and didn't care if it showed.

Amanda came out to them and they went quiet. "You'd best come eat a bite," she said. "It's only sandwiches and coffee, but it's something to put in those hungry stomachs. It's been a long day for all of us."

She led the way and they took seats at the kitchen table. Doctor Cutler had removed all the surgical evidence from the one under the window and they enjoyed a happy meal. Helen was asleep, and so was baby Reed.

જીહ્લજી

It was late in the evening—after the meal. Lamps had been lit long ago, and Amanda felt restless. She faced Reed. "I know it's late and dark outside, but I think we need to get on home." She looked at Herb. "The doc says he'll stay another night here, to see how she does, before he leaves. I think you'll do fine, helping, and might end up being a good nurse in the bargain."

"Why sure, Amanda." Herb looked puzzled. "Why not bunk in here with us, late like it is? We got plenty of room."

"I feel like we need to get back and see to things with the boys gone off to town and all."

"Well then, I thank you for coming and bringing this gentleman with you." He indicated Reed. "Don't know what might've happened if you hadn't come along." Herb shook his hand and held on for an extra moment as emotion tried to get the best of him. He fought it down and called Bennie, his voice rougher than usual. "Son, how about you get their buggy hitched up, will you?"

"Sure will, Dad." Bennie looked about. "It's way after dark, why they leaving out now?"

"They want to get on home, son."

Bennie turned to his little companion. "Maybe you'd better sit right here on the porch so you won't get in the way."

He strode manfully to the corral and Marianna burst into tears.

Reed took her in his arms and coddled her. "Now, honey, he's right. That old horse might decide to step on you."

"Won't neither," she sobbed.

Marianna was disappointed, but the little minx didn't try to leave his arms. She nestled there, taking in the warmth and masculinity of him, something she'd never had much of. Reed knew that about her and vowed he'd never turned her away. He enjoyed the feel of her delicate little form as he held her.

Amanda went to sit beside Helen's bed. "We'll be leaving now, I know it's late but we need to get these children home and tend to things. The boys went to town and haven't bothered to return as far as we know." She still had no idea who'd watered her garden. *Could it have been Reed?* She decided she'd ask him when the time was right. Whoever it was had done it on the sly.

"Helen looked up at her, drowsy and pale in the lamplight, but clearly awake after her surgery. "Thanks for coming. It was a long way for you with the babies. Won't it be long after midnight before you get home?"

"Reed'll do the driving so no need to worry about that."

"You set a lot of store by that man, don't you? Are you sure you're doing the right thing, placing so much trust in a total stranger?"

"I did that once—the day I married Harvey." Her voice took on a determined edge. "From now on, I'm my own woman and place my trust in no one and no man." She shrugged and uttered a small helpless sort of laugh. "But for the present, I need this stranger and I'll do what I have to."

"I hear the bitterness in your voice, Amanda," Helen replied. "I knew all along how it was for you with Bradshaw. No woman could have been happy in that situation." She smiled. "You'll be all right, dear girl."

After a flurry of activity, Reed, Amanda, and the children set out for home. Amanda was glad to be alone with him again after the long exciting day. Helen's words came back to her. She sat close against his shoulder and they bumped along over the crude wagon trail. Marianna slept in the back and baby Reed lay asleep in her arms. Amanda held her chin firm, her lips tight, and her back stiff as she decided. *I will be all right. I will.*

CHAPTER 21

Amanda had no idea how late it was when they returned to the ranch nor did she care. Paralyzed with fatigue and nearly asleep herself, she collapsed in Reed's arms as he helped her down. He held her longer than needed to steady her, pressed her tired body close against his, and she allowed it. Why it felt so good, she didn't understand, but the closeness and warmth of him felt like heaven. Being held in his arms this way seemed like a safe haven.

It was something that constantly drew her thoughts, and she smiled, her face pressed against his shirt. She had no way to stop the errant thoughts that crept into her mind, nor did she want to.

When Marianna moaned in her sleep, Reed released Amanda. Saying nothing, he picked up baby Reed and placed him in her arms. Then he reached into the buggy, took up the sleeping girl, and together they entered the darkened home.

The warmth and familiarity of the place, and the little wiggling dog, reached out to welcome them and Amanda heaved a sigh of happiness. Unused to the feeling, she wondered what made her feel that way.

But for Reed, holding her close that way had sent his pulses rising high. He felt his heart leaping in his chest and his breath caught in his throat. The feeling of welcome in this home made a bit of moisture creep into his eyes. "I'll put this little girl in her bed," he murmured to Amanda.

He headed down the hall with the child. Amanda lit a couple of lamps, changed her baby, and fed him. A bit later, with the children settled and asleep, she sat in the big room, overly tired, yet the riotous feeling, stirring her into a frenzy of torment, made it impossible to seek her bed. She looked intently at Reed.

He spoke first. "Amanda, I don't know where we are headed but I—"

Suddenly fearful, she raised her hand to stop him. "Please, don't say anything now, Reed. I don't know where we're going, either, but please, don't tell me you're leaving me. If you're thinking to push on to the north like you said in the beginning—"

She got up and stepped close to him. "I might be crazy to say it, but right now I don't know what I'd do without you." Flushing, she added, "Not to say anything against my husband, but looking back, I wonder what possessed me to think I had what it took to become a rancher's wife."

He took her in his arms. "Amanda, I'm not planning on leaving you that way. Whatever made you say such a crazy thing?" he asked, pulling her close. "You and those kids have become a part of me. And don't forget that boy carries my name. I'm not letting go of that." He held her out from him and looked into her troubled eyes. "What's got into you?"

"I hear so much about the Saldana woman, how beautiful she is and how men love her so much. I know you've been in her arms. I've caught her perfume on you. You're a man—how do I know you're not like Harvey?"

Reed pulled her close and chuckled softly, his nose inhaling the scent of her thick, lustrous hair. "My dear, don't you know that already? I've been around, and I've seen plenty, but I'm not fool enough to let anything like that happen." He shook her gently. "Tell me, what's come over you—what are you thinking?"

"I got to worrying about it on the way home from Helen's. Can't you see how on the edge we live—not knowing from one day to the next if we'll be here on this ranch tomorrow?"

He held her close against his body. She trembled in his arms, not from fear, but at the gentle way his big hand stroked gently down her back. The way he bent his head down to lay his face against her cheek, made her nestle closer against him. His scent filled her mind and she soon felt those strange, insidious, tiny flames flickering through her body. Those small heated barbs set her to worrying. *What is he doing to me? I don't know what's happening.*

He moved to take her mouth and kiss her. Gentle at first, he deepened his kiss when he felt her respond. The way she tightened her arms around his neck and pressed ever closer set his blood on fire. He ravaged her lips over and over, murmuring his loneliness and longing until she cried out his name.

"Reed, you make me feel like I'm on fire. What are you doing? What is happening to me?"

"My darling woman, nothing is happening that you wouldn't want. Certain things can be a wonderful, beautiful, thing between a man and woman. Amanda, this is only a small part of it, only a beginning." He fell silent, letting his arms and lips speak for him.

She was alone in the world and fearful. Reed understood that and comforted her. "I'll never leave you now, Amanda, unless they haul me off to that hell-hole in Yuma. I don't know how this business will end, but if God lets me live through it, I'd be proud to take care of you, and those babies of yours, too. And I mean forever, if you'd consider it." He held her away and looked at her. "You hear what I'm saying, Amanda?"

She pulled away from his embrace, her face white in the lamplight. "Yes Reed, oh yes, I do hear you, but what can I say?" Struggling to regain her composure, she lifted her chin as she pulled away. "It's so soon after my husband's death. I couldn't consider such a thing. Wouldn't that be wrong?"

Away from his embrace, she stood before him, feeling ashamed at the wanton way she'd responded to his kisses. "My God, he isn't even in the ground yet. How can you ask me that and how can I possibly answer you?"

Amanda moved away from him and sat in her own chair, remembering once again, how she'd been feeling the past several days. How greatly she'd enjoyed her sudden release from male domination, reveling in it, and how firmly she'd vowed never get in this situation ever again. She laughed aloud at herself and faced him. "Do you have any idea what sort of things I've been saying to myself since I've become a widow?"

Watching her face change and her dainty chin tighten, he replied with a soft chuckle. "Right now, I'm not sure I want to know." He stood silently, leaning against a wall, watching this soft, lovely creature, who'd felt like heaven in his arms a moment ago, change into a resolute young woman, one who sat up straight, with lips firm, and chin jutting out.

Seeing that, Reed began forming a few doubts of his own. Maybe he shouldn't have said anything about marriage. It *was* too soon after her husband's death, and what business did a homeless saddle bum like him have in offering himself to this woman, or any woman? The realization of his situation hit him with a crushing blow.

"Perhaps I've spoken too soon." It was all he could think to say.

"It's not you Reed. No finer man lives as far as I'm concerned." She gave him a quick smile of affirmation before she went blithely on with what she had to say. "But after my years with Harvey, I've decided I cannot put myself in another situation like that, ever again. I certainly know well enough, that I'm not a good marriage prospect for any man. I've plenty of proof of that." She huffed and crossed her arms. "Nothing about me ever pleased Harvey that I know of and, most likely, I wouldn't make you happy either." She sniffed, her nose in the air. "If you were married to me, you'd soon be running to town after that Saldana woman, just like him."

Fighting the laughter that rose in his throat, Reed choked out a few words. "Woman, you've wandered way off the range with that kind of thinking." Trying to keep the amazed grin off his face, he added, "It's time to catch some sleep. I think we could both use some of that."

Choking back his mirth at her declaration of inadequacies and shaking his head, he left her and headed down the hallway to the darkness of his room. Right now, he was just grateful she allowed him to sleep beneath the same roof.

Amanda sought her own bed, her mind racing with the words just spoken between them. *That man just proposed marriage!* Her mind swirled with agony over thoughts of what that meant. *If I got married again, it would start all over. No! I can't let myself get tangled up like that again.* Remembering her years with Bradshaw, she sighed. *Aside from all those disgusting things a man makes you do to please his own selfish needs, I never drew a peaceful breath what with him staring at me with those cold, blue-gray eyes for letting the dog in or forgetting to water that damned garden!*

Amanda scoffed at herself. "And now just thinking about it has got me to swearing." She pulled a pillow beneath her head, turned to her side and, smiling to herself, remembered how Reed's body felt, how his kisses burned. In spite of it all, she drifted off.

ᏗᏕᏗ

The moon had gone dark, and it was coming up on dawn. Sleepless, the black-eyed woman lay awake in her bed. Though she'd given him every invitation, that icy-faced sheriff had never failed to rebuff her. He'd rejected

her offers and hints of feminine comfort and, for that, she
bore him a seething hatred. Being snubbed by the sheriff
had certainly made her resentful, but it had also made her
rather nervous.

She fumed and writhed in her luxurious bed, while
running her slim fingers over the smooth edges and fine
embroidery of the silken sheets, thinking of that fancily
dressed dude with the sheriff. Yes, her thoughts strayed to
him constantly. At last she'd found among the *gringos,* a
man she truly wanted, money or not. She burned inside for
that tall, handsome male, imagining how those long hands
would stroke her body. Her thoughts dwelled on the fine
figure of a man he was. *Ah, si*! *He is no same like los other
miserable gringo. Oh no, none so fine like that one*!

She squirmed and twisted her body beneath the sheets,
imagining how his passion for her would rise and how he
would take her.

She'd slowly accumulated many lovely things. The
mere possession of them made her feel equal to or above
any of the other filthy *gringos* in this town. Yet the owning
of those precious trivial things never lessened her hatred or
her thirst for revenge upon those who'd stolen her inher-
itance, those lying, cheating devils, each and every one of
them.

Her forbearers had been the lords of this land, owning
acreages so vast, a good *vaquero* couldn't ride across it in
two days. She felt the pride of it swelling within her breast.
But now, because of them, *los gringos,* she and her people
had been systematically reduced to the status of the lowliest
of peons.

She'd learned her history as a child, at the knee of her
loving father, Armando Leon Saldana de Los Portales. Her
heart swelled with pride, remembering the fine man he'd
been. He'd cut a fine figure riding his blooded horses, until
the gradual loss of his vast properties had transformed him
into the pitiable lost soul she'd barely recognized at the end
of his life.

By that time, the evils of *los gringos* had turned him into a stingy, cruel old man, she thought with disdain. Because of his abusiveness, she'd grown to hate what he'd become. He was gone now and she barely gave the man a thought anymore. He'd struck her once too often.

Mercedes breathed in a huge breath of fresh air. She wasn't the kind to suffer that treatment from any man, including that empty soul she'd once called Father. But the fine *estancia* they'd once owned was gone, too, and that fact never left her mind for a moment.

Recently, things had gone according to plan. She was very close now to recovering a good part of that once splendid rancho, but more must be done. She gave thought to the fine-looking man who'd came in with the sheriff, the brother-in-law of that disgusting fool of a *gringo*, Harvey Bradshaw. She'd welcomed that incompetent man into her musky, enticing embrace too many times over the past year.

Remembering her encounters with Harvey Bradshaw, she shivered. It'd been a sacrifice of the greatest magnitude, but the rewards would be worth every sickening moment she'd given the fool. She laughed aloud. "What that disgusting fool knew about women wouldn't fill the inside of a gnat's ass."

Laying there, seeing herself as mistress of a large expansive rancho once again, she smiled into the swiftly fading night. The luxurious touches of her costly furnishings made her smile, and finally, lascivious thoughts of that fine new male filled her with a burning need she could not extinguish alone.

As the cravings within her body intensified, she writhed with need until the intensity of it forced her to seek the relief she craved. She slipped out of her soft bed, padded to a door toward the back of the house, and knocked softly. It opened rather quickly. Her heart raced wildly as she reached out to the handsome black-eyed man waiting there. Barely clothed, he'd waited for her call as he had done so many nights. She breathed her desperate need softly, *"Ah, mi Ramon, amore."*

She took the black-eyed man's hand, placed it on her swelling breast, and pulled him against her body. The heat in his eyes and the odor of his nearly naked body filled her with stinging fire. She rubbed her hand over his engorged member and led the big male to her bed.

Falling on the bed with him, she sighed with sensuous pleasure as he took hold of her. He used his hot mouth and seeking hands to send waves of desire burning through her. He tore at her, seeking, pulling, and touching her in those places he knew so intimately. Her aching breasts were only the beginning. He knew her body completely and stood ready and waiting, at her service.

He loved her desperately and continually waited, readily available to bring her body to the final and total release she craved. Ramon's chest expanded in his power over her. He was the man, the only one who knew her well enough, who had the skills to bring her to the point of ecstasy, over and over, and well beyond. Though he had many other uses, it was in this way she often used him. He'd become a demanding, mind-bending narcotic to the lovely Mercedes, and he allowed her to believe she used him at her pleasure.

But to himself, Ramon burned with hatred at her many infidelities. He shook internally with a damning rage, coupled with his wild passion. He took possession of her, using her lush, exotic body to avenge his savage anger, mastering her in every cruel way he could devise or imagine. He took her rough and hard. He made her suffer long and forcefully in atonement for her wayward attentions elsewhere.

Secure in the knowledge that she thirsted for him only, he made her pay hour after hour. He tortured her. He soothed her and, in exultation, heard the agony in her voice. He rejoiced as, during his savage mastery of her body, she cried out his name over and over during the heights of her release. *"Ah, por Dios! Ramon, Ramon, mi amore."*

CHAPTER 22

Sleepy-eyed, Reed stepped out onto the porch and looked about. The sun barely peeped over the eastern horizon, casting the soft pinks and pale lavenders of early morning over a lightly clouded sky. He'd slept little and now paid scant attention to the beauty of his surroundings, his mind on the conversation he'd had with Amanda during the night. After that, he had a lot of thinking to do. Shaking his head in wonder at her impassioned declaration of her inadequacies as a wife, he murmured softly into the fresh morning air, "That woman is dead wrong in what she believes."

He chuckled softly, remembering her outburst but, more than that, he recalled the softness of her body so warm against his as he pressed her close. He remembered those full lips he'd kissed and smiled as he thought, *Lady you'd make any man alive happy, and that includes me. You just don't know it.* He couldn't stop the smile spreading across his face,

Piddely sat beside him, tail wagging, seeking attention. Smoke poured from the bunkhouse chimney. As late as it was, he ought to walk out there and have a word or two with those useless bums, but instead, he turned his thinking to the situation with the bank. *With all the loans on this place, she'll not be able to keep it, regardless of who's at fault. Money's been borrowed against the place and that's that.*

Amanda had let him know that losing the ranch would not be an emotional hardship for her. She'd made it clear to him that she longed for the rugged mountains of her home country and would be happy to return to Colorado. That sounded fine to him, being as it was that much farther from the hated Yuma Prison.

He'd grown attached to both her children and had smiled many times, thinking of watching Marianna grow into a young woman, and a boy who'd grow up calling him, Dad.

The door opened and Amanda came out, hugging her robe against her ever-slimming form. "I've made breakfast."

Her words, terse and unemotional, sounded cold but he noticed the cup of coffee in her trembling hand. He couldn't read her expression, or figure what she thought of him this morning, but something was on her mind, that was plain enough. Had she given further thought to his proposal of marriage?

That he'd asked her surprised him as much as it had her. He hadn't planned on it, hadn't even thought of it. A man in his situation was hardly in a position to take a wife. In the heat of the moment, it'd just happened.

Yet, with all that had passed between them since the day he'd found the place, he felt ever more bound to Amanda. Her daughter already loved him, and though she thought she could make her own way, Amanda needed a man to take care of her. He smiled into the soft morning air and swore in amazement. For the first time in his life, he was ready to make a life with a woman he cared for and loved.

He looked at her standing there. She'd mostly regained her slender figure, yet he remembered all too well, the swollen look of her before she'd given birth. Looking at that slightly built female body, it amazed him what a woman was able to withstand. Females were strong, in ways he couldn't imagine, and mystifying as hell. Trying to understand a woman would take a lifetime, and he'd reached the point in his life where he was more than ready to give it a try.

"Sounds good," he finally replied, got up, and gave her a good look square in the eyes, taking in the sight of her soft female figure and shimmering golden hair she'd twisted into a knot at the back of her finely shaped head.

Amused, he smiled. She was all business this morning. When she turned to enter the kitchen, he followed her.

At the stove, she dished up potatoes, bacon, a platter of eggs and set them before him. The biscuits were still in the oven, but he caught the smell of them and swallowed in anticipation. He sat at the head of the table and waited for her to sit down.

She set her food on the table and turned to fetch the biscuits. The heat of the oven had flushed her features to a rosy hue. As she brought the basket of those fluffy wonders to the table, she looked absolutely delicious to his hungry eyes. He fought a strong urge to grab her and kiss her into the kind of passion he'd discovered she was capable of, carefully subdued beneath that cool exterior.

Thoughts of exploring those forbidden boundaries held a magic for his imagination that continually tantalized the hell out of him but never so much as right now. But he refrained.

"Thanks, looks mighty good," he said as the fork lay unused in his hand. He'd forgotten the food in front of him, shocked at the intensity of his wayward thoughts.

"Better eat while it's hot," she reminded him, but her own trembling hands easily told him she remained in a whirl of emotion from last night. Maybe she'd hadn't had enough time to sort out his idea of marriage and likely spent a good part of the night giving thought to it. He hoped she had.

Marianna came straggling out, dragging a blanket, with a ratty teddy bear clutched to her chest. Spying him, she dropped the teddy bear and sidled close to his side. "Weed, you here."

His closeness to the child was not lost on Amanda, and he enjoyed every moment of it. If she didn't want him for a husband, her child wanted him for a daddy and that certainly pushed the odds in his favor.

"Marianna, set and eat now." Amanda took her up, set her in her padded chair, and put too much food on her plate. "There you are."

She sat at her place and began picking at her own plate of food. "I wonder how Helen feels today. Do you have any idea how she might be after an operation like that?" She directed her query to Reed, keeping her tone businesslike.

"A mite sore and stiff, I imagine." He grinned at her as he tore into another biscuit. "You're mighty good at making these, aren't you?"

"Cooking is one thing I seemed to have gotten right," she said, referring to her conversation of last night.

"I'd say you've done just right at bringing forth some fine looking children, too." He sighed. "Amanda, I've more to say to you when I can."

"I won't hear any more of that business from you. You know my feelings on it." Her tone curt, her face flushed red, she kept her eyes on her plate.

"How wrong you are, my dear—so very wrong." He smiled at her, shaking his head, and shot her a heated look. "I imagine, your past experience makes you say things like that, but it'd never be that way between us. Don't you know that?"

"I don't know any such thing!" she gasped. "Please don't go on about it. My mind is set. I've given a lot of thought to being married and, for the life of me I can't see what all the fuss is about." She raised her head and smiled at him, her lips and chin firm. "I've been thinking I might open a nice little shop in some small town where I'd only have to deal with women folks. That'd be a whole lot better for me." She hadn't touched a thing on her plate, and her hands trembled so much she nearly dropped her fork, but her clenched fists and tightly set jaw told him she believed what she was saying.

"Well, you might just have that shop in town one day, but we have a long way to go in getting things on this place settled." His referring to sterner matters turned her face pale. "You may have to sell it or let it go to pay Harvey's debts."

"You believe it's that bad, then?" she asked as her eyes darkened with worry.

"I didn't say that, but a debt is a debt and has to be paid one way or another. When I rode out with the boys the other day, I saw very few cattle and couldn't get a word out of Jud or Buddy about what's happened to the rest of them."

"Neither of those two are worth their hire, even Harvey said that."

Amanda shoved her plate aside and put her head down. "I truly don't know what to do about it. I hate feeling helpless like this." She raised her stress-filled eyes to him. "When I asked you to stay and help me sort things out, I wasn't trying to find another husband."

"Believe me, I know that. But at the time I was the only help you had, and since then, I've become attached to certain things around here." He bent his eyes on the little girl, doing her best to eat her food, and chuckled at how the dog kept close enough to catch the errant droppings. He noticed how coyly Marianna made sure they were plentiful.

"She never went to her father the way she does to you," Amanda admitted in hushed tones, not wanting her daughter to hear anything derogatory about her sire. "You handle her gently and never turn her away. Because of that, she knows her feelings are safe with you. I appreciate that about you, more than you'll ever know. But I can't imagine putting myself under a man's thumb that way again—even yours. Being married just isn't worth what a woman has to go through."

"It'd never be that way, lady." He softened his tone. "Don't worry your head about it now—we'll get it worked out." With a smile aimed deep into her eyes, he rose from the table. "Mighty fine chuck, Amanda Thank you, I believe I'll have a word with the boys now."

He headed out the door, his head held high, whistling some tuneless melody.

Amanda had to hold Marianna in her seat. "No darling, Weed has to work, today. You can't go out there. You'd be in the way and a horse might step on your toes."

As she said it, she stood in the open door herself, watching Reed's lanky figure walk to the bunkhouse. He had a swinging gait, like many men, and on him it looked more than fine. Imagining herself in his arms, letting him do those secret and intimate things to her, she shivered. *He wants to marry me. Could I possibly go through those disgusting things men make you do again? I hated that with Harvey. Of course, Reed's not the same sort. I'd really have to love someone desperately to put up with certain things, when they get the way they do.* In a quandary, grabbing plates and dropping cutlery, Amanda started clearing the table and doing the dishes before the baby awakened.

ℰↈℰↈ

The men rode out and had been gone for several hours when she heard a horse approaching. Looking out, she saw Sheriff Toliver riding up. He watered his horse and tied him out near the corrals where he could reach the swatch of hay he'd tossed to him.

"Looks like he plans to stay awhile," she muttered and met him at the door. "Sheriff Toliver, is everything all right?"

"Nothing to get in a twist about. I wanted to see Reed about something."

She informed him of Reed's whereabouts, led him inside, sat him down, and brought him a glass of apple juice which, after taking a good whiff, she decided it had begun to ferment. "Hope it's not too strong for you. Need to use it up before it gets any stronger."

"It's just right, ma'am, but I believe you could bottle this stuff and sell it in another week." He laughed as he swept his hair back, making a smooth area, wet from the sweat under his hat band. "As to why I'm here, all hell's breakin' loose in town, and thought to get Reed's take on things."

"What's happened?" She found it hard to believe he'd seek Reed's input, him being an escaped convict and all, but couldn't imagine voicing a question about it. "How can he help with any of that?"

"He's very sharp, ma'am, might could use some lawyering on some of these things."

"Lawyering? He's never said anything about that to me." Amanda felt a shock hearing it. "He did look like one in those nice clothes, but that's not the same as being one." She shook her head "That man never stops surprising me with all the things he turns up knowing."

Little more was said until Amanda decided to check the garden. She hadn't even looked at it and didn't know if it had been watered again. If not, she was sure everything had died by now. "I'm going to see to the garden. Just sit here and rest while I'm gone." She rose to leave and Marianna quickly left her scattered toys to join her.

"We go pick, Mommy?"

"Maybe. We'll see, honey."

They headed to the garden, and Toliver joined them, matching his long strides to her shorter ones.

"Haven't seen a nice patch for a while. We don't keep one," he said, referring to himself and his wife. "Nellie isn't up to it anymore."

They entered the garden to see it moist, watered, and everything growing wildly.

"I don't believe it! It hasn't rained lately, yet look how it grows. It's wet between the rows."

Again she wondered who'd been so kind. With his talk

of marriage, she'd forgotten to ask Reed about it. She allowed Marianna to pick a carrot this time. Pointing out a nice sized one, the child pulled it up. It was about five inches long.

The child wiped it on her dress and began chewing on the tender growth. "It tastes good, Mommy, I eat it."

"Yes, along with a peck of dirt. The garden has a ways to go yet, but it's doing fine," she told Toliver,

She walked through cabbages beginning to head, sweet corn that had tasseled and ears begun, even the potatoes had flowered and tiny ones would be growing beneath the vines in the dark, soft soil. *Who does this? Who waters this garden?* she wondered as they walked back.

"You've got a right nice place here, ma'am," Toliver said.

"I suppose it is, but my heart is in Colorado. That's where I came from before I married Harvey." Remembering her dead husband, her face flushed with embarrassment. "Has my husband been buried, as you said?"

"Yes, we took care of it." He grimaced. "Had to, if you know what I mean, couldn't wait for Reed to come in and take care of it. Even had a few at the service, too."

"Did that Mexican woman attend?"

"Didn't see her, but a good-sized Mexican gentleman came. He was wearing some mighty fancy duds—maybe just looking things over. I figure Harvey's killing was possibly his handiwork since he works for her."

"Probably would be the one who did the killing, if she had a hand in it,"

Amanda realized with shock, she'd separated her feelings so far from Harvey it was as though she spoke of someone she barely knew. Maybe she should feel ashamed, but she didn't, and felt only a small tinge of guilt about it. She flushed at how quickly and easily she'd distanced herself emotionally from her husband. Wrinkling her brow, she wondered if Reed had anything to do with how she felt.

"I heard Harvey was a real hard man, Mrs. Bradshaw,"

Toliver commented. "This country makes men that way sometimes."

"Does it make them run to town and take up with the first woman who asks them?" She couldn't hide the anger that still burned within her after learning she'd been deceived by her husband. "Nothing like a cheating husband to make a woman feel like an ignorant fool." She turned her face away as she bit off the words.

"Some men are that way, ma'am. I don't know why. Never knew anyone who did," Toliver offered, hoping that small factor might comfort, but it didn't seem to settle her anger.

When they heard the men in the yard, Toliver heaved a sigh of relief and quickly left to see Reed. The men shook hands after a perfunctory greeting and stood facing each other.

"What brings you out this way, Toliver?" Reed felt uneasy. There was always the possibility of a new warrant being sent around. He saw the sheriff had something working on his mind.

"A lot's happened and I wanted a confab with you on it." Toliver nearly pawed the soil beneath his feet and wore a smirk on his face in the telling. "Seems our esteemed banker has got himself in a peck of trouble. The fool's been seeing that Saldana woman, right along with a few other men in town. It seems his wife's left town in disgrace, but not before she shot a hole the size of Texas in his leg." He couldn't hide his grin. "He's under investigation by the bank examiners for fraud, on top of that."

"Any help in that for the lady here?" Reed had a one track mind when it came to Amanda's problems.

"Well, dunno about that. As you know, a loan is a loan, as they say. Needs some sorting out and thought you might be some help in that, being you've had some lawyer trainin'."

"Damn! That devil-woman's had her hand into every money pot around." Reed sighed then chuckled. "Wonder how much she got off old Blankenship?"

"Word is he was up to his neck with loans he couldn't repay. Been helping himself right along with the other loans. Seems the wife couldn't handle the heat from her society friends. She went back to Missouri, to a sister, so I hear."

He frowned. "Her fancy club members turned into a nasty bunch of cutthroats when they got wind of his trouble. My wife wasn't good enough for the likes of them and I told her at the time, she was better off. Hope she believes it now."

Reed heard the wistful note in the man's voice and guessed most men liked to see their women satisfied in her social life. Toliver was no different.

"Anything else?" Reed felt the man had more to say.

"Well, that warrant is still out on you. I found an old one in the office under a few others. I stashed it away, but not before my deputy, Bart Day, got a good look at it. Never forgets a face, he says—brags on it."

"I was afraid of that happing one day. I hoped I was far enough away from that hell-hole, so as not to worry." Reed felt sick with apprehension but not for himself. "I'd like to stay around long enough to help Amanda with this place. It's hard as hell figuring what to do if I'm sticking my neck in a noose and running a chance it'll send me back to that damned Yuma hellhole."

Toliver grinned. "Reckon he wouldn't recognize you a'tall dressed the way you do, coming into town looking like a damn lawyer or gamblin' dude. I'll do all I can. I'm asking around about that sheriff in Prescott. If he's crooked, it'll catch up to him one of these days."

"Maybe not in time for me," Reed replied then changed the subject. "Any more on the Saldana woman? She can't be doing all this killing and cheating without leaving a trail of some kind."

Toliver shrugged. "Our lovely Mercedes has a man working for her that's a hell of a lot more than a hired man.

He's with her near day and night, closer'n a husband, or every bit as close. With her tom-catin' around the way she does, wonder how that works for him? I've known of this business for a year or two. I believe he does her bidding and for that, receives plenty of attention from her, enough to keep him at it. But hell, any man's got his share of pride, don't he?"

"Could he be the killer of Bradshaw?"

"Sure as hell could, and that's what I came to see you about. What I need to find out is this: does that Ramon own a Springfield rifle?" Toliver became thoughtful. "I'd like to get a good look inside that house, but I can't raid the damned place without cause." He shot Reed a sideways look. "Any chance you could get in there and check that out for me?"

CHAPTER 23

Goddamn! You ask a lot of a man." Reed imagined himself in that house with Mercedes Saldana flaunting her luscious bosom in his face and pouring that potent Tequila down his throat. "Why not ask a man to go shoot himself?"

"I think I just did, Reed." Toliver was serious. "Putting away that mess of hornets would go a long way to help your case if it ever comes up."

"I'll think on it." Reed changed the subject. "Come on in the house and set a spell. Have a bite of supper with us."

Reed sounded like the owner, a man with a home, family, and the ability to offer hospitality, though he had title to neither.

And when the sheriff replied, "Why, sure, it'd be my pleasure," Reed saw curiosity building in the man about his status with the missus of the place. He decided Toliver was eager to get the feel of the climate inside the home of a newly widowed and beautiful young woman and a fugitive from justice.

But Toliver only said, "I'm hungry as hell."

They walked inside to behold Amanda holding her baby, the smell of food cooking on the stove in the kitchen, and a small girl playing on the floor with her doll. Piddely rose to meet them, wiggling and letting out a low, joyous growl. Amanda, still cool toward him after last night's dealings, said nothing, only nodded at them and turned to the stove, her chin set firm.

Reed smiled at the cool greeting. But he broke into a wide grin when he heard Marianna cry out. "Weed!" The little girl rushed to wrap her arms around his leg and looked into his face while dancing on her toes, eager to be swept up into his arms.

"Looks to me like something's in the works between you two," Toliver murmured to Reed. "If so, I'd be mighty proud to see it. I have to say, I've had my hopes up for you both all along. You deserve the best for all you've suffered in your young life." He grasped Reed's hand. "Folks just like you are what we want here in the West. You have what it takes to become one of our finer citizens, and this country's growing real fast," he added. "We need you, Reed."

Reed had little to say, but his crooked grin and the sparkle in his eye said it for him.

Toliver nodded to Amanda and stepped close to look at the new child. "A fine boy you have there, growing like a weed. That Harvey would have been proud as punch over this little fella."

"Yes he would have." Her answer was short, knowing she'd have had her husband's wrath to face if the child had been female. "Like to hold him? I need to tend to supper and he's been a bit fretful today."

"Why sure, it's been a long while since these old arms have held a little mite like this." Toliver took the baby and, without thought, gently jostled the boy to settle his fretful cries. He shot a look at Reed. "Named him after you, she told me last time I was here."

"Reckon she felt a bit emotional right about then." Reed flushed, remembering the circumstances of the birth. The sheriff didn't know all the particulars, but he knew enough. "It'll be kind of nice having a little namesake running around." He planned on sticking around to see the boy walk.

They settled in the large sitting room to await the supper meal, and Toliver commented with a sly smile. "There's a plenty going on between you two, now isn't there? It's none of my business, but after hearing about the namesake, I had to ask."

Reed laughed a little. "Not right now, there isn't."

Toliver nodded, understanding the increasing intensity between Reed and Amanda, and said quietly, "There's gonna be fireworks galore around here one day as far as I can see. You two'll make a hell of a pair if you're lucky enough that she'll have you." He glanced out the window. "It's getting on into night. Might need to spend the night, Reed. That possible?"

"Sure, you're welcome. I'll ask the lady of the house." He sauntered into the kitchen. She was about to set the dinner on the table. "Say, Amanda, sheriff needs a place to bed down for the night, any chance of him finding a place in here?"

"He can bunk right in there with you, then." She had her nose in the air, and her jaw clenched tight. "What's that man cooking up for you, now?"

He didn't miss the suspicion and fear for him in her bitter tones. "Needs me to make another trip into Artesia." He let that bit of information work on her for a while before he offered even more tantalizing news. "Heard another interesting bit of news too," he said, deliberately dangling the hint of gossipy news before her. She'd have to ask him about it if she wanted to know the particulars.

"Like what, then? Toliver mentioned something about it but never said what it was." Curiosity urged her to ask, and it aggravated her to distraction that Reed deliberately held back what he had to tell. "News of any kind is hard enough to come by living so far out without having to pry it out of a body."

Seeing her tightly clenched teeth and flushed face, Reed was satisfied he had her upset over it, but he kept on. "I guess it'll wait awhile, seeing as how supper's about ready. Toliver's got that baby sleeping like an angel right now. Want me to tuck him in his bed?"

Her tone cold, she sniffed. "Yes, if you would, please." She busied herself pulling the biscuits out of the oven, keeping her back to him. When she turned to face him, the hot biscuits near burning her hands, she accused him. "You're going in town to see that Saldana woman again, aren't you?"

"Only because the sheriff needs my help with something. He's got a plan and I'm aiming to help him out." He lowered his voice. "Amanda, he'll be in my corner if they arrest me one day, don't forget that."

Her face went white. "Arrest you?" Afraid she'd drop them, he reached to take the biscuits from her trembling hands. "Reed, is that likely to happen?"

"One of the deputies has seen the flyer and Toliver says he never forgets a face." Seeing the desperation in her face, he decided to water it down a bit. "No need of worrying on that. He wouldn't know me dressed in those fancy duds of Harvey's I wear."

"Yet, you're willing to take that kind of a chance— why?" She came close to him. "It's hard to admit after that business of last night, but I don't think I can get along here without you. I wouldn't know what to do or where to begin." She fought her rising fear. "Why must you take the chance of being arrested again? Why do that?"

He saw tears beginning and, right now, wished that sheriff was a hundred miles away. After Marianna was put to bed, he'd have it out with this woman. A lot of feeling had built up between them. And after what he'd said to her last night, his own feelings had, all of a sudden, increased to the boiling point.

They needed time alone to sort things out and he was more than ready to get into everything with her. He looked at her slim body and the way she had her golden hair twisted into a glossy knot. Thoughts of unpinning those glistening coils, to let them fall in shimmering folds down her back

like she did at night, took a deep hold on his mind. He
dwelled constantly on a whole lot of other things he wanted
to do with her as well. Secret things that needed to wait until the dark of night, with the babies asleep in their beds. He
felt himself responding to his wayward thoughts and turned
away before she saw how it was.

Amanda took hold of herself and stiffened her spine.
"Better call that sheriff to come eat." Smiling, she added in
a lower tone, "Right after you put the baby in his crib."

The mood had changed between them. She'd put her
own intense feelings on hold, needing to attend to her family and their guest. Reed was family to her now and, if he
was arrested and taken away, she'd be left alone with two
small children and two very poor cowhands. The reality of
things came home to her plain as day: *This is the reason
women get married and put up with those disgusting things
her man does. It's in order to have her babies, make a
home, and do those things that make up a woman's life.*

She shrugged and started putting the food on the table.
This was her life right now and most likely on in to the future—hungry men to feed and babies to tend. She huffed in
futility and laughed at herself, wondering, *Will my own life,
or any woman's, ever be any different?*

As Amanda saw it, men were a separate breed completely, especially in thought and action. They held the
power and control of things, yet sometimes she'd discovered, they needed tending to, just like babies in some ways.
Wondering if women were merely put on earth to serve
them, she couldn't figure it out.

She called supper and Reed came to the table carrying
Marianna, sat her in her chair, and took his seat at the head
of the table where Amanda had placed him. Toliver found
another seat and Amanda noticed the way he watched them
both. She knew he liked and respected Reed, maybe her,
too. Without comment, she piled a good amount of food on
Marianna's plate and urged her to eat while Reed dug into
his.

Toliver followed suit and, after biting into a biscuit, he exclaimed, "Ma'am, these are the best I've ever tasted. I won't go bragging your talents to my wife, but any man eats at your table is mighty blessed indeed."

Amanda received the comment as a warm flush of pleasure spread across her face. "Why thank you sheriff, it's the one thing I've gotten right in my life."

"Aw now, ma'am, the way I see it, you've done a whole lot right, and I'm mighty surprised at hearing you say such a thing. Look at those fine younguns of yours. Any man'd proud to call them his own."

Amanda flushed again at his words and kept her eyes on her plate. Reed winked at the sheriff, smiled in his quiet way, and kept on eating.

The meal finished, Amanda cleaned the kitchen, and Reed settled Marianna in her bed before retiring to the large sitting room. They took up the discussion of town events and Amanda, tired and upset at waiting to hear Reed's news, asked Toliver, "Sheriff, anything of special interest happening in town?" With a toss of her head, she shot a look of disdain at Reed.

"Well, yes, quite a lot. I guess you wouldn't have heard what happened with the banker and his wife."

He went on to tell the events of the banker's downfall. She listened intently, no longer needing to hear what Reed had to tell. She gave him a knowing glance, her nose in the air.

In time, the men sought their beds. The house was dark and quiet, but Amanda, too restless to settle for the night, headed for the porch and a breath of soft night air. The baby would awaken a few times and disturb her rest, but she'd regained almost all her strength. With her children sleeping, she sought time for herself—time to think. Her world remained so unsettled that she needed to find enough quiet time to figure how she might proceed with making a life on her own.

She walked out onto the porch and sat in a chair, think-

ing and pondering her future. She could see most of the
ranch yard in the faint glow of a rising moon and leaned
back to relax, heaving a tired sigh.

Nearly drifting off, she heard a soft voice come out of
the darkness. "Amanda?"

She started at the whisper-soft sound of her name and
called softly, "Who is it?" A stab of fear shot through her.

"It's me, Reed."

He'd been there all the while, and she'd never seen
him, so intent upon her own thoughts, she hadn't thought to
look for anyone else. He' sat quietly in another chair,
watching her.

"I couldn't sleep either." He rose to drag his chair next
to hers. "You worrying on something?"

"No, just feeling restless and needing time to think.
Finding a quiet moment isn't so easy these days."

He moved a bit closer. "Anything special on your
mind?"

"I can see that something's on *your* mind, mister." Her
voice took on a warning tone. She drew herself up, crossing
her arms as if to shield herself from an unwelcome presence.

"Aw, why do you say that?" He knew exactly why and
kept on. "We have a few things to work out between us, you
and I, you know we do."

"What things?"

She knew full well what he meant since he'd asked her
to marry him. The entire idea had been ridiculous from the
beginning. She couldn't imagine it happening and didn't
want to think about it. Being married again and forced to
submit to those intimate things a man wanted and seemed to
need, turned her insides to ice if she gave it one moment of
thought.

"With you being a new widow and all, I should have
kept my ideas to myself, but it just came out. Things have
been heating up between us and I need to know where we're
headed." He looked intensely into her darkly shaded eyes.

The moon lent very little light, but he could see her face well enough for his purpose. "I meant what I said last night, Amanda. I believe being married to the right person can be mighty nice."

"For the man you mean. I know enough about that part of it and I'm not speaking of cooking and cleaning," she retorted. Her pulses raced so madly, she could scarcely catch her breath or feel the heat flushing over her face. She felt she had to fend him off, though he hadn't made a move to touch her. But he would, and she knew it. "I can't allow all that to happen to me again. I won't."

Reed struggled to contain his amusement. "All *what* again?" he asked, his eyebrows high and but his face straight and stern.

Amanda couldn't answer that. She couldn't speak of such things even to Helen, let alone this man or any man, whether he'd delivered her child or not. "I can't talk about it and I don't want to think about it." She turned her face away, unable to look at him, wrapping her arms tighter about herself. Then remembering his words, she turned to face him. "Just what do you mean, things heating up?"

"Nothing much, except that things in town might get hot and heavy for me in more ways than one. If that deputy happens to recognize me, I don't know if the sheriff can hold him off from throwing me in jail," he said, deliberately adding to her worries over losing him, and if it made her more receptive to his ideas, so much the better. She said nothing, so he continued. "Amanda, another thing, I'm guessing things weren't all that good between you and Harvey, but it doesn't have to be that way in a marriage. Haven't you ever seen two people who were really in love with each other, a couple that seemed more than happy together?"

"I don't think I know what love is, if that's what you're talking about. It's more like taking on a job, with some parts beyond—" She couldn't go on and dropped her head into her lap. "Why aren't you in bed, anyway? You must be tired, aren't you?"

She jumped in surprise as his arms enfolded her and pressed her close against him. He was on his knees before her chair, and she felt his heart hammering as hard as hers against her breast.

"Amanda, you're way off kilter about things between a man and a woman. Don't you know God meant us to be together, instead of at war with each other?"

"Well, I know what I know and I can't answer for God," she declared, sticking to her beliefs about the rigors of marriage. She'd had enough of it.

"What do you know? Who've you spoken to about these things?" He pressed his point while hiding his smile and disbelief at her thinking. "If you weren't a happy woman, it was never your fault, never! I can easy see that and I've only been here a short time." He put his hand under her chin and lifted her face to him. By the pale rising moon, he looked into her eyes. "Harvey must have been blind or crazy not to see what a treasure he had in you."

She saw him shaking his head in disbelief and uttered, "You're most likely just saying that for some fool reason of your own. I certainly never felt like a treasure. More like a work horse or brood mare was how it was, being married, and I'll not go through that again."

Yet, while she remained unconvinced of what he said, she did like the sound of his deep, soft voice as he talked to her. The sounds of it held a kind of gentle warmth she'd never heard from any man, not from her father, her brothers, and certainly never from Harvey.

Reed remained where he was. "No need to go worrying about it now, Amanda. I won't leave you, even if you refuse me. I couldn't go off and leave you to the wolves, and that's what it would amount to." He loosened his hold on her. "It's way too soon to be talking about something like this to a new widow. I should have held back."

He sat back in his own chair and leaned toward her, his arms resting on his knees. "The thing of it is, I see that you're hurting and it's all for nothing. None of what's happened here is any fault of yours. It isn't, Amanda. It never was."

"You really believe that, don't you?" She raised her head and smiled. "I will say this. You know how to make me feel better." She got up from the chair. "I guess I'd better get some rest, the baby will be waking me soon enough."

"Baby Reed." He chuckled, got up, moved close, and pulled her into his arms. "I love hearing you say his name and I'm crazy as hell about this, too." He kissed her lips over and over, across her face and down onto her neck until she struggled against him, gasping for breath.

"What are you *doing*?" Her heart beat like a trip hammer while she felt the ice melting inside her body from his heated kisses. "You have me in a dizzy spin. I can't get my breath!"

"Just saying goodnight, ma'am, like it ought to be said to a lovely, sweet woman like you." Reed released her and steadied her on her feet. "I think I hear my namesake calling for you."

Hearing the lusty wail of her baby boy, she took another look into Reed's glowing eyes and quickly turned away. "Good night." She nearly ran to the darkness of her bedroom. Once reaching the safety of her room, she shut the door and stood inside trembling. No closeness, no embraces she'd ever known from Harvey had ever made her feel like she felt now. The heated, burning waves of thrilling desire that tore through her body, made her legs feel weak. Those were sensations she'd never imagined possible.

Looking down at the struggling, snuffling infant, who cried with his need for nourishment, she stroked his fuzzy head. "You precious thing, you cried just in time."

She had a lot to think about and, at this moment, none of it included how to save the ranch or pay off the enormous debt against it. Shrugging, she settled against the head of the bed, put her son to her breast, and relaxed as he fed, giving way to the feeling of wild satisfaction common only to mammalian mothers.

Later, lying awake, trying for a bit of rest, Amanda heard a clinking sound outside the house. Alarmed, she rose to the window and pulled the drapery away. The area around the well lay bathed in the same subtle moonlight she'd enjoyed earlier on the porch with Reed. It gave enough illumination for her to see a figure carrying two buckets from the well toward the garden.

After watching for a long while, seeing the many laborious trips he took, she knew who'd done the faithful watering of her garden. "Bless his heart," she said, as she took to her bed.

CHAPTER 24

Amanda slept little and in the beginning light of early morning, rose from her bed, changed her infant, and nursed him. Leaving him gurgling in his cradle, she wrapped her robe snugly about her body and left her bedroom.

The delicious aroma of coffee filled her senses, and the snapping sounds of frying bacon welcomed her, as she edged into the kitchen. Reed stood at the stove, deftly laying thickly sliced potatoes into the pan of bacon fat to fry. A bowl of flour mixed and ready to make into biscuits waited only for those long, brown hands. The tantalizing odors made Amanda faint with hunger this morning.

Fascinated at the picture he made, going about the tasks of preparing a meal, she slipped into the nearest chair without a word, positive he was unaware of her presence. Shortly, he filled a thick mug to the brim with the freshly made coffee and turning, set it before her. "Morning ma'am." The mischievous twinkle in his eyes set her to wondering what other wild ideas were spinning about in that head of his.

"Morning, yourself. Did you sleep at all?"

"Plenty." He stirred the snapping potatoes, and then finished rolling out his biscuits. He had everything well in hand and the smell of the forthcoming breakfast made her swallow without thinking, reminding herself of Piddely at the sight of food.

"A woman could get used to this sort of thing." She'd had to say it, despite knowing how he'd respond.

Their closeness had intensified, and she'd noticed he watched for any small opening to make up to her. It dawned on Amanda that Reed was courting her in every way the man could devise. The realization hit her with an excitement she hardly dared to believe. She couldn't hide the wide smile crossing her face and wondered: *Does he realize what he's doing?*

If Reed had a retort in mind to go along with the burning look he cast her way, it was cut short as Toliver came sauntering in, booted, belted, and ready to ride. He took another chair at the table. "Say, Reed, taking on the cooking now, are you?"

Reed turned back to the stove, poured the man a coffee, and set it before him. "Morning sheriff."

Without another word, he returned to his task of cutting the biscuits. Amanda believed he'd made enough for half of Artesia again this morning as he placed them in a large pan with those finely formed hands of his and shoved them into the oven.

To her, he had the hands of a city man. Though browned as they were, they were finer than that of a cowhand, and the sight of them made intensely heated images race through her mind. She couldn't stop imagining Reed's hands on her body, doing those intimate things that she worried so much about. Somehow, the thought of *this* man doing such things didn't seem so dreadful. She shivered, hoping it didn't show.

"Ready to ride, later?" Toliver asked, seemingly unaware of the tension so rampant in the kitchen.

"I reckon so,"

Reed avoided looking at Amanda. He knew how she felt about his visits to Artesia and was delighted in the fact she'd shown a good bit of jealousy. He didn't mind edging her a bit, but with things unsettled between them, he wanted to go carefully and not worry her unnecessarily.

Marianna came into the kitchen, dragging her ragged blanket. She never noticed her mother, but spotting Reed, went straight to him.

"Weed, I hungy."

He picked her up and settled her beside Amanda, her blanket across her lap. "Here you go, Marianna," he said. "Get ready to eat a big breakfast."

She raised adoring eyes to him, giggled, and looked at her mother. "Weed cook, Mommy."

He winked at Amanda and again the thrills raced through her. After last night, the sight of that lanky man working in her kitchen made the heated memory of his kisses return full force.

Reed had lit a fire inside of her and left his mark on her, far deeper than she'd realized. She had no defense against how she felt. She couldn't stop thinking about the gentle, caressing way his hands had felt going down her back and across her body. Her welcoming cup of coffee sat cooling in the cup as she relived the way his kisses had burned on her lips.

They sat to eat. Few words were spoken except for Amanda helping Marianna. She cut her bacon and buttered her biscuit, all the while worrying that Reed was headed into Artesia and, without a doubt, into the arms of the Saldana woman. Amanda couldn't help the sick feeling in her stomach at the thoughts of Reed in that woman's embrace.

Whatever reasons the sheriff had up his sleeve, she disliked the burning jealousy that raged in her mind about his involving Reed until she sternly reminded herself: *He is not my man and will be drifting away when he's ready, so why do I worry about it?*

She directed a question to the sheriff, her eyebrows raised. "What are your plans when you reach Artesia, then?"

"I've a few ideas roaming around in my head," Toliver replied. "Reed seems to have attracted the attention of a certain suspect and it's my hope he can find certain evidence I need if I'm ever to solve your husband's murder."

"If Harvey was killed near Albuquerque, why don't *they* solve it?" Amanda questioned, her eyebrows drawn into a straight line. "How is it your responsibility?"

"I believe it was a suspect or suspects from Artesia who planned it and benefited from it. I've forwarded that information to Albuquerque."

"Who is it—that Saldana woman?" She couldn't help the suspicion in her narrowed eyes and voice. She'd had a good sniff of the woman's perfume on Reed, and on Harvey, too.

"Could be. I've been suspicious of that and more from the likes of her." Seeing her start in alarm, Toliver hastened to explain. "Ma'am, I see your worry about Reed's involvement, and it's true, she looks for men with money and shines up to them." He shook his head. "And as we know, all too often, they end up like your Harvey. I've got to put a stop to it."

And place Reed's life in danger to figure it out? Sick inside, she couldn't say it aloud. She merely looked at Reed, feeling the blood drain from her face.

Seeing the stricken look in her eyes, Reed spoke to reassure her. "I'll be on watch. She thinks I'm this fancy dude with a bundle of money, so she'll be careful of me."

"Enough people know you aren't. If she's as smart as everyone thinks, will she not know about that, too?"

Amanda got up from the table and left the room, frustrated and frightened by the latest attempts of these two fools trying to bring that evil woman to justice. *The sheriff hasn't caught her in all these years, how is he going to do it now?* She went into her bedroom. With a defeating sense of hopelessness about the outcome, she didn't want to look at either one of them.

The men were ready to ride and Reed sought her out, knocking on her bedroom door. Amanda opened it to see him wearing those fine-looking clothes again and her heart took a wild leap that left her breathless.

His dark eyes burned with feeling. "We'll be leaving now."

She took in the fine figure he cut, dressed fit to kill in those clothes. She looked up at him, wondering if it might be for the last time. "Will you please be careful?" She could barely speak because of her fear for him.

Anything could happen when he reached town. She might never lay eyes on this gentle, caring man again. She hesitated, but had to say what was on her mind. "Reed, after last night, I've come to see that things between us maybe could be…" She didn't have the words to go on.

Her heart was in her eyes and he saw the shimmer of tears. She worried about him and cared for him. His heart soared to the heavens.

"I know, Amanda my dearest, we'll have it out as soon as I return." He grabbed her and kissed her deeply. His kiss was so much more than a goodbye peck. The intensity of it left a turbulent trail of heated streaks that swept through her body like a rapidly striking lightning storm. He released her, turned away, walked out of the house and mounted his horse.

Watching out the kitchen window again, she saw the men ride away. Reed rode Spotty beside the sheriff, heading for Artesia, and into that devil woman's arms. He never turned to look back before they disappeared from sight, and desolation filled her mind. She worried she'd seen the last of him.

"He says it's to find Harvey's killers, but how do I know? How does any woman know what her man is up to?" She fought her tears as she turned to care for her fussing infant, never realizing how easily she'd referred to Reed as her man.

℄ℨ℄ℨ

Reed and Toliver reached Artesia in the early afternoon and entered the sheriff's office. He stood face to face with Bart Day, carefully observing the man's face for signs of recognition and, with relief, saw none. *The man who never forgets a face, eh?* With a slight smile across his face, he decided to let the devil take the hindmost and not fret about it. He had bigger worries ahead.

"How you plannin' to handle seeing what kind of rifle she might have on her premises?" Toliver asked.

"You mean how do I keep from getting myself killed?" Reed snorted. "Which way do you want it? I've had a bullet or two thrown my way already."

"You ever plannin' to tell me about that?"

Reed went on to explain about the shot fired when he'd left town after the last visit to Mercedes.

"Like that, is it? Saldana might be on to you then, or could be Ramon's takin' things into his own hands."

"Getting more of the Saldana woman's perfume on my clothes won't set well with Amanda." He shook his head. *All this for a damned Springfield rifle. Is it worth it when so many folks about carry the same weapon?* As far as Reed was concerned, he wanted nothing more to do with that devil female. Facing his next encounter with her to please the sheriff was more than he'd asked for.

"Hungry, Reed?" Toliver winked. "Ready to stick that good-looking neck of yours in the noose?"

Reed shrugged, "Starving, you bastard."

Returning Harvey's nice Silver Beaver to his sweat-streaked black hair, Reed headed down the boardwalk to the cantina with Toliver. It was too early for supper, yet the place was humming. Music blared out into the dusty street, and Reed's heart rate increased with every step.

They entered and took seats at a small oilcloth-covered table of a size to fit two patrons.

A young boy murmured, "*Hola, señores,*" and laid a menu before them, spotted and tattered as before.

Reed made a pretense of reading it while glancing about the room. Few tables were open. The place bustled with sounds of clinking crockery, muffled conversations, and the odor of sweating males intermixed with tantalizing odors of Mexican cuisine. His stomach rumbled and, being damned hungry, he looked forward to the meal in spite of the deadly side issues associated with it.

The wafting of her perfume preceded her presence. With racing heart, he looked up into the sultry eyes of the lovely Mercedes. But, the glittering message written there was not the same inviting one he'd expected. Something had changed inside her. She offered no seductive come hither looks and, by her icy glare and rigid jaw, he saw he'd lost her favor.

He nodded to her, made his selection, "*La especial, por favor,*" and returned his gaze to the table top. Something had happened. *Did she suspect him of playing falsely with her?* He'd let things ride at present. She hadn't finished with him. Somehow, he knew that, too.

Toliver had a question in his eye, as he gave the same order. "Looks like she don't cotton to you anymore, don't it?" He coughed and reached for the water the boy had brought. After a few swallows, he went on. "You do or say anything to make her suspect you?"

"Not that I can think of." Reed felt his own brow tense. "Of course, I didn't hand her a bundle of money the last time I saw her, either." Things weren't going right, not for what he was expected to do. He felt a sense of relief about it. "Let's see how this meal goes. She took to me once, maybe she will again," he muttered. "Then, again, maybe I've lost my charm for the ladies. More likely, she'll be looking to slit my throat."

"I don't think so, you good looking bastard. I see how that pretty lady out at the ranch eyes you. If I don't miss my guess, she's got you in her sights."

Reed laughed. "Maybe you don't know what you're seeing, then. I could tell *you* a tall tale." He felt the heat rising in his cheeks and hoped he wasn't blushing like a damned fool.

Mercedes brought both heavily laden platters, interrupting their conversation, and set them before the men. She stared into Reed's eyes with a chilling gaze as she set his meal down. She said nothing, nor made any of her usual sultry moves to display her ample charms—other than the clothes she wore. Those were still seductive, in any case. He kept his eyes peeled, but noted no overt movement—no pushed out breasts or swaying posterior. Perhaps if he was a lucky man, she was done with him.

Yet he had the feeling she had more to say to him—alone, away from Toliver. "She wants to say something to me, sheriff, but you're in the way."

"How the hell you figure that?"

"She does, I can see it. Any chance your office needs you right away?" he asked, urging the man to make an early departure.

If the lovely and deadly Mercedes wanted a confab with him, he'd give her the chance and see what was on her mind.

"Not until I eat, son." Toliver leisurely finished his meal, then rose from the table, announcing in a conversational tone. "Well, I've got things to do, might need to see you later on before you head on home." He laid money on the table, enough for two, and took his leave.

Reed sat alone, nursing the coffee he detested. As good as the food always proved to be, the coffee remained distasteful. "Maybe it's only me, never could get around the taste of this damned chicory," he murmured as he waited.

Before long, she sidled near enough to say in a lowered voice, "I must speak with you, only you, *señor.*"

Her message, accompanied by a withering look, was not the one he expected. Yet what she had to say might be worth hearing and he planned on listening. He nodded his assent.

CHAPTER 25

After another half hour, he moved out onto the street, unhurried and watchful. He strolled aimlessly, waiting for her contact and his heart rate increased with the waiting. From his prison days, he'd learned to have eyes in the back of his head. It'd kept him from assault more than once. Wary that the big Mexican, Ramon, often followed him, he saw no sign of him, but couldn't be sure.

In time, a small boy came close, grasped his sleeve and tugged. "You c—come m—me, *señor*." He stuttered the unfamiliar words, pulled, and beckoned.

Reed went with him, down the same street as before. This time of day, with the illumination of the sun, the house was cast in a different light. A very fine-appearing hacienda made of thousands of sun-dried adobe bricks, the home appeared to be well-tended and gracious. The clinging feel of evil was not dispelled by the sunlight and he shivered involuntarily. Was it because he knew the evil that lay within?

Entering the cool shadows of the entryway, he waited. The boy pulled a finely braided rope and quickly disappeared. After a few short moments, the inner door opened and Reed was rewarded by the sight of Mercedes gliding toward him on bare feet. She'd changed into a satiny, clinging blouse, gathered so loosely about the neck, it revealed more than it covered.

He gasped, seeing her erect nipples pushing outward beneath the shimmering fabric. The wildly colored skirt, spread out from a tiny waist, flowed with the motion of her swaying walk. Her finely shaped feet, well-manicured, peeped from beneath. He wondered why she wore no shoes.

"*Ah, señor,* you come." She wore the same perfume and the heavy, seductive scent of it seeped into his senses as she came close. Friendlier now, she still carried an icy edge. She did not touch him or grasp his hand. He kept his guard up and his hidden pistol handy while he waited to hear what had gotten into her craw. She was angry; he had no doubt, and she hid it poorly.

She led him to the same wide, softened-leather couch strewn with soft pillows of many bright colors. The very appearance of it suggested the many love trysts he'd heard about and imagined. He was only guessing at that, but it fit with what he knew.

She said nothing for several long moments then came right to the point, staring coldly into his eyes. "You have woman?"

"No woman, only my sister."

"You lie to me, *señor*, you lie!"

Her anger boiled over so quickly, he watched for the hidden dagger she'd been known to use. A slim, razor sharp stiletto, he'd heard about, but he didn't plan to be among the chosen few who'd felt it sliding into their flesh, beneath their ribs, and into their vitals.

"I have said nothing to you of my personal business. Not one word, ma'am. Not one word." He grasped her shoulders. "What is it you want with me?"

She twisted away from his touch. "What I want of you?" She uttered a mocking laugh. "I only want what is mine, *señor. Por Dios, que mucho.*"

She suddenly became hopelessly enraged, rattling on in rapid-fire Spanish. He could not grasp enough meaning to make sense of it. With clenched fists and the snarling features her face had assumed, he realized she verged on hysterics, but in Spanish, he wasn't sure of that either.

After a while, she settled down a bit and faced him again. "You lie, *señor*, I know thees." She laughed in his face. "I take care *your* place, I take care good. Ramon, he go, see your woman." She spit out the words. "My man, Ramon, he see you. He say, she *your woman*—no *hermana*." She shook her head then nodded knowingly. "He see you kees her, love her."

Her face darkened with pent-up rage. Her clenched teeth and tight fists were in his face. Her speech became increasingly laced with her own language. He believed she was becoming rabidly violent. Perhaps she'd use her little knife.

"Ramon was out there—at the ranch?" In fear for Amanda, he reached for her, ready to strangle it out of her. "He's out there, now?" He kept away from her slender throat, clutching firmly onto her velvety shoulders, and shook her. "Tell me!"

Hate emanated from her black eyes and, in amazement, Reed watched hatred destroy the beauty of a woman's face. Mounting anger and greed changed the lovely Mercedes into an ugly, enraged harridan right before his very eyes.

In frustration, he shook her again demanding, "What the hell do you *want* of me—what am I to *you?*" The knowledge that Amanda's place had been under observation for this woman's purposes, filled him with anger.

"It was you, *señor*, I wanted you. Many nights I long for you—so much."

She wriggled her hips, suggestively touching herself in the groin. Then she tossed her head and stamped her bare feet, to show her seething hatred of a man she believed had rebuffed her, betrayed her. Then suddenly, she changed and softened toward him.

"I wanted only you, *mi amore*." Her voice softened with those last words, as if hoping her desperately uttered words of love and burning desire could entice him if she tried hard enough.

She's fallen in love with me, and wants me? Sick with disgust, Reed wanted to reason with her, but he'd seen her anger for what it really was. *This fool woman is mad—stark raving mad! Her nefarious scheme to regain what'd never belonged to her in the first place has become an obsession to the point of insanity.* He'd never seen madness before, but he'd read of it and heard about it. And he certainly recognized insanity in this woman's actions—and in her erratic beliefs.

No one would be safe with this woman running amok. In her state of rage, Mercedes Saldana would readily kill, without guilt or remorse, anyone who stood in her path.

Reed, desperate with fear and worry for Amanda, shook Mercedes again. "You say Ramon is at the ranch now?" Facing her, and forgetting his own danger, he held his rage inside, trying to use the voice of reason. "If he touches Amanda, or her babies, he'll answer to me. You'd best call him off, my dear." His voice had become a low growl as he clutched her even tighter by the shoulders. "He lays a hand on her, I'll find him and kill him. You have my word on that."

Reed, unable to abide another moment in this monster's presence, turned to head out the door. Mercedes leaped in front of him, barring his escape, her teeth bared, and eyes glowing wild as a rabid wolf.

"Ramon, he do what I wish. I say go your ranch, he go!" she panted. "You no leave me, *señor*, you stay weeth me."

She reached out for him. No seductive moves now, only the insane grasping of a mad woman. Her lovely painted nails had become claws, and her flowing black hair like that of a hag from hell!

He no longer cared about looking for a Springfield Rifle. Fear for Amanda and her children had frozen his insides. Having no time to lose, he shoved her aside to gain the door. Within a split second of hearing the whisper of sound behind his back, he felt the sharp burning pain of a knife wound.

She'd missed his heart, her chosen target. He felt the graze and the warmth of flowing blood. It left a trail of crimson streaking down his arm, soiling the shirt he wore. It didn't slow him. It only infuriated the hell out of him.

"You crazy bitch!" Reed roared.

Turning, he raised his right hand, back handed her across the face, and left her lying on the floor of her entry-way. He left her door and raced frantically down the streets toward the sheriff's office. By the time he reached it, he was wheezing and gasping for air.

"What the hell!" Toliver rushed to his side, sat him in a chair, and pumped him for information. He listened as Reed gasped out his story.

"You're saying that Mex bitch has sent that damned Ramon out there to that ranch and Amanda's alone with those babies?" Toliver swore. "Son of a bitch! We've got no time to lose! That Saldana woman's gone off the deep end of the damned river, Reed. We'd better get to hell out to that ranch." He grabbed his hat and left orders for his deputy. "Bart, if you can shove that she-devil in a cell for assault and attempted murder, please, go and do it. Be damned careful and take some help. The woman's gone plum loco."

They saddled their horses as fast as they could. Their own excitement transferred to the horses and, when they mounted them, the agitated animals provided a few hump-backed bucks and end-swaps, until the men applied their spurs and tore onto the trail, their mounts in a dead run.

Fearing what they'd find at the ranch, Reed maintained a stony silence, his eyes grim and jaw tight. His face felt like granite as he rode. They urged the horses as fast as they dared and still get them to the ranch alive. Five miles seemed like five hundred.

CHAPTER 26

Mercedes Saldana rose from the tiles of the entry-way and sat up. Shaking her head to clear away the confusion, she crawled slowly to her couch. The tall, fine-looking man was gone. She groaned, twisting the fringe off the pillows, stamped her foot, and threw the glass of tequila she'd made for the finely dressed *gringo* smashing against the far wall. "He very strong. I want him. He care nothing for me or what I can give to heem. *Por Dios*! What must I do to make him want me?"

He'd aroused a desperate need within her then refused her lush body and all she'd offered. She cried out, flinging her arms about in rage at his rejection, and drew her eyes into narrow slits. "I see if he have woman, I must know!"

❦❦❦

Amanda, seeing no smoke pouring from the bunk-house, surmised Reed had given the men their orders for the day. It crossed her mind that she no longer worried about Jud. He never approached her now, realizing she'd let Reed know if he did.

Marianna and Piddely accompanied her to the garden. She knew it'd be well watered and now she knew who her benefactor was, too. As they walked among the green rows, Amanda carefully explained how to choose the right plants to pick and allow the others time to grow bigger, selecting several for Marianna to pull.

"See, Mommy, I pick it!" Her small hands barely grasped the green fronds of the carrots, but she pulled one out and soon had the dirt from it smeared across the front of her dress and face as she nibbled on it.

When they returned to the house, Amanda cleaned the kitchen, bathed her infant, dressed, and fed him. Restless and worried, not knowing how things would go in Artesia, she changed her worries to Helen and decided to drive over and see her.

It took a while to get the buggy out and the old mare harnessed but the children cooperated and finally, with baby Reed tucked the large padded box behind the seat, she and Marianna drove away. It was near five miles, she guessed, but she wanted to know about her friend. Aside from that concern, it felt good to be out and doing things again.

It took nearly two long hours on the roughened trail to the K Bar O ranch. She pulled up in front of the house, and Bennie ran out, his mouth forming an O at the sight of her driving the buggy. He quickly recovered his manners, doffed his hat, and said, "Howdy ma'am, get down and come on in."

He reached up to help Marianna down. Amanda got down, handed the reins to Bennie, and took up her fussing son, who was hungry again and in need of care. She entered the home to find Helen dressed and sitting in a chair. Her color had pinked up nicely, considering what she'd suffered. She looked good, and she was alive.

Amanda stood looking at her friend. "Helen, you look just fine. I had to come and see how you were making out after that operation."

"Those two men saved my life, and I'll never forget it," Helen said, waving Amanda to a handy chair. "I was terribly sick for a few days with a fever, but I'm on the mend, now." She changed the topic from Amanda's interest to her own. "And how is it with you—and that wandering savior of yours?"

Amanda hastily put her baby to her breast to stop his fussing, but she couldn't stop the blazing rush of heat that flushed up her neck and into her cheeks. "He's all right, just fine, Helen."

Her answer was in no way satisfactory to the older woman. With a look of exasperation across her face, Helen said, "There's more to tell, now isn't there?" She laughed. "You'd better tell me, I can see for myself, things have progressed between you two." Helen frowned. "Please don't mind my saying so, but I knew how it must have been with Harvey. I've known it all along and I didn't see you suffering all that much at the loss of him. I believe we're close enough that I can speak plainly."

She reached out to pat Amanda on the shoulder. "Reed is no way the same kind of man. You must know that. There's a lot more to him than he's saying. How could he know so much about that operation business, when the doctor didn't even know?"

"He said he went to school in Kansas and has studied law."

"Law, now is it? Looks to me, like he's studied a lot more than that." Driven by curiosity, Helen continued. "I'm seeing, by the look on your face, there's something going on between you two. There is, isn't there?"

Amanda flushed again. "He's mentioned marriage to me, but after my first try at it, I don't think I have what it takes to make any man a decent wife. I don't know how I could possibly go through all that again."

"Mumph—in light of the warrants out against him, that's a mighty bold thing to ask a woman. Hasn't got a dime to his name, either, has he?"

Amanda changed the baby to her other breast. "I wouldn't care about money, but Helen, if they took him away, I couldn't stand that." Amanda's lips tightened and worry lines crossed her brow. "The sheriff told us that one of the deputies in town has seen the wanted poster on him and that man never forgets a face. He brags on it." She felt her face grow cold. "What then?"

Helen sat back in her chair. "Lord have mercy— Toliver told you that?"

"Yes, he was out to talk Reed into getting involved in some fool notion of his, trying to get evidence on that Saldana woman," Amanda huffed. "Now he's gone off to Artesia to help the sheriff with some other hair-brained idea to find something to convict her or the man who works for her. Toliver wants him to play along with her to see if he can find a certain rifle." Amanda sighed. "He knows full well that men who mix with her are usually found dead."

"Huh! Play along with her? Amanda, if she finds out he hasn't any money, she'll likely want to do the killing herself."

"It's no joke Helen. I'm worried for so many reasons."

"I can think of one good reason, my dear."

What do you mean?"

Helen flashed a knowing smile. "You're crazy in love with that man, I can see it on your face plain as day—you are!"

"Impossible!" Amanda flushed hot to the roots of her tresses. "I've already told him I'm planning to open a dress shop or restaurant to support myself and my children." She was adamant. "I'll never be able to pay off the debts Harvey's put on our place, and at home, I never had anything to do with running cattle. My father didn't think it seemly for womenfolk to be out among those terrible cussing cowboys." Amanda got a dreamy look across her face. "I believe I'd do well enough on my own. I'd like to have a dress shop or something, and support myself and my children in a small town, preferably in Colorado."

"I doubt that will ever happen." Helen laughed. "In this country a woman needs a husband to take care of her and her children. Life is tough enough for females in this western country without you trying to go it alone." She bent

closer. "And, dear girl, have you looked into a mirror lately? You are a very beautiful young woman. With all the
lonely men in this territory, they'll make your life a living
hell, sparkin' after you and trying to get you to marry one of
'em. You'd never have a peaceful moment to yourself, my
dear." She chuckled softly. "No, Amanda, you sure
wouldn't."

"Well, you certainly paint a dismal picture of things.
But getting married to Reed or any other man, means putting up with certain things. It's something I can't speak of—
but I refuse to go through all that again."

Seeing the distress on Amanda's face, Helen patted her
shoulder. "You poor soul, don't you know? It can be so different! I can't prove it to you, no one can." She lowered her
voice. "Well, excepting that long drink of water off the trail.
He could—he's got the look."

"What look is that?" Amanda felt light headed with all
this crazy talk.

"Never mind, dear, it's not something for a body to
speak of it, but I must tell you, with the right man, certain
things can be mighty close to heaven, they can." Helen
smiled, nodding. "Herb's the right man for me, always
was."

Amanda couldn't argue with the serene look on Hel-
en's face. Baby Reed had fallen asleep, and Amanda, glad
to get away from Helen's discussion of intimate things,
rushed away to lay him down.

When she returned, Helen rattled on. She wasn't done
with Amanda as far as her ability to be a wife. "Amanda,
down on his luck or not, I'd say you're one lucky woman
that tall drink of water came riding along. You've got a
ways to go, girl, but if that Reed is the man I think he is,
he'll bring you around." She chuckled. "My dear, you are in
for a real special ride down the man-woman trail."

Speechless, Amanda stared as Helen got up to make a
bite to eat. Thinking and wondering at Helen's words, she
went to help her lay out cold beans and biscuits with a pan

of apple crisps that Bennie had made. She called the children in to eat. They enjoyed a quiet meal and drank diluted apple juice, or cold milk.

Helen's fare was simple, the best she could do in her state of recovery. Marianna yawned, tired after playing so hard with Bennie.

Amanda grew restless. "We'd best head on home if we're to get there before dark. I don't know when to expect Reed back from Artesia—if ever."

Hearing the forlorn note that had crept into her voice, Helen couldn't help her parting comment. "My dear, I still say you're crazy in love with that man whether you know it or not."

She sent Bennie to hitch the horse to the buggy again and soon waved them away.

With the children settled, Amanda drove toward her ranch. It'd been a good visit, and one she'd needed. Talking with another woman was always a comfort. With Marianna settled on a layer of blankets alongside the baby's box, Amanda drove in a dreamlike state thinking and remembering how Reed's lips had taken possession of hers to the point she had no will of her own. *He isn't at all the way Harvey was. Could Helen be right about things being good, or maybe even wonderful between a man and a woman?*

As she neared the ranch, she saw an orange glow shimmering against the few clouds in the sky. "Could that be fire?"

Her heart leaping in her chest, she slapped the reins against the horse's rump and hurried onward. Close enough to smell the heavy acrid smoke of burning buildings before she saw the fire, Amanda hoped and prayed it wasn't her home with all her possessions.

She flapped the reins harder over the mare's tired back, urging her into a trot. It made the ride much rougher, but fear of seeing her home destroyed, pushed her on. The frightened cries of Marianna and her baby never stopped her onward rush. "My God, the house is going up in flames!"

Reaching the ranch yard, she saw with relief the house remained intact. But the barn appeared fully engulfed in flames. Jud and Buddy ran madly with puny buckets of water from the horse trough trying to put it out. They scooped water and rushed to throw it into the roaring flames. In spite of their efforts the barn rapidly reached the stage of total loss.

Their reddened faces looked scorched and blistered from the heat. Finally, in utter futility, the men stopped and stood back, silently watching. The major supports had burned through and the roof crashed to the ground sending out a rush of flames, smoke, and burning ashes. Her horse reared up at the sight. Amanda pulled on the reins to settle her.

Marianna, staring at the flames, grabbed at her mother's shoulder with fearful hands. "Mommy, it burns!"

Amanda got her down and told her to go to the house. Taking up the fussing baby, she went up to Buddy. "How'd this start? Any animals in the barn?"

"We didn't see it start, but kind of sudden-like, we heard the crackling and ran out to find it going like blazes." He remembered her question. "No animals was in there, none of 'em needed bein' there just now." He shook his head. "We just rode in a while ago and everything was fine. But later as we made supper, we heard popping an' cracklin'. We come runnin' out, seen it going like blazes, nearly all through it. We started fighting it right away, but she's sure enough a goner," he said, "Ma'am, we got out all the saddles, harness, and tack we could but we lost some of it."

His words were punctuated by the last few timbers crashing to the floor, sending the flames flaring momentarily higher.

Jud came up to them. "Sorry for this to happen, ma'am. Didn't see no one around here, but when daylight comes again, I'll be looking for tracks. No way in hell this barn caught fire on its own, no way a'tall." He shook his sooty head, looking at her through reddened eyes.

Amanda nodded to them and, holding baby Reed, walked slowly to her home. He was awake but not crying, as if he knew a part of his heritage had just burned to the ground.

Buddy took care of the horse while she entered the safety of her house, glad it'd been spared. Jud's suspicions took hold in her thoughts, "Is someone out to ruin me even further?"

A cold chill settled over her, setting her on edge. Nervous, she took comfort having those two cowboys nearby and turned her thoughts to caring for her children.

She lit a lamp, settled the baby, and fixed something for herself and Marianna. She didn't bother to look out the kitchen window at the smoldering embers of the barn. It was more than she could handle right now. A few tears coursed down her soot-laden cheeks.

She sat quietly at the table eating a cold biscuit and apple butter. Marianna sat on the floor with Piddely, giggling and petting him. The dog appeared uneasy. He growled frequently and paced about. Amanda paid little attention to the dog's restlessness.

But at the sound of a footstep—or was it the creaking of a weighted step on a wooden floor? —a chill coursed through her body. Her head went erect and her heart began to hammer. That strange sound came from somewhere inside the house and, hearing it again, she knew instantly something or someone was lurking in her house. It wasn't—it couldn't be one of her men! They were outside. She heard someone moving about in another room, listened a moment, then called out in a tentative voice. "Is someone in here?" She heard no reply.

Piddely growled louder, his hackles up as he faced her bedroom. Amanda took it as a warning and raced to that dark chamber to check on her baby. Inside the dimly lit room, she heaved a sigh of relief. He slept peacefully, yet something made her stop.

She caught the scent of male sweat and, listening carefully, heard breathing. *If I had hackles like Piddely, they'd
be flaring like blazes right now.*

Icy with fear and anger, and desperate to protect her
children, she sidled to her low-slung dresser and leaned
against it. She slowly slid open a drawer. Harvey always
kept a loaded pistol there, and that was one thing her father
had taught her—how to use one.

Feeling the cold, hard steel of it, she furtively took it up
with a folded bit of diaper cloth and held it close in the folds
of her dress. If the man had seen her take up the gun, hopefully he'd think she picked up an item of clothing for the
child.

As she grabbed up her infant and headed for the door, a
solid figure stepped in front of her, blocking her escape.
Piddely, snarling low, advanced on the man with bared
teeth.

She heard a low chuckle as the man faced the dog.
When Piddely flew at him, snarling, with teeth bared, the
man gave him a vicious kick, flinging his small body
against the wall. He yelped and slunk down, growling deeply and readying for another charge. This time he leapt for
the man's leg, his small teeth bared, and met another vicious
kick that left him in a motionless heap on the floor.

"*Hola, señora,* we are meeting at last." Ignoring the
moaning dog, Amanda froze as an accented, male voice
came out of the darkness.

CHAPTER 27

"Who are you and what are you doing in my home?" Though terror filled her veins with ice, she held herself solidly together. She had babies and would readily give her life for either of them. Her hand gripped the cold steel of the revolver. The feel of it settled and comforted her.

"*Su casa, señora?*" He asked with a low, guttural laugh. "Nothing here belongs you, *nada.*"

She heard his snarl of disdain. "Get out now, I warn you." She kept her voice, low and intense. Knowing the man thought her a defenseless female he need not fear, she had an advantage. Holding her infant close in her left arm, she lifted the gun in her right hand, cocked and ready. "Step outside and leave this property. If you do not, I will do what I must for my children—but I will protect them."

She meant every word and stood ready to prove it, finding an inner strength she hadn't been aware of until this moment.

"I go, *señora,* but I soon return. All this is for me and mine." He snarled the words, steeped in disdain, as he edged for the door. Amanda stood back to allow his exit.

"If all this is yours, as you say, why burn the barn?"

"To make warning for you." He backed into the larger room, heading for the door, but he stopped his exit at seeing Marianna. He started for her. "Ah, I so long time wish for *la*

nina. Esta muy bonita. I will have her, too." He laughed at
Amanda as he reached for her daughter. Piddely had recovered enough to leap toward his bare arm. "Iyee-ee *car-
umba!*" he cried in pain.

Flinging the dog aside, he clutched his bleeding arm.
Marianna, unaware of her own danger, sat on the floor, staring up at him.

Tears formed in her deep blue eyes. "Hurt my doggie!"

The strange man, big and powerfully built, blood dripping from his torn arm, reached out for the child, seeking to
steal her away from her mother.

Amanda screamed, "No!" The strange dark-eyed man
turned to face Amanda with a laugh on his lips and raised
his fist toward her. Without another word she brought the
pistol up and shot him full in the chest. "No you won't!
You'll not take my child!"

She watched in silent horror as the man gasped in
shock and surprise, grabbed feebly at his chest and, with a
look of utter disbelief on his dark face, crumpled to the
floor. He lay motionless, gasping out his last few breaths.
Amanda stood frozen, prepared to fire again if he moved.

He lay dying, blood oozing from his mouth and, and by
the dimness of lamplight, she saw his vision fade and die
away.

The icy coldness of terror left her, and the shock of
what'd happened in her home, settled over her. At the sound
of running footsteps, she turned to see the comforting sight
of Jud and Buddy come roaring into the house. "Oh, thank
God, you're here!" she cried.

Jud looked down at the man crumpled on the floor,
blood draining from beneath him. His head was turned
enough to see his open mouth draining blood. Amanda
stood motionless. Marianna had reached her side, and stood
huddled against her, clutching her skirts.

Standing there like the avenging angel she was, her infant in her left arm and a smoking pistol in her right hand,

Amanda began sobbing in great gasps. "He tried to take Marianna," was all she could manage to say.

"Good God, Buddy, look what she done!" Jud prodded the man with his foot. "Shot the bastard right through the heart, lungs, or both. He's a goner, that's for damned sure."

Piddely, hackles raised, limped over and sniffed the man's body.

Jud looked at Amanda with new eyes. "Ma'am, you 'spose he's the one started the fire out there?"

"He said this place was his and he set the fire as a warning." She drew a ragged breath. "That's all he said. But I can't imagine why he'd want to burn the place down if it was his, like he said." She laid her struggling baby down in one of the chairs, set Marianna beside him, and cautioned her as she dried her eyes. "Keep him from falling off now; you mind him."

She straightened up and drew a deep breath. "I gave him the chance to leave, but not with my *daughter*—he—he tried to take her." She barely whispered the words, refusing to give in to hysterics before her daughter or either of the men. "I had to do what I did and I'd do it again." Her jaw firm, she took another deep breath and reached over to pat her daughter's head. "Either of you know who he is?"

"Looks like that big Mex, Ramon. He's always hanging around the Saldana woman," Jud put in. He looked at Amanda. "Ma'am, your face is real white. You all right?"

"I will be—just a little upset after something like this."

"I hear he does a lot of work for her and none of it good. Looks like you done the sheriff a real big favor, ma'am," Jud said.

Amanda wasn't so upset that she missed the renewed look of respect in his eyes. Jud glanced at Buddy and nodded. "Maybe we might pull this carcass outta here. He's messing up the floor, looks like."

Their unhurried discussion about attending to things tended to sooth Amanda's roiling nerves. She sat beside her children, shaking and sweating. She'd never imagined shooting or killing anyone. It'd happened so fast she couldn't grasp the reality of it.

She kept seeing it over and over in her mind, playing out what she might have done against what she'd had to do. But uppermost in her mind lay the fact that she'd never allow any man to lay a hand on one of her children and that was all there was to it.

"What was he to The Saldana woman, and why was he here? What'd that have to do with Harvey?" she asked the empty room.

The two men were outside tending to Ramon's body. She supposed those things were connected somehow, or had to do with that Spanish land grant business. Right now, Amanda wished she'd never heard of it. And Reed had gone in town to see that evil woman. *What was happening to him*? Those images took hold in her mind, adding to her distress.

Gathering her strength, she took Marianna into the kitchen and poured her a glass of milk. "Drink this sweetheart, it'll help you sleep."

"I 'fraid, Mommy. Where Weed?"

"He's not back yet, but maybe when you wake up in the morning, he'll be right here. You can sleep in my bed with me tonight and we'll have Piddely on the bed, too." She squeezed her daughter. "What a good dog he is, going after that bad man."

With a lot of coaxing and, with her sitting on the bedside, the child finally drifted off. Amanda covered her with a quilt. Her dog lay beside her, looking at Amanda with woeful eyes. She patted him and left the room.

She wiped up the blood and scrubbed the site with lye soap until she couldn't find a trace of it in the dimness of the lamplight. What the boys had done with the body, she had no idea and didn't care. She only wished for the sight of Reed and imagined herself being held in the warmth and comfort of his arms when he came home—if he came home. She had that worry, too. Maybe the evil woman had used her knife on him. Amanda knew it was possible, certainly, after what she'd just encountered.

If he made it home and wanted to, she planned let him hold her as much as he wanted. He always had a way of making things right for her. She'd grown used to his being there, always competent, never intrusive, warm and support- ive.

Thinking about him, she realized he'd more than prov- en himself to be a man a woman could trust and lean on. She'd rapidly begun to face how lonely her life would be when he left her and headed north again. The loss of him meant loneliness and desolation for herself—and for Mari- anna, the loss of a wonderful man who would gladly be her father.

She couldn't remember ever having these feelings about Harvey. He'd been so severe about everything, more of an overseer in her eyes than a husband. She smiled to herself, able to forget what had just happened for a moment. *I could have done without the intimate benefits of married life from him, but from Reed? I wonder.*

She sat in a chair, tossing the idea of life with Reed about in her head until she nearly forgot about shooting the Mexican. Tired as she was, she'd never sleep this night without Reed in the house. Remembering her life with Har- vey, she decided his only real gift to her had been the two children. Of him, she had no fond memories, not one.

Jud and Buddy returned, and she asked, "Where did you put him?"

"Well, ma'am, we drug the big fella as far as we could," Jud answered. "He's under a tarp out there until the sheriff can take care of him," he added with a worried ex- pression on his face. "You gonna to be all right, ma'am?"

"I think so, but I keep seeing him reaching for Marian- na." She shivered and fought tears, now that it was over.

"That big *hombre* didn't get very far on that, now did he?"

Appreciating the note of pride in Buddy's voice,

Amanda just smiled. She sat there, tight lipped and tense, trying to understand what Ramon had said. His words kept returning to her. "He said he owned this ranch." That and the terror of seeing the man reach for her daughter, haunted her, chilling her. She saw it over and over again in her mind.

"Wonder what made him say a thing like that," Buddy muttered. Jud said nothing.

Marianna had awakened and crept into her mother's arms. Amanda comforted her. "Don't be afraid, honey, the bad man's all gone."

She raised her eyes to her mother. "Bad man fall down."

Amanda comforted Marianna, crooning to her that the man wanted to take her away, and her momma wouldn't let him.

Marianna smiled. "Weed find me, Momma?"

"Yes, he would, but he went to town, darling."

She rocked and soothed her again until she fell asleep. As for herself, she couldn't sleep without having her daughter close for this fearful night. She laid Marianna in her big bed again. Her baby slept in his crib. Seeing that all was quiet, she crept silently out of the room to wait for Reed.

Buddy and Jud stood waiting for her to return to the room. "We'd best sit with you, ma'am, for the night," Jud said. "No telling if there's more of 'em out there."

That Jud wanted to spend the night in the house, sitting with her, made her skin crawl.

He'd shown himself to be a lot of help during the fire and with the big man's body, but she'd never abide that odious man in her presence that long and didn't want him in her house as she slept.

Remembering his constant hassling of her, she was irritated and angered at the sight of him. "Buddy, would you to sit in one of the chairs here for the night and keep watch?" she asked. "I'd sleep better knowing you were here."

"Well, now, ma'am, I can do that just as well as Buddy

here. Man needs his sleep." Jud wasn't about to let this chance pass him by.

Amanda faced him and declared. "I've used this pistol once tonight, mister, and if you don't get your carcass back to the bunk house, I'll use it again." She was in no mood for Jud's nonsense. "Buddy will do just fine and I won't be sleeping much in any case. I don't think I'll ever sleep again."

The look in her eyes was one Jud hadn't seen before tonight and, after the way she'd dispatched Ramon, he wasn't about to test her further. He left the ranch house with only a few grumbles and cussed angrily as he stepped off the porch, his boots making more noise than needed. Being angry as hell and stomping along in rage was all he had left. Hearing his complaints made Amanda smile for the first time this evening.

"Thank you, Buddy," she said, deciding to let him in on what she knew. "I know you've been watering my garden. I saw you the other night from my window."

He flushed bright red in the lamplight. "Aw, ma'am, it wasn't nuthin'. I seen how you was having to carry that water before and never liked the idea. Just helping out is all." He tried to make light of what he'd done to help her, but he was proud she'd taken notice of his efforts, and that she appreciated it. His face flushed with pleasure and Amanda could see it.

The baby's fretful cry bade her get up and go to his cradle. "Thanks," she repeated. "It's good to know I can depend on you." She smiled over her shoulder at him. "I'll be in here a while, might even try to sleep with you on guard."

She watched his chest swell until the buttons nearly burst on his shirt. He settled back into one of the chairs. "I'm right here, ma'am, and will be as long as you need me."

Amanda had seen Buddy in a new light since she knew of his watering and believed he was a quiet soul who'd never been noticed much in his life. Perhaps, her complement and confidence in him, would give him a well-needed boost of importance.

She tended little Reed and relaxed on the bed. His nursing helped sooth her frazzled nerves, but it would take a lifetime to blot out the way Ramon had crumpled, bleeding, to the floor from her bullet. In her mind, she saw the man clutching his chest, trying to stop the pain. And that sudden look of surprise she'd seen in his eyes continued to haunt her.

She stepped to the bedroom door and bade Buddy good night before settling to sleep, curled snugly around Marianna. Exhausted with the care of her children, recovering from childbirth, the loss of the barn, and the trauma of shooting a man, she fell into a deep sleep in spite of her agitation.

CHAPTER 28

Amanda awakened to the sound of footsteps and the deep tones of male voices. Her heart began a rapid tattoo in her chest and only one thought came through to her senses—Reed was home!

Alert and excited to see his face, she hurriedly pulled on her worn robe, tied it snugly about her waist, and stepped into the sitting room in time to hear Buddy going on to Reed and the sheriff about her deed of the early evening. Shocked at hearing it again, everything came crushing back upon her.

"Yessiree, shore enough, she shot the bastard right where he stood. He was a trying to kidnap her little girl, that's what," the nondescript little cowboy told them, his chest puffed out, embellishing where he could.

Amanda stood there, wrapped in her robe, rubbing her eyes, looking at his rangy form. "Reed, you're home."

So grateful and excited at the sight of him, she felt a flush of heat creep into her cheeks as she slumped into a chair.

"Amanda, I guess I'm a bit late, seeing as how you've taken care of things just fine." He chuckled softly, "My god, woman, you are—"

He couldn't seem to finish his words, but she didn't miss how his eyes shone with his pride. She saw his worried mien and how pale he looked in the lamplight as he came close and looked deeply into her eyes.

"You all right, Amanda?" he asked, his voice husky
with worry,

She wanted to let loose and cry her heart out at the
sight of him, but she got hold of herself and met his gaze.
"Yes, Reed, I'm all right, or I will be if I ever get over what
happened."

Seeing the sheriff standing there, she motioned to a
chair. "Sheriff Toliver, won't you sit down?"

Both men had a multitude of questions on their faces.
She really didn't know where to begin with all that had
happened. She only wanted to crawl into Reed's arms and
rest there.

"We got word you might be having an unwelcome visitor out here and rode as fast as we could, getting here," Toliver said, pride and amazement written all over his face.
He'd already had a lot of overly excited information from
Buddy's detailed story of the burning barn and the way
she'd protected her family. "Looks like you handled it on
your own, right enough."

"He tried to take my daughter, Sheriff, I couldn't let
that—" Her throat closed and her voice trailed off at the
thought of what could have happened.

Reed moved closer, ready to take her in his arms if she
needed him.

Toliver uttered a chuckle and sought to settle the score
on part of it. "You did what had to be done. Of course, you
couldn't let him lay a hand on your girl."

Reed said little, but the shine in his eyes and slight
nodding of his head, made her heart swell nearly out of her
chest. A deep respect shone in his eyes, and pride in her as a
woman and mother, standing up for her family the way she
had.

He cleared his throat, needing to know. "He laid a hand
on you?"

"Ramon never got that close. He wasn't interested in
me, just my little girl, for God's sake! He kept saying this
was *his* ranch. Why would he say a thing like that?"

"Likely has something to do with the money your husband borrowed or the plans he had with the Saldana woman," Toliver told her. "Maybe the bank can straighten that out for us. Borrowed money leaves a trail, one that can be followed. Ramon was a close associate of that Saldana woman. That tells us something." He nodded at the faint stains on the floor. "She used that big Mex for most of her dirty dealings, and I've no doubt at all he was the one who killed your husband."

"But he said she sent him out *here*, why? And why burn the barn down, why that?" Amanda felt her anger rising. "Is she everywhere?" She shook her head in anger and frustration. "What I wouldn't give to get my hands on her scrawny neck."

"The woman's gone plumb loco from what Reed tells me," Toliver replied. "I sent Bart Day to arrest her. I'm hoping he lived to tell about it."

"Was Ramon the one who burned the barn?" Reed asked.

"He said he 'make warning for me,' but didn't actually confess it." Amanda replied automatically, using Ramon's actual words.

"It's late," Reed told them. "I'll send this fella back to the bunkhouse."

He rose and invited Buddy to accompany him. They stepped out into the darkness and the cowboy, upset that his position as protector had been circumvented, slouched off to his bunk, scuffing his boots and kicking rocks as he went.

Reed returned and Toliver told him he was going outside himself and have a good look around.

Alone now, Reed stepped close to Amanda and pulled her into his arms. "You all right after what went on here?"

"I'll never stop seeing that man fall to the floor—or that awful look of surprise on his face as he died."

She sank her body into the strength of him and flung her arms tight around him. Reed's smell was familiar and comforting. She'd never had this sort of closeness with

Harvey, but Reed was a different kind of man. She was completely certain about that.

Clinging to his strength and taking in the warmth and safety she found in his arms, she felt right about it. In spite of her fears of the intimacies of marriage, she faced the fact she never wanted to be away from him.

She gazed up at Reed with hungry eyes as if seeing him for the first time. Having come to rely on his quiet strength, she'd missed him terribly in her hour of need.

Looking at him now, she noticed he seemed to be someone else, when he wore the fine clothing, and looked so natural and right in them. It made her want to know more about him.

Who is this ragtag stranger off the range? Escaped convict, killer? Never! Not the way he'd been with her and her children.

To Reed, though she felt soft and helpless in his arms, and trembling the way she was, he'd seen the steel in that slender body. Amanda was one hell of a woman and she'd more than proven it tonight in defense of her child.

He wrapped his arms tightly about her, nuzzled his nose into her fragrant hair, and whispered, "Amanda, I'm sorry I wasn't here when you needed me."

"Reed, he reached down to take Marianna." She shuddered and clutched him tighter. "Oh, Reed, I couldn't let that happen."

She noticed the blood on his shirt. "You've been hurt!"

"It's just a scratch. Saldana went for me with that damned knife of hers."

He laughed it off but Amanda knew about wounds, how deadly they'd become if left unclean.

"I'd better take care of that right away." She pulled off his shirt and took a look. "I'd say you were lucky, it is only a bloody scratch." She set about cleaning it with strong soap and applied aloe juice when she finished. "It'll heal in no time with this stuff." She uttered a soft, satisfied sort of hum. "Tried to get you, eh?"

Reed reached out to grab her but she shied away. "You'd better go change your shirt," she said, forgetting everything for a short moment. With a glow of happiness, she sent him down the hall.

After donning a clean shirt, he went back to take up their earlier discussion about Ramon. "You're one brave woman, Amanda. What you did was right. It was what you had to do."

Holding her, he wondered if what she'd just been through had changed her mind about marriage or needing male protection. After handling the situation with Ramon, he realized she certainly knew what to do when things went south. If Amanda needed male protection, she hadn't shown it tonight.

She stayed in his arms, letting him hold her. But what were her thoughts? Had they changed in his favor? Reed didn't know, but decided to have his say. "Amanda, maybe it's too soon after the loss of your husband, but I'm very much in love with you." He lowered his voice to a soft whisper. "I've known it for quite a while. I've nothing to offer a wife and family right now and can't support you the way things are, but I don't want to be apart from you."

"You love me?" She drew back and searched his eyes, seeing his dilemma written across his face. "I hear what you're saying. I don't know how to answer you, but I do know this. I don't ever want to be apart from you either, Reed, not ever." Flushing a deep rosy red that the flickering lamplight could not hide, she shyly added, "When you hold me and kiss me the way you do, you make me feel strange inside and I can hardly breathe. I don't know why you make me feel that way, but I think I like it."

Tossing the idea of life with Reed around in her head, she'd forgotten shooting the Mexican. As tired as she was, she'd never sleep this night, and her mind had gone numb as she struggled to understand.

He saw her distress. "I'm guessing you just might be in love with me, too. It's possible, isn't it? Have you given thought to that?" It was in his mind to show her how much he loved her and let her know how it could be between them. It had burned in his thoughts for days.

"I'd love to show you how things could be between us, but I reckon it'd be too soon after—" He stopped, embarrassed at what he'd said. "I don't want to get ahead of myself, talking marriage this way, but woman, you need someone to help raise those kids. I love them Amanda, and I do have possibilities."

"Possibilities?" She'd wondered about him so many times. Maybe he'd finally tell her more about himself. Curious, she waited.

"I've thought of starting a law practice somewhere out here in the West. I played cowboy long enough to get myself sent up for murder and now I've got paper out on me for escaping from that hell-hole in Yuma, but this country's a big place. Maybe Colorado would do for a place to live." He looked her in the eyes. "What would you say to that?"

"You're a lawyer?" She looked at him in amazement. "Not live on a ranch anymore?" Her brows furrowed with her questions. "Will I ever know who you really are?"

"I'm just Reed," he said softly. "I've told you the truth all the way, Amanda, but not everything I've ever done. That'd be a long story."

"I'd love to hear it sometime." She nestled her head against his shoulder. "I could easily live in a town, and I've thought of that rather often. I was never cut out for ranch life, never learned much about it either. My father never let us girls ride along with the cowboys, didn't think females ought to be out among the men, doing such things and hearing them cuss the way they do." She looked up at him, smiled. "I never got the hang of it." Hugging him, she whispered in a wistful tone, "I'd only ask one thing. I'd love to live where I could see those wonderful, soaring mountains again."

"Are you saying you'll marry me, then?" He held her out to look into her eyes. "Are you?"

"Yes, I will, Reed," she panted, suddenly afraid. "I don't know what love is and the thought of being a wife again scares me to death, but I can't face living without you in my life. You've been a life saver, not only for me, but Marianna—even for Helen." Excited and apprehensive, she babbled on. "I'll never forget how you came along that evening—I never will." She finally stopped and, embarrassed, put a hand to her mouth. "Not a great answer to your question, is it?"

"It's answer enough for me. I've been thinking of Colorado Springs. Ever hear of it?" He went on without waiting for an answer, his enthusiasm increasing with every breath. "It's near Cripple Creek. That's a big gold-mining area and the town is full of men with money. Those sort always need the services of a good lawyer, and I'm a good one, Amanda."

"All this time, you never said a word about it," she chided, embarrassed and excited in the same breath. "Reed, I never wanted to marry again. Some parts of it are more than a decent woman can tolerate and keep her sanity." She blushed hard again. "Yet Helen tells me it isn't always like that. That it doesn't have to be. Is that true?"

"It most assuredly is true, my darling girl, and I'll take all the time in the world to show you how fine it can be when a man and a woman are in love. Working and living together to make a life. Oh yes, my darling, it was meant to be wonderful and it will be for us. Remember, God made us to be together, sweetheart. He meant male and female to mate, and he made it so very right." He crushed her against his chest and kissed her fully on the mouth. "Especially, with the right person, it can be so very wonderful."

"I'll have to trust you then, to make it that way. I wouldn't know anything about—well, except that everything seems right nice with you." She hid her face from him and her face burned so hard, she was glad for the darkness.

Reed just held her, thinking of the glory days ahead with her as his wife and Amanda settled close against him, pressing herself against his body, until finally, he sensed a change in her.

She straightened up, moved away a bit, and turned to the business side of things. "We'll need to go to the bank again, and see what's to be done about those loans. Maybe I can salvage enough from this ranch to get you started. And Reed, I'd be pleased if I could do that."

"We'll head for town as soon as we can and maybe get us married while we're at it."

"I'd want Helen to be with me for the wedding, and Marianna." She hesitated. "And I couldn't sleep with you in that bed in there. Reed, I—I could never do that," she stammered, gesturing to the dark bedroom.

They were interrupted by a knock on the door. Toliver had stood out there long enough to grow whiskers while they talked. Now he wanted to go to bed. He faced them, a knowing grin on his face.

"I know it's not my place to say it, but you two love each other. Maybe you don't realize it yet, and with her husband dead so short a time, it might not be thought proper. Yet, Amanda—" He turned to her. "—a woman alone has little chance to survive on her own in the rawness of this country. You've been around long enough and must realize the way things are around these parts. A quick wedding is not a bit unusual."

Amanda blushed and said nothing, but Reed winked and nodded, giving Toliver a signal that things were settled between them.

"You young folks can stay up all night and talk, but this old man has got to get some sleep." Toliver grinned and headed down the hall.

Left alone, they sat together on a wide settee. Reed held her close against his side and stroked her hair. "I don't want to frighten you but holding you like this is something I'll never have enough of. I wish we were married right now—my God, I do!" He pulled her against him and kissed her mouth until she struggled against him and pushed him away.

"Stop, oh please stop. I don't know what's happening. You're making me dizzy and I'm worried my heart is about to explode in my chest."

"And that's only the beginning, my dearest darling. There is so much more ahead. We'll be happy together, you and I." He loosened his grip on her and sighed. "I supposed we'd best get some rest ourselves, but letting you that far away from me will be a real tough trial for me from now on."

"You've made me forget about that evil Ramon." She uttered a laugh, but sobered quickly. "I haven't even seen my husband's grave or been to see it." She shrugged. "I should feel ashamed about that—but I can't."

"Don't think about it now. We'll need to go to Artesia very soon to see what's to be done about this place," he said. "You can visit it then and I'll be with you." He rose and pulled her to her feet. "Go and rest now. My namesake will be calling for you soon enough."

"Mister Big Reed, would you carry Marianna to her own bed? With you and the sheriff in the house, she'll be safe tonight."

"Sure enough, darling."

He went into the bedroom, gently picked up the sleeping child and took her down the hall to her own bed. Piddely trailed behind. When he returned, he took her into his arms again. Amanda leaned close against his body and looked into his eyes.

"We will be happy, won't we?" she asked.

He saw the doubt in her eyes as he smiled down on her, knowing he'd have the chance to change her thinking about being married. He looked forward to that lovely task with unbelievable eagerness. "Yes. Yes, we will."

Amanda left him and crawled into her bed, worried she wouldn't be able to make a good enough home for Reed or make him happy.

If he was so sure about things, why couldn't she feel the same? Thinking back over her years with Harvey, she wondered about her many failures. He'd never seemed happy. Was it her fault?

Why was he so domineering and why did he marry me in the first place if he sought another woman's arms for his comforts?

CHAPTER 29

Struggling to sort things out, Amanda finally drifted off until, awakened by her hungry infant, she sat with him against the head of the bed, thinking.

"Reed says it's no fault of mine. Maybe he's right about that. He's been right about so many things," she said to her infant in the quiet of her early morning bedroom, a place that held few good memories for her.

"He'd better be right about it. I'll never live that way again," she murmured, curled up with her nursing baby. Drowsy, wanting to sleep, she saw the sky getting lighter and the beginning light of a new day. When the baby finished nursing, she got up, changed him, squared her shoulders, and got dressed. Tired clear through, she hadn't gotten around the events of last evening, but she had men to feed.

She hadn't had time to think through the fact that she'd killed a man. She'd had to defend her child, but it hadn't really sunk in that she'd taken a life. Putting those thoughts aside, she thought about heading for the kitchen. Reed didn't need to do the cooking for her. Being fully capable of tending to those things, she would do it from now on.

Her infant had gone back to sleep, now tucked in his cradle. His little belly was full again and his diaper clean. Looking down on his tiny form, she told him, "You'll have a good father. He's a loving man with children, I know that much." But as good as things seemed with Reed, she couldn't shake the niggling doubts that clouded her mind and made her shiver with apprehension.

She walked to the kitchen and took out the things for breakfast. When she had the bacon sizzling, Reed came to stand in the doorway.

"Morning ma'am." A lazy smile spread widely across his deeply tanned face.

She took a closer look at this man she would marry. How dark his eyes were, and how black his hair was, and how he'd slicked it down out by the horse trough again. The sight of him sent wild thrills coursing through her. And lately, she'd noticed a heated sensation warming her lower parts. Was it some wonderful kind of magic he'd woven over her? She wasn't totally sure what was happening to her when Reed was around, but merely looking at this man made her burn with fire and flames, and it kept getting worse. She wanted to fall to the floor with him in her arms. *How can he make me feel that way, merely looking at me?*

He'd filled out some since he'd been at her ranch, yet he remained the slim, whip-cord sort of man she'd seen that first day when he rode into her yard. *He looks just the way God made him, and He did a fine job of it at that.*

"I've been out tending the stock and looking over the ruins of the barn." He shook his head. "Total loss out there, burned all of the hay we had. Have to put the horses out to pasture now to feed them. Wonder what got into that fool, setting it afire like that?"

"I imagine the Saldana woman put him up to it, being he worked for her. Did all sorts of evil things for her, didn't Sheriff Toliver say?"

"Why yes, I did," Toliver said, making his appearance. "Sure smells mighty fine in here." He moved to the stove and helped himself to the coffee. To Reed, he made an aside remark, "Pretty bad out there?"

Reed nodded and winked at Amanda as she set the food on the table. "Where is Marianna? She ought to be out here by now, sun's coming up."

Amanda flushed a rosy shade and laughed. "If she knew you were here in the kitchen this morning, Reed, she'd be right out here."

"I'll go get her." He walked down the hall, his heart filled with joy. He was going to be the girl's father. He'd see her grown into a lovely young woman, just like her mother. Entering the small bedroom fitted out for a girl, he saw no child snuggled in her blankets, but only an empty bed with sheets awry and toys strewn about. "She's up already?"

But he hadn't see Marianna in the kitchen or anywhere else. Her shoes and clothes were lying about. He saw no sign of Piddely either. A cold feeling struck him. Something was wrong. "Oh God! Could she be missing?" He raced to the kitchen, sick inside for the child.

Seeing the look on his face, Amanda cried out, "What?"

"She's gone from her bed and not in that room. I'll look in the yard. She may have gone out to see what's left of the barn or the garden—loves that place." But he had a feeling as he went into the yard, Toliver right beside him.

"She's gone, you say?" Toliver asked as they raced about looking for any sign of the child.

They called her name repeatedly and heard nothing in return. After searching in every imaginable place and finding no trace of her.

Reed looked at the sheriff. "Saldana?

"Who else would be that evil?" Toliver replied.

Reed's face went tight. He felt his anger soar, knowing and fearing the evil that was possible from the madness of Mercedes Saldana. His jaw set tight with determination, he growled. "The woman's gone mad, Toliver. She is capable of anything." Imagining Marianna in those cruel and heartless hands, he feared for the child. "If she lays a hand on that girl, I'll wring her damned neck!"

"Reed, you go tend to the mother right now," Toliver said. "I'll have a close look around out here. She'll be here

somewhere, because if I know that she-devil, she's not
through with you yet—because—son, you ain't dead." He
grimaced. "She wants your hide for some reason, and no
doubt, Amanda's, too."

"She wouldn't hesitate to avenge herself on a helpless
child, not that evil bitch. She's gone completely around the
bend, Toliver. I saw that with my own eyes. Hell, I was
lucky to escape with a scratch after she took a swing at me
with her little knife. You'd best be damned careful," Reed
warned and went in to Amanda.

Inside, he met her frantic gaze and took her into his
arms, trying to soothe her with a voice that lacked conviction. As she sobbed in fear about her missing child, he
smoothed and caressed her back then kissed her trembling
lips.

Hearing the swish of skirts across the room, Reed
pulled back in shock when Mercedes Saldana leapt in front
of them. She waved her clenched fists and screamed, "You
kees her?" She let out a screech of rage amid a burst of rapid-fire Spanish. "*Bastardo,* why you do thees to me?" she
demanded, venting a long string of invectives into the shadowed room that, if fully understood, Reed figured, would
have curled the hair on them both. "If thees one is your
woman, why you come to me?"

Startled, Reed quickly shoved Amanda behind him and
faced the enraged harridan. Her face had gone dark red with
hatred. She flashed her small, sharp knife in his face.

"Where is that child?" he growled, breaking into her ti-
rade. "What have you done with her?"

He had to bargain for time. The woman was crazy as
hell, and Toliver was outside somewhere. Mercedes had
seen them embracing, affirming what she'd claimed earlier.
And now she thirsted for revenge against them both, though
Reed feared Amanda was her real target.

"I never came to you, *you* came after me," he reminded
her.

"Where ees *mi Ramon*?" she screamed, heading off on

another tack. She glanced about with a worried, puzzled expression on her face, her accent thickening as she nearly screamed, "Where, ees he?"

"Who is Ramon, and why would he be here?" Reed asked, stalling.

"Thees my *ranch*. I take from this pale-faced bitch." She bit off the last word. "I send Ramon—he kill her, burn her out." Her laugh held no humor, only madness. "You think I live in this hovel? *No, señor*. I make *estancia* for me, *La Reya*. I take land from *gringos*!" She uttered a high-pitched cackle. "Is mine, *señor*, all mine!"

"By what right do you claim anything here?" he asked, hoping Toliver had the woman in his sights by now. "Why this place?"

"I own everything. I buy paper thees place with money from bank *señor* Bradshaw bring for me." She shrugged, her nose into the air, sneering at Amanda. "Big fool, that one. He love Mercedes, no want you. He love me *que mucho,* he crazy for me."

"You killed my husband, didn't you?" Amanda asked, her voice calm and cool. "You shot him down like a dog." She stepped from behind Reed, her head held high, facing the enraged woman. "He had a family!" She growled like a stalking cougar, as she moved toward Mercedes. "If you've hurt my child, you won't live out this day. Where is she?"

"You want that squalling brat? I shut her up—she no crying now." She glared at Amanda, her features swollen and ugly with the insanity and rage that had claimed her soul. "You no find her—"

Amanda struck with the swiftness of a rattler, slamming her body into the woman with enough force to knock them both to the floor.

Reed breathed a sigh of relief, seeing the small knife go clattering across the kitchen floor. Amanda smashed her fist into that once lovely face then wrapped her hands around the woman's throat.

Mercedes' screams were choked off, but her long nails

reached out, seeking to rip long gouges in Amanda's face, though she only managed to tear at her hair.

Amanda straddled the Mexican woman, banging her head against the floor again and again. Reed stood transfixed at hearing her dire threats,

"Where is my daughter, you rotten devil?" She squeezed Mercedes neck tighter. "I'll wring it out of you," she hissed and pounded the woman's head against the floor, several more times. "Where is she? What have you done with my child?"

Mercedes struggled to answer, her voice choked and hoarse. "Weeth your filthy cheeckens."

Amanda jumped off her and ran out of the house, leaving the woman to the men. Toliver had entered and seen the action. He stepped over and snapped cuffs on the shivering Mercedes as she sat on the floor, shaking her head.

Reed chuckled. "It's not a good idea to mess with Amanda's babies," he said then frowned. "I wonder where that dog is." He had a sick feeling about Piddely.

"You weel pay for thees," Mercedes replied with a vicious snarl. "Ramon, he take care you."

Reed laughed in her face. "I don't think so. Your man's gone."

Mercedes never heard his words as, in her rage, she fought the metal cuffs hard enough to cut her wrists and start them bleeding.

Amanda came in carrying Mariana. The child's tear-streaked face was dirty, and she had scratches bleeding on her arms.

Sobbing, she clung to her mother, bits of straw and dirt clung to her clothes and hair. "Lady hurt me, Mommy."

"She can't hurt you any more, dear. Look at her. She's right there on the floor," she said, holding her child out to look at the handcuffed woman on the floor.

"Bad lady!" Marianna scolded. Spotting Reed, she cried out to him, "Weed!" She wriggled down from Amanda to run into his arms, sobbing out her fear and pain. "Bad lady take me, hurt my doggie, Weed."

Seeing Reed with the child, Mercedes turned even darker with rage and she opened her mouth, poised to spit further venom until Toliver moved close to her, looked down at her, and threatened, "You'd best keep your mouth shut, ma'am. You're in trouble enough."

"Where ees Ramon?" she snarled.

"He tried to steal this little girl right here," Toliver replied. "And Amanda shot the bastard. He's dead."

"Yes, I did," Amanda confirmed. "I shot that devil and he *is* dead. No one touches my children." She flung her words in the Mexican woman's face, letting her know she was all alone in her crimes.

"No! Eet cannot be! You take my Ramon? You keel heem?"

Her accent deepened yet again, and Reed surmised it was in her shock at the loss of her faithful escort, servant, and partner. Ramon had been, no doubt, the only man in the world who'd truly loved her in every way, body, and soul.

She tried to lunge at Amanda, her mouth open to emit a deathly, enraged scream, but the sheriff's hand on her cuffs restrained her. Amanda stepped closer to the defeated woman, and softly asked a question that silenced her, "Did you enjoy your time with my husband? Wasn't he wonderful?" The mocking tone in her voice spoke the exact sentiment she wished to convey.

"Slut!" Mercedes screamed.

Amanda had scored a hit to the woman's tender, most, intimate spot. From her own experience, Bradshaw had been an ugly man in many ways. Amanda smiled knowingly at Mercedes. Understanding that both women had barely endured their intimate moments with him, no further words needed be spoken on the subject. Mercedes caught her meaning and could not avoid her revulsion at the unfeeling, brutish ways of the man, any more than Amanda could.

Harvey had been a clumsy, selfish clod in the bedroom and, as little contact as Amanda had had with Reed, she'd begun to realize, albeit unwillingly, that all men were not the same, in the bedroom, or out of it. That mystery lay before her, and she shivered at the thoughts of it. Her anger at Saldana faded rapidly. Sidling close to Reed, she looked with pity on the pathetic soul Mercedes Saldana had become.

"I've got to get this woman to jail and check on Bart Day," Toliver said. "I've got a bad feeling about him."

Mercedes had enough hate left in her to rejoice over another *gringo's* fate. After seeing the gloating look and wry smile on her face, the sheriff's worries increased. She smiled up at him and, had he looked, the sheriff would have seen the gleam of vengeance still burning brightly in her black eyes.

Amanda shivered at the evil in Mercedes eyes and looked away. Buddy and Jud appeared at the open doorway with questions on their lips.

"What's all the screamin' an' yellin' about?" Jud asked. "We heard the ruckus clear out to the bunkhouse."

They entered the ranch house and Reed saw Jud flush white as a ghost when he saw Mercedes sitting on the floor in handcuffs.

"What's going on in here?" Jud asked them, his voice faint and shaky.

"Little dust up with the lady on the floor right there," Toliver said.

Mercedes looked up. Spotting Jud, she laughed, unable to keep the rising note of hysteria from her voice. "*Hola, señor* Jud. You work here? For man you like to keell?" Knowing her words of accusation would help in the demise of another hated *gringo*, she grinned.

Her words shocked Amanda, as well as drawing the full attention of Reed and the sheriff. She looked at the man and gasped. "Jud? It was you? You killed my husband?"

Stunned, she glared at him, her hands on her hips. "Why, for God's sake? Why?"

"Why, no, I never—Ramon did the shooting. That bitch is a lying through her teeth."

But the obvious guilt written across his white face made *him* the liar.

Buddy shook his head. "So was that where you was all them days when we was needing to be out on the south ranges and I was all alone out there?" he piped up, not helping Jud's case at all.

Jud advanced on Buddy, his fist bunched, ready to punch his saddle pal in the face. "Shut the hell up, you damned fool!"

Mercedes felt no joy as she watched the ruination of Jud's plan to own the ranch and have the blonde woman for his wife. "You one vera beeg fool, Jud."

"That lying whore sitting on the floor right there's the one who done it. She's got them big plans." Jud pointed to Mercedes, anger and desperation plain on his face.

"He go weeth Ramon. They bring big money back for me." She laughed in Jud's face. "You help Ramon kill her man." She nodded to Amanda then went quiet for a thoughtful moment.

Seeing Amanda, quietly standing in shock at all that'd happened, Mercedes uttered defeated snarl. "I think this pale-haired bitch ees one vera lucky woman. She no have you, Jud, and she no have her husband," she sneered then slumped into silence.

A tear streaked down Saldana's cheek and, seeing the defeated expression on her face, Reed understood that she knew her dreams of an empire were finished, smashed—in ruins. Her faithful lover and henchman was gone as well. The woman sat there in the middle of Amanda's front room, in handcuffs, saying nothing more.

CHAPTER 30

Amanda took Marianna into the kitchen, cleaned her of chicken feces, straw, dirt, and tears, then she treated the cruel rope burns on her fragile little wrists, medicating them with the healing juice of the aloe plant.

"You'll be fine, honey, and guess what? Reed is going to be your daddy. Would you like that?"

"He'll be my daddy? All the time?"

Peeking around Amanda, she cast adoring eyes on Reed as he helped the sheriff bind Jud's hands. Marianna let out a giggle or two then burst into a fresh round of tears and ran to him. "Bad lady hurt my doggie, Weed."

"I can't leave here until I see what happened to that little dog," Reed told Toliver. He took Marianna's hand. "Do you know where Piddely is?"

"She hurted him. He sleep by my bed."

Reed raced down the hall and, searching Marianna's room, found the small dog lying in a pool of blood beside the bed, his body hidden by bedding that had been tossed aside. Kneeling down to touch him, Reed felt a faint quiver of life. The small dog tried to raise his head to lick his hand. After a quick exam, he believed the dog would survive. The poor creature had received a vicious blow to his skull and, likely, a stab wound. It would take some time to be sure. He carried the dog out to the kitchen and laid him on a rug beside the stove.

Amanda knelt beside the dog to check his injuries. She cleaned his fur, medicated his wounds, and then stroked him with loving caresses, murmuring soft words to him. "What do you think, Reed? Will he live?"

Marianna sat close to Piddely, white-faced and shocked at the sight of her dog so wounded. "Doggie gone away?" she asked, her voice quivering.

"He'll be all right in a few days if you take good care of him, little darling." Reed gave her a confidant smile and rose to his feet. Mariana stayed at her dog's side.

Toliver looked at Reed. "All right, daddy dear, I've got these two to haul into Artesia. Any chance of getting you to help? Wouldn't do to let either of them get away from me, now would it?" he added. "I'll check the bunkhouse for rifles while I'm here. Wonder what I'll find."

Reed turned to Amanda. "I'll need to help Toliver. We can handle the other matters when I get back."

She understood he meant the arrangements for their wedding. "Reed, put on those fancy lawyer duds you wear so well, and while you're in town, and go see the banker, whoever that may be with all that's happened."

She smiled down at Mercedes and let out a chuckle. "I'm sure in the light of things, Blankenship surely will be gone. Let me know how things stand. Being a lawyer as you say, I guess you'd know what to do."

"I'll do that—dear." He added the last endearment with suggestively raised eyebrows.

She'd allow a small recap of their intimacy when he got back, in light of her acceptance of his proposal.

The sheriff came back, carrying a well-maintained Springfield Rifle slung across his arm. "Here's one of them. Wonder what we'll find at the Saldana home?"

He already had his guilty suspects and Reed figured he really didn't care if he found another rifle, but fear for his deputy was written on his face, and he was in a hurry.

They brought out enough horses to accommodate the prisoners, as well as Ramon. They'd dragged his body out from where Jud and Buddy had hauled it and Mercedes, seeing the body, let out a scream of anguish.

Amid her tears, she rattled off a rapid-fire stream of Spanish invectives that all the men, as well as Amanda, were glad they couldn't understand.

They tossed the bound and silent prisoners on mounts, put lead ropes on their horses, including the one selected to haul Ramon's body, and headed for Artesia.

Reed didn't look forward to the ride. He hated to leave Amanda with the way things were. He'd been to that town too often already and wanted to stay home, to comfort Marianna. And he was worried about that silly little dog, Piddely, in the bargain.

ᘓᑍᘓᑍ

The ranch yard was empty of activity just now, and outside the bunkhouse, Buddy walked about with his head hanging low. Amanda thought he moped over the shocking turn of events for his saddle mate, Jud. Sure that she wouldn't come home to a devastating fire, this time, she stepped out on the porch and called him. "Will you drive me to Helen's?"

Receiving an affirmative, she returned to the kitchen and knelt beside the faithful little dog. She stroked his fur and received a lick from his tongue. He took a few laps of water and then a bit of milk. His tail wagged at the very tip, letting her know he'd be all right and it was safe to leave him.

Buddy hitched up the buggy with what harness he could put together, while she got her children ready. Amanda packed up the baby's things and they were soon off. Marianna sat between her and Buddy. Baby Reed slept in his box.

Buddy was very quiet. Fearing that he suffered anguish because of what his saddle mate had done, she offered what comfort she could. "Buddy, it wasn't your doing. Don't take on so," she said, patting his arm in sympathy.

"I know we wasn't the best of hands, ma'am. I went along with whatever Jud said, like I always do, an' I feel bad about the way your husband got killed. Maybe I could've—"

Amanda stopped him. "Just keep driving, Buddy. It's done now, and there's no turning back—never is. You know that."

"Guess not, ma'am."

He settled to do the driving and guided the mare over the easier places, trying for a better ride. Amanda, tired from all that happened yesterday, and this morning, enjoyed having someone drive. It made the long trip easier for her and she relaxed in thought. Many questions had been answered and her future settled as well. A smile crossed her lips, trying to imagine living her life with that long drink of water off the trail, as Helen had called him.

When they pulled into Helen's yard, she came walking out to meet them, surprised and curious. With her eyebrows raised, she asked, "You're back so soon. What's happened?"

She's standing up real straight these days. Amanda smiled, recalling with a deep sense of pride how her man Reed had had a hand in Helen's recovery.

After getting down and entering the home, Amanda poured her heart out to her friend, telling her everything that had happened in the past several hours. It felt good to tell it over again, like a cleansing of the soul. Afterward, they sat together discussing it and sorting it out. Baby Reed slept and Marianna ran off to play with Bennie. With no one to hear them, they could speak freely.

"I'm worried she'll have nightmares over what that woman did to her. And her poor little dog, he can't even walk right now. Reed thinks the dog will recover and Marianna will get over it in time." She sighed and leaned back against her chair. "I'm just grateful that neither of them was severely injured."

In time, their chatter turned to wedding plans, and they laughed and talked with joy. Amanda felt an unexpected soaring of happiness. "Oh, Helen, will certain things be wonderful like you said? I'm afraid and I worry I won't be woman enough to make him happy. In fact, I'm scared to death."

"Honey, don't you worry your head on that score. You've got yourself some kind of man, if I don't miss my guess." Helen nodded and deepened her voice as she continued with confidence, "That man will take care of everything, including you."

"I don't know what you mean by that," Amanda admitted, puzzled.

"Honey, you will—you surely will."

Helen smiled at her and Amanda felt a burst of unexpected tremors pass through her at Helen's admonition. Her thoughts ran rampant. *I'm scared to death to be married again, but I can't get along without him!*

℮⌘℮

With the accused incarcerated in their jail cells, Toliver asked Alonzo, "You seen Bart?"

The man looked puzzled. "Dunno, he wasn't around last night, and I was supposed to have the night off. He never showed. Ain't he supposed to be here today?"

"I sent him to arrest the Saldana woman yesterday—it was late in the day."

Reed saw the sheriff's face turn six shades of white as he shoved his hat back on his head.

"Come on, Reed," he hissed and flung orders over his shoulder to Alonzo. "Keep a close watch on those two.

They're in for murder and kidnapping." He rushed out and mounted up.

They quickly rode the distance to the Saldana home. It sat eerily silent, standing in the lovely grove of cottonwoods that towered and swayed high above. Brilliant splashes of crimson Bougainvillea, growing about the place, mocked them with the purity of growing things. No birds sang in the trees as they dismounted and rapped on the door.

Doors were rarely locked but Toliver knocked out of common courtesy. Expecting no answer and receiving none, he shoved it open. They stepped into the murky dimness and within a few short steps, encountered the body of Bart Day. He was sprawled facedown just past the entryway, cold and stiffened in death.

They turned Day over to see the finely edged cut from a very sharp knife. His throat had been neatly slashed. "That evil bitch!" Toliver cried, shaking with rage and futility. "Used her knife on my man, here. She's for murder now, that's for sure. Damn me for rotten luck, I sent him over here!"

Reed hurt for the man. He stood there, shaking his head, knowing full well it could have been himself laying there so still in death.

"Best call the undertaker soon's I get a few witnesses in here to see this." Toliver said, more to himself than Reed, regret burning in his eyes. "Should've damned well known better. I did tell him he ought to take some help along. Wish to hell he had."

Reed shivered, having little to offer except condolences. He remembered the silky hiss of the knife as she'd tried and missed in her attempt to kill hm. "While you're getting this straightened out, I'd like to visit the bank and see what's to be done for Amanda."

He took his leave while the sheriff headed for the needed witnesses and the undertaker.

Inside the bank, he asked to see the manager. The clerk, a new face also, had the thin figure and the pale complexion of a man who seldom saw the sun. He nodded his head of scant reddish hair and blinked his watery blue eyes. Dressed nicely in a business suit, he wore an air of importance and held his head high. "I'll see if he's busy."

He hurried away and, once again, Reed, dressed as he was in the fancy clothing, knew he made an impressive figure, one to command attention. He planned to use it to Amanda's advantage in any way he could.

After a few moments spent looking about the interior of a typical small town bank, Reed saw the clerk beckoning to him.

"He'll see you now, sir."

Ushered into Blankenship's former office, Reed met an older man, wearing a nicely cut suit of a fine gray broadcloth. The man bade him to take a seat. A newly made sign on the desk informed him that this was, Arnold J. Worthington, Bank Manager. The man extended his hand in greeting.

"I'm Arnold Worthington, just transferred to this area. How may I be of assistance?" His educated voice was nicely modulated, and his eyes, alert and sparkling, expressed both an interest and competence in his work.

"Welcome to Artesia." Reed didn't want to hurry yet he felt the need to head back to the ranch. "My name is Leroy Hardesty. My sister is the widow of Harvey Bradshaw and she's very worried about keeping the ranch after learning of the many loans made against it. My purpose today is to learn if you have any information or assistance you can provide in settling this matter. It would be much appreciated." Reed took a deep breath and waited to hear the man's reply.

"Yes sir, I know about that situation. You are aware of course, that the indebtedness equals, or somewhat exceeds, the value of the property in question. My predecessor made some imprudent loans to your brother-in-law." He stopped for a moment and fiddled with the blotter on his desk, making Reed wonder what else the man had on his mind. "Of course it is apparently a valuable parcel of land for cattle ranching." He looked up and smiled. "I have reason to know, as there is an interested party seeking such a place. His group is willing to make an offer on the property. It happens to be generous enough to pay off all outstanding encumbrances and leave your sister a small sum."

Reed was delighted to hear that Amanda might be able to leave the area with a few dollars. He held back a quick, positive reply, and casually gave a reluctant shrug. "I'll see if she's interested. Being newly widowed, things have been exceedingly difficult for her these past several weeks as you might imagine." He sat quiet for a short time, as if in deep thought, then added, "She loves the place and hoped to keep it, but it appears to be a decent offer. I will pass the information on to her."

"Yes, please do so. They are awaiting her reply. I had planned to drive out tomorrow with the offer, but you've saved me a tedious trip." It was obvious to Reed, the man, a city dude, was greatly relieved that he no longer faced a long drive over rough roads through brush country.

Reed broached another question, heavy on his mind. "We've been informed that the Saldana woman had bought up these loans on the ranch. How much credence can we give to that?"

The man uttered a soft chuckle. "None at all." He splayed his hands out, and smiled. "She signed a few papers, but Blankenship, my predecessor, made sure they were improperly written and certainly never notarized. As it stands now, they are essentially worthless. She had no legal assistance and he'd apparently begun to question her motives. More than that, I am not at liberty to reveal, but be sure the bank holds all the essential papers regarding the loans made to the deceased."

He finished his statement and Reed knew he'd reveal nothing regarding the riotous gossip surrounding Blankenship's departure.

"Thank you, sir. I'll explain what you've told me to my sister." Reed took his leave, chuckling under his breath.

"That banker must be the only man in existence that still believes I'm Amanda's brother."

Eager to return to the ranch, he was about to leave town when he met the sheriff again. Toliver quietly handed him a rolled up, yellowed paper torn on the edges with visible pin holes.

Reed knew without looking what it was and stuck it inside his jacket. He had time enough later on to look at a thing that had haunted him for so many months and so many miles.

"Bart was the only one who'd ever taken notice of it," Toliver said as he slapped Reed's roan across the rump, setting him off on a trot.

With a light heart, Reed headed for "home." He reached the ranch well after dark and went into the house, hoping to find Amanda still awake. He needn't have worried. She met him at the door, waiting to hear what had happened at the jail as well as the bank. Anticipation shone in her eyes.

"Please, Reed, tell me everything. What did they do with that woman, and Jud? I couldn't believe he did what she said." Breathless with curiosity, she added, "And what about the bank? What did man have to say?"

"First, how is that little dog?" Reed asked. He didn't mind holding back a bit on the information he had for her. It wasn't right, but he couldn't help creating some suspense.

"He's taking a little food and was outside for a bit, today," she answered. Not to be put off, she kept after him. "Tell me everything."

"Those two are safe in jail, now." He shook his head sadly as he told her, "Just as he feared, Toliver found his deputy dead." Reed grimaced. "That crazy woman had slashed his throat, like she tried to do to me."

He touched the healing scratch on his arm, taking his time, setting her on edge with waiting. But seeing her temper getting the best of her, he decided he'd better get to the news she awaited more than all the rest.

"Amanda dear, you might like the offer the new banker has on the table for you." He took his time with that too until she headed for him, ready to squeeze it out of him. "He was about to pay you a visit, until we talked." Chuckling, he put his arms up defensively as she advanced on him.

"Well?" She grabbed his shirt. "Reed! What?"

He wanted to laugh over the way he'd caused her agitation, but the fun had to end. "I'll tell you everything, but I need you right here."

He pulled her onto his lap and held her so tight she could scarcely catch her breath. After several deep searching kisses which she put up with partly so he'd tell her what she needed so desperately to know.

"He said the loans pretty nearly exceeded the value of the property, and he also knew how many cattle you had, and their worth." He grinned. "More than I ever got out of Jud. But looks you might make out right fine, since a group from Texas is offering a sum which, if you are interested, will leave you with a few thousand dollars to the good." He hugged her again. "How's that, then?"

"If it's enough to leave this miserable country and get us set up in Colorado Springs like you said, I like it fine." She smiled at him. "You made me drag it out of you, Reed. There will be severe penalties sometime in our future for your doing that."

"What kind of torture you planning for me?"

"You won't know what's coming, but I promise you that and more, Mr. Twining."

Happy together, they spent time holding each other and laughing, but Reed kept from going too far or letting things get too heated between them. He'd wait until he had the right, and she was his.

CHAPTER 31

Amanda made one trip into Artesia. She visited her husband's grave. But looking at the freshly turned earth, she felt sorrow only for the way he died. At the loss of him as a husband, she shed no tears. Her life with Harvey had been hard. That and her bitterness at his infidelity, greatly lessened any grief she'd ever felt as his widow. After only a few moments standing there, she turned away. Harvey belonged to her past.

Now through happenstance and good fortune, she looked forward to a future filled with the promise of far greater happiness for herself and her children. She would marry that ragged stranger who had come in answer to her desperate prayer.

She found a new dress at the general store and with a few alterations, made it into a better than passing wedding dress. A pale creamy shade of muslin, with embroidered tiny blue flowers scattered across the wide full skirt, it only wanted a dark blue sash around her small waist to complete it, and Amanda was fortunate enough to possess one from her girlhood.

Two weeks later, Samantha and Reed were married at Helen's ranch. He had purchased a strong team, and solid wagon to hold those few things Amanda had wanted to keep, and it was very little. She planned to begin life anew with very few reminders of her unhappy days in New Mexico as Harvey Bradshaw's wife.

Though neither of them eagerly looked forward to the need for a long wagon drive, they decided it was the best way to move Amanda's things and spend time alone after the wedding.

Marianna, knowing she wouldn't see Bennie anymore, cried bitter tears about it until Helen said they'd try to find a way to visit in a few years. Not knowing how long years were, the little girl was satisfied.

૯౨౯౨

Amanda had no flowers. She held only a small bible she'd kept tucked away. Deep in her heart she firmly believed God had sent Reed to her in an hour of deepest need and she honored that belief.

Toliver and his wife attended. Amanda asked the sheriff to give her away as she had no family close. There hadn't been time enough to inform many of them, but enough nearby neighbors and friends attended to make it a festive occasion.

Reed stood straight and tall beside Amanda, his warm hand holding hers and that devilish twinkling in his eyes kept going right through her to add to her stress. Yet his strength and deviltry helped her make it through a ceremony she'd sworn never to repeat. However, that twinkle in his eye did nothing to settle her nerves.

The minister, Jedidiah Rathborne, a tall skinny scarecrow of a man, came from Artesia on his boney old nag, to read the time honored words. Reading the vows from the good book, he wed them in proper fashion.

Marianna, with Piddely at her feet, stood at her mother's side in her own new dress and preened like a peacock before

Bennie who sat with his mother on the sidelines.

Amanda leaned down and whispered to her, "This makes Reed your daddy for real, sweetheart."

Helen held baby Reed during the service and, afterward, one old gentleman provided fiddle music. There were some who danced while others circled tables, set out under the trees of a wide patio, that groaned with roast beef, chicken, biscuits, preserves, pies, cakes, and any number of side dishes. Liquor flowed in a few areas as well.

Amanda was so tense from getting things in order for the long trip ahead, preparing for the nuptials, and with the wedding, that she found it difficult to keep her senses straight. In a dizzy whirl, she took care of baby Reed and helped where she could, but more than once, she was laughingly told her trembling hands were no help.

They'd left the Bradshaw ranch for good the day before and, after the wedding festivities died down, they'd be heading northward to their new home. After thinking it over, they decided to make the trip a long honeymoon on the way to Colorado. Those thoughts kept Amanda in a tizzy of apprehension, but she'd made sure there was a decent bed installed in the wagon.

During a lull in chatting and eating, Reed swept her aside. "How are you holding up, my darling wife?" His eyes were kind, but glowing with desire, as he gazed into hers. "Don't you be nervous about us being together later on, and don't ever fear being with me. We have a long way to go in life and I'll see you a happy woman, you know that."

She loved him all over again for his caring and understanding. "Thank you, Reed. I know you will, and I'll do the same for you. You're the best man I've ever known." Though there was a tremor in her voice, she smiled at him. "The way you came into my life was an answer to a prayer. Did you know that?"

"You never mentioned that, Amanda. Will you tell me about it?"

"Yes, Reed, I will." She smiled again. "When you rode into my yard right then, I was in a bad way and prayed for help. I told the minister who married us about it. I thought he ought to know something about you."

He tried to sound offended. "But you never told me about it."

"I'll tell you everything about that day—if I have time." Now that she had something to tantalize him with, she planned to use it as he'd done with her too many times. The man was a devil of a tease, and the twinkle in his eye confirmed it. He deserved teasing and she was learning how.

"Any other surprises in store for me?"

"Might be, when we're alone tonight." She smiled bravely, all the while quailing frantically inside at thoughts of the night ahead. Insensible with unrealistic apprehensions despite Helen's assurances to the contrary, Amanda totally feared her wedding night. Could she endure the physical side of being a wife again? In her panic, she'd lost sight of the heated and frenzied way Reed made her feel when he held her and kissed her.

Helen approached the couple. "I've made up one of the rooms way in the back for you two. The baby is right next to you and Marianna is sleeping close by." She took Amanda's hand. "It's the room with a silver bell on the door so you'll know the right one."

It had grown late and most of the partiers had either left or found beds in their wagons or camps. Most usually stayed awhile for a wedding, and if they could, would create a wild *shiveree*. In this case Helen did her best to make sure they didn't and told Amanda, "I tried to hold them off, figuring you'd be nervous enough without them *shivereein'* you into a nervous breakdown." There were tears in her eyes. "I'm going to miss you sorely when you're gone. Never had a neighbor I liked more."

"I feel that way too, Helen, and I feel bad for Buddy. He's lost without Jud to boss him around. He's at the ranch taking care of things around the place until next month when the new owners come in." Amanda looked at Helen.

"He's not much, I suppose, but if you folks could use him, I think he'd be happy here."

"Why, I'm sure we could. We need someone to tend our milk cow, chicken, hogs, and such. Herb hates it and so does the hand that usually does those chores. I believe your Buddy'd be just right for that. And we have a good sized garden, too." She laughed. Amanda had told her of Buddy's late night activities.

"Thanks, Helen. We can leave New Mexico without a worry then, knowing Buddy has someone to look out for him."

"You'll be a happy woman with Reed. But I wish you lived next door." Helen added in hushed tones, "Let him lead you along, and you'll be just fine." She gave Amanda a warm hug. "You've got a *good* man there, my dear."

And somehow, Amanda knew she meant far more than she'd said.

Reed came to her and, seeing how edgy she was, held her close for a while. But when he said, "It's thinning out some. Maybe we'll be able to get some rest before morning." He felt her tremble and took a firm hold of her hands. They were cold as ice and trembling.

Holding her shaking hands, he moved along the hallway. "Let's get to that room with the fancy bell on it, my dear Amanda. We have a long drive ahead of us in the morning."

Leading her along until they saw a silver bell decorating the door, he opened it and drew her inside. Baby Reed's cradle stood in the corner, and he slept. They peeked at the sleeping baby with his pink cheeks and dark hair.

"Here we are." He drew her into his arms and held her close for a long moment. "I'll be the best husband a man can be to you, Amanda," he whispered in her ear as he kissed her and pressed her ever closer until he felt the beginnings of her tremulous response. "Will you be all right?" he whispered.

Amanda knew exactly what he meant. "I don't know,

Reed." Her voice quavered and she shook as she looked at
the wide white bed, made especially nice for their use. She
glanced back at him. "I'm proud to be your wife and I'm
scared to death, but I—I do trust you." She couldn't stop
shaking.

He said no more and tenderly kissed her lips. Taking
his time, pressing her close against his body, he kissed her
neck, ears and, after unbuttoning her dress, he kissed her a
bit lower.

"Reed, the things you do make me feel weak and burning inside. I don't know what's happening, but when you
touch me and kiss me like that, I feel a strange need burning
right through me. I don't know what to do. You know
what's happening, don't you?"

"I hoped for it, my darling wife. I've been in love with
you for a very long time." He buried his face in her breasts.
"And darling, someday when my namesake is finished with
you, I'd like to help myself right here, too."

At her shocked gasp, he kissed her full breasts, removed her dress and let it fall to the floor.

"Oh, the air is so cold," she cried and shivered.

"Come into the bed with me—let me warm you." She
heard his clothes hitting the floor and, trembling life a leaf
in the wind, she slipped beneath the sheets with as much of
her under-clothing in place as she dared keep on.

But as he slid beneath the sheets, he moved against her,
kissing her deeply. He slid his hands around her back and
pulled her against him. Slowly, he succeeded in removing
every stitch she wore. But by this time, she was past caring
and gasped as he pressed himself against her. She felt the
man he was and frantically began to help him, moaning and
eager for what awaited.

"Reed, I'm not afraid any more. Nothing is the same
with you, nothing at all."

They came together at last as he slowly and carefully
brought her to those towering heights she'd never imagined
or knew existed. She came to know at last that magical un-

ion between male and female. And it was more than she'd ever imagined—so much more.

After several hours in his arms, she marveled once again how he'd come to her. Lying close in his arms, she smiled into the darkness of the night.

"Are you still afraid of me?"

His voice, so soft and deep, came from his chest, where her head rested. She lay calmly in his arms marveling at how he'd managed to take her, gentle her fears, and make her soar to the heavens with his fine, skillful lovemaking.

"No more do I fear the marriage bed, Reed. If I shed a tear, it's because of how you are with me, my children, and those yet to come. And in the bargain, I'm waiting for the day I can look out the windows of our home in Colorado and see those majestic peaks again." She snuggled closer as his arms tightened about her. "Reed, I love you so."

"Oh, my darling," he replied and reached for her again.

THE END

About the Author

Ramona Forrest is a retired RN. She keeps busy writing novels—and traveling whenever possible. Forrest has resided in the back country of Arizona, assisted in round-ups, worked in Saudi Arabia, and has had the pleasure of traveling extensively. She now resides in Phoenix and spends much time in gardening, writing, entertaining friends, and family.